C000090403

FALLING

FALLING

Adalta: Vol. III

By

Sherrill Nilson

Illustrations and cover by
Kurt Nilson

COPYRIGHTS

This is a work of fiction. All characters and events portrayed in this novel are fictitious and are the product of the author's imagination. Any resemblance to actual places or persons, living or dead, is entirely coincidental.

FALLING: Adalta Volume III

Copyright (©) 2019 by Sherrill Nilson
Cover art and illustrations copyright (©) 2019 Kurt Nilson

All rights reserved. No part of this publication may be reproduced, distributed, or transmitted in any form or by any means, including photocopying, recording, or other electronic or mechanical methods, without the prior written permission of the author, except in the case of brief quotations embodied in critical reviews and certain other noncommercial uses permitted by copyright law.

ISBN 1978-1-7322729-8-9
ISBN 978-1-7322729-7-2

Published by Green Canoe, LLC
PO Box 401
Locust Grove, OK 74352

For my Family
Wherever you are,
You are where home is.
No wonder I'm so scattered.

"To me, the thing that is worse than death is betrayal.
You see, I could conceive death, but I could not conceive betrayal."
— Malcolm X

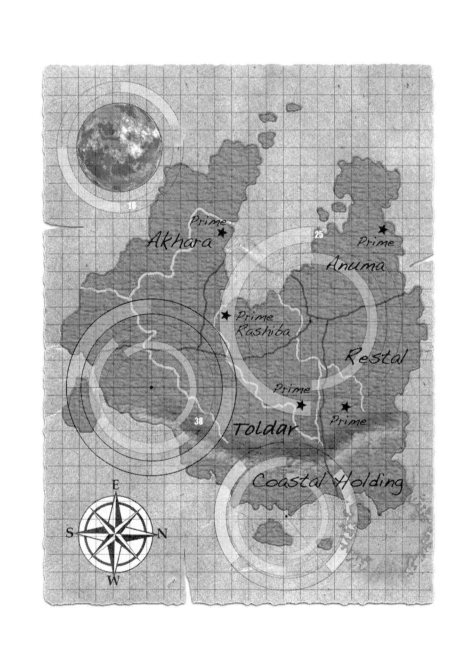

CHAPTER ONE

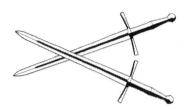

My brother has tried to kill me three times, at least three times. Maybe more. I understand. I have watched him all my life. Watched how he coped with being the only person on Adalta with no magic, the magic we call talent. Watched how he coped with being the oldest son and not the heir because he had no talent.

He learned to defend himself with swords, the one in his scabbard and the one in his wit. He learned to earn the respect of his men despite his terrible handicap.

I wondered at his ability to live a full and productive life without even the talent of a farmhand who can barely encourage a few seeds to sprout and grow faster.

I loved him. He tormented me, true, but isn't that what older brothers are born to do? He never hurt me, not until the assassination attempts began. I loved him even then. I still do. He's all the family I have now.

He cannot have done what so many others believe he's done. My brother would not ally himself with the creature that is causing so many deaths. The one I'm fighting now. The creature who will destroy us all if it isn't stopped.

He cannot have. Whatever others think, he's a victim. He's the controlled, not the controller. I know when we kill the Itza Larrak, he'll be free. Somehow I will free him.

Guardian Daryl Me'Vere looked up from the side of the wounded trooper to see a small dot in the sky grow rapidly larger. Mi'hiru Philipa flying on the back of Cystra, her Karda, approached too fast. So fast he knew they were not carrying an ordinary message. Dread landed so hard on Daryl's back if he weren't kneeling already he'd be prostrate on the damp, stinking ground.

He lifted the ravaged arm of the soldier he knelt beside. The young man hissed with pain. His moan blended with the moans and cries that surrounded them, sounds that haunted Daryl day and night and had since the urbat attacks started again with the first warming of spring. They never seemed to fade.

Today's fight was over. The urbat were gone. Daryl didn't want to get up and go to the landing field to meet Philipa. He wanted to stay here in the stink of blood and urbat ichor and heal this bloody gash in his trooper's arm, then move on to the wounded woman on the next pallet and the next and the next. He tried to let their moans and cries for help block the message he knew she was bringing, but they couldn't.

He didn't want to wait for Philipa to land and tell him what he knew she was going to. He tried to let them block out what he must do next. He didn't want to call his tired troops together again and lead them to another village under attack and another and another. He tried to let the cries block his doubts. How could he plan defenses against the urbat attacks that seemed to him to rise up everywhere anytime? Was he even the right person to lead this fight?

He worked to close the ragged rip from an urbat's claw in the troopers arm, drawing on the power of Adalta, concentrated on knitting the tiny vessels and nerves, the muscle fibers. He thought about nothing but this wound before him and the soldier who would be able to use the arm again when Daryl finished. This work helped heal his own wounds, the ones inside him.

The small village reeked from the battle with the urbat. Stinking miasma clung to the ground in a thick, yellow fog that stuck to his clothes, to his skin. Even the cloth wrapped over his mouth and nose and smeared with pine-sap salve didn't help. He cleared it from the wound it clung to so the arm could heal without infection and ignored, as best he could, the infectious black cloud of dread approaching with Mi'hiru Philipa.

His troopers were scattered along the edge of the small landing meadow, some helping the two village healers move the wounded outside the walls to the inn they'd taken over. They piled dead urbat and salvaged arrows; some worked with villagers gathering too many dead in a too long line just outside the too short walls. The villagers' voices were low and somber and scared.

As well they should be. Daryl was too polite to curse their obliviousness. He'd sent messengers to warn all the villages near the Circle of Disorder of the dangers. Too many hadn't listened, hadn't made the preparations he ordered. What a waste. Did they think he was so young and inexperienced he exaggerated the dangers out of some bloated sense of self-importance? Should he insist Prime Guardian Hugh Me'Rahl take control of this fight? Someone older, wiser, and time-tested?

He closed his eyes and clamped his jaw against seething, fruitless frustration. Then he forced his shoulders to straighten, shoved his worries and doubts inside where they belonged. He couldn't afford to indulge them now when it did no good. He went to meet Philipa. He had no choice. This was his duty, and these were his people. Show no doubt. Show no fear. Don't let that seed of panic in his belly take root.

A flash of the library at Restal Hall bit him. How he longed for books and boredom.

Cystra cupped her wings to land and loped to a stop in front of him. Philipa didn't dismount. "Flat Rock. About fifty urbat are headed for Flat Rock, Daryl. And they're moving in organized ranks. I think the Itza Larrak is with them. Flat Rock needs help now. The Karda's best estimate is they'll be there in less than thirty minutes."

Daryl's eyes burned with fatigue, and he scrubbed at his face, wanting to scrub away her words. They'd barely get there in time. The small town, almost a village, was thirty minutes away. Behind him Armsmaster Krager bellowed, "Troopers, arm up and mount up. Fast. We've got another fight."

"Get to Me'Mattik Hold, Philipa, it's not that far from Flat Rock," Daryl told her. Abala, his Karda, was already approaching the landing field to pick him up, back from hunting. He drew up a mental map of Me'Mattik Hold where Flat Rock was. "We'll approach from the Southeast. Have Holder Me'Mattik's flyers move in from the North. Maybe we can drive them away from the town and trap them between us. Be sure to tell the holder to watch for the Itza Larrak—and for Adalta's sake, don't let any of his flyers—I mean troops—approach it. Just let me know where it is." There were no Karda, no flyers at Me'Mattik Hold.

It was another plan on the fly. Maybe he and his troops would have help this time. Maybe not so many people would die. Maybe he was the wrong person to lead this battle, but he could fight the fight in front of him. Then he would look at the big picture. Something had to change. Even if he had to step down and let someone else take responsibility because maybe—. But he couldn't think about that now. There was no one else right now. He couldn't even shrug his shoulders, the weight was so heavy. And the battles had only just begun.

The Itza Larrak was intensifying its attacks. Daryl knew it was drawing attention away from the growing Lines of Devastation creeping out of the Circles of Disorder toward each other, building its continent-wide antenna to reach into space and call to other Larrak to come. The parasitic aliens would destroy this planet.

Cystra and Philipa, the little Mi'hiru, one of the all-women cadre who served the Karda, whirled, loped away, faster and faster, and lifted from the ground they had only just touched.

"Me'Mattik." Krager's voice was flat. "Don't count on Me'Mattik, Daryl."

"You don't trust anyone, Krager. I told him to be ready, to be on the watch. He'll be there." He'd be there. Me'Mattik had to be there. The village was part of his holding. Daryl refused to let the doubt claw free.

"We can hope."

"Always the voice of doom, Krager. Check to see every one who's able to come with us has enough arrows, and don't let anyone come who's too wounded to fight. No matter how badly they want to. I'll be with the healers as long as I can."

His Karda Wing was mounted and ready in ten minutes. His big hawk-headed, winged mount Abala was saddled and stomping with impatience when Daryl finally stepped up on his knee, threw a leg over and settled in the saddle. Abala took off at a lope while he was still buckling his leg straps. Then they were in the air. Daryl pulled down his flight goggles against the rush of the wind. Only the thunder of Abala's wings filled the silence of flight, the comforting sound of wings beating up and down as they climbed.

Perhaps the Itza Larrak would be at Flat Rock. Maybe he'd be able to assess the damage it had taken in the last battle when the approaching cold of winter had weakened it, and it disappeared back into its Circle of Disorder with its urbat. Tessa and Kishar had almost severed one of its wings.

He could still smell the stink of urbat on his clothes. He drew on his Air talent and let the wind suck it away until he could smell the cold, clean air of flight. He'd been flying Abala since he was a child. Daryl relaxed into the big Karda's movements. Rested. Let the wind pull his hair loose from its tie. Closed his eyes and rested. Let the wind pull the fears, the doubts, the anger, the tiredness out of him, let it flow through him and out the ends of the hair streaming behind his head.

As soon as spring began to fight off the icy hold of winter, the urbat attacks had renewed in earnest. The Itza Larrak, the awakened alien, was sending them at the small towns and villages all over the south end of the Circle of Disorder where it laired over the winter. Sometimes it was with them—those were always the most devastating attacks—sometimes they appeared without it. The season had barely begun to warm, and already the alliance's troops were tiring trying to counter the scatter-shot tactics it used to keep the planters away from its circle with their remediating trees and plants. If it didn't, the plants would eventually destroy the circle, its refuge.

Abala tilted his wings and began to drop, startling Daryl awake. ~Are we already there?~ Daryl spoke mind to mind to the Karda. ~It's a thirty minute flight. Have I been asleep?~

~You snored so loud I could feel it rumbling through the saddle.~

Abala's telepathic voice was bell-clear in his head. As usual, the big Karda's voice anchored him.

Daryl's fifteen riders on their magnificent hawk-headed flying horses circled the landing field outside the small town of Flat Rock. Huge, monstrous doglike creatures, half metal, half flesh, shoulders and necks covered with triangular metal scales, surged over the walls into the village. They'd arrived just before Daryl's flyers. From high in the air Daryl could hear the ringing beat of their stubby metallic wings. A sound he'd grown to hate. A sound that sang sorrow to his ears. A song that sang failure in his ears.

At his signal, Karda and riders swooped across the field. Daryl watched Karda snatch unwary urbat in their needle sharp talons, carry them high above and drop them to their deaths in the middle of the throng attacking the gates. The gruesome sight roused sickening satisfaction inside him. Sickening to the gentler part of him, satisfying to the fighter part—the part he called on now.

Their riders aimed arrows at the urbat below them as they poured through the gates their long metal claws shredded like tissue. They tore through the streets after townspeople and his few guards stationed there who fought with swords, spears, axes, even hoes—whatever they could grab. His people were tough, resilient. They wouldn't stop. His pride swelled when he spotted two half-grown children, a boy and a girl, tucked next to a chimney on a roof where the urbat couldn't get at them, firing arrows with careful shots at the monsters in the street below.

The Karda patrollers didn't need his guidance—by now they knew only too well what to do, how to attack. His mouth pulled back in a fierce grin. A wide sortie to assess, to look for the Itza Larrak, and he could join the fight. This wouldn't be another Ardencroft, unwarned, undefended, unaware.

Daryl and Abala dropped down to twelve meters, twice as high as the urbat could reach with their stubby wings and massive bodies. They crossed the wall he noted with irritation was too short and made a circle above the small, slate-roofed stone houses and shops of the village. There was no sign of Me'Mattik. Only a scattered few of his troopers fighting with the villagers. Anger at this betrayal added to the despair that drooped like a stubborn shroud over Daryl's shoulders. Even the anticipated fight couldn't dispel it.

Why was Me'Mattik not here? Why was there only a small number of his troopers below? This small farm town was part of his hold, and not far from his keep. It was his responsibility to protect it. Where was he? He must have defected to Readen's rebellion against the so-called aristocracy of talent, weakening the battle against the alien Itza Larrak and adding to the problem Daryl would have to confront when, or was it if, he won this war. Hot blood flooded him. Icy dread fought it.

He didn't have time to think about that betrayal, that future, not now. Screams and urbat snarls and howls rose beneath him. The clang of swords and hoes and scythes against the urbat armor rang, shoving those thoughts out. The savage brutes swarmed through the small town, and the people fought with everything they had. His people. This wasn't the time to think about Me'Mattik and Readen; it was the time to think about defending his people.

Below him, a terrified unarmed villager stumbled to his knees, an urbat half-flying, half-falling at him. A second villager ran to shove his short-bladed spear overhead at the creature's belly and impaled it. The impact knocked the man down, but he scrambled to his feet, put his foot against the urbat, pulled his weapon free and slashed it across the throat. Thick yellow ichor ran in runnels between the cobblestones. Daryl swallowed at the sight of the thin tracery of red human blood that threaded through it, forming a picture of terrible, shocking beauty.

Daryl flew on and the picture disappeared behind them. He drew on his talent. Firebolts—long, narrow projectiles of flame— shot from his spread fingers, one after another. He incinerated every urbat he caught in the open, careful of the villagers and the buildings. He fired and fired until Abala peeled away to beat his way up into the air and beyond the walls. He jerked around in the saddle trying to turn his Karda back. There were still too many urbat on the ground.

~What are you doing, Abala? They're still fighting.~ He didn't have to think about speaking the words from inside his head to Abala's. He'd been doing it since Abala came to him when he was a lonely child of three.

~And you have depleted your talent. You are so tired I can feel you sway in the saddle. We have other work to do. Another kind of monster to find.~

Daryl scrubbed his hands through his hair. He wasn't tired, he was angry. He needed to fight. But Abala circled ever higher, and Daryl slumped in the saddle. This gave him too much time to think, and thinking wasn't what he wanted now. Thinking brought a thin tracery of doubt running through his battle rage. Was he the right person to be leading this battle? He wasn't ready for this responsibility, didn't want this responsibility, didn't want to think about the larger battle picture. He wanted to fight. He wanted to kill urbat.

Then he saw Philipa and Cystra. They flew close, and Philipa held up both arms and shook her head. Daryl's shoulders slumped lower before he caught himself and pushed away all those thoughts he didn't want. Me'Mattik wasn't coming. Now wasn't the time for self-reflection, for doubt. He watched Philipa pull out her bow and head for the town. Like most Mi'hiru, she was deadly with that bow from the air. He wanted to follow her, but Abala was right on both counts. The Itza Larrak had to be found, and Daryl's power had to be replenished.

He'd misread Me'Mattik. The nowhere-in-sight Me'Mattik. Trusted where trust wasn't returned.

He took several long, deep breaths and pulled strength from the air, the clouds, the sky. Restoring his power through elemental Air without touching the ground was difficult—impossible for most— but there wasn't time to land to draw power from deep in Adalta. Slowly it built like thunderclouds roiling and boiling in the sky, filling him, pushing away his uncertainty, giving free rein to his anger and determination.

While it built, he and Abala flew a sortie over the fields and trees around the village, searching for the Itza Larrak. He knew it needed to be within sight of the gates to control its urbat. Daryl strengthened his shields against a possible attack from the alien's powerful psychic force field and flew low, searching, searching. All too aware of the fight in the town. All too aware he was needed there. All too aware he needed to be in six places at any one time.

Off to his right, a small group of men trapped in a red stone quarry fought off ten urbat with picks and long, heavy pry bars—only two of them armed with swords, another with a short spear. They would lose.

Abala pathed to Daryl, ~You are too depleted of talent to use firebolts.~

Daryl stopped him before he could go on. ~Just get us a little closer.~

Abala dove. Daryl extended his arm, spread his fingers, and a bolt of fire flew toward an urbat, burning it to stinking cinders. Abala flew, wings near vertical, in tight arcs around the fight, and Daryl struck another, and another—every urbat far enough from the fighting men, who finally drove the rest of the monsters off and ran for the town gates waving their thanks to Karda and rider. A small victory, but Daryl could use every victory that came along.

Abala straightened and beat his wings hard to gain altitude. They wheeled around again, widening their search over brown fields near the river and the forest to the East wearing a haze of new green leaves and purple buds, but never out of sight of the small town. Daryl split his concentration between drawing power from Air and searching for the Itza Larrak—the alien driving the urbat, controlling them—its minions, its creations.

~There, in that small grove of pines at the far edge of the runway,~ Daryl pathed. ~I can feel the Larrak.~ A flash of anger and denial shuddered through him like a comet trailing a smoky tail of doubt. His brother Readen couldn't have, wouldn't have willingly loosed this monster on Restal Quadrant.

Daryl knew better than to waste power attacking it. The Larrak's shield was too strong for one fighter. Ten of Adalta's powerful talents had fought it in the battle last fall. It had killed one, almost killed another, and escaped. Not unhurt, but it had vanished into its Circle of Disorder where they couldn't follow. Daryl looked as closely as he could through the monster's pearlescent shield. The wing that Tessa, the Austringer, and Kishar, her Karda—the only ones who could follow it into the circle that was its refuge—had nearly severed was repaired. The circle where nothing lived but the Itza Larrak and the urbat spawned there. This was the first time he'd gotten a good look at it since it reemerged. The frustration and anger he'd felt when they couldn't follow and finish what they'd started surged, and he tensed against the grief for the friends lost, for his troops who'd fought and died.

Merenya. For a moment, all he could see was the spray of blood from her Karda's wing and the vision of their twisting, turning fall to earth. Too many friends, too many of his patrollers gone because of this alien being. Such unnecessary deaths. What did it want? What did it fight for?

He was fighting for his people. The Itza Larrak had no people. It had creatures but not people, not beings like it. Survival. It needed to survive. Perhaps, like him, like a human, survival wasn't possible for it alone. Daryl cursed his need to understand everything. It was simpler to have an alien enemy than an enemy he could understand, could imagine, could see what it fought for. It wasn't human. It didn't think in human terms. But survival. Survival wasn't only a human need.

If it had to exterminate humans to survive, it would. If Daryl had to exterminate it for his people to survive, he would.

~We've found it, Abala. Now let's go see if our new tactic works.~ The big roan peeled off toward the village, landed, and loped to a stop beside Philipa and Cystra.

Philipa unfastened her quiver of quarrels from the saddle rig, pulled her small crossbow from its holder, and slid to the ground. She adjusted her sword belt, and started after Daryl.

He stopped and turned to speak to her.

She spoke first, her small body tense. "Don't tell me to go back up there and just watch that monster."

Her face was as tight as her white-knuckled grip on her cross-bow. Daryl didn't dare tell her she couldn't go, and they headed for the gates.

Outside the wall, a ring of six people, six people with strong Air talent, formed, securely guarded by armed villagers and four troopers wearing tunics in Me'Mattik's colors, the only ones Daryl had seen. Two women ran through the gates to join them, a young boy right behind them. One of them called to Daryl, between pants for air, "Where is the Itza Larrak? Are we close enough? I think I can feel it."

"The stand of pines to the southeast of the landing field. I felt its force field shoving at Abala and me. Form up here against the wall close to the gates. I'll help you locate it and monitor you until you find it." Daryl didn't let a hint of his worry about how prepared they were show on his face. He swallowed the bitter taste of it.

A woman already seated cross-legged on the ground, her skirts tucked under her, looked at the boy, anguished questions in her eyes. He spoke between panting breaths. "Mom, Maddy is all right. She's on the roof of the cottage with three quivers of arrows and a spear, firing as fast as she can. Do you need me here to back you up? If not, I'll be with the healers."

She gripped his hand hard. "Don't worry about me. Go to the healers and stay out of the way of the urbat. Don't get killed. You'll be in big trouble if you get yourself hurt." He headed back toward the gates and bumped into Daryl. He stopped, his face bright with relief and a tinge of hero worship."Thank Adalta you're here, Guardian Daryl, now we have a chance."

The boy ran as fast as he could back to the village and the heal-ers, and Daryl bit his lip and watched him go. A chance. He hoped so. In the final battle last fall his troops had trapped several urbat alive. He, several Karda, and the best Air talent minds he could find had studied them and the Itza Larrak's connection to them as long and as intensely as they could. The vicious doglike armored monsters had kept fighting with a singleness of fury—until the alien cut its tie to them, and they milled about in confusion. Daryl could fight with singleness of fury, too. The thunderhead of Air talent inside him roiled with fury and arced with a lightning-arrowed singleness of purpose his doubts couldn't confuse. Not right now. He watched the boy run for the gates and the healers.

The eight people, the village's strongest Air talents, sat in a tight ring on the ground— still, knees touching. This was the first time anyone had applied the spell techniques developed over the winter. Daryl and several of the best Air talents in the Prime had spent long, cold hours in the air flying to the bigger villages near the circle, spreading the spell. This time the urbat had attacked a town big enough to have enough Air talents. A chance. Daryl forced himself to breathe. It had to work. He watched them settle in, gather their Air talent, and reach out to one another to connect. He touched one man gently on the shoulder. "Ground, first." The man straightened, then relaxed into the cross-legged posture these people would hold for hours fighting the Itza Larrak's psychic attacks.

The Itza Larrak stepped out of the pine grove to the edge of the landing field. A tall, broad figure of light-absorbing black chitinous armor. Part metal and part flesh, the Larrak was a grotesque blend of insect and humanoid. Its enormous pierced metal wings never stopped moving, sounding a soft, singing susurrus. It raised its hands, and long, taloned fingers wove complicated symbols in the air.

Despite himself, its eerie beauty caught Daryl. Shaking his attention loose, he drew on Adalta and strengthened his shields just as it threw wave of terror across the field—a psychic wall of terror that froze anything without strong shields, human, animal, or Karda. The eight people swayed, straightened, and held firm, whispering the spell they'd worked on for the past four tendays.

After a few minutes, the ring swayed again then righted itself, pushing a psychic field that rocked the Itza Larrak. They settled in for the long battle for control. He hoped the spell they'd developed worked. If it didn't, troops, villagers—anyone trying to fight who didn't have strong, very strong personal shields were vulnerable and helpless against the urbat. Those with strong shields would be left to fight alone. They wouldn't be enough and another village would be lost.

Daryl breathed deep. The ring swayed and recovered again. The mix of anger at what he fought and the fear for his people that clenched his belly muscles eased. He dropped to his knees, placed his hands flat on the earth, drawing strength from Adalta, restoring Earth and Water talent power inside him, feeling it move up through him from deep in the heart of the planet. He knelt there for several long minutes strengthening his life connection to the source of his talent, sinking into it, into the rocks, the soil, the underground streams, into the heart of Adalta. Until the headiness of the power of the planet flowing through him and the sounds of the battle in the village pulled him back to his purpose.

Finally replete, he sat back on his heels and took a last look at the ring of eight Air talents. They swayed and recovered, swayed and recovered, but held against the Itza Larrak. The power of Adalta surrounded them in whirling wind that lifted their hair and tugged at their clothes.

Then he stood, drew his sword, flexed the fingers of his left hand, and headed through the gates at a fast walk. Abala thundered back into the air to search for unwary urbat. The armor on their necks protected them, but it also prevented them from looking up to see a Karda bearing down on them, long, needle-sharp talons extended. Daryl ran through the gates, Philipa on his heels, and grabbed the arm of the first patroller he saw. "Krager? Where's Armsmaster Krager?"

"Sir, the fiercest fighting is between the grain storehouse and the tavern. You'll find him there. I was waiting for you. To watch your back."

"Let's go then, Wingman Arden. Tell me what you know on the way." As long as Krager was still alive, all was right with the world.

The two men and the Mi'hiru jogged toward the center of the small town, checking each intersection for signs of fighting. Suddenly Arden grabbed Daryl's arm. "Over there, sir. Look." His voice rang, not with danger, or with the thrill of the fight, but as if he saw something impossible.

There, in the middle of the next intersection were four urbat, milling aimlessly and weaving around each other. Sometimes a head would droop, the urbat shaking it furiously. One pawed at its face, leaving deep scratches weeping yellow down its muzzle.

"What's wrong with them?"

Philipa fired her crossbow, crippling one. Daryl waited till the others were as close together as he thought they would get, shook out his left hand and shot three firebolts, incinerating them just as their heads cleared and focused on the three of them.

His lungs filled again. The Itza Larrak had lost control over these urbat for a moment. A significant moment.

He didn't stop to explain or celebrate but headed around the corner to the town square where the fighting was most intense. In the midst of it, Armsmaster Krager watched, shouted orders, and fought, never missing a smooth stroke of his two swords aimed for the urbat's few vulnerable spots. He beheaded an urbat on a backstroke and shouted to send two troopers to a corner where three more urbat appeared. He was alive and unhurt—a flash of relief went through Daryl.

He took a couple of seconds to orient himself, then he didn't have time or thought for anything but his sword and his firebolts and killing monsters. He fought, lost all track of time, keeping his feet in the rivers of blood and gelatinous yellow ichor running between the cobblestones, keeping track of where he was, where the troopers and Krager were, where Philipa was shooting from. She moved along the edge of the square, loosing bolt after bolt from her crossbow. Tipped with razor heads of salvaged urbat metal bones, they could pierce the creatures' armor, sometimes killing, sometimes wounding them for swordsmen to finish off.

An urbat faltered, dropped its head and shook it, an easy target for the farmer's scythe behind it. Another faltered, and another. Then every urbat head snapped up, and the creatures ran for the gate or flew over the wall, some stumbling, a few confused and wandering, soon dead at the swords of the following patrollers and fighting villagers.

They were leaving—running, flying, leaping the wall, tearing through the gate. What happened? He didn't care. They were leaving. The psychic circle. What happened at the circle? He started toward the gates.

Krager walked beside Daryl. "What in the name of our lady Adalta happened here?"

"I hope the ring of Air talents worked, thank blessed Adalta. I hope it was because they held off the Itza Larrak's psychic field and interfered with its control of the urbat. It had to call them back or lose them."

He scrubbed his hands through his hair and rubbed at the back of his neck, feeling the adrenaline sustaining him leach away. His head ached, and he forced himself not to tremble by gripping his sword hilt so tight his hand hurt. "Send small teams through the village. Check every house, every building, under every rock. Gather the wounded here in the main room of the inn." He waved at the building behind Krager. "I need to check on the Air team, then I'll be back here with the wounded." He walked faster and faster until he was running toward the gates, fearing what he would find. Krager, already shouting orders, headed in the other direction.

When he cleared the gates, the clamp of fear tightened on his abdomen again. All eight of the Air talents lay sprawled on the ground, eyes closed, bodies not moving. He skidded to a stop when one of the men rolled over, pushed himself up on one arm, and raised the other, hand fisted in a victory sign.

It had worked. The experimental spell had worked. The circle of Air talents had disrupted the connection between the Larrak and its monsters. More urbat had been killed here than at any of the other villages they'd attacked this spring. With hope and relief, he watched the other members of the circle stir and sit up, tired faces lighting with elation and triumph. He had a new tactic in this war for survival.

The man's voice hoarse and weary, he grated out, "We did it. We forced it away. We forced the Itza Larrak to back away and sent the urbat home with their damn tails between their legs." Then he fell back, exhausted.

CHAPTER TWO

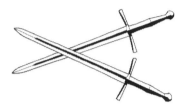

Cedar's ears popped like a cork out of a bottle. The quarantine pod shuddered. The watering can fell off the bench. She lost her balance and smacked her hip on a seedling table. The light over the containment hatch blinked red—on-off on-off on-off—again. Shit.

Cedar moved to the control panel. Oxygen levels were down but climbing. Pressure was down but climbing. Her stomach was down but climbing. And climbing. Climbing a rope in her throat on its way to panic.

The light switched to steady green. Her stomach slid back down the rope, and the breath she didn't know she was holding burst out of her chest like missile propellant.

Another glitch. More every week now on Alal Trade Consortium's five-hundred-year-old-and-then-some spaceship.

She stumbled. Galaxies curse her bionic left leg. Bionic, ha. How did it become a hunk of metal, polymers, and wires that only worked when it chose since they'd first settled into their first orbit of Adalta?

One eye on the light over the door, Cedar moved from plant table to plant table with a carrier of slides, collecting soil samples. The soils from the ship and the soils from the planet had been mixed together for a year now. She should have a definite picture by this time of how well they mixed. Or not. Her hands shook, and she almost dumped the latest sample on the floor. If what she suspected was actually happening, this was the most vital experiment she'd ever attempted.

The lights in her gro-pod were on full-sun. The air was steamy with humidity and smelled of sweet soil. Her favorite place to be. It was a quarantine pod. No one could bother her here. She loved people, but sometimes—well, she'd be lost if the directors ever admitted they had to abandon ship for the anti-tech planet below, and she had to leave this behind. Quarantine gro-pod six was on the perimeter of the spaceship's network of living pods, warehouse pods, manufacturing pods, administrative pods—little pods like this, big pods like the assembly hall and living pods. The ship spread for hundreds of meters in all directions. She thought of it as an enormous fractal net with hiccups.

Her seedlings were fifteen centimeters high, full-leafed and ready to transplant. With care, she uprooted a last seedling with a sample of soil, spread it on a glass slide, slipped the slide into the carrier and moved to her electron microscope. If they had to leave the ship she'd miss her microscope as much as she'd miss her bionic leg. She didn't want to think about how she could work without her equipment. How she would walk without a working leg. Would it fail completely? Would she be a useless cripple? Was leaving an if or a when? If she had so much trouble accepting the when, how did she expect anyone to believe her warnings?

She dipped her head to the eyepieces and watched the dance of organisms. They made her happy as much now as when she'd forced her way, still a child, into the grumpy Director of Bio-Systems's labs as soon as she could walk after her leg was fitted. She was close to certain the microorganisms from the planet were compatible with the ship's ancient Earth soils, preserved so diligently. Today's tests would tell. Plants and microorganisms were so much simpler to deal with than the consortium's directors. And possibly smarter.

The pod shuddered again. The red light over the door blinked again. This time the shudder didn't stop. Neither did the blinking. Not good. Not good. Not good.

Cedar looked for her mother. Ahnna was three tables away, repotting seedlings. "We need to leave, Mother. Now. The containment status—" Her mother didn't look up.

Shit shit. Cedar dropped her slide, slipped in a puddle of water, ran for her mother, and stumbled. Again. Shit shit shit. Now wasn't the time for her leg to freeze. Now wasn't the time for her mother to freeze.

"Mother!" Cedar yelled, and her mother looked around, her eyes wide with an oh-gods-what's-happening-now look. "Get to the hatch. Now!" Oh, galaxies and nebulas, don't let her mother lose it now.

Cedar's ears popped again.

"Now, Ahnna! Now! The containment is breaching. Move!"

Her mother didn't move. She looked like she was staring into a black hole.

The klaxon blared. "Containment failing. Exit pod immediately. Containment failing. Exit pod immediately."

Cedar ran as fast as the solid clunk of her frozen-again leg would let her, grabbed her mother, dragged her to the airlock hatch, and shoved her through.

The door behind them didn't close.

She couldn't panic now. She slapped her hand on the button to open the second portal, shoved her mother again and dove.

The second containment hatch slammed down behind them.

She lay there, flat on the floor, afraid to move. She couldn't look. She couldn't look to see if her foot was smashed. She couldn't look to see if her leg was still attached to her, couldn't breathe. She was useless enough with it. What, who would she be if it was gone? How could she survive on the planet with only one leg? On sheer bravado? How could she be useful? She couldn't feel it. No need to panic; she hadn't been able to feel it for some time now.

Gradually the racing rhythm of her heart slowed. She could breathe again, but the sharp smell of the worn rubber tiles on the floor filled her nose and woke the blank spaces in her brain.

She looked down. She moved her leg. It wasn't caught. And the foot was right there at the end of her bionic leg where it belonged.

"Oh, dear."

Cedar looked up. Ahnna stared at the closed hatch.

"Oh, dear. I think your quarantine gro-pod is gone." She looked down. "I'm sorry, Cedar. I know that experiment was important to you. But I don't think it can be recovered."

Cedar wanted to bang her head—shit—on the floor—shit—three times—shit. But she already had a headache sharp enough to shatter a diamond. She pushed herself up, stumbled to the control panel, switched on the camera and watched her precious plants drift away.

Her knees threatened to give.

She wanted to throw up.

Her mother reached a thin arm around her and flipped the com switch. Cedar alerted the captain's deck. In less than four minutes two tugs appeared and attached themselves to the loose pod. Through its wide-open hatch, she could see her seedlings. They looked fine. And they would be for about twenty more minutes.

Then they'd dehydrate, wither, and die. Like her heart. All the experiments she'd worked so hard on for transferring plants from the ship to the planet.

Gone. Dead. Lost.

And there wasn't a thing she could do about it. The microorganisms might last a bit longer—if the techs could get the hatch closed and the environmental systems back up. Big if.

Her mother took her arm, her fingers gentle on Cedar's clenched muscles. "Let's go, Cedar. There's nothing more we can do here. We'll start over somewhere else."

But there would be no somewhere else. This was the beginning of the end to a familiar somewhere else. She looked past the floating pod to the planet beyond—the only somewhere else left. If she was right and the ship was failing. The loss of the gro-pod was like an exclamation point at the end of that statement. The ship is failing! Please, someone believe me.

Ten minutes and three walkways later, she left her mother with a cup of coffee in the small café near their quarters and headed for the Captain's Meeting Room. "Glenn," she said to her Cue.

"Voigt. Don't call me to fix anything. I'm retired." Grumpy, cryptic Glenn Voigt, Cedar's former boss and still mentor, clicked off. The old man could be more mothering than her mother in his own crusty, crotchety way.

She called him again. "Don't click off. I need you in the director's room. Now, Glenn. The unthinkable has finally happened." She could be just as abrupt and cryptic as he was. And right now it brought a bit of warmth to her middle. Something normal.

By the time she got to the Captain's Meeting Room, Captain Kendra Pathal, and Clare Taylon, Director of Engineering and Maintenance, were seated at the table. Papers and schematics and cups littered its gleaming white surface. Random doors hung open in the wall of cabinets on one side. On the other side of the table was a wall-sized screen. Director of Security Sharon Chobra stood in front of the wall opposite the door filled top to bottom with overflowing plant boxes. Every room on the ship had a plant wall—part of the bio-system that was Cedar's responsibility. Sharon's usually immaculate blond hair was a mess, her uniform half buttoned.

All of them were older than Cedar's nineteen years. Which made it even harder to convince them the ship had fatal problems. They still thought of her as the little girl who lost her leg, her father, and a good bit of her mother on an inhospitable planet. When Glenn retired, they'd probably let him talk them in to letting her serve as Director of Bio-Systems as a sop, a place to put her where they could watch over her. Because she still needed rescue.

Cedar swallowed hard. She stared at her favorite place on the big screen. Her gro-pod, two small one-person tug-shuttles clamped like parasites to its sides, hung in space, the brown and blue planet of Adalta beyond it under patchy gray and white cloud cover. Through the still open maw of the hatch she saw her electron microscope toppled over in pieces. A pile of glass slides lay scattered and broken, glinting ruby crystals in the on-off on-off blinking red light.

Some of her seedling flats had slid off the growing tables to the floor. How was the grav still working? The little green plants looked forlorn, withering but upright, as if all they needed was for her to give them a drink. She blinked hard. It wasn't just the loss of the plants, of the microscope, of the microbes she was studying. She could start her experiments over any time. It was that there wasn't going to be time. Cedar looked around, hoping against hope someone else would finally recognize it. There wasn't going to be time.

Clare's face was white, and Kendra, the captain, shook her head back and forth. Cedar could almost see the words No No No spinning over her head. She wanted to shake her own head. Or bang it against the wall. She'd told the captain. She'd told the directors collectively and individually, again and again. She'd told them the ship was failing—not just old, not just needing maintenance, not just damaged. Capital F Failing. But she was young, they said, and unnecessarily worried, needed more experience. Her fists clenched against her legs.

She was glad she hadn't told them the ship was being sabotaged —maybe by the planet below them. If it was all but impossible for her to believe, once again they'd smile indulgently and remind her she was young, that her plants' roots were invading the systems everywhere on the ship because she didn't have the experience to control them. Did she need Meta from housekeeping to take over some of her duties with the plants?

The ship wasn't ever going to leave this planet. And if she couldn't convince them of that, they'd all die up here in orbit far from hope.

Now they were probably going to make this her fault since it was her plants sending rootlets and tendrils into sensitive places they didn't belong. Sometimes shit doesn't float, it just sinks, and she was at the bottom of this wobbly pile of hierarchy.

The captain, stocky, short, hair going gray over her square face and stolid expression, looked up. "What did you do, Cedar? What happened to your pod? What has happened to my ship? Is it that alien? Are the other aliens coming?"

Cedar couldn't even roll her eyes. She was too sad, too scared to be angry. "I decided the ship was taking up too much space in space, Kendra, so I lopped off a piece." She slid into a chair opposite the captain, her back to the screen. "Mother and I are both okay, by the way. In case, you know, you might be concerned." She turned to the engineering director. "I don't think this is a fixable problem, Clare."

"I'm sorry about your plants, Cedar, and your experiments. We've pushed the pod a safe distance from the ship. I'm not sure how it broke loose. Well, I know how—the sudden escape of air acted like a rocket engine and blew it off. Why it broke loose we don't know yet."

How could Clare be missing the point? It wasn't just the pod that wasn't fixable.

Mark Kelton, Director of Finance, walked in, immaculate in his tight white shirt and black trousers with a knife-sharp crease, blond hair slicked back off his face. "You're just going to let it fall? Letting it drop on some farmer's head is not a good way to let the people down there know we're here."

"I've got two tugs on it now, keeping it in orbit till we figure out what to do." Clare gave Mark a duh-you-idiot look. "And do you actually still think we're a big secret? After what Kayne did? After Galen and Marta? After the rulers and important people on the planet witnessed their marriage ceremony?"

"Galen and Marta? I didn't know they were still together."

"What ship do you live on, Mark?" asked Cedar instead of slapping the back of his head. "What obscure galaxy do you inhabit when you have your nose in your figures?" And your thumb up your nose. Or somewhere else. "Galen is bonded to a young woman, Tessa Me'Cowyn, from the planet and has been for most of the year. Marta is bonded to Altan Me'Gerron, guardian-heir to Toldar Quadrant. Just so you're up to date in the romance department."

Director of Security Sharon Chobra pulled out a chair and sat, ignoring Mark, and brought them back with one word. "Kayne."

Cedar could almost smell the disgust in Sharon's voice.

"Selling akenguns to a primitive planet where such armaments are not only unknown, but their tech forbidden—and stealing Marta's inheritance to do it. If the Trade Federation ever finds us he'll go from our brig to 43Beck b in the Dorma galaxy. A nastier planet doesn't exist—a fitting end for such a nasty man. Unless, of course, this new, interplanetary alien species finds us first."

Mark said, "What do you mean, Sharon, finds us? And, oh great galaxies, we have no defense against an aggressive alien species. Not one of the colonies nor any of the trade ships have ever seen any sign of another sentient species traveling space. I don't believe it."

The four women looked at him, speechless. How could he not know this? Cedar propped her elbows on the table and dropped her face to her hands. She was so tired of willful ignorance her head was too heavy for her neck. Their survival was at stake here. They'd die when the ship fell apart. Or they'd die when the aliens found them. Or she'd die of frustration first and not have to worry about anything anymore. Which death would come first? Frustration. Definitely frustration.

Clare said, her words slow and clearly enunciated, as if she spoke to a five-year-old—a particularly dim one, "The com satellites are gone, Mark."

"Oh, yeah." He glared at her. "Do you have any idea what those satellites cost, Clare?"

Cedar took a deep breath before she loaded Mark the Math Geek in a shuttle and aimed it at a black hole. "No one out there in the wide wide universe knows where we are, Mark." She avoided looking at the others, who still turned deaf ears to her warnings about the ship's failing systems. "And this pod breaking loose is only the biggest and latest in a long series of system failures. The ship is dying, Mark." She didn't add, "As I have said over and over and over to you all." But she had to glue her lips together to keep the words behind her gritted teeth.

Glenn Voigt said it for her as he came through the door. The tall, handsome, silver-haired man's voice was a terse growl. "Face it, people. You have to start planning to abandon ship. And pray that this planet will prove hospitable after what Kayne did. We ain't going nowhere, boys." He pulled out the chair next to Cedar and sat. "How's your mother, Cedar? She okay?"

Cedar waggled her palm. She didn't want to smile, but she did.

The remaining directors arrived, and the conversation ebbed and flowed, drifting like a cloud of galactic gas for another three hours before those whose heads had been mining the asteroid-of-denial were willing to take action. Cedar's rear end was numb, and her nonexistent leg itched like crazy by the time they finally made a sort-of decision. The captain managed to push the threat of the Larrak as a hostile species in interplanetary space out of sight behind a distant nebula.

Clare, Glenn, and Cedar were to do a systematic study of the ship's condition. Cedar knew they only included her because Glenn insisted. After all, she was young and excitable—and had already made up her mind. But it was a start.

They even went so far as to appoint Glenn Voigt the ship's ambassador to Adalta. Whatever they decided about the ship's condition, they were known and official contact needed to be initiated. Cedar could see he was pleased despite his grumpy, grudging acceptance. Assam Kamal, Kayne Morel's replacement as Director of Planetary Affairs, would accompany him. Cedar was appointed to tag along as the Glenn babysitter and if-needed scapegoat.

Assam, a big, shambling, deceptively athletic blond with the kind of face so ugly it was sexy, walked out with her. "You have your work cut out for you, handling that old man, but I guess you've been practicing for it most of your life."

"But your mess is bigger, Assam. Kayne left you a big pile down there."

On her other side, Sharon said, "Do you think you'll get a chance to ride one of those flying hawk-horses? Handling Voigt is a small price to pay for that chance. I'll envy you forever if you get to ride one before I do."

Cedar's eyes rolled as she limp-clumped out the door. She'd rolled her eyes so many times in the last few hours they ached and didn't roll out of her head only because she refused to let them, closing them tight when the urge got too urgent.

Ah, yes, riding a flying horse hundreds of feet above solid ground covered with sharp rocks—there was the bright side to this debacle. The sudden glare was blinding.

CHAPTER THREE

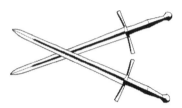

After Daryl was certain the village was clear of the vicious creatures and the Larrak was gone, he moved along the makeshift aisle between pallets crowded into the main room of the village tavern, which stank with the thick miasma of urbat. He knelt beside a young guardsman, his arm torn, one side of his face shredded. He was half-healed and half-conscious. "I'm going to finish healing your wounds now, Boren."

There was comprehension and not a little fear in the boy's eyes. Daryl should have been faster. He should have left the clean up in Krager's capable hands. The village healers and the two from his Karda patrol were overwhelmed. He should clear the stink from the room, but there were still too many half-healed or not yet healed to use his power for that. He'd clear it from the wounds as he went. Galen and Tessa, the Kern and the Austringer, would be here momentarily according to Abala. Galen could clear the room faster and more easily with his powerful Earth talent. And he'd bury the bodies, human and urbat.

"How many did we lose, sir?" The boy's face was tight with pain and Daryl could see it hurt to move his mouth, but that was his first question.

Daryl made a mental note to talk to his lieutenant. He might make a good squad leader. "Not as bad, this time. And you're not one of them."

"Will it hurt?" Boren's voice was faint, as if he was afraid he didn't have enough breath in him to speak.

"You'll feel some heat, but it's okay if you decide to sleep through it. You've done your duty. Now it's time to let someone take care of you."

The urbat left horrible ragged wounds. The hastily slapped on bandages told Daryl he'd gotten enough triage healing to stop the bleeding, but the sick, stinking miasma the urbat left over every battle lingered. It was always strongest where there were wounded, and if it wasn't removed, the wounds festered and turned putrid.

He cupped his hands a few centimeters from the boy's face. His eyes never left Daryl's.

Daryl concentrated, ignoring the weariness that threatened to prostrate him. He reached down through the bedrock beneath the village, searching for rivulets of underground water. A surge of power reached for him, and he drew on it, siphoning away the heavy, sick urbat stink from the wounds, letting it pass through him, pushing it deep into the ground. He couldn't do this as well as Galen, the Kern, who could clear the whole area, but he could do this much.

When it was gone, he sent his consciousness back into the ground, searching out a strong rivulet of water, anchoring himself in bedrock far beneath him, sending his request to Adalta. Earth, Water and Air power moved through him. He twisted Air and Earth into a fire scalpel and focused on the shredded cheek, burning out a few pockets of infection and one hiding patch of urbat miasma. With Earth and Water, he searched for severed nerves to join, knit together torn, cut muscles, and closed the long gashes in the surface of the skin with delicate care. Time passed. He didn't notice. Unable to knit the skin well enough to eliminate scarring, he sat back on his heels and shoved away his frustration that he could do no more—as usual, not letting a hint of that emotion make it to his face. "You'll have scars, Boren. It's been too long since the battle with the monsters for the healing to ensure smooth skin. But they'll be superficial."

The boy tested the muscles in his cheek and discovered he could smile, even if it was a small smile. "There was others hurt worse'n me. I told the healers to let me wait."

Daryl turned his attention to the injured arm, drew more talent force from the planet, and concentrated on the healing. He lost himself again as he knitted blood vessels, muscles, and tendons, repaired a deep score in the bone, and finally closed the final layer of skin.

"You'll have scars here, too, but you'll have full use of your arm." No one could have done better. He had no doubts about his ability to heal, and it felt good. If he could devote his life to something other than this battle and solving the problems of Restal, it would be a close struggle between healing and books. That's where his strength was. Could he ever find that strength as a leader? Would he?

The young man made a fist and grimaced.

"I know. It still hurts. It takes a while for your body to finish the healing. Your arm will be sore, and you won't be able to use it to the fullest for a tenday." Daryl patted his good arm. But Boren was already asleep.

"At least the urbat stink is gone—from you if not from the room," he said to himself. The smell was thick, nearly palpable, toxic and infectious. It permeated everything around them, settled in wounds, on walls and floors, bodies and bedding. It took a long time for it to dissipate naturally and left lingering sickness behind. Galen needed to get here soon.

With effort, Daryl levered his tired body back to his feet and looked around. He dabbed more pine sap salve under his nose and under the boy's. The wounded lay on pallets with a few cots for the more severe cases. The less severely injured leaned against the walls, waiting their turn. With so many, the healers were forced to ration their battlefield triage, only doing what they must to stabilize the worst and get all of them inside the tavern.

He let his eyes and his talent senses roam over the room and noticed fever spiking in three of the guards lying there. He caught a healer's eye and motioned to the three men. She nodded.

He raised his head and sniffed. At last, thanks to the healers with strong Earth talent, the foul, stinking miasma hovering over the wounded was less thick. One more reason they were tired and their talent stretched thin. One more reason why the less severely injured, like Boren, had to wait so long for healing. Many would have scars they shouldn't have. He closed his eyes and opened them quickly so he didn't fall down in a heap on the floor.

Then he felt something. A tiny nudge at his senses. He wound his way through to a young woman lying on a cot near the doorway and knelt beside her. Ana, one of his regular Karda Patrol wing and fiercely loyal to him. She had taken a slash low to her side. He searched it. It wasn't the wound he felt. That was closed and shallow enough the intestines weren't compromised. He searched further and found the tiny nudge—a faint, fast thready beat. Not *her* heart, though. She was pregnant. The shock of her wound and a hidden pocket of foul urbat taint threatened the small life inside her.

He took her hand, and she opened her eyes. She trembled with fear. "I thought I would be all right when the healer finished with me, but there's something else wrong. I have just enough talent to know it, but not enough to fix it. I don't know…" Her hysteria rose, and her words faltered.

"May I?" he asked, with his hand just above her belly. She nodded, and he rested his hand on the blanket. He closed his eyes, firmed his connection to Adalta, and sucked the contamination through him into the ground beneath. His attention sank into her and found the little spark that was new life. Daryl grounded it, strengthened its shaken connections to the larger life that was the planet Adalta and to the mother-to-be. He felt the muscles of her abdomen relax.

"What is it?" she asked. "Did the healers miss something? A leaky blood vessel?"

He sat back on his heels. "You have something to tell Jack, Ana. I'll send him to you as soon as I see him."

Her eyes widened, and both hands flew to her belly. "I'm pregnant?" Her eyes went frantic. "Is it all right?"

"It's decided to stay." He put a large sword-callused hand over hers, his smile as light as his heart. "A new life. I'm glad I'm the one who discovered it. A sign of hope and regeneration. Thank you, Ana."

Something in him relaxed for the first time in months since he'd first learned of Readen's perfidy, since he'd been shot with a poisoned arrow—at Readen's order—since he'd come too close to being garroted—again at Readen's order.

Too pragmatic to believe in signs and portents, nevertheless, irrational as it might be, Daryl felt a tiny bit of joy nudge away a tiny bit of self-doubt, at least for the moment. He walked on through the wounded, speaking to each one as he passed. Thanking the troopers and assuring the villagers that they would have the help they needed to rebuild and repair the damage from the urbat attack.

Flat Rock's three village councilors—two women and a man—waited for him on the wide covered porch of the tavern, their faces drawn with pain, anger, and fear.

Headwoman Surana's right arm was in a sling, her left arm supporting it. She shifted on her feet, and pain flashed on her face. "Perhaps we could meet in my home. It's not far."

He followed them to a small, one-story brick home. A young girl sloshed buckets of water across the steps. It ran red with blood and strings of gelatinous yellow ichor. Her skirt was tied up out of the way showing bulky bandages wrapping both legs.

She noticed his look. "I been to the healers. I be all right." She moved aside, and they entered, doing their best not to step in the bloody water.

Inside, a small boy slumped half-asleep in a chair at the stone table that took up much of the kitchen-living area, both arms wrapped in colorful bandages torn from the curtains on the window beyond him.

Surana shook her head at Daryl's questioning look. "My family is not as bad off as some of the others. My bonded is unhurt. He's our blacksmith and made sure to keep one of the weapons made of the monster's metal bones close by him. Unlike some, who thought since we'd heard of no attacks all winter that they were over, that our walls were high enough, strong enough, and we'd be safe inside them."

She sat, almost fell, into a chair, and he felt her weariness. "They were wrong. Please seat yourself. I can stand no longer. Mina will finish washing the blood and ichor from the porch and come to make us some tea. And we could all use a sandwich, I think. You are welcome in our home, Guardian. May our table provide you sustenance, may our land provide you work to suit your heart and hands, and may you find safety within our walls for your rest." She paused. "And may the work our land provides you be less bloody than this day's."

The boy lifted his head, and his mother said, "Go to your bed, son. You've helped as much as you can. Now you need rest."

He looked at Daryl, at the sword on his hip, and his lips went tight and thin. He forced words between them, "We all knew Me'Mattik was gone. We all knew he wasn't going to show up. How could you not know? You're the guardian. You're supposed to know."

"To bed now, Arlen," his mother said, her weary voice sad, one wary eye on Daryl.

The boy backed away into another room, his eyes never leaving Daryl's. The anger and accusation blazing in them arrowed deep into his chest. It would do no good to tell the boy he and his patrol had been fighting at a village forty kilometers away—an attack even more devastating than this one. That one of his patrol wing members and a Karda were dead. That he'd been fighting urbat in village after village since winter season changed to early spring. That every Karda patroller he had was tired to the bone or injured or both.

"He lost his best friend. He's an apprentice healer, and he couldn't save his best friend, Guardian. Please forgive his anger," said Surana, her words low, weary, unapologetic.

Daryl nodded. He could take the boy's anger. He was angry too.

The male counselor, Davris, said, "You are always too easy on that boy, Surana. He needs discipline." His tone was harsh until he turned to Daryl. "We hold no blame for you, Guardian. We are grateful that you arrived when you did. Your Karda Patrol saved us." His switch to a fawning tone grated on Daryl.

The other woman, Bettis, spoke, "And we wouldn't have needed so much help, Davris, if you had agreed to spend enough to raise our walls this winter—like we were told. Or agreed to pay our blacksmith to forge more weapons—like we were told. Or agreed to train our young people to fight—like we were told. I think it might be time to change our town charter. If all three of us have to agree on an action, too often no action is taken, and today we've had a harsh lesson."

His instructions, his exhortations—he'd practically begged the holders and villagers to listen—had too often been ignored or at best resulted in half-hearted efforts. It reinforced his doubts of his adequacy as a leader.

Bettis pulled her blue cloak, banded with the distinctive dark red embroidery of a healer, tighter around her. "I'm exhausted, and I still have patients to see to. Let's figure out what we do next and get this meeting over with." Bettis looked at him. "We won't let those monsters defeat us."

Surana ignored Davris. "Three young men cutting wood in the forest spotted the urbat. They warned us. One of the monsters they saw was taller than a man and walked on two feet clawed like a Karda's. It was dark as night with yellow eyes and enormous wings. It had to be the Itza Larrak. Thank Adalta, Surana had organized our Air talents. They, at least, paid attention to your warnings and directions."

"We worked hard on our defense against its terror attack, said Surana. "Without the spells you and Finder Mireia sent..." Her words trailed away, and her eyes looked at empty distance.

Davris snapped his words out. "We had prepared, whatever these women tell you. We had. And we killed a lot of urbat. We drove them off."

Daryl straightened in his chair. The last thing he needed was to get in the middle of a village squabble. The girl Mina handed him a mug of hot, strong tea. The warmth on his hands was welcome. Early spring might be warmer than the cruel winters on Adalta, but sometimes it was hard for him to believe the season was actually changing. "You are fortunate you have enough strong Air talents to block it." He didn't tell them that had they not been able to block the Itza Larrak, many of them would be dead. He'd found too many villages, too late, that hadn't been so fortunate. Even one was too many. He dropped his eyes to the steaming cup. There'd been more than one.

A Karda screamed its hawk cry from the sky, and Daryl heard Abala in his head. ~Tessa, Kishar, and Galen approach.~ There was a pause, then Abala added, humor in his voice, ~Yes, Ket, too, of course.~

Daryl caught himself before he slumped in relief. "Surana, the Austringer and the Kern are approaching your landing field. Galen will clear the diseased stink from the urbat, salvage the armor and metal bones from the dead ones, and bury them for you if you collect them in one spot. We'll leave the metal with your blacksmith. Tessa will talk to your village defenders about strategy. I see your walls almost reach high enough. You'll be able to repair today's damage and finish them, with luck, in possibly a tenday and a half."

He looked at Davris. "Do not worry about the costs. Restal's treasury is hard hit, but I'll see about resources for you. Planting season is still tendays away, so every worker you have can be put to building up your walls."

He put his untasted tea on the table and pushed himself to his feet. He'd find them help somewhere, somehow. "I'm heading for Me'Mattik Hold to find out why he didn't come. He'll provide funds to help you."

No one spoke. No one looked at him. The three village leaders stared at the table.

"What is it? Do you think he won't help? He's your holder. It's his responsibility."

They didn't answer. Now he didn't want to hear their next words.

Surana finally looked up. "He's gone. He and his troops are

gone. Meryl went to see him to ask for help on our walls on Deciday and find out why his troops left us unguarded. His hold is abandoned; only servants and a few guards remain."

Daryl looked at her. Her words hardly registered. Dread opened a deep, gaping hole inside him. "Gone?" That was all he could say, could think.

Bettis said, "Gone. North. To your brother Readen's hold, or so the rumors say. Word is, he's joined Readen's revolt against you."

Daryl looked back and forth between the three of them. His mouth wouldn't form words. Me'Mattik wouldn't be at his keep. And he wasn't off fighting urbat somewhere else on his hold. Daryl deserved the boy's anger. He'd failed to keep track of Me'Mattik. What other holders would he lose to Readen? He fought to keep his despair from showing on his face.

Bettis's face twisted in disgust. "Me'Mattik is not a strong talent for a holder. Probably doesn't have much more than I, a simple village healer, do. He believes your brother is fighting you on behalf of those with weaker talent—against the custom of rule by strong talent."

Surana snorted. "His excuse, you mean. He is a traitor to Restal."

"I hope you will not hold his treason against us, Guardian," said Davris. His eyes shifted back and forth between the other two councilors. "We are completely loyal to you. You are the true leader of Restal Quadrant."

Was he the true leader of Restal? It wasn't Readen—not so long as he was under the Itza Larrak's control. Who else was there? He was failing in his responsibility to Restal. The elation he'd felt when the psychic circle had broken the Itza Larrak's grip deflated to a tiny meaningless triumph in the overwhelming battle. If more holders defected to Readen, the Itza Larrak would win, and Adalta was doomed.

He wanted to close his eyes as if it would block the betrayals. Me'Mattik's betrayal. Readen's betrayal. His own betrayal as an unsure and inadequate leader.

CHAPTER FOUR

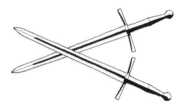

Daryl, with Restal's Commander Kyle, walked into the long narrow council room of the keep, lit by small balls of light in bronze brackets on the red sandstone walls. Two ornate, open iron stoves with glowing magma stones warmed it. A polished granite table surrounded by carved wooden chairs in the center of the room were the only furniture. Daryl pulled out a chair and sat at one end of the long table. Prime Guardian Hugh Me'Rahl from the citadel at Rashiba moved to the other.

Guardian Turin of Akhara took a seat midway between them in front of the floor to ceiling small-paned windows. Two of his guards stood behind him. The mountainous man sat unmoving. Daryl noticed his closed eyes, as though he were meditating. It wasn't bringing him peace if the lines of cruelty carved deep in his face were to be believed. He turned one open eye on Daryl as if taking his measure then closed it again, hands folded on the table in front of him.

Marta Me'Rowan, from Toldar Quadrant, and Tessa Me'Cowyn, the Austringer, came through the door laughing and talking. Galen Me'Cowyn, the Kern and Tessa's bonded, followed them.

Three of Restal's largest holders arrived and arranged themselves around the table. Already seated was Anuma Quadrant's new guardian, Ballard Me'Karyl, whose face, whose whole demeanor, shouted anger and grief for the mother he'd lost to the Itza Larrak in the battle just before last winter set in. Tessa and Marta stopped laughing.

Finally, Daryl stood and began, "Welcome, all of you, to Restal Prime. May our table provide you sustenance, may our land provide you work to suit your heart and hands, and may you find safety within our walls in your rest. And may we find mutual benefit and agreement in the issues before us today." He turned to Turin. "Guardian Turin, I want to particularly welcome you. I know your winter was long, cold, and arduous, and you would much rather have been able to return to Akhara than spend the winter in the cold here."

Turin put his huge fist on the table and looked at Daryl, eyes slits, mouth a straight, thin line. He rolled his shoulders and said, voice flat in a tell-me-no-lies tone, "I kept my troops here because Hugh asked, and because I deemed the threat of the monster your brother released a serious one. But Hugh is not leading this fight. You are. Which gives me pause."

Daryl felt Commander Kyle lean forward.

"Why should we—" Turin gestured at Ballard, inclined his head to Marta. "Why should we other guardians trust you to lead this battle given the deplorable history of your family's rule here and given the fact that your family brought this curse upon us?"

In the devastating silence Daryl wondered if the others could hear the whistle of steam from his boiling shame, his doubts about Readen, his roiling anger. That Turin could be right only added more pressure. He had a right to question Daryl's leadership, but Daryl would never admit that Readen was more than a victim of the Itza Larrak. Not to Turin, not to himself, not to anyone.

Daryl shoved his way through his frustrations and doubts, unlocked his clenched jaw, and walked around the table to get as close to Turin's face as he could and let anger give power to his voice. Turin might be right, but Daryl wouldn't, couldn't let this go.

"I am not my father. My brother is not responsible for loosing the Itza Larrak on us. This is my quadrant. I am not asking you to fight with me against Readen. I am calling on you to fight the threat against all Adalta."

Turin didn't look away and neither did Daryl. Finally, Daryl said, "Perhaps you could start with what you saw of the urbat, and what you could see happening at the Circles of Disorder you passed on your way up from the eastern border?"

Tension held the room in thrall for a minute that threatened to become eternity, then Turin's chair creaked, and he leaned into the table. "We couldn't ride near the circles, but the Mi'hiru and my one Karda Patrol wing were able to see farther as they flew above us."

Daryl moved back to his chair. He wouldn't show relief that Turin had backed down. Wouldn't show how fragile his bluff had been. He kept his face impassive. Stone, but stone that paid attention to every word and expression.

Turin's voice was deep, his eyes narrowed slits in his broad face. "There are lines of dead trees extending for kilometers from all four quadrants of the three circles they scouted. All of them reaching toward a line from another circle. The last word I received from my people is that whatever your brother set free, *accidentally*, here in Restal has spread as far as Akhara, and there are lines growing out of the circles there. Our last guardian was also lax about keeping up the remedial planting around the circles, but it didn't go on for generations, and I have reinstated it."

Daryl saw a flash of what might be concern cross his face. Maybe the rumors about his ruthless ambition were exaggerated. Then the flash was gone. And maybe not. If he had to trust Turin, it couldn't be blind trust. Ever.

"The villagers, by the way, gave us what supplies they could spare, but they were too often sullen and suspicious. It wasn't because we were from another quadrant. The Mi'hiru did a good job of spreading the word that we were here to fight urbat and the alien monster, not conquer them, but the resentment was strong. Not directed at my troops, but at me—as a guardian."

Turin leaned back and his chair creaked again. "We encountered no urbat coming from any circle we passed, but it was apparent that remedial planting around the ones in this quadrant had been abandoned too long, and they are spreading."

Turin nodded his head toward Marta in what Daryl thought might pass for respect if he stretched the word to its limit. "Mi'hiru Marta, congratulations on your bonding to Toldar's heir and your new position. I was privileged to be invited to witness." He nodded to Tessa and Galen who were bonded in the same ceremony in Toldar Prime before winter closed everything down.

He continued. "Toldar and Anuma have been more diligent in their care of the circles. The lines were there, leading out of every circle we passed, but they were only a few kilometers, sometimes only a few hundred meters long." He turned back to Daryl, and his look couldn't have passed for friendly. "I cannot say the same for the circles in Restal. Not only are the lines longer, but the circles are larger, far worse than Akhara. As I said, I resumed the remedial planting as soon as I became guardian."

The Circles of Disorder—bleak, deadly areas, roughly circular, created by the alien Larrak race millennia before—were enormous. When the colonists from a devastated and close to uninhabitable Earth arrived, they found themselves in the middle of a war between the Larrak and the planet, Adalta, which the Larrak wished to take over. They were well on the way to stripping the planet and making the entire world as toxic as the circles. The soil over much of the continent was sterile. When the Larrak were done, they would have moved on to find another world to sustain them. It was the Karda who asked the humans for help, and between them, they destroyed all but one Larrak, the Itza, the last Larrak.

The colonists' Ark ship was loaded with the seeds, the embryos, the DNA of every species of life that could be rescued from Earth. And after fighting centuries of pollution, they had many remedial plants. When they succeeded in crossing an Earth poplar, long used for pollution remediation, with a native dalum tree, they began planting the resulting abelee trees around the circles. Over the five centuries since they began, and with much work, the circles diminished and forests grew. From the spaceship now above they looked like great green bowls with a sick canker in their midst.

Now, with the escape of the Itza Larrak from its cavern prison, Lines of Devastation had begun to snake out of first one circle, and then another and another, reaching for each other to form a net that would extend across the continent. A net that the ancient Kishar, the last Karda of his kind, said would become an antenna for the Itza Larrak to use to call back Larrak ships. The parasitic aliens would destroy Adalta.

Prime Guardian Hugh spoke up. "You are right, Turin, it is Readen who is responsible for the Lines of Devastation. It was your brother, Daryl, who loosed the Itza Larrak on us. I will accept you believe it was accidental, not intentional, and he is a victim. Perhaps that's true. But, make no mistake"—he looked directly at Turin—"it is a curse that affects all Adalta. If we do not stop it here we are lost. And Daryl is the one who knows this quadrant and its people."

He turned to Daryl. "I know with spring coming the urbat attacks have started again here, and it will get worse as the weather continues to warm. How bad has it been?"

Not for the first time, Daryl wished he could turn the responsibility for war against the Larrak over to the Prime guardian. But the laws limiting a centralized government forbade it. He bit down on the inside of his cheek and swallowed the copper taste of blood and the taste of his doubt about his ability to lead this fight—not for the first time.

"We—" Daryl nodded at Commander Kyle and at Armsmaster Krager on his right—tall, rangy, his face all hard planes with a thin scar across his cheek, "have stretched our troops as far as we can. We developed a spell to be used by a circle of Air talents to disrupt the link between the Itza Larrak and the urbat. It worked, and since that last attack all has been quiet. It won't last."

"The Karda tell me the ice in your harbors will soon start breaking up, Guardian Turin, and two large bands of mercenaries, maybe fifty or so each, were spotted loading supplies onto ships in Port Exhallan on your border with Toldar's Coastal Holding." Marta had the unique ability to speak to any Karda and used that ability to collect information from all across Adalta. "I assume as soon as they can safely leave harbor they'll load their horses and embark. They'll head for Me'Bolyn Hold to try to cross through Revka Pass."

Daryl looked at Turin and waited for a response—and waited.

Finally, Turin turned to look at Daryl.

He always looked like he was half asleep. He wasn't. Daryl needed to remember that.

"What colors did they wear?" Turin asked.

"Colors? Oh, yes, one band wore maroon and the other dark blue."

Daryl couldn't interpret the look that flashed in Turin's eyes before they turned to dark, still lakes.

"Stephan will not allow them to cross Toldar," Marta said. "They'll have to land in Restal's Coastal Holding."

"It's a long coast," said Krager. "With far too many inlets and coves where they can disembark without being seen."

Hugh spoke up. "If he knows, that would explain why we haven't heard from Holder Me'Bolyn. He'll be protecting his own. He's not one for asking others to help protect what's his. Me'Nowyk will let us know as soon as any ships are spotted off his coast."

"Yes, if they are spotted. The Karda can't fly too far from land. They could slip by." Marta agreed. "Mi'hiru Dalys is there. I'll send word to her. She speaks telepathically with—I can't remember the name of the Karda who partners her. And so does Me'Nowyk's daughter."

Daryl cocked his head. "Jenna? I thought she was terrified of Karda."

"No, his youngest daughter. She's only ten but an accomplished flyer, and she flies all along that part of the coast." Marta's voice lowered until her words almost couldn't be heard, and her mouth quivered with the effort not to curve into a nasty smile. "I bet that infuriates Jenna." They weren't friends.

Turin slapped a hand on the table. "I'm not here to talk about little girls and Karda. I'm here to talk about what your brother unleashed on us, Daryl. I want to know what the situation is now.

What else are we going to face?" He looked across the table to Marta, Galen, and Tessa. "While it was an honor to be invited to attend your bonding ceremony, I need to get back to Akhara. Let's get to the real issue here."

Hugh Me'Rahl spoke in a quiet voice that commanded attention. "Since one of the real issues is the expected arrival of two mercenary troops from your quadrant who were not invited by Daryl, perhaps we can start there."

Turin's ponderous head turned to the Prime guardian. "I do not control all the mercenary troops in Akhara. Those are not my troops—wrong colors. Frankly, I'm glad they are out of Akhara and not my problem."

Commander Kyle spoke, "Yes, the problem seems to have been handed to us. But our most immediate problem is the urbat and the Itza Larrak that controls them."

Hugh's eyes hadn't left Turin's face. "I repeat—this problem is not just Restal's. That's the reason you and I, Ballard, and Marta as Toldar's representative, are at this meeting. These monsters must be contained and defeated here, and Daryl needs help defeating them. He's fighting another front to recapture Readen, which isn't helped by your mercenaries, Turin. If we do not help here, we risk once again plunging all Adalta into a war with aliens we know next to nothing about. The Itza Larrak cannot be allowed to build his planet-wide antenna to call other Larrak. And you do not want another Ardencroft in Akhara if the urbat from your circles are released."

Tessa spoke up, her voice low and intense, "No, you do not want an Ardencroft, Guardian Turin. The urbat killed every person in that village and in the prison where Readen was being held. every one. We had to bury them all in a common grave. I had to put a baby in that grave with no way of knowing who his parents were. He still haunts my dreams, crying for his mother. You do not want that."

Daryl watched Turin's face. It seemed a placid blank, but around his eyes and mouth the lines deepened. He would have to be told about the other threat—the akenguns smuggled to Readen from the spaceship. "Since this is my quadrant, and Krager, Commander Kyle, and I are most familiar with the terrain and have experience fighting the urbat, Hugh has agreed that we—I should take the lead. You've had troops stationed here all winter, but what I need to know is how many more troops you can send. The urbat have started to attack with a vengeance as the weather warms and they can move again. Several villages have been hit."

"Altan will be in Restal with four hundred troops from Toldar within a tenday," said Marta. "He stopped at two circles with his strongest Earth and Air talents and burned through the Lines of Devastation growing in this direction. We know that's not a permanent solution. They grow back. He cannot bring his troops directly to Restal Prime. He and his father, Toldar's Guardian Stephan, do not want their movements misconstrued as a threat. But Stephan also knows the akenguns smuggled from the spaceship are a threat to all of Adalta, and Altan *will* attack Readen if he leaves his hold with them. Altan is skirting the mountains to get close enough to Readen's hold to gather what information he can."

"Weapons from the spaceship?" asked Turin. "What kind of weapons? How useful, or dangerous, are they?"

He suddenly appeared to come alive, his frown no longer one of boredom and distrust, but one of intense eagerness. Daryl didn't like that quickened interest.

The akenguns were an advanced technological hand weapon. They could be fired fifty times before they ran down, and because of Adalta's ever-roaming magnetic energy fields, they couldn't be recharged. Nevertheless, they would devastate a force armed only with bows, spears and swords.

"I have a hundred troops inside your borders, and a hundred more preparing to deploy from Anuma," said Guardian Ballard. "From the reports I've gotten, the attacks that began this spring have been between Restal Prime and the circle to the north where we fought when winter began." He looked at Turin. "I understand your hundred-fifty troops are moving up from the border in the direction of the urbat's circle now."

Turin looked at Ballard and Daryl looked at Turin. There was a long silence, then Turin nodded. Daryl calculated how many Karda and Karda Patrol he would have to divert to keep track of Turin's direction. The guardian was impossible to read.

"The problem now becomes the Itza Larrak. We don't know where it is. It has powers of illusion. If it acts as it did last fall, it will not leave us alone to cut the lines and to reestablish the remedial plants that reverse the circle's growth. It and its urbat will attack all efforts to do so," said Daryl. He knocked his knuckles on the table. "So once again we'll attack the circle with all the planters Master Planter Andra can find. Only this time we won't be in only one place. I intend to surround the circle. She's preparing for that."

Tessa spoke, her words low and hard and pointed as one of her arrows. "The Itza Larrak and the urbat both get their power from the circles. It will defend the circle with all it has. Surrounding the perimeter with planters will scatter its forces in groups small enough that we can decimate them. It will have to show itself and make a stand. And we know it can be hurt. We know it's possible to kill it."

Daryl noted Turin's reassessing look at young and beautiful Tessa. It was Tessa and Kishar who'd come close to killing it, who'd wounded it, who'd almost severed one of its metal wings. Young and beautiful silver-haired Tessa was also fierce and dangerous Tessa. Between them, she and the ancient Kishar knew more about the Itza Larrak than anyone alive on Adalta.

Daryl broke the silence that followed her words. "Hugh, perhaps now is the time to tell us of the other problem we face."

The Prime guardian pushed his chair back and slowly walked to stand near the stove. He looked at each of the other guardians in turn. "As most of you are aware, for the first time in five hundred years we have been reached by other humans. The ship orbiting above us has dropped its mirror shields and is visible in the night sky. I have been contacted, through Marta and Galen on their communication devices, with a message that the ship is failing. It is one of the original Ark ships peopled by trader families who elected to stay in space rather than on a planet."

"So it's leaving," said Ballard. "And we've been discovered."

"We've been discovered. But the ship's not leaving, Ballard.

They want permission to send envoys to ask for a place here. The ship cannot leave orbit around Adalta. It is failing. Its people have no other place to go."

Readen Me'Vere looked up from his desk. Closing the journal he was writing in, he stood, and reached out a hand to grasp Holder Me'Mattik's forearm.

"Anson, may my table provide you sustenance, may my land provide you work to suit your heart and hands, and may you find safety within my walls in your rest. Welcome to Me'Vere Hold." His smile was broad—this was his genial, friend to all half. The one most people knew. The one that most people believed.

But something—something other—watched from inside his head—cold, assessing, uncaring—and too familiar. Too much like that other half of him. The cruel, power hungry, half. The half that thrived on torture and pain. Readen blinked and it was gone.

"I'm gratified you decided to answer my invitation. Tell me how matters are at your holding, Me'Mattik. I understand there have been some troubles with strange creatures. Are your people safe?" The watching thing in his head wondered why Readen had asked. Neither he nor it cared about Me'Mattik's people. "Have a seat and I'll order something hot for you, with an extra kick. It may officially be spring, but it's still damned cold out there, and I imagine the roads and trails were deep with mud. My people said you rode in, not flew in."

He knew all too well no Karda would ever land at his holding. No Karda would ever carry him. And he suspected they had refused Me'Mattik too.

He listened to the holder's words with half his mind while the other half tried to free itself of the alien presence intruding again. It had the feel of the Itza Larrak. But how could that be? He pushed it away, and it disappeared, leaving a tiny worm of unease he ignored. He was used to living with two halves of himself. He didn't need a third half.

Me'Mattik pulled off his gloves and shed his heavy lined coat. "Cold isn't a strong enough word for the weather. But spring will come. It always does." Every sentence tilted up on the end, like he was asking permission to be there, like he wasn't sure of his balance. Was there ever anyone as boring as this man? "I've come to talk to you about Daryl."

Readen dropped his head, shook it, and looked away out the window, forcing the muscles in his face to pull down, sighed deeply, raised his head and looked at Me'Mattik. "I hope you've come to tell me he's ready to apologize for..." His words trailed away, and he looked down again. His fingers picked up the pen, twirled it, then dropped it back on top of the slim leather journal he'd been writing in, every move practiced, studied. He was so accomplished at duplicity he didn't need to think about it.

Me'Mattik reacted just as Readen intended at this show of sadness and humility.

"It's a crime the way he's treated you. First locking you in prison, then isolating you in your hold. I had a hard time talking myself and my guard through the ring of watchers he has around you here. I've come to ask what your plans are. It's high time someone realized the smaller holders with lesser talents should have their say in the quadrant's government. And you're the one to lead that fight."

Me'Mattik had never had an original thought in his head. Every word he said was a word Readen worked to plant for years. They were finally sprouting out of the fertile ground of stupidity in this idiot's brain.

Readen pulled his face down again and shook his head, slow movements side to side. "I tried, Me'Mattik. I tried. Perhaps it was too early. Perhaps the others like you and the smaller holders weren't ready. Perhaps they're not ready now. I'm isolated here. I can't get much information about what's going on in my—in the quadrant. It's frustrating and distressing to me. Daryl is so young and impractical. I'm afraid he's just going to make things worse no matter how hard he tries. He has so many new ideas and so little real-life experience. I just hope the quadrant is ready for him. And that he's ready for it. He has no idea of the weight of duties he faces. And I worry about the people he's surrounded himself with—two of them from Toldar."

And he'd worked hard to instill doubt and guilt in Daryl almost from the moment of his birth. To make him feel incompetent and unsure. It would have worked if it hadn't been for Krager. At the thought of Krager's duplicity, rage almost broke through his practiced geniality. If not for his betrayal, Readen would still be in control of Restal Prime, and by now the entire quadrant.

He stood and walked to the window, his back to the room and the holder. His voice low, he said, "I wish I knew more about how the others like you feel. I can't begin to tell you how it gratifies me that you came. That you are willing to talk to me."

He turned back around, one hand on his heart, and Me'Mattik reacted exactly as Readen intended.

His voice stronger, Me'Mattik said, "You have more support than you know. The quadrant is in chaos. Daryl is chasing his tail all over the northwest of Restal fighting little battles with monsters they call urbat. And the people close to him are blaming you for their appearance. Saying they are controlled by the Itza Larrak you supposedly released. Daryl doesn't believe that, but every one around him does. I don't know how long it will be before they convince him."

Readen moved back to his desk, elbows propped, head in his hands to hide his smile. Daryl would never believe his brother could be anything but a victim of evil. His voice low so Me'Mattik had to lean forward to hear him, he said, "That woman spy from the spaceship, Marta. I liked her." There was a long pause. "Why is she telling such horrific stories about me? That I tortured her, when there wasn't a mark on her body? That I somehow released the alien Itza Larrak from the prison it had been in for centuries? How could I even know how to do that? How could I even know it was there? What does she gain from these lies? What do the people on her spaceship plan to do to us, to Adalta? What do they want—with all their forbidden technologies?"

CHAPTER FIVE

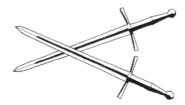

"No. I will not allow you to go, Cedar. I cannot allow it. Astarte15 isn't safe."

Cedar closed her eyes and took a long, slow breath. "This isn't Astarte15, Mother. That was years ago. This planet is Adalta, and it isn't the same at all. Galen is down there. And Marta. Glenn is going with me. And Assam. It's safe." She squeezed her mother's shoulder. "I've been ordered to go. I'm one of the ambassadors, Mother. It is an honor."

Truth be told, she'd begged and pleaded and coerced whomever she could corner to finally admit the ship had major problems. Not every one was yet convinced it was failing, but at least most of the directors finally admitted the ship was never leaving Adalta's orbit. She didn't think the captain had. Not yet. Not completely.

"You understand that. I've asked Amalie to come stay with you while I'm gone. She'll help you start packing."

"Pack? Why should I need to pack?" Ahnna's voice rose higher with each word. Her thin hands, blue veins showing through translucent skin, traced back and forth on the folded coverlet at the end of Cedar's bed, never stopping. "I don't understand what I would need to pack for. You're not going, Cedar. I won't pack your things."

Apparently being appointed an ambassador wasn't an honor to her mother. Her fear for Cedar was stronger. But Cedar'd been so young and only half-conscious when they'd been stranded on Astarte15, hiding from the men who'd killed her father. For ten days her mother kept them hidden, tended Cedar's leg as best she could, and never let her child see her fear, holding them both together until they were rescued. It was only when the infection in Cedar's leg couldn't be healed, and it had to be removed that her mother fell apart. She'd not been whole since. Sometimes Cedar thought her mother had lost more than she had on Astarte15.

"My things are packed, Mother," said Cedar, her voice calm, her words evenly paced. "See? This is the last of them—" She tucked a jacket in an outside pocket of her soft-sided duffel. "every one will leave the ship over the next months, Mother. We discussed that." She took both her mother's frail hands in hers. "The ship is failing. It's dying."

"I'm not leaving." Ahnna snatched her hands back. "I'm not. Not ever. I will not set one foot on another planet. You know that. I won't. I lost your father, and you lost—you lost your leg on that planet." She turned and left Cedar's room. "I will not go down there and neither will you."

Cedar fastened her duffel and carried it into the central room of the apartment. Ahnna sat in her chair, her body curled over her tablet reader, locking reality away again, probably looking at ancient videos of Earth, the place she dreamed of being, the place no longer like the blue and green planet the videos portrayed. Cedar stood at the door for a long moment. "Watch over my plants for me, Mother."

Ahnna didn't look up. Cedar opened the door and walked out, closing it quietly behind her. She leaned back against it, her eyes closed, her head aching. A frond from one of the plants that lined the hallways of the ship brushed her leg. Would she have to drug her mother and wheel her to the shuttle on a gurney? If she stayed here she'd die alone and afraid. If Cedar stayed with her they'd both die with the ship. How could she make a new life on the planet when every time she looked into the sky she saw her mother dying? A cloud of pain swirled through her, then she stepped on the walkway to the shuttle bay.

Two hours later, the cloud dissipated, and Cedar braced as the shuttle slowed. It jerked and the four rotor arms deployed, slowing them further. She stayed glued to the camera screens, excited, fascinated, and not a little scared. This was the first time she'd been off the ship since Astarte15. Since she was six.

She tried to wiggle the foot at the end of her bionic leg. It didn't move. She smoothed the unfamiliar wool skirt and looked down at her hands. Her clean hands with not a speck of dirt, not even under her fingernails. That had taken a while.

"Look, Cedar. Over toward the mountains. Those must be Karda. If we can see them from this far out, they must be. They're too big to be birds." Assam's voice shook with excitement. Imperturbable, unshakable Assam's voice shook. The screen showed more planet and less empty space. In the distance below them six birdlike dots drifted in and out of low clouds in wide circles and wandering arcs.

As the shuttle got closer to the ground the Karda disappeared, and the forest surrounding Restal Prime appeared beneath them. And what a forest. The trees, spears of green conifers and leafless black skeletons with a hazy hint of spring green, were enormous.

If she hadn't been buckled in, she'd be bouncing in her seat. Of all the diaspora planets, Adalta was the most like Earth because most of it was barren and ripe for terraforming. Like Old Earth, not the devastated ruin Earth was now. So many plants to study that she'd never seen growing before—only in pictures and vids. The barren areas were so extensive, the planting was still far from finished even after almost five hundred years.

And the trees. Oh, the trees. There were trees on the ship, of course. They were essential to the life systems. But they grew in pots, or in soil that couldn't be deep enough for truly large trees. Her palms itched to touch these trees, to feel the bark, to rub their leaves between her fingers, to sink her hands into the humus of the forest floor.

She pushed black curls away from her face, tucked them behind her ears, smoothed the front of the unfamiliar tunic, and fisted her hands on the awkward skirt that almost reached her ankles, covering the tops of her boots. Leather boots. Real leather boots. She grimaced. Real, stiff, uncomfortable leather boots. On a foot that didn't work.

Assam looked at home in his tunic and tight trousers, a sword on his belt and tall riding boots on his feet. Glenn, on the other hand, wore his ship uniform. At least he'd consented to wearing long pants instead of the shorts he usually wore with his skinny hairy legs hanging out. It was cold on-planet. But blending in had never been part of Glenn Voigt's repertoire. Cedar laid her hand on his arm.

"Scared, missy?" he asked. He glanced down at her foot. "I won't let you fall. Just hang on to me, if you have to. You'll be all right."

She glared at him. She hadn't thought her leg might be a problem till he mentioned it. Or thought to be scared. She'd forgotten there was a war going on here. A war with an alien species. She'd be a burden, not an asset. Not thoughts she'd wanted to have at this moment.

Then—Thunk. They were on the ground. The rotor whine curled down, and Cedar was on a planet for the first time in thirteen Earth years. She bounced out of her seat—or tried—bounced back and unfastened her harness. The hatch ramp lowered, and she gasped at the icy air rushing in. Finally fumbling free, she wrapped the thick cloak around her and headed out the hatch, her hand heavy on Glenn's arm so she could walk, not lurch.

She breathed in a long lungful of the cold air and sneezed. Oh, the smells. Hundreds of new smells. She'd never smelled anything like the clean, clear smell of the forest. The air on the ship, even in her gro-pods, was nothing like this. She stood, eyes closed, and drew it deep through her nose, again and again. Until Glenn pulled her arm, then had to keep her from falling. A burden, not an asset.

Oh, great galaxy. Five enormous saddled Karda stood in the

clearing, horse bodies gleaming, hawk heads high. That sharp spicy smell came from them. One, a soft, luminous gold, stood next to a smaller black Karda. There was a thunderous sound, and Cedar turned to see a sixth Karda cup its huge wings, glide to land at the far end of the long, narrow field and canter toward them. She recognized Marta on its back. Her back. Cedar remembered Karda were not "its," and Marta's partner Sidhari was a female. Thank you galaxy. Marta was here.

Galen was leaping up the ramp toward her. Cedar looked around him at the people standing in a half circle at the end of the ramp, three very large men and one small woman, all armed with swords in well-worn scabbards. Then she was enveloped by his large body, and Galen said, low in her ear, "Welcome to Adalta, Elf. I got you." He took her arm from Glenn and began the introductions, beginning with the girl with spiky silver hair, a coffee-with-cream complexion, a sword on her hip and a bow and quiver strapped to her back. "This is Tessa, Elf, my bonded. Tessa, this is my friend, Director of Bio-Systems Cedar Evans."

Cedar grinned. "He actually looks nervous. Like he thinks we're going to bite each other. I am so very glad to meet the woman who can make Galen Morel nervous, Tessa." And she reached to clasp Tessa's forearm. "Oh, I forgot. He's now Galen Me'Cowyn. My sincerest best wishes on your bonding. And my thanks for puncturing his ego. That must have been difficult."

Tessa widened her already wide brown eyes. "Ego? Galen has an ego?"

"He used to." Glenn growled. "How deflated you look, Galen. Perhaps you could introduce us to the others in your party."

But he was interrupted by Marta, who came flying off her Karda and ran to hug Cedar. "I'm so glad you came. I was worried they'd send Glenn without a keeper."

"Where is he, Marta? Which one is your handsome fairy tale prince?" Cedar looked back and forth between two tall, dark-haired young men, one whose face was all hard angles and whose hand looked like it never left his sword grip, and the other, equally large, with I-hold-the-world-on-my-shoulders hazel eyes, sun streaks in his hair, and a sword on his hip. He didn't look much older than she was. Both men's eyes constantly flicked back and forth between the landing party and the surrounding forest as if disaster were moments away, hiding in the forest, and they were all that stood in its way. The smells in the air sharpened in her nose, and her eyes flicked to the looming trees, too.

Marta's mouth twisted down. "He's halfway between Toldar Prime and Restal Prime with his troops, trudging through ice and mud. But let me introduce you to Prime Guardian Hugh Me'Rahl from Rashiba. His presence, and that of the two other quadrant guardians, is why you were asked to land in Restal instead of Rashiba Prime."

The third man, a large, burly older man grasped Cedar's forearm, his fingers nearly encircling it. "Welcome to Adalta, Cedar Evans, Glenn Voight, and Assam Kamal. May our table provide you sustenance, may our land provide you work to suit your heart and hands, and may you find safety within our walls for your rest." He turned and stepped back. "And may I present Guardian Daryl Me'Vere of Restal and Armsmaster Krager?" So Daryl was the man with the troubled eyes.

Assam stepped forward and grasped each man's forearm in the traditional greeting. "We accept your gracious greeting, and may we offer peace, harmony, and service to your planet, Guardians, Armsmaster." He turned to Galen. Cedar saw the wariness on his face. "Galen, it's good to see you. I hope we can work together here as well as we did when we worked with Marta and her dad on Baldur4."

Galen grasped his forearm. "We're both a lot older and wiser now. Maybe we won't get in so much trouble."

Assam's shoulders relaxed. He'd been the one to arrest Galen's father for smuggling the technologically advanced akenguns to this low-tech planet.

Daryl looked like he didn't know how to smile, and Cedar saw tiredness beyond exhaustion in the deep lines on his face. She wanted to ask about the war, where things stood, how much danger were they in here, because that's what the tension was telling her:

that there was real danger.

But he spoke before she could, as if he knew what she wanted and didn't want to give it to her. "I extend welcome to Restal to you all. Our early spring must feel like the coldest winter to you, so I suggest we begin our journey to the Hall. We have a light wagon for you. Forcing you into your first flying lesson right off the shuttle didn't seem a good welcome. It's a short ride back to Restal Hall. The wagon is covered and heated, though not the most comfortable, so it might not seem short to you."

Moving as though impatient to get them off this field, Daryl picked up Cedar's duffel, took her arm and started to lead them at a brisk walk toward the wagon at the edge of the clearing. She stepped off with her nonworking foot and stumbled. He caught her easily, looked down, frowned, and slowed his pace.

Cedar fumed. Had Galen not told them about her leg? Or was this tall, handsome, too-busy-for-this person just oblivious? His eyes still flicked in unceasing survey of the forest around them.

She shook off his hand and walked as fast as she could without lurching like a robot with its systems out of whack, seething. "I can assure you I am able to walk without assistance. I can take care of myself." Well, she probably couldn't, but she'd never admit it. Not to him.

He looked at her as if seeing her for the first time. She couldn't think of a word insulting enough to make her feel better. She took a deep breath of the enchanting forest smell and felt better. And sneezed.

Cedar looked around the quarters she, Glenn and Assam would share in Restal Hall. She felt like a character in a novel set in the Middle Ages of Old Earth. Tall, mullioned glass windows filled one wall, overlooking extensive, untidy, winter-bare formal gardens. The small glass panes were thick and wavy and looked to be handmade. Vibrant rugs covered the floors in the five rooms—one central space with two bedchambers on either side. The furnishings were heavy, beautifully carved and upholstered. Tapestry hangings on the stone walls and the iron stove on the hearth took the chill from the room with its high, beamed ceiling. It felt so safe here. The horrifying monsters Galen had described to her were all but impossible to believe.

Glenn poked at the glowing stones in the stove with an iron rod. "I've been wanting to get a look at these since I heard about them. There's no ash here at all. They just sit there and glow hot. How can they possibly work?"

Assam dropped his duffel in his room and came back out. "They're called magma stones, and they work with some kind of magic."

"I'm gonna have to see that to believe it." Glenn picked up his duffel. "I can't wait." Then he went into his room and closed the door.

Cedar knew he was tired. Glenn was an old man, and he was failing. No one had mentioned his age when it was decided he would be the ambassador, and she hadn't either. She hoped this mission wouldn't be too strenuous for him. How would he take to flying on a Karda? At least Assam had ridden horses, but neither Glenn nor she had, and she wasn't sure she could manage it. Well, she'd do it, but she didn't have to like it. How embarrassing it would be to fall off—except splatted on the ground, she wouldn't be alive to be embarrassed so why worry?

The feeling of absence below her thigh wasn't reassuring at all, but at least right now it didn't itch. Or ache with phantom pain. That kind of hurt was a double pain she hadn't had to deal with since she was a child. It hurt physically, it hurt emotionally, and it forced her to remember part of her leg was gone.

Falling off a Karda was probably the least danger she might have to face.

Tall as he was, Daryl had to reach up to brush Abala's shoulder. ~You are covered in dry grass and mud, and you have a couple of bent flight feathers. Where have you been, and what have you been rolling in?~ he complained.

~You've been in meetings all tenday, and I was bored and hungry. I found a tasty kurga and what I thought was a nice dry meadow. It wasn't dry.~

~You must have flown pretty far into the foothills.~

~Ket and I thought we'd do some scouting while you and Galen were otherwise occupied. Kishar went with us.~ He stretched his big hawk head out when Daryl's brush reached his neck. ~You might want to know he and Ket had an intense conversation they kept private from me. Ket didn't look happy. Kishar and I hunted, and Ket flew off toward the mountains. He just got back.~

~What did Kishar say?~

~He did not abandon his mysterious and inscrutable air.~

~Any sign of urbat? Please tell me you didn't see urbat.~

~You'd have known immediately if we had. You missed a spot.~ Abala twisted his huge hawk head to expose the underside of his neck.

Daryl heard the door open from the street side of the mews, and Cedar walked down the aisle toward them. She held to Galen's arm with one hand and linked arms with Tessa on her other side. Her face was set in a stubborn show-no-pain smile, and her walk was more lurch than walk. He ached to get his hands on her bionic leg —that was what Galen called it, bionic. It was somehow linked to the nerves and muscles of her thigh, and he said it worked like a normal leg—when it worked. He wondered, with the kind of technical and medical knowledge that must have been available on the ship, why did she lose her leg in the first place?

But it was the kind of advanced technology that didn't work on Adalta. It was now nothing more than a mostly immobile block. He ached to examine it. Did it come off? How did it work when it did? In his need to study everything he almost blurted the questions out.

"Don't tell me you walked all the way from the Hall." Daryl was half-angry.

"All right. I won't tell you we walked all the way from the Hall." Tessa laughed and tossed her saddlebags into a stall where a smaller black Karda waited. Galen's face was a study in embarrassment. "But it was worth it to hear Cedar's stories about Galen as a boy."

Cedar looked up, and her show-no-pain smile changed to a don't-pity-me glare.

Daryl went back to brushing Abala's mane to hide his suddenly hot face. He wasn't sure what he felt about her, but it definitely wasn't pity, and it wasn't something he had time or energy for now. She was an ambassador from the ship, that's all she was.

Galen leaned against the opening to the beautiful golden Ket's stall, dropping two sets of loaded saddle bags at his feet. "Save me, Daryl. Send me on a dangerous journey far far away. Cedar is destroying my glamour. Tessa's going to think I'm ordinary."

"Oh, galaxy gods forbid, never ordinary." Cedar laughed and sat on a hay bale in the aisle next to Ket's stall. She looked around. "What a beautiful space. What did you call it, Tessa? The mews?"

Large, open stalls lined the flagstone alleyway, separated by rare, polished, wood-paneled walls taller than most men. High in the stone outer walls, a row of clerestory windows let in light. Curious Karda poked their fierce hawk-heads over the stalls to look at the newcomer.

Daryl watched as Cedar took a deep breath in through her nose, and a look of surprise lit her face. She jerked around and looked at him, puzzled. Then she frowned and closed her eyes—which he couldn't help noticing were big, brown, and beautiful under her glistening mop of curly black hair. Finder Mireia sat down beside her, shoulders touching, and Cedar relaxed.

Daryl shook himself. He hadn't even noticed Mireia come in.

Abala shoved at him with his shoulder. ~You need to check my flight feathers before we take off if you want to go very far today. Pay attention.~ Daryl could feel his laughter.

The alleyway filled as two wings of the Karda Patrol arrived for this expedition to show the village of Ardencroft to the emissaries from the spaceship. Mi'hirus Tayla and Philipa came out of the tack room carrying saddles with coiled straps. Patrollers and Mi'hiru passed back and forth retrieving tack, and the mews came to life.

Assam and Galen arrived. "Good, I see we're taking two wings of Karda Patrol to Ardencroft. I hope sixteen flyers are enough," said Galen.

Ardencroft was an empty village—all its inhabitants were killed the year before by urbat—all its inhabitants. Daryl chose it for the first landings of the refugees from the ship in spite of the war going on. All the quadrant guardians who needed to be consulted were in Restal, and other places to settle them were still undecided.

"Me'Fiere's troops will also be there. All he can spare. The urbat hit another of his villages last Deciday." Daryl's mouth tightened. "They were prepared. The holders and villagers are learning. They are not such easy targets anymore. Their losses were not heavy, and they kill more of the monsters every time they attack now. But it's still cold. The urbat will get faster and stronger as the weather warms. Troops, mount up."

"Time to fly, Cedar. You'll love it. It's incredible." Galen laughed at the little flash of terror on her face.

"I'm not sure *incredible* experience is the same as *good* experience. I have to admit, I'm terrified," said Cedar.

"And you should be." Galen mock shuddered.

"She'll fly with me," Daryl found himself saying. Why did he say that? She obviously wasn't terrified, there was laughter on her face as she stuck her tongue out at Galen. Why did that make him feel lighter?

"If you loosen your arms every few minutes, I'll be able to breathe and maybe still be alive when we get to Ardencroft." There should have been at least a hint of humor in his words, but Cedar didn't hear one.

She unlinked her hands from their white-knuckled grip and grabbed fistfuls of Daryl's tunic instead. Pompous ass. Those were the first words he'd spoken since she'd managed to clamber in place behind him on his Karda. She'd fallen the first time a patroller gave her a leg up—with her artificial leg, of course, which failed her, of course. Finally Galen boosted her with his hands on her leg and her bottom instead of her foot. She'd pasted her smile on her face and willed it not to turn red. Which wasn't possible. It did anyway. How could she ever get used to being a cripple, because that's what she apparently was doomed to be?

Abala adjusted his wings, Cedar's stomach went somewhere else, and Daryl's body stiffened when she grabbed onto him again. Why does he need to breathe, he's not human. "Just don't fly too close to the sun." Was that a slight humanlike twitch?

A full two minutes later—she ticked the seconds off—Daryl said, "Don't worry. I don't use wax to repair Abala's flight feathers, and I've been flying too long to get so excited I fly into the sun."

Cedar felt heat in her face. "How do you know the ancient story about Icarus and his wax wings?" She was surprised she didn't stutter.

"Abala likes me to read to him." He didn't say another word.

Cedar was so embarrassed, that, for the first time, well maybe not precisely the first time, she didn't have a quip on the tip of her tongue. The only sound for several hours was the rush of Abala's wings through the air. She watched them, marveling at the way they moved, the way the long feathers on their outside edges opened and closed as they beat up and down, the efficient way they cupped the air. She'd never even seen birds before except on vids. She was living a miracle.

Then she concentrated on controlling her stomach and looking down at what they flew over: bowl-shaped forest, villages surrounded by fields, and kilometers of desolate, barren land that made her queasy in the middle of this miracle. Nothing without a price.

Abala's flight wasn't smooth. Every small adjustment he made, every tilt of tail or wing, every strong wing beat, stopped her breath, and she clutched harder around Daryl. Finally he put a hand over hers and held it there.

She closed her eyes, took several long, deep breaths of the air redolent with scents even this high, and gave herself a talking to. Think about the job to be done, not about falling off. She forced her mind away from how far she was from the ground and thought about the assumptions she had about this planet and its people. Those thoughts needed to open up. Adalta was primitive, yes, but maybe she needed to redefine primitive. every one kept talking about the magic they called talent, but even the magma stones didn't seem magic, they just worked. And without smoke and ashes and cinders and burning wood or coal or poisoning the air. How was that primitive?

Maybe she ought to redefine mobility, too.

And she needed to reassess the needs of the people of the ship. She might have been six years old when she was last on a planet, and it might have ended in loss and trauma, but she'd loved every minute before the attack. She'd loved the openness, the freedom, the skies, the non-digitized *realness* of it. She'd been young, injured, traumatized, and terrified when she and her mother finally made it back to the ship, but the feelings and images had never left her.

There were people on the ship who spent entire long lives never experiencing anything other than ship life. If the emptiness of the barrens below made her queasy, when she was enjoying every minute on this planet, how would it affect those people? Some of them had grown up on one section of the ship and seldom ventured into another. How could she mitigate that problem, because she had no doubt it would be a problem. She could look at the sky, and as long as she was in the city or the forest there was no problem. But even thinking about the open space on the ground was daunting. She'd talk to Assam and Galen and Marta about how they dealt with open spaces when they were first on a planet.

The sun was midway to the mountains in the west when Abala led the Karda down toward a broad green spot in the middle of the bare brown landscape they'd flown over for the last few hours. The ground came up so fast Cedar clenched her eyes shut and grabbed Daryl's waist tight again, her face mashed into his back, her insides left high in the sky. The landing was rougher when Abala touched down and loped to the end of the long runway outside the green oasis. Cedar's thighs ached, her bottom was numb, and she didn't know how she would ever get down. Or if she wanted to.

They loped across the wide green field and stopped at a small stream surrounded by immense trees. She could see their small round leaves twisting in the breeze with a soft clattering noise, and there was a cloud of what looked like feathery down floating in the air. She'd ask what kind of trees these were. Oh, there was so much to learn, to explore.

Then Daryl slid his right leg over the front of the saddle and landed on the ground, and all she could think about was getting down—or not. "Abala would you mind if I just sat here all night? I'm fine right here. I'm sure I can sleep sitting up. You can just have someone bring me dinner and a blanket." She showed Daryl a toothy smile. Her hands clamped so tight on the saddle she didn't think she could let go. Abala shifted under her, Cedar's breath stopped, and she closed her eyes again. "At least I didn't scream 'eek.' That would be a little melodramatic and girly."

Daryl's soft laugh startled her.

"I didn't know you could laugh. Are you laughing at me? That's not polite at all." His whole face changed when he laughed. Maybe he was human after all.

"Abala is going to get down on his knees—no, no, don't panic— then I can get you unbuckled and lift you off." He almost smiled. "Just close your eyes and hang onto the saddle. Meanwhile I'll celebrate being able to breathe again."

"Maybe you do have a minuscule sense of humor." She closed her eyes, and Abala made a snorting noise. "Did he just laugh at you?" Then the big Karda lurched under her, throwing her around in the saddle. She clamped her lips tight. She was sure a "Mmmeeek" like sound escaped. Then his hands were around her waist and she was on the ground. He let go, and she was really on the ground. On her bottom.

"He finds me very amusing."

She wasn't amused at all.

CHAPTER SIX

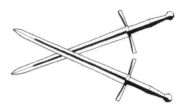

Daryl pulled the small saddle bag off Abala's back and reached down to give Cedar a hand up from her unexpected seat on the ground. Her eyes got larger and larger as Mi'hiru and troopers all around them unloaded the rolled blankets and small tents from saddle bags and the cargo harnesses of the un-partnered Karda who accompanied the group. Karda hated to be used as pack animals and didn't make it a secret, but they agreed to carry the extra supplies the humans would need, willing to do a lot of things they hated in order to defeat the Itza Larrak. Pack horses couldn't keep up with flying Karda.

They'd landed in one of the small oases that dotted the immense barrens of Adalta established by First Planters, who planted trees, bushes, and grasses around the springs they found as staging areas for later groups of the Planter Corps. It was too early for cotton-woods to release their flying feathery seeds, so he wasn't surrounded by sneezes, dripping red noses, and watering red eyes.

"What's all that for?" She turned to Daryl, hands on her hips. "We're staying here all night? Outside?" The word "outside" squeaked out.

"I thought you understood. I informed Glenn and Assam. It's a three-day flight with so many people. Especially people who've never done anything remotely like this before." Daryl's eyes never stopped surveying the surroundings, but he noticed Cedar's glare at Glenn. It could burn a hole in his back. Glenn turned, and Daryl struggled not to laugh at his delight at her disgust.

"Well, he didn't tell me." Indignation growled in a voice he didn't think she intended him to hear.

His eyes followed Cedar making her awkward way through the bundles and packs to Marta, who told her, "Finder Mireia has offered to share her tent with you. I figured you would be more comfortable sharing than alone this first night under the stars. And it will be good to have her near you if your talent manifests. It took a crisis for mine to show up, and it blasted through me. I hope you don't need her like that, but she'll feel better if you're close. She asked that Glenn and Assam share a tent next to hers."

"I know we were told every one will manifest some kind of what you call talent ability, Marta, but I'm finding that hard to accept. And what stars?" She waved a hand at the gray sky. "We won't see any stars tonight."

Assam stood by the creek, staring down at the water. "The clouds will be gone soon." Not a hint of doubt in his voice. Daryl didn't think he even realized he spoke aloud. He watched the current swirl around and around in front of Assam. Tiny fingers of the stream reached toward him then splashed back. Assam was entranced. No one but Daryl noticed. A Water talent. And not only a Water talent, but a very strong one, and Assam didn't know. He made sure Mireia noticed, and she moved to talk to him.

Daryl set sentries around the edge of the oasis. He didn't think the urbat attacks had spread into the barrens, but this group was a large target, and Galen, the legendary Kern with his incredible Earth talent, was one of their preferred targets. He, Tessa, and Kishar had destroyed hundreds of urbat. Tessa and Kishar had nearly killed the Itza Larrak at the end of fall last year. An attack wasn't probable, but not probable wasn't not possible.

A number of Karda, relieved of riders and packs, flew watch in coordinated circles beneath the thinning clouds. Daryl noticed

Abala among them. He felt one knot of tension relax. Karda could see a long way even at night and the barrens were wide open.

More and more Karda had shown themselves in the skies over the past several tendays since winter lessened its icy hold and allowed spring to edge its way in. Karda in colors Daryl had never seen before. There were even a couple of white Karda with bright yellow flight feathers. Bays with dark blue heads and tails. Sorrels with primary colors on crests, on wings, on tails. And every once in a while, so high they were little more than shiny Karda-shaped dots, Daryl saw gleaming golds like Ket, the Karda who partnered Galen. Those gold Karda never landed anywhere they could be seen. He noted that every time they appeared, Ket acted like he wanted to hide behind something, except there was nothing big enough to hide him.

No one knew where Karda came from, other than from the mountains. The only fledgling Karda ever seen were the two rescued by Altan Me'Gerron when their parents were killed. Karda showed up when they were needed as they had when the colonists first arrived on Adalta and joined the war between them and the Larrak.

They were cared for by Mi'hiru, with whom they bonded in a mystical, unbreakable connection. Sometimes a Karda would also choose another, as Abala chose Daryl when he was a child. Un-partnered Karda carried others, such as members of the Karda Patrol, forming friendships and alliances. every one knew there were more Karda in the inaccessible middle of the mountains. Many disappeared from the rest of Adalta when that first war ended. Or rather paused for five centuries. Until the last of the alien Larrak escaped its prison. Now it was back. With luck not tonight. Not here.

Daryl shook himself free of the mystical sight of Karda in coordinated swirls like flocks of enormous swallows against the colorful dusk sky. He didn't bother setting up his tent. The clouds thinned as Assam predicted. The cooks' three fires burned to coals, and faint smells of dinner drifted. A few Karda patrollers were still setting up tents. The rest of the party perched around the fires on rocks or fallen cottonwood trunks dragged into a rough circle. There were stories, laughter, and chatter between the Adaltans and the ambassadors from the trade ship falling apart above them.

He made a round of the sentries, satisfying himself that they were spaced well, that most of them were experienced patrollers, that there were no new and young troopers who might be tempted to fall asleep, or panic over things that weren't there, or were. Daryl made three more rounds in the quiet night. The stars shone bright every time, shadowed only by the swirling Karda taking turns keeping watch above.

As usual his sleep was fitful. Second guesses circled doubts, circled insecurities, but by first light, he was sound asleep. Until Abala screamed inside his head, ~Ware, Daryl! Urbat come. From the west.~

He heard Marta yell the same and saw Galen buckling his sword belt, looking toward the sky, probably telling Ket to fight from above. Daryl hid his eyes and nose in the crook of his elbow when coal-black Kishar landed beside him and scattered dust and leaves, unlike other Karda, able to touch down directly in camp without having to lope to a stop. Galen helped Tessa saddle him. She leapt to Kishar's back from his bent knee. Galen strung her bow and handed it up with two quivers of arrows.

~How much time do we have, Abala?~ Daryl asked.

Before Abala could answer, Marta yelled at Daryl, "Fifteen minutes, Daryl. Fifteen minutes. I'll fight on the ground."

Daryl knelt on the ground, pulling strength from rock and soil, water and air, until he was as full of talent as he could get. He finished jerking his boots and sword on and told Abala, ~I'll fight from the ground, too. The ambassadors must be protected. How many come?~

The swirl of Karda above him swerved west, eager to meet the attack. Abala answered, ~We estimate two hundred, Daryl.~ Alarm shaded his usual unperterbable telepathic voice.

The urbat poured over the hillside a hundred and fifty meters from the edge of the oasis. Karda swooped, tearing at the urbat's stubby wings with long, fierce talons. They snatched them, flew high, and dropped them in the middle of the urbat force racing toward the camp. Everywhere one was dropped, there was a confused swirl of urbat tearing at the dead one, stripping away its metal bones.

Daryl's stomach muscles tightened. Adrenaline flooded through him, and he gripped hard on his sword hilt. He'd thought two wings of Karda Patrol would be enough guard, along with himself, Marta, Galen, and Tessa. They might not be. He shook away visions of the dog-like half metal half flesh urbat tearing at Cedar who was trying to run, stumbling with her non-working leg. Two hundred. Two hundred against twenty-one fighters and at least two who couldn't fight at all.

He relaxed a little when tiny Mi'hiru Philipa grabbed Cedar's arm, pulled it over her shoulder, and ran with her to the center of the clearing. There Finder Mireia sat cross-legged on the ground in a ring with two troopers and one of the cooks, all with eyes closed, intent in deep concentration. One of the troopers already had Glenn there. Assam stood close to the small stream, his sword drawn, looking back and forth between the other two, Daryl, and the creek, confused, as if he knew he was where he needed to be, and torn because he knew he must protect Cedar and Glenn.

Sentries ran in and joined the others around the camp in a tight double circle. Galen, his scars morphed into the beautiful root, tree and leaf tattoos that were his gift from Adalta, walked the circumference deep in concentration, and a two-meter wall of brush loaded with long, razor-sharp thorns sprang up behind him, closing them inside a living fortress. He reached where Daryl stood. "That's the best I can do now. It won't keep them out, but it might slow them down. It's too much to hope that they will attack in a close swarm so I can bury them."

Daryl grimaced. "They can fly over it. Burying them will be difficult if they're in the air." The urbat's high pitched howls spread around the thorn hedge.

Assam moved up beside them. Daryl started to tell him to move back, but a look at his face stopped him. "I trust you can fight?"

Assam's nod was tight. "Galen and Tessa described them to me, found me a sword they said was made of the monster's metal bones, and told me where they were most vulnerable." He paused for a minute, then turned and smiled a twisted smile, "I've fought monsters on other worlds, some of them bigger. How can this be worse?"

~Abala.~ Daryl pathed. ~Is the Itza Larrak with them? He can't hide himself in this barren landscape.~

Marta moved up next to him. "None of the Karda have seen the Larrak, Daryl. But they didn't see the urbat until it was almost too late."

Abala echoed her words from the air. ~Something was hiding them with an illusion, Daryl. A strong illusion.~

Daryl looked at the tight ring with Finder Mireia and the three others in the center of the clearing. Cedar sat right behind her, and they were well guarded. Fear loosed something in his chest right before it iced again. She couldn't fight. She couldn't run. She could barely walk. She was too vulnerable. He looked away. He couldn't thaw now. Wouldn't.

Then the keening howls of the urbat changed to loud, vicious snarls, and it wasn't time to think anymore. He and Galen moved through a gap in the brush fence.

Galen was the first to react. He knelt on the ground and shoved. A wall of dirt and brambles and wicked thorns buried the first thirty urbat before they were fifteen meters away. The urbat behind them scattered too far apart for Galen's first defense to work again, and some of them took to the air for the short hop over the bramble fence. It was time for swords and lances and arrows.

Kishar and Tessa swooped down, and a swift-moving storm of arrows felled seven. Kishar veered up, went wings-vertical in a sharp wheel and dove back down.

Then Daryl was too busy fighting to worry about anything else. He shook out his arm and long, slender bolts of fire hit urbat after urbat, burning through armor and turning them into fiery torches. The stench of burnt urbat and hair filled the air.

Four urbat bulled their way through the thorny hedge near the creek, tearing at a trooper. Assam ran toward them, Marta beside him. They fought side by side with two more troopers. Marta screamed instructions about the urbat's vulnerable spots, "Neck in front of the armor, throat, legs, lower spine behind the armor." Someone dragged the wounded fighter away, and Marta, Assam, and the two troopers fought to hold the opening.

But Galen's hurried fence didn't slow the monsters for long. Daryl yelled at him to fall back into the circle filling with urbat and fighters. Blood and thick streams of stinking yellow ichor were everywhere, the grass slick with it.

Galen plugged a hole in the brush barrier by shoving a wall of soil at the six urbat coming through, burying them alive, then he turned to the next opening. Flying over the fence left urbat undersides vulnerable to upraised lances and swords, and urbat-metal tipped arrows.

The fighting got too close for Daryl to throw fire without hitting his own troops. He pulled his sword and shoved it halfway through the soft spot at one urbat's throat as it leapt at him. He jerked it free, and beheaded another. Eight urbat broke through the brush to his left. He shouted for his fighters to fall back and called for archers. They hit the beasts with a storm of arrows, and Daryl threw bolt after bolt of fire. Galen closed the hole with thorny growth that surged up around seven trying to get through, entangling them, killing them with curved, wicked thorns.

Six creatures pushed through on the other side of the little creek, and Daryl started that way. Assam and one trooper were the only ones near, and they weren't enough to stop the raving creatures, or even slow them. But when the urbat splashed into the stream, water swirled up around them, a powerful whirling spout that caught all six of them.

Daryl looked at Assam, who stood, right hand holding his sword and left hand raised, palm toward the water, a mix of terror and jubilation holding his body rigid.

"Guard me," Daryl yelled at the three troopers nearest him. He closed his eyes and concentrated. Pulling deep from Adalta, he reached the magma at the heart of the planet and threw a meter-round red, yellow, and blue ball of fire at the pillar of water. Steam billowed, and the urbat fell, dead and cooked.

"Welcome to Adalta, Assam," he shouted to the astonished man. He turned to check on the small ring of Mireia and the three troopers. They were swaying, murmuring the arcane words of the spell to disorient the urbat, but to little effect. Three of them weren't enough to affect the horde of urbat. The Itza Larrak had to be close, hidden behind a shield, controlling them.

There were too many still attacking, and the human fighters were tiring or wounded or both. He didn't want to think about how many were dead.

Daryl saw Cedar look around her, both hands over her mouth and nose against the terrible stink. Three urbat were almost through their guards. She looked lost in a daze of unbelief and terror—her hands clenched tight, her body shaking all over. Suddenly her hands fell away from her face. She straightened, her back arched, and her head stretched back so far the tendons in her neck were taut ropes.

She fell to her knees, grabbed around Mireia's shoulders and pressed her body against the finder's back. All four members of the ring sat bolt upright, galvanized. Their heads fell back, their mouths opened, and the words of the spell screamed loud over the clamor of battle. The urbat stopped. All of them. They just—stopped.

every one stood still. Then they fell on the urbat with no qualms about killing a monster that didn't defend itself. Some of them they threw in piles, still alive, and Galen pushed soil over them.

It was quiet. Not even a stem of grass moved. Then the moans and cries of the wounded broke through.

Daryl organized the injured under the cover of a tree. Clouds closed in, and it began to drizzle. Three troopers grabbed tents, ropes and pegs flying, and ran to cover the injured as best they could.

He shut out the rest of the world and went to work, sorting out the severely wounded and sending three of his men with healing abilities to tend the others and stabilize those only he could heal. There was nothing but himself, anchored deep in the bedrock of Adalta, reaching into the streams of water that ran deep in her, pulling Earth and Water talent through his body and into the ripped muscles, tendons, bones, and slashed organs of the first fighter, a young woman. Mending, stabilizing, closing wounds, fusing broken bones until another healer pulled him out. "I can finish this, sir. You need to tend to that one."

Daryl moved from fighter to fighter until he was certain all were cared for. Angry at the urbat, angry at the Itza Larrak, angry at himself for not knowing how to stop this never-ending slaughter.

In the background the sound of urbat metal popping out of mounds of new, green grass rang. Long metal bones and razor-sharp triangles of urbat armor were all that was left of the two hundred urbat that attacked their small group.

Daryl sat back on his heels and saw Mi'hiru Philipa run for Mireia's tent and back to her with a small capped jar. Mireia, barely able to stand herself, held Cedar's shoulders while she heaved, though he could see there was nothing left in her to heave. Mireia smeared something under Cedar's nose. She stopped retching.

Daryl couldn't help himself. He started toward them, but Mireia held up her hand and mouthed, "Talent surge," and he stopped.

Cedar looked up at him with a smile that didn't even hint at the usual sunshine on her face, and toppled over, unconscious.

Every time Readen Me'Vere pulled one of the ancient books from his library shelves he heard Daryl's voice. "Wear the cotton gloves. These books are precious and fragile." It irritated him, but he always did it. Why had no one ever made copies of these?

He knew the answer. Few remembered the books he'd brought to Me'Vere Hold over the years. Daryl had already read them, and no one else cared. No one had expected the Itza Larrak to reappear. But Readen did it. He brought it back—freed it from its prison in the columns of the now blocked cavern beneath Restal Hall. He discovered it as a child, by accident. It had never stopped teaching him its magic and the dark magic Readen could raise himself. He was more powerful now than the strongest talents. He had the Itza Larrak. Or so he told himself.

All the long winter Readen spent every spare moment perusing the ancient books. The stories of the war against the Larrak fought when the colonists first arrived on Adalta. The stories they'd learned about the first war, fought a millennium before between the Karda and the newly invading Larrak. He turned the last page of the last book, closed it, and pushed back from the table. No one, either Karda or human, had ever connected with a Larrak like he had. He put it back on the shelf.

All that time wasted, all that power wasted unlocking the preservation spells on the five-hundred-year-old books, and he'd learned nothing. He didn't bother putting the spells back. His head heated with the familiar surge of frustration. He didn't have talent. He'd never had talent. He was never going to have talent. The only person on Adalta ever born without talent. Readen pushed the old frustration back down—a distraction, a waste of time. And irrelevant. He didn't have talent, but he had power. A little worm of thought asked, was the power his or was it borrowed? It was his. Yes, and he was determined there would be more. The Larrak needed him as much as he needed the Larrak in their conquest of Restal and the planet. There would be more.

He pulled the silver medallion from beneath his tunic. Well, silver-colored. He had no idea what the metal was. The Itza Larrak gave it to him when he was twelve years old, the first time Readen released it from its imprisonment in the inscribed pillars of the cavern—with his own blood. every one thought of the Larrak as a boogey man to scare children into behaving. A legend. A fireside tale. It was real, now. It and its creatures, the urbat.

For several hours, he'd felt it calling him. The pressure of the Itza Larrak's call was growing more and more insistent and painful. Readen's resistance was weakening. His power reserve was weakening. He hadn't had a chance to bolster it for too long. Where was Samel with the prisoners he'd sent for?

When Readen finally brought the Larrak into material form, he'd woven a protective web between him and the Itza Larrak to keep it from killing him, from stealing his body. But it was becoming something more now. He could feel it sucking holes in him. Holes the Larrak was trying to push tentacles into. He could not allow the

Larrak to subsume him. He could not sacrifice himself for the Larrak. He could not let the Larrak control their connection.

Readen concentrated, sending an image of Daryl, sending the message that attacks on Daryl's villages should be the focus of the urbat to take Daryl's attention away from him until he was able to retake Restal Prime. He was so close to ready. The mercenaries he'd hired from Akhara would be here within a month, he was certain.

A knock at the door startled him. He gathered his thoughts and his meager notes and walked out into the hallway. A guard said, "Sorry to disturb you, sir, but there is a man with a closed wagon here who insists on seeing you."

Samel. It had to be Samel with prisoners. Days late. A fire of relief kindled inside him. Now he could regain the power he needed to resist the Itza Larrak's call. Anticipation lent fuel to the fire. Perhaps even call it to him instead. He didn't run down the stairs ahead of the guard, but he took the last steps two at a time and opened the small side door out of the hall. What prisoners had Samel brought? How many? If they were strong one or two would be enough. He could make them last for weeks.

The driver pulled the wagon close to the entrance. Illias—not Samel—dismissed him and rolled off his horse, groaning. Tall, pale-faced, his black curls in an artful toss, he bent and stretched and smiled at Readen and the expressionless guard. "I want to kiss the ground. I am not used to—"

"Why are you so late?" Readen's words snapped. "And where is Samel? Why are you here?"

Illias straightened as if a whip popped him. A forced smile twisted his mouth.

Readen dismissed the guard with instructions to find Pol, his oldest and most trusted guard, and turned back to Illias.

The man's forehead was wet with sweat and dark with dust, but answered with calm. "I'm afraid Samel is in prison, and no one can get in to see him. I didn't enjoy making—"

Readen grabbed Illias by the shirtfront and pulled him close, nose to nose, toes stretching for the ground. Illias's eyes bulged. Now the fop was frightened.

"How did that happen?" Soft menace leached from every syllable.

He let go of Illias, who scrambled back with a look of horror. Readen had made a mistake. "I'm sorry, Illias. I've been alone here for too long. My temper is as bad as my manners. It is good to see you. I'll have a room made ready for you. And I'll be sure there's wine for you. You've made a long journey."

Illias straightened his jacket with a petulant shrug and nodded. Readen would have to be more careful with his allies. He couldn't afford to lose this messenger.

Pol unlocked the wagon door and pulled out the two people inside. A tall, slender young man and a young woman, almost as tall, but far less slender, both dazed, disoriented, and terrified. He led the pair away to the cells in the depths of the hold. They could hardly walk. Pol had to hold them upright and push them.

Readen felt nothing but cold relief and cold satisfaction. No rush of heat deep in his belly. No shiver of sexual anticipation like usual. A faint buzz of confusion at this absence fluttered in the back of his mind. He slapped it away, like swiping at a mosquito. No matter. They were nothing more than power sources. He'd make good use of them in his special room below.

"Drugged. You over-drugged them. How much did you give them, and how long before it wears off?"

Illias reappeared and shrugged, his shoulders so high and tight they almost covered his ears. "I had no choice. They are both strong. And loud. How else could I keep them quiet? It takes more than a tenday to get here in the best conditions, and we didn't have the best conditions. The mud was axel deep in places." He cleared his throat, and his voice steadied—almost. "The effects will be gone in a couple of days." His hands wormed around and through each other close in front of his belly, his usual aplomb nowhere in sight.

Readen sniffed at the fear smell pouring off Illias. It fed his power, but there was no familiar arousal. Even more confusing, there was nothing but a faint distant alarm at the lack of it. "Go settle your horses and guards and come to my study. I need your report." He went back up the stairs to pace the length of the room.

Samel arrested and incommunicado. How had that happened? How had he been discovered? Readen depended on Samel to stir up and organize opposition to rule by talent in the Prime so when Readen acted to take it over, there would be support. He'd not done that the first time. It had been a mistake.

He raised his hands to his head and pressed on his temples. For an instant it felt as though his mind was cleaved in two. Then the feeling was gone, replaced by the relief that he would soon be able to replenish his power.

Illias knocked on the open door.

"Who exposed Samel?"

Illias froze, fist still upraised, swallowed, and took a step inside. "I don't know who. Or how he was discovered. Although I suspect it was too many unexplained absences from the Prime."

"How are you explaining your absence? Can I depend on you, or are you next to be imprisoned? And spill what you know to Daryl? Or Krager?" Readen felt his forehead crease in a frown, but what he didn't feel was the familiar rage at the thought of his brother and the duplicitous Krager. Then that thought drifted away, or was pushed away by something. He shook his head as if something inside it was out of place.

Illias's voice was thick, as if he needed to force control over his lips and tongue. "I'm checking on my hold, which as you know, is not far from here. To set up defenses against the urbat attacks."

"Ah. yes. I'd forgotten you have a small holding." Readen rounded the end of his desk and sat, his back to the light from the window. Illias frowned and squinted at him. "You needn't worry about the urbat attacking." He forced a genial tone. Holding his long-practiced facade was becoming difficult. It shouldn't be.

Illias looked confused.

He shouldn't have said that. He couldn't afford to inadvertently confirm any suspicion that he released the Itza Larrak. He was forgetting himself too often. Rumors of his connection with the urbat and the Itza Larrak must stay rumors. His troops, even the mercenaries would walk away on the instant if they didn't. "Your hold is close enough to mine. The mercenaries I've hired will be here soon. I can protect it." He relaxed his shoulders and smiled the old, familiar Readen's-your-friend smile.

Illias smiled a shaky smile of relief. His hold was small and wasn't rich.

"Now, tell me about Restal Prime and your journey here. Are my rumors about the revolt against repressive rule by the strongest talents spreading? What news from the guards inside the hall? What is happening with the struggle against the urbat? Are they attacking? What has become of the Itza Larrak?"

Illias began to talk. The longer he talked, the stronger his voice became and the straighter he stood. "We traveled by night, wrapping the horses' hooves and harnesses to muffle them. My two outriders spotted a number of Daryl's sentries, but we were able to avoid them. We weren't spotted."

Readen didn't believe that. Of course they'd been seen. Illias's only hope was that no one had recognized him. Readen's hope, too. Illias was accomplished at ingratiating himself with the powerful, and Readen needed his information. So he listened to Illias's reports for a long time, unspeaking but for the occasional question. His expression was genial, but inside he might have been one of the stones in the wall of his study. Nothing mattered except power and his conquest of the planet.

CHAPTER SEVEN

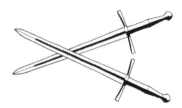

"How many are there, and how close are they?"

Jenna Me'Nowyk stopped with her hand on the door to her father's study. There was a wasp buzz of anger in his voice with a note of fear behind it. She'd never heard fear in his voice before. It scared her. Her home might not always be happy, but it had always been safe.

She stepped back. Who was he talking to?

"Five ships, two with mercenaries and three with their horses."

That was Mi'hiru Dalys's voice. Mercenaries? She edged closer to the door. If she went in, her father, Toldar's coastal holder, would halt the Mi'hiru's report. He'd never allow her to hear a report about mercenaries approaching their harbor. She was a girl, and what did girls know about war?

"Why am I just now hearing about this? If they're close, I should have reports."

"The Karda Patrol saw them two days ago when a storm drove them to shelter in a cove not far from Amarena harbor. After the storm they headed too far out to sea for the Karda to keep track. The wing leader sent word. As soon as I got it, I came directly to you. That took a day of hard flying. The ships will pass the border into Me'Bolyn's Hold in not much more than a tenday."

Jenna heard her father's chair creak and slide back.

"The spring storms may delay them. Show me on the map where they were spotted." Footsteps sounded, and paper crackled. "That's north of anywhere they might land to get to the pass over the mountains through my holding. They're headed for Restal's pass. That makes them Holder Me'Bolyn and Guardian Daryl's problem, not ours. Just make certain you don't let ChiChi fly anywhere near them and alert the Karda Patrol to be on the watch. I'll need to know immediately if they try to land anywhere along my coast."

"Should I find a Karda to take word...?'"

"Don't bother. Me'Bolyn's patrols are always out. They'll see them in plenty of time."

Jenna clapped one hand over her mouth and fisted the other tight against her stomach to keep from barging through the door and objecting. This was wrong. Her father was wrong. Restal needed to be warned as soon as possible. Karda didn't venture far from the coastline. The mercenaries might not be seen until they were close to shore. Me'Bolyn needed to be warned now. Guardian Daryl needed to be warned. The battle with the Itza Larrak and Readen could turn on those mercenaries.

Dalys came through the door. Her blond hair flew around her head, and her riding skirt swirled. Anger and distress stirred her Air talent as if she were in the middle of a tornado. The little Mi'hiru started to speak to Jenna, who shook her head. Dalys paused, breath whistling between her clenched teeth. Jenna whispered, "The mews," as Dalys's storm swirled by. She patted her smooth dark hair, straightened her dress, and stepped into the study.

Even behind his desk, her father was tall, with a slender, spare frame, and a fringe of dark hair around a bald pate—dark hair Jenna knew wasn't a natural dark. Ruben Me'Nowyk's eyes narrowed so they were slits in his lined face. "I suppose you were listening outside the door again."

"Father—"

Me'Nowyk leaned back in his creaking chair behind the broad desk and held up his long-fingered hand, palm toward her. "I don't want to hear it. I've already sent more troops than I can spare through the pass to join Toldar's troops. They're halfway to Restal by now. There's no guarantee those mercenaries won't try to raid one of our small harbor towns before they sail past us. I need every patroller we have to protect this holding. It's time you stopped listening at doors and interfering in holder business. As I've told you over and over, I'm the one running this hold. You need to be watching your sister. Chiara is off with her damn Karda when she's supposed to be at lessons. Sorrows of Adalta, Jenna, your step-mother says she's taken to wearing a long knife in a sheath at her belt like a sword. You need to take hold of her and put a stop to that." He waved a hand at her. Dismissal in so many ways.

Jenna pulled on her Earth talent to ground the fury rousing her strong Air. The battle inside was fierce enough to burn through stone if she let go and twisted the two talents into flame. She concentrated on the coolness of the flagstone floor and pulled on the tree-calmness of the walnut desk between them until she could speak coherently. She was so far outside her body and inside her talent elements her voice was a muffled echo in her ears. "Yes, Father." If she did what she knew she had to do and warned Holder Me'Bolyn, what would she do then? If her father let her come back at all it would be as his prisoner. She had little freedom now—she'd have none then.

She stalked down the hallway and out to the Karda mews. If she were wearing boots instead of slippers, the boom of her stomping, stamping steps would have brought down the ceiling. every one she passed drew away from her as though she were a flaming torch that would burn them to cinders if they got too close. She wondered if her hair was on fire.

Jenna stopped at the mews entrance to let her eyes adjust to the dark and adjust her temper. Warm air blew down the flagstone alleyway from the open door of the tack room, chasing away the cold smell of the sea from the rocky shoreline with the spicy scent of Karda and the clean smell of straw. Several deep breaths helped her step inside and walk down the wide space that separated the two rows of elegant stalls. She stuck to the middle. She hated flying. She was terrified of Karda, but she had no choice. The decision to warn Holder Me'Bolyn hardened in the kiln of anger inside her.

"Your father wasn't alarmed about the mercenaries." Dalys jerked a comb through the reddish mane of her Karda. Seralla's head and wings were every shade of brown from pale orange rust to nearly black, with long white tips on her flight feathers.

She stopped combing and leaned against Seralla's shoulder, frowning. She'd calmed down enough that her hair was back in place. She was one of the advance agents from the spaceship and had kept her secret until she was told it was safe to admit it. Controlling her new talent wasn't easy for her. "I don't know what to do. Seralla can alert every Karda we see, and there are a lot of them in the air I've never seen before. We can hope word gets to Holder Me'Bolyn and to Guardian Daryl Me'Vere in time."

"Dalys, you're a Mi'hiru. You don't have to listen to him, much less obey him. You can leave anytime. This is an emergency. I'll explain it myself to Mother Cailyn in Rashiba if anyone objects. But they won't."

"But there's Chiara."

"ChiChi can survive without you. You and I need to leave. Now. As soon as I'm back with my things and before the other Mi'hiru get back with the patrols. Or else we'll have to make up some story. Can you find me a bedroll and the things we'll need to camp? It's a tenday flight to Me'Bolyn Hold. And we'll be racing the mercenaries' ships."

Dalys's mouth opened and closed. Opened and closed. "You and I? But Jenna, you don't fly. And horseback—"

"I can do the calculations, Dalys. I know horses can't keep up. I fly if I have to. Just please ask a Karda to carry me who's...who's...gentle?" She flushed at the way her voice squeaked up at the end of her sentence.

She turned to leave. There was a loud scuffling in the next stall. It was just Mia, the Karda ChiChi flew, folding her knees under her to lie down.

Thank Blessed Adalta ChiChi wasn't in there. They'd never get away without her. She was perfectly capable of throwing a screaming fit loud enough to be heard all the way to the Great Hall.

Back in her room, in spite of the tremble in her hands—she really really hated flying—Jenna packed what she needed in less than thirty minutes. The clothes she wore for riding would do for flying, and her hooded, barla-hide coat would do for inevitable rain and sleet. Even this far south it was still too early in the spring for anything but scattered promises of warmth. Halfway to the door she stopped, stripped the heavy wool blanket from her bed, rolled it tight, and looked at her saddlebags. They were designed for horses, not Karda, and someone was sure to see her and wonder where she was going with stuffed full packs. She wondered herself. However was she going to do this?

Finally, loaded with two lumpy pillowcases and her blanket, Jenna left and promptly bumped into the housekeeper.

"What are you doing, Jenna? Let me get someone to take those wherever you need them. Have you been cleaning out closets?"

"Yes, and my blanket needs washing. But The Step Mother wants to see you right away. I'll manage," Jenna never used her step-mother's name. Both she and ChiChi pronounced the words as if they were capitalized, with a hard popping "p" on "Step."

ChiChi was in the tack room when she got to the mews. "What are you doing here, ChiChi? You're supposed to be with your tutor." This was not good. Keeping secrets from ChiChi never worked. Mia must have told her.

"Yes, yes, I know. But Miss Fidelia is still fiddling around with her 'Plan For Chiara's Day,' so I told her I'd be back in an hour. She was fine with that." ChiChi didn't look up but went on rolling a bedroll and tying it tight. She glanced at Jenna's bundles, her head still down. "I'll take care of those. Oh, good, you brought an extra blanket. We—You'll probably need that."

Jenna dropped her things and hugged ChiChi from the back, laying her dark head of curls on ChiChi's red-gold and ever-wind-blown tangles. "I'm sorry, ChiChi. I'll be a dead person to Father after this. I don't want you to be one, too."

"Any more than I already am?" Her voice was small and shook.

"It's going to be a fast, rough trip. Too rough for a ten-year-old. And yes, I know you're a better flyer than I'll ever be, and Dalys is a Mi'hiru, but we can't ask her to take responsibility for a child in addition to leaving her post here however dire the emergency."

"I'm not a child. I'm almost eleven." She swiped hair out of her face—chin out, mouth tight, eyes narrowed into her angry, stubborn-like-a-rock face.

Jenna grabbed a mane comb from a shelf and attacked the long, heavy tangles of ChiChi's stick-straight hair, getting it back in a leather-wrapped tail that brushed the girl's waist. Wrapping her arms around the narrow, tense shoulders, Jenna whispered, "I have my journal. I'll write down everything we do and see, even the things that scare me, and you can read it when I get back."

ChiChi's voice was little more than a whisper. "What if you get —what if you get killed? What if you don't come back? What if The Step Mother convinces Father that you should be banished forever?"

"I'll just have to come back from the dead and rescue you, won't I?"

"Without a sword or anything?"

"With a stick and a stone and my unshakable promise." Jenna kissed the top of the gold head. "Thank you for packing this for me. I haven't a clue how to pack for flying."

"Yeah. You need to meet Mirjana, anyway. I know you don't like Karda, but you'll like her, and she's really smart. You won't even have to think at her very hard for her to know what you want. She'll keep you safe."

Jenna leaned against the wall outside the tack room, her eyes squinched so tight her eyelids might have been welded shut. Her arms wrapped around her as if to keep from falling apart. A big, clumsy moth banged around inside her chest trying to beat its way out, pushing all the air from her lungs. It wasn't dislike of the Karda. It was terror. Every time she mounted one, the world tried to go black, and she had to force herself to breathe. Two years ago, she'd flown from the west coast to the east coast for the annual assembly at Rashiba. Her terror never left her. She hated it. She'd sworn never to do it again, and here she was. So much for never again.

"Jenna?" Someone took hold of her shoulder and shook it. "Jenna?"

She pushed herself away from the wall and opened her eyes. It was all she could do not to turn and run. Behind Dalys stood a silvery gray Karda, its predator head almost on Dalys's shoulder. Jenna couldn't look away from the dark, dark eyes.

"This is Mirjana, Jenna. She told Seralla to tell you the first and most important thing you need to know is, she will never drop you. You will never fall off her. She will never have to dive and catch you by the seat of your pants?" Dalys's voice rose a little at the end in a half-laugh, half-question.

Mirjana held Jenna's eyes. Peace. Deep, solid, abiding peace started at the top of her head and spread down through her body, her arms, her legs until it was as if she stood in a deep, warm pool of it. Peace.

From somewhere a high, thin scream sounded and went on and on and on. Jenna looked up to see a tiny body falling from a blue sky, arms and legs flailing, trying to grab the air. An enormous dark shape swooped on it, grabbing it in long, sharp talons. The screaming didn't stop. Her body jerked, and she was back, standing outside the tack room, caught by Mirjana's dark eyes.

"I fell," she whispered. "I fell off, and a Karda caught me." She'd been seven years old.

She'd lived with that terror hiding inside her for thirteen years. She breathed in air with the spicy scent of Karda. It filled a vacuum inside her she didn't even know existed. The moth banging around in her chest folded its wings and shrank back inside its chrysalis.

Dalys moved away. Jenna laid her hand on the side of the silvery head. "I can do this. I'm still afraid, but I can do this. I can fly with you." Her voice was a whisper so low only she and Mirjana could hear it.

Mirjana took a long curl of Jenna's dark hair in her beak and combed through it, gentle, calming, mothering.

"She's grooming you," said Dalys. "I think she likes you."

Dalys wasn't able to hide the bit of doubt in her voice.

Today, for the first time, Jenna helped with the rigging. It slowed them a little—leaving before the patrols were back would be close—but within the half-hour she and Dalys loped down the landing meadow to take off. The last thing she saw when she looked back was ChiChi, standing with her hands on her hips, staring after them. She couldn't see the expression on her face, but she hoped it was her sad and angry face and not the determined one.

Because she wasn't terrified and grabbing the arched saddle handle in desperation, Jenna discovered it was much easier to move with Mirjana. She wasn't being thrown around like a ball in a game of keep-away. It was already easier to feel the way Mirjana moved. She'd get better. What Jenna felt in return was another wave of peace, and she settled in to learn and feel the way the Karda moved, to feel the way to move with her. It wasn't easy, but still easier than flying stiff with fear, eyes shut, hands gripping the saddle handle until they cramped.

They flew north for four hours along the coastline. The sky darkened in the east, the sun dropping behind the spikes of the mountains, and the few clouds in the west shone pink and silver, gold and crimson over a midnight blue ocean. Four riderless Karda flying spirals around and around each other arrowed toward them from the east. They spread out and incorporated Mirjana and Seralla in a V formation and headed inland to a landing meadow in the middle of a small forest of bamboo.

Mirjana's landing lope was smooth, but Jenna's legs were on fire. The Karda knelt, and she climbed carefully down, stepping from saddle to Mirjana's knee to the ground. Everything hurt. Everything. She hung on a stirrup until her leg muscles stopped quivering, and she thought maybe she could walk or hobble or crawl. Unbuckling the saddle pack and hauling it down was excruciating. She looked from the packs to the fire circle several meters away, took a deep breath, and started dragging them. To pick them up and carry them was not an option. If they weren't in a desperate hurry to warn Me'Bolyn, she'd have stayed here splayed out on the ground and not moved for three days. In the rain. In the snow. In the burning sun. She'd never notice.

Dalys looked up from the small fire pit. She looked closer. "Oh, my, Jenna. I'll unload and unsaddle for you. You can hardly walk."

"I'll let you tonight. I have salve and aspirtea in my pack if I can find it. I hope ChiChi didn't forget to put it in."

Dalys settled Jenna's packs near the fire pit, and Jenna started fumbling one open. "Please, Adalta, let ChiChi not have forgotten my salve." Everything hurt except her hair.

"Uh oh," Dalys's tone was a resigned I-was-afraid-of-this-and-I'm-not-happy-about-it.

Zigzagging, side-slipping, almost turning upside down, a small dark gray Karda with long, slender, wine-dark wings and a tiny, wildly waving figure on its back flew toward them and landed, prancing and dancing down the runway.

ChiChi and Mia had arrived.

Jenna dropped her head in her hands and muttered, "Chiara," followed by a vividly descriptive sailor word. This was one of those times when only a sailor word would do.

The intrepid ten-year-old bounced off Mia and ran to Jenna, throwing her arms around her.

"I found you! I didn't get lost!"

CHAPTER EIGHT

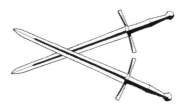

Cedar's eyes flew open. She tried to sit up, but someone had her cradled tight, and there were straps criss-crossing her belly. She was shifting and jerking up and down and sideways, and her stomach couldn't keep up. Daryl looked down at her, nothing but blue sky and a pair of enormous wings appearing, disappearing, and appearing again above his face. Oh, purple nebula, she was in the air again. She curled her body tighter, grabbing onto his arm.

"You're awake, good. Stop struggling. You're safe."

"Sick. I'm going to be sick." Saliva flooded her mouth. She tried swallowing. It didn't help.

Daryl shoved a large rough cloth at her and turned her onto her side. Her belly tried to turn itself inside out. Fortunately, there wasn't much left in her stomach. But when she opened her eyes, the ground below her was far away, way too far away. She closed her eyes against the terrifying distance and the constant shifts of Abala's flight. Surely this was a nightmare, and she was sleeping safely in a bed somewhere. Somewhere on the ground.

Wiping her mouth, she wadded up the cloth and slowly, carefully shifted back around. Daryl's mouth turned up in an unconvincing smile. There was a flash of can't-stop-smiling smirk that looked like it hurt, then turned into a concerned upside-down smile. His thumb rubbed up and down on her arm. She liked his smile, but she was too terrified to return it. There was a strong sense of "this man needs me" that came out of nowhere, and her terror wound down into big fear. Her stomach lurched again, but whether it was Abala's unpredictable movements or that strange feeling, she didn't know.

Daryl dropped the smelly cloth. The upswing of Abala's wings caught it, and it swirled away like a little white bird. Then Cedar was smothered in smells. Smells that spoke of power from the air, smells that spoke of the spicy scent of mystery that was the Karda they rode on, smells that spoke of worry, overwhelming responsibilities, self-doubt. And—love—love and safety, from deep inside Daryl? It felt like a landing place and made her want to curl tighter against him. This wasn't in her job description. Not at all.

"It's too much." Her head spun. "It's too much." She covered her mouth and nose with hands that smelled of vomit. They stank, but the pressure helped. She still felt the power of the scents around her, but the emotions faded. Afraid to move her body, she raised her eyes from Daryl's face to the wings moving above her, to the clouds too close above her.

She mumbled through her hands, "What is it? What's happening to me? Why are we up in the air?"

The taut muscles of his face and the sharp lines across his forehead relaxed, but the arms holding her tensed. He propped her feet on his leg and reached a hand around to his packs. She wrapped both her arms as tight as she could around the one arm holding her and curled her legs up to her belly. Only one arm holding her. She froze.

"Are you going to be sick again?" He handed her a clean cloth and a small jar, and his other arm curled around her legs, drawing her closer. "Mireia said to smear a little of this under your nose. It'll help." He put his arm under her legs again.

She felt like a baby, but she managed to move a hand to grab the jar. It took every bit of her courage to let go of him long enough to open it. She smeared the strong-smelling salve under her nose and on the cloth. A tiny bit of tension left her body. "No. Even if I were, there's nothing left to come up. I won't spoil your clothes." Her voice sounded squeaky even to her. It took more than a little of the pungent salve that smelled like trees to block out the smells—the smells that were so much more than simple smells they were confusing her there was so much in them. Amusement—that was coming from Abala. That wasn't possible.

She eyed his jacket and shirt and the lines of tiredness on his face. "Although they look like you've been sleeping in them for days. You don't look like the smooth, immaculate guardian I met when we landed." She tried a smile. It didn't work.

The only sign of humor on his face was a faint crinkle of lines at the corners of his eyes. "I'm not as worried about my clothes as I am about my saddle. And Abala hates to be thrown up on. It messes his mane."

"How did I get up here, flying too close to the clouds?" The cloth muffled her voice but she didn't dare move it away. She could smell doubt and a hint of dread, but over that, his laughter, his relief, and his love even through the wad of wool and tree smell. How could she know what doubt and fear smelled like? What love smelled like? How was that possible? But she did. Somehow she did. She tried to shut it out. She shut her eyes tight, pressed the cloth tight over her nose, and breathed through her mouth. It didn't help. This was too scary. This was impossible. She had to figure out what was happening to her. Then she could control it.

The constant movements of Abala's flight, his little adjustments to air currents, the thunder of his wings when he gained altitude, and the soft silence of gliding began to soothe her fear. She ever so slowly, ever so carefully wiggled around to look up, not down at the faraway ground, and concentrated on watching his wings. The flight feathers tilted open when he raised his wing and closed tight when they moved downward, cupping the air and carrying them forward and up. Concentrating on seeing, not thinking, made this better, bearable. She relaxed a fraction.

Something warm and wonderful spread into her wracked stomach. Love—he loves me. And he doesn't know it. The warm feeling spread. Oh, the complications. How could she know this? And know he wasn't ready. She wasn't either. How could she possibly know this? But the surety of his love for her was there. Solid rock surety. She wasn't even confused by it. Which confused her. Love didn't happen this way—it grew, slow, like a plant from a seed. It wasn't an instantaneous fall-on-your-head-knock-yourself-out thing.

"You've been unconscious for two days. Since the attack. Mireia says your sudden surge of talent is what saved us."

She jerked at the sound of his voice and grabbed his arm tighter. "Surge of talent? Saved us? Saved us from what? I don't understand. Two days? I've been unconscious for two days? Have you been carrying me for two days?" The world wasn't making sense, and she was shrieking again.

"Definitely two. Somebody had to do it, and no one else volunteered. You don't smell very good, you know. Assam said you'd be grumpy when you woke up. And full of questions."

"Beware, Daryl, a sense of humor might soften your soberness." Cedar was quiet for several minutes. Even with her eyes closed, she smelled Daryl's watchful look. She smelled worry. How could she smell worry? And a seed of love didn't have an odor. The forest had an odor. The Karda had a spicy smell. Her clothes had an odor. Oh galaxies, did they ever. But worry, doubt, love? They didn't have odors. But still, she smelled them. More ointment. Her limpet grip on Daryl's arm had to loosen to open it, but she managed a swift smear.

Then her body went still, like the air in a pod when the circulators failed. "Those weren't cuddly puppies or faithful flying dogs, were they?"

"No, they weren't."

"Am I hurt? I don't hurt anywhere except my stomach. Did they attack me?" She started patting herself all over, nearly falling out of Daryl's hold. She grabbed the arm around her chest with both of hers. "Was anyone hurt? Oh, supernova take me, was anyone killed?"

"No, you weren't hurt." Daryl's hold tightened. "Quit wriggling, you'll tip us over."

"Oh, don't let me do that." She clamped both arms on his. Her fear of falling disappeared in a flood of memory. Monstrous, snarling, dog-like winged creatures with long razor-sharp claws and vicious, tearing teeth swarmed through her head, darkening the edge of her view of Daryl's face. That was all she saw, his face, and she latched onto it as if it were an emergency oxygen mask in a spaceship pod. "I remember the monsters." Her muffled voice was tiny in her ears. "If they didn't attack me, why have I been unconscious for two days? Did I fall over and hit my head on a rock? Did I —oh my, what did I do?" Had she humiliated herself and fainted from terror?

His glance at her was a now-what-do-I-do. "Uh…"

She waited. Not for very long. "What won't you tell me? What aren't you telling me? Are you hiding something bad I did?"

"Do you ever run out of questions? I know Assam warned me, but…"

"Not often, and why won't you answer them?"

"We're landing at Ardencroft now. You can talk to Mireia. She can help you better than I can."

The word she uttered with her muffled voice came through loud and clear. "Coward."

Cedar thought for a moment he was actually going to smile again.

She didn't feel like smiling. What kind of talent did she have? If she was going to have magic, why couldn't it be a magic she could understand, could control? How could she control something she didn't believe was possible? It certainly wasn't helpful. Throwing up all the time was not a useful skill, and it sure didn't seem like a magic thing.

He tightened his grip on her. Abala hit the ground running. And Cedar did her best not to scream.

Galen and Tessa met them at the end of the runway. Daryl slid out of the saddle, still holding her tight. Finder Mireia thundered to land just behind them, jumping to the ground before her Karda stopped. She grabbed Cedar's shoulder, and immediately Cedar could breathe without the wad of cloth over her face.

Still looking at Daryl's face, she said as sweetly as she could manage, "Thank you for carrying me here. You can put me down now."

A moment passed.

"You can put her down now, Daryl," Mireia said, her eyes on Cedar's face. "When did she come to?"

"Oh." Daryl set her on her feet and held her arms until her legs were steady. "Just a little bit ago, Mireia. And she's full of questions. Full."

Galen choked back a laugh. "I'm sure." He took hold of one arm, Mireia on the other side, and they started toward the village at a slow pace. Cedar's legs shook. She was still learning to maneuver with her clunky leg. After several paces, she shook loose from Galen. "I can walk now." But she walked closer to Mireia, who felt like a comforting blanket. The protection was smothering, but Cedar couldn't trust her stomach or her nose. Her jar of strong ointment was still gripped in one fist. She made use of it again. It helped.

Patrollers and Mi'hiru passed, carrying packs and saddle rigging. Other patrollers came from the village to help unload the supplies. When they finally reached the town gates, two large freight wagons were parked just inside, empty. There was scaffolding against the walls in several places. They were working hard to make the town ready for her shipmates.

She had a brief memory flash of one of the vicious creatures flying to attack and shivered. Galen touched her arm, and she shook her head. Sometime soon, she'd sit down and try to come to terms with what she'd experienced. But not now.

The village of Ardencroft was full of workers repairing doors and windows and walls. Cedar wondered if Mireia removed her protective blanket, would she smell terror or peace in this place filled with temporary people, no families, and a mass grave? Images of the village attacked by the monsters she'd seen, unwarned, unprepared, unaware that the creatures even existed flooded her—she held the open jar close under her nose. They faded, but they didn't go away.

Tessa and Galen walked in front of her, holding each other's hands so tight it looked like it must hurt. They were the ones who found the massacre that emptied this town. They were the ones who'd buried the entire town of victims, who'd buried the few dead urbat they found. Was this a place she could recommend as a home or even a staging depot for the people from the failing ship?

There was another question she pushed to the back of her mind. Could she live anywhere on this planet if she couldn't breathe without the overwhelming strange smells that didn't smell like smells should smell? Were they the reason she was unconscious for so long? Unconscious on the back of a Karda kilometers in the air. Two days an unconscious burden. Awesome. Swirling galaxy awesome. She was a helpless, useless lump, like her leg.

Marta walked toward them. "I've found our quarters, Mireia. You and Cedar and I will be in a little house on the next street. It has...had a big garden around it, so it will be quiet." She looked at Cedar. "You'll be glad for that while you're adjusting to your talent. It's easier for some than for others. And you and I seem to be of those others."

"You know how to build up a girl's confidence. I feel better already." Cedar smacked her on the arm. "Someday, I may even be able to stumble around without Mireia attached to me and propping up my sanity. Why don't you have a place for yourself and the awesome Altan? When will you introduce me? I promise not to poach, even though he'll prefer me to you. My iron self-restraint will let you keep him." She was prattling.

"I'm not worried. I'm good with my sword, and you've never even held one. And Mireia will sort you out. She won't turn you loose on this world with talent you don't know how to use or control. It wouldn't be fair to the rest of us." She put her arm through Cedar's and pulled her closer.

Cedar dropped her head and watched her feet move unevenly up the street before she looked back at Marta. "How often do those creatures attack? I'm supposed to be finding us places to settle before the ship fails entirely. It doesn't feel safe here. I can't even defend myself, and few of the people coming can either."

She looked ahead at Galen with his arm now around Tessa's

waist as hers was around his, as though they propped each other up. Cedar heard her own voice, too soft with the self-doubt and fear she hadn't allowed herself to feel since she lost her leg and her father. She asked, "Will I be able to do what Galen did? Pull a thorny hedge out of the ground? I don't think so. I'm not going to be able to do my job if all I can do is vomit." She had to get past this. And somehow she would. She looked up at the sky where the ship hung, a tiny silver dot. She would. She'd do her job.

Marta whirled around and looked up. "Oh, no. There's another attack somewhere."

Tessa and Galen spun and sprinted back toward the landing field and the Karda. Cedar heard Daryl yelling orders. Patrollers dropped packs wherever they stopped and took off at a run, some with saddles over their shoulders trailing straps behind them.

Mireia looked at Marta. "Go. She'll be fine with me." And Marta took off with the others.

"What's going on, Mireia?" Cedar covered her nose and mouth. The smell swirling in the air was tangible. Smell of alarm? Fear? Terror? The glory of flight and fight? So many smells, so many feelings that weren't hers. She stumbled. The air swirled around her—a tempest, a cyclone of feelings screamed through her nose. She would not faint again.

Mireia knelt on the ground and dug into her pack. "Try this, Cedar." She dabbed a smear of stronger ointment on Cedar's upper lip and put her hand back on Cedar's shoulder. The insulating blanket descended.

Trees—the redolent trees she'd smelled when she first landed. She closed her eyes and breathed it in through seared sinuses.

"It's pine tree sap ointment. Does it help?"

Cedar nodded, breathing through the growling cramps in her empty stomach. "We'll keep it handy." Mireia tucked the small lidded jar of it in her pocket. "The Karda must have spotted urbat and the Itza Larrak heading for a village between here and the Circle of Disorder."

Cedar closed her eyes and concentrated on pine trees and not smelling. The empty houses along the now-empty street stared back at her, their windows blank, sad eyes. In spite of the chaos of patrollers leaving, the thunder of Karda taking off, and the sounds of workers readying the village, the silence grew. It was a heavy silence without the sound of people going about their business, of children playing, of neighbors calling to each other. Sounds of life that filled the living pods on the spaceship were absent here. Oh, would they be able to turn this town from a tomb into a home? Then she heard a voice call, "Let's get back to work. These walls need to be higher."

Her people, her soon-to-be-homeless people would bring life back to these empty windows. She would organize that. She would borrow her mother's knitting needles, knit the rip in her self-confidence back together, and get that organized.

Mireia tugged at her, and they picked up the packs, theirs and Marta's, the troopers had dropped and walked on, turning the corner to the small house with the big, straggly garden where they were to stay. It was hard to breathe without Mireia's hand on her shoulder, but she fought the nausea, and they made it to the house.

Cedar dragged one of her packs toward the larger of the two bedrooms. "Marta and I can bunk in here. You should have the privacy of your own space. I expect you'll have lots of confused visitors soon."

"I don't know that I need it, but I appreciate it. But we need to start working on your talent. You don't want to spend the rest of your life smelling nothing but pine sap and holding your hand over your nose and mouth. So dump your packs in there, wash up, and we'll start. That's more important than unpacking anything but a change of clothes." Her nose wrinkled and her eyes crinkled.

They settled in comfortable chairs beside the rock fireplace. Mireia waved her hand, and the bed of magma stones glowed, spreading heat.

"You don't even need a sparkly wand and magic words. What happened to me? I can't remember anything except helplessness at the horror attacking us."

"Would you like a cup of tea, Cedar?"

She shook her head carefully. Tea? Tea when she was busy

fighting not to throw up? All she wanted to be able to do was not throw up every time she met someone.

"Your talent manifested, Cedar, and I'm alive now because it did. So, thank you. I know there are talents like you, but I've never found one so strong. I'll check in a minute, but I believe your major talent is Air. Your Earth is a bit less strong. What I need to do now is to help you get a handle on your *very* unique talent."

"Does that mean you don't know how to help me?" Cedar looked down at her fists clenched in her lap. "Voices. I hear not voices but the emotional *smell* in voices, and—I know this sounds dumb—but I *smell* anger. And grief. And love and responsibility. How can I smell responsibility? And responsibleness, which is not the same, somehow. I smell—so many emotions all at once. How is that a talent? It's more a curse, and it burns my nose. How can you smell emotions?"

"Well, I can help you control it so you can understand it and learn to work with it since I'm the best there is at working with talent." Mireia laughed. "Or so I like to tell myself. It seems to me you have an extraordinarily useful ability. Bring the cushion from your chair and come sit on the floor in front of me."

Mireia placed her hands on either side of Cedar's head. Calm soothed the prickles in her body, and Cedar drifted away, through a stillness that smelled of ageless peace.

Mireia squeezed her shoulder, and Cedar found her way back from wherever she'd disappeared to. How could she know what peace smells like? How could she know that's what she smelled? It must be imagination—her brain finding a familiar pathway for a new experience. Peace doesn't smell. Anger doesn't smell. Her nose filled with a sharp odor. Confusion doesn't smell. Oh, galaxy, how could she know the odor was confusion?

She hadn't been this confused, this bereft of words and vacant of coherent thought, for a very long time. A big part of her wanted to climb back on the shuttle and lift back to the ship.

"You have no defenses, no shields. I've been trying all along to shield you, but I didn't realize how very vulnerable you are."

"Is that why my head feels wrapped in a thick blanket with prickles?"

"Prickles?" Mireia tilted her head to one side. Surprise flicked across her face. "I've put a psychic blanket, a damper, around you until you're able to do it for yourself. That's the other part of what I'm to teach you."

"Oh, that's why it prickles. I've never liked being protected from myself or anything else."

Mireia laughed. It smelled of flowers and cookies. "And I imagine a lot of people in your life have tried."

Cedar lifted her prosthetic leg and glared at it. "Since this. Can you take the insulation off my mind so I'm not listening to you through a tunnel stuffed with curtains?"

Two creases appeared between Mireia's brows. "Yes, I will, but first I'll help you learn to ground and build some shields."

"Ground is not a good word to use to someone whose home is about to fall out of the sky, Mireia." The blanket lifted slightly, and now her head was aching, assaulted, afire with smells.

The finder laughed. "Tether, then. We'll try to teach you to tether yourself. And build your shields."

"Will it make my head hurt worse? Because the pile of blankets is preferable to lightning striking my head and not bouncing off." She leaned back.

"It will make it better. It helps if you close your eyes, take long, slow breaths and let them out through your mouth, counting them one by one. Picture a wall empty as space."

"Space isn't empty." Cedar opened one eye. Her right foot bounced up and down.

Mireia laid her hand on the bouncing knee. "Picture a blank wall, then, and put a bucket of dark blue paint with a wide brush in front of it." She moved around and put her hands on Cedar's shoulders, massaging lightly. "Put your thoughts on that blank wall." Her words were slow and soft. "Every time a thought enters your head, pick up the brush and paint over it with long strokes until thick blue paint covers it."

She continued to knead Cedar's shoulders.

Cedar started painting. Then she started making designs with the paint. Then she wiped imaginary blue paint off her hands onto her skirt. When could she have a long talk with Marta? How was Glenn doing? She remembered the blue paint and started slopping it again. For a long time thoughts bounced in and out of her head, not always landing on the wall.

Finally, there was nothing but the wet, glistening blue wall and slow, faint words. "Now feel a tether reaching down through your body into your foot, into the ground, like the first root pushing out of a seed. Feel it branch into more roots and rootlets, working through the dirt and rocks, drinking from the small streams of water that circulate through the planet like blood vessels. Feel the tether anchor itself—wind its roots around the stones that are the bones of Adalta."

Cedar felt as though she were becoming part of the planet, as though she were that green shoot pushing down roots and reaching for the light above. The soft voice said, "Now, Cedar, from the living soul that is the planet Adalta, build your tree around you. Your special tree—with strong thick bark, with a myriad of branches reaching into the world, with thousands of leaves filtering the emotions that surround us all. Feel your tree shelter you from them, from the intrusive emotions of others, emotions that do not belong to you. Feel it separate you from them. Feel it let you know what you need to know like spots of sunlight filtering through the leaves. Feel what you don't need to know travel down your tether back into the planet to be cleansed and used as food for new growth."

She could feel the smooth bark of her own trunk, the wind in her tiny leaves, the sap coursing through her. She felt belonging. Belonging with the sharp, clean smell of pine and cedar, the Old Earth tree her mother named her after. Even her absent leg was there. For the first time she since she was six, she was nourished, was whole. She could rest.

She stayed there, rooted, tethered, for a long time. Then she opened her eyes. The thick blanket was gone. The lightning flashes were gone. A light, sweet fragrance swirled around her. It was from Mireia, and Cedar knew it for what it was—satisfaction and approval—then she let it go. She leaned back against Mireia's knees and felt the fragrance filter through her leaves, flow down her furrowed bark and into the ground, letting only a slight hint of scent reach her. She still knew what it meant, but it was a knowing, not an assault blasting through her sinuses and dizzying her mind.

"Wow." She blinked several times and turned to look at Mireia. "Could we go outside and walk in the gardens? I know it's cold, but I need to be outside. I don't think I'll ever get enough of outside and the way the air smells—the real smells."

"Are you sure you are ready for this? Control takes a while."

"But you'll be right beside me, and I have to master this. There's not a lot of time to pamper myself." Getting up from the floor wasn't easy, so Mireia extended an arm, and Cedar levered herself up.

"Well, it's only the garden, not a crowd of people. But if you…. You're not a patient person, are you Cedar? I doubt if you've ever pampered yourself." Mireia found Cedar's heavy cloak and her own, and the two women walked out to the garden, straggly and overgrown. Twice workers passed outside the low wall. One pushed a wheelbarrow, fighting it as it wobbled on the cobblestones. He smelled of something ugly, the other smelled of contentment as he rushed by. She had to bolster her tree-shield around her both times. Even the contentment smell felt like an assault until she did. She felt like an intruder, peeping into someone else's mind. She didn't like that.

"It will get easier. You will need to concentrate on your shield all the time until it becomes automatic and permanent."

"Do you have to do that? Does every one?"

"I grew up doing it, from the first time I heard my mother's voice as words rather than sounds. And, no, every one doesn't need such strong and continuous shields."

Mireia talked to her of Air talents who could do anything from foretelling the weather to calling up breezes, to manipulating wild storms, to healing damaged minds. Water talents who were often healers of both mind and body, as well as diggers of wells and irrigation systems, firefighters, sailors. Earth talents ran the gamut from simple farmers to earth movers who built dams, smoothed washes and gullies, and miners who, even with a small Earth talent, could extract minerals and ores from the ground. They nurtured growing things as farmers and foresters and were strong fighters. Those who could twist Air and Earth could forge metals, light candles, create light balls, and shoot firebolts if they were strong enough. They made excellent swordsmen and warriors.

"The ways of talent and talent manipulation are endless and as varied as human minds and abilities. And they are so commonplace, most of them, that they are seldom noticed or remarked on. A farmer with Earth talent is just a better farmer. He doesn't need to consciously call on his talent to plow a field or scatter seeds."

They walked in silence for a time. Then Cedar asked what she'd been itching to ask from the beginning. "And me? What am I? A miner or a farmer?"

Mireia laughed. "Actually, neither."

"But I've worked with plants all my life." Cedar heard her voice rise toward whiny and pulled it down. "That's all I know."

"Did you play hide and seek when you were a child?"

"Hide and seek? What does that have to do with—with anything?" Memories of that childhood game were loaded with pain. She always found whoever was hiding—quicker than anyone else by a lot. But she couldn't run. Not until she stopped growing and they could fit her with her permanent no-longer-works bionic leg. By then, every one had outgrown the game and wouldn't play anymore. "I always lost."

"But not because you couldn't find the hiders, I bet."

"I always knew where they were. No one could hide from me. They pretty much quit hiding and just outran me. That was no fun."

"I know Galen thought you would be a planter, as he is, or wants to be when he can stop fighting. But you won't be."

"But that's all I know." Cedar knew she repeated herself. She chewed on her lip to keep her mouth shut. It didn't work. "So, what can I do?"

Mireia cocked her head and smiled. "Yes, you were Director of

Bio-Systems, but it's the systems part where your people skills lie. An important part of systems analysis when you apply it to situations involving people, maybe the most important part, is emotion. You have a strong Earth channel, but your largest channels are Water and Air. Water makes you a strong intuitive, Air manifests as logic, and Earth as the ability to categorize. My theory is Air carries the smell, Water activates the feeling, and Earth gives the feeling a name. We will have to work hard on the ethical aspects of your talent."

"Why are the smells so strong? Will I always be struggling with them? It's not comfortable for anyone if I'm always on the verge of losing my last meal." Ethical aspects? What could she possibly do with smells that would harm anyone? Throw up on them? Then she remembered the uneasy feeling that she was intruding into that gardener's mind. If she couldn't control this, she wouldn't be able to do what needed doing. So she'd learn to control it.

"It's because it's new. It manifested all at once with full force, and it's strong. You didn't gradually grow into it from childhood. Some from the ship will have the same problem, although such strong talent is rare. And this talent is exceedingly rare at such strength. You'll discover there are some ethical issues with it as you learn to control and use it."

Cedar was silent for a long time. Then she laughed, or rather she tried to laugh. It came out as more of a choking noise. "I have to tell you. There are a lot of people who could use some strong emotion soap. Maybe I could be an emotion soap maker." Ethical issues?

CHAPTER NINE

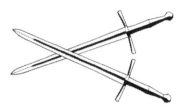

Jenna, ChiChi and Dalys flew as far off the coast as the Karda felt safe, but Jenna saw no sign of the mercenaries' ships. Lots of fishing boats, small coastal hoppers, larger trade ships—but no mercenaries. Every night, to her tired dismay, Dalys insisted they fly inland almost to the edge of the mountains, making the trip even longer.

"We don't want to get grounded by the fog that rolls in on the coast," she explained to Jenna when, after the third exhausting day, she complained. "Karda will fly in rain, even sleet and light snow, but not fog. They need to see."

Jenna shuddered. Her fear of flying was mostly gone—mostly. But a fog blinded Karda—the thought blew away her tiredness. She wouldn't complain again.

Even with a favoring wind from the south it was a long, hard tenday to reach Me'Bolyn Hold. Klaus Me'Bolyn was in the mews when they finally landed in the coastal town of Me'Bolyn Hold, tired, dirty, and hungry. A great, hairy medgeran of a man, he enfolded Jenna, squeezing her breath away. "You outran your father, I see. He's a fool to let two such beautiful ladies—no, three, I see— fly off ahead of him. I think I'll hide you and keep you captive till he gives up looking. Then you'll be mine. Good evening, ChiChi,

Mi'hiru Dalys. Welcome to all of you. May our table provide you sustenance, may our land provide you work to suit your heart and hands, and may you find safety within our walls in your rest."

His deep, steady voice hit her like a warm blanket, a soft bed, and a glowing magma stone stove. She wanted to hand the problem to him and fly back home. But the blanket, the bed, and the warm stove would become her prison, and she knew Me'Bolyn had sent all the troopers he could spare to Daryl already. The responsibility was hers. She sighed. She'd accepted that before they left the Me'Nowyk mews.

"Let me unsaddle Mirjana for you, Jenna." Dalys reached for the rigging, and Jenna pushed her hands away.

"No, I want to do it. And I'll groom her too." Her fingers still fumbled the buckles like a two-year-old learning to fasten her boots, but she managed to get the rigging off and the straps coiled. "See, I'm almost moving like a human again. I'm learning to live with my aching muscles and bruised bones." Her voice sounded falsely bright, even to her, but she'd done it by herself for the first time. A small triumph with a big feeling and a pair of aching wobbly legs.

Me'Bolyn took the saddle from her and tossed it on a saddle stand. He turned back, pulled on his short, black beard, the broad smile gone from his face, and handed her a brush from the tack cabinet on the wall above the stand. "Your father's not ambling along behind you, is he? What's going on, Jenna? Why are you flying with one Mi'hiru, your little sister—excuse me, Chiara, your intrepid younger sister—and no troopers to guard you?" He looked at her smudged face and the clothes she'd worn too long. "I don't need to make arrangements for the wagon train coming along behind carrying your clean clothes, do I?"

Jenna's face heated. How could she explain her father's negligence? The two holders were supposed to be allies in the efforts to separate the Coastal Holdings from Toldar and Restal. But she knew her father. His idea of being an ally was being the ally on top.

ChiChi's mouth started to open. Jenna laid a hand on her shoulder for fear she'd say something that didn't need saying about their father.

She stood as straight as her aching body would let her and used her calm, diplomatic voice. "Two ships loaded with Akhara mercenaries accompanied by three ships with horses and equipment are coming up the coast, sir, probably making their way to your pass across the mountains to join Readen Me'Vere's fight over who will rule Restal. They will pass through your hold on their way. By the time they get here, they'll need supplies."

Me'Bolyn looked at her so long and so hard she was sure her feet had sunk into the ground half a meter. It was all she could do not to hide her face in Mirjana's mane with shame for her father. It wasn't the first time she'd been embarrassed by him. As diplomatic as she was, he was not.

"I see." He crossed his arms and leaned against the wall. "And you're on your way to warn Daryl."

ChiChi stood on a stool, unfastening and coiling Mia's saddle straps. She stopped. Her eyes flicked back and forth between Jenna and the holder, getting bigger and bigger, her face hot and red and angry. She clenched her fists, arms stiff at her sides.

Jenna braced herself. She didn't even try to stop ChiChi.

"He wasn't even going to warn you." Her words were a whisper of shame. "Jenna, he wasn't even going to send Holder Me'Bolyn or Guardian Daryl a warning, was he? That's why we flew so fast and hard."

Jamming his slouchy hat over shaggy hair and a dirty stubbled face, in his shabby but heavy shirt, patched sheepskin jacket, worn trousers, and scuffed boots, Krager finished the illusion and changed his face. He leaned against a wall in the alley beside blacksmith Kobe's shop and enjoyed the heat from the forge that warmed the square-cut red stones. He hoped the political temperature of the city he was out testing was only warm, not forge-fire hot. He doubted he would gather much information, but he had to make his rounds anyway. Any information was useful. No information would be useful too, he supposed.

A woman in a voluminous shawl walked toward him with a heavy basket, trailed by a small child in so many clothes it looked like he or she could roll faster than walk. She saw Krager, grabbed the child's hand, pulled it across the street, and walked faster.

When she was out of sight, he slipped farther into the alley, counted up from the bottom row of stones and wiggled out a loose one. He put the paper he found in his pocket and walked without apparent purpose to the tavern down the street. A faded board over the door read *Bloody Talons*, and true to the spirit of the sign, the stains on the floor were often from blood. At ten in the morning, the room was empty.

Krager sat at a table in a back corner. The tavern owner, a small, wiry, ageless woman, a big bat in her shapeless black clothes, sat on a high stool at the end of the bar beside him.

"Morning, Payne. Who you gonna hurt today?"

"Nobody on my kill list right now, Mother Girt. What do you have for me? Or who?" Krager knew there was a stout club, a long knife, and her cash box within finger reach under the bar. He also knew by the unguarded tone of her voice they were the only two in the tavern, which was why he'd chosen this time.

"Name's Derrick. Thinks he missed his chance when Readen's forces left, and he didn't. Thinks he should be a sergeant by now. Never will. But he's got what amounts to a squad of men he's talkin' to, tryin' ta get 'em all movin' in one direction. Not a direction you'd choose."

"They got a place?"

"Don't know where they meet. I seen 'im in here a lot with one or two at a time. Usually careful not to talk louder'n whispers."

She slid off the barstool, "S'all I kin tell ya," and disappeared to the kitchen in the back, cash box tight under her arm.

Krager finished his ale and mentally flipped through his lists to find someone who'd become a regular in this tavern, or might be already, then he left to find another of his spotters or watchers.

They didn't actively spy for him. He wouldn't ask that of them. They were the kind of people who just watched their neighbors, their customers. Who knew them and whether they supported

Readen or Daryl. It was up to Krager himself to decide how to use the ones they found for him, and what would work on them—money, ideology, ego, blackmail.

He'd been doing this on Daryl's behalf, sometimes with and sometimes without his knowledge, for years. Daryl might choose to believe Readen wasn't allied with the Itza Larrak, but Krager knew better. He'd studied Readen since he arrived in Restal Prime as a child and become Daryl's best friend. Readen's too, or so Readen had thought. Now, of course, he knew better. Keeping track of the political temper of the city was more vital than ever since Readen's failed revolt and subsequent escape from his prison.

Finding people who could ferret out Readen's supporters and spies wasn't the tricky part. That was communication—getting information from them and to them.

A young boy, tall for his age, came up beside him, stretching his legs to match Krager's pace.

"Good mornin' to you, Becca." Krager kept his head and his voice low.

"Don't call me Becca." She looked around. "Someone might hear you. Bek. I'm Bek. I found where three of that evil Samel's servants went. Two of them ain't any innocents. I got a job in the stable there so's I kin watch them."

"Becca—sorry, Bek—I don't think that's a good idea. You won't be able to pass as a boy for much longer."

"I gotta eat. I need a job, they need another manure picker, and I owe you big. Nobody pays attention to me. I fork stinkin' straw and keep my ears open and my mouth shut. Wish I could shut my nose, too, sometimes. It ain't the best run place I ever been."

She skipped a couple of steps to keep up. "You wanna know where they are so you can arrest 'em?"

"Yes, and I'll not be arresting them till I know what they know and what they plan. Now, tell me what you know quick and get back to the smelly straw before they get suspicious. Or you get fired for being lazy. Be careful, Becca-Bek. I don't want to lose you."

"Aw, Krager. It's nice to know you care."

"I care that you always bring me useful information." He

smiled, careful not to let it show too much, and gave her the names from the piece of paper he'd found behind the brick. "Ears open, eyes wide, mouth shut, Bek. I'll be out again in a couple of days."

"Next time bring two sausage rolls." She skipped away, out of sight in a second.

He knew where Samel's men were. He knew to watch Derrick. He knew a lot of other little things. Not big breakthroughs, but information he needed. Little parts to the puzzle that could save Restal. He headed for a quiet spot to lose his illusions and get out of his smelly clothes.

Me'Bolyn hoisted Jenna's heavy packs to Mirjana's back like they were packed with nothing more than an afternoon's picnic. She checked the straps and buckled one side while he did the other.

"There's no need to worry about us, Holder Me'Bolyn."

"Klaus, call me Klaus. Are you sure, Jenna? Are you certain the three of you have enough energy and talent strength to block the pass? You had a hard tenday flight and only one night of rest."

Chiara walked up, shoulders back, face drawn into the perfect definition of determination. She opened her mouth to speak, but before she said anything rash, Jenna spoke.

"ChiChi is an exceptionally strong Earth talent despite her age. My Earth is almost as strong as my Air. Dalys's Air is powerful enough to raise a tornado that could blow rocks off the side of the mountain herself. She has to have significant Earth, or she'd float on the breeze."

Me'Bolyn crossed his arms and tilted his head to one side. "A strong Air talent with little training. I know she's one of the advance agents sent by the spaceship. Talent is new to her."

"She's been working with our finder every day since we discovered who she is." She tried not to think about the inept Miss Fidelia and how much she'd had to discover about her talent on her own, learning from the powerful talents she met when traveling with her father.

"We can shut off the pass. Not permanently, no one wants that, but if we find the right spot, your forces can come from behind to block the mercenaries in and harry their efforts to clear a way through." Jenna's voice wanted to quake like abelee leaves in a breeze, but she didn't let it. She cleared her throat. "At the least, we can give Daryl more time. And the mercenaries will be mired in mud by the time they manage to work their way through. The thaw will be at its worst. Even when they manage to clear the pass it will take them at least two more tendays to reach Readen's Hold."

"Don't make it so bad they decide to turn around and come back through my hold. Mad mercenaries who haven't been paid I don't need. And I also need the pass back so don't completely destroy it. I'm sorry I can only send two patrollers with you. I need every fighter I have to keep the mercenaries away from my hold and villages and keep them headed for the pass. I'll delay them as long as I can. And I'll let them spend their money here on supplies. We've sent word to every village between here and the pass to prepare to come in with all the livestock they can bring or fade into the hills if they need to. My walls are strong, my people are tough, and burned villages can be rebuilt. Walls that fall can be built back up. We'll let them get to the pass, but we won't let them back out."

He tapped the side of the stall with his fist, punctuating his words. "As much as I agitate for independence, I am still a Restal Holder, still one of Guardian Daryl's holders. For Readen to win this battle would be disaster for Restal, and maybe even the whole of Adalta. I know in my bones his ambition knows no bounds. So, here we are, one little girl and one old man to stand in his way and hold our ground."

Jenna laughed. "Except I'm not a little girl, and you're not an old man."

"I'm almost eleven. I'm not a little girl either." One of ChiChi's hands was on her hip, the other on the handle of her long knife/short sword. Her chin was stuck so high in the air she looked eight centimeters taller. Jenna suspected she was on her tiptoes.

"All right, one almost-eleven ChiChi, one tiny Mi'hiru, one tough woman, and one middle-aged, battle-scarred holder. Who could beat us? We'll save the world all by ourselves, right, ChiChi? Maybe before you leave, you could give me a bout with your sword. You can hack at my knees, and I'll swing my sword around over your head."

Jenna turned away to brush Mirjana, hiding her fear in Mirjana's mane while ChiChi argued with the laughing holder.

The three girls took off with the two patrollers, Arron and Kory. Mirjana's lope was smooth, and Jenna's seat in the saddle was more sure every day. She rose and fell in time with the thunderous beats of Mirjana's wings as they hooked air and drove them up and up and up. Navigation wasn't a problem. They just followed the road, widened by countless traders between Restal and the Coastal Holding. It was a day-and-a-half flight to the middle of Revka Pass, so they spent the night in the foothills where the pass began.

The next morning, the Karda climbed to a higher altitude than Jenna had ever flown as they passed beyond the foothills, and the mountains began to rise, stark, white, and sheer beneath them. The air currents grew rough and unpredictable. Inside her gloves, Jenna's hands were cold and white-knuckled around the arch of the saddle handle on the pommel. Her insides stayed two wingbeats behind and were running to catch up. She let go one hand at a time, checking straps and buckles over and over until she caught ChiChi laughing at her. Or maybe ChiChi was just laughing at the sheer joy of flying in the mountains. ChiChi had never been this far into them before in the air. Their father often traveled the Southern Pass by caravan, which suited Jenna just fine and frustrated ChiChi when she was old enough to go with them.

What was she doing here? Taking off to warn Daryl with only her little sister, a tiny, if fierce Mi'hiru, herself—who didn't know the pointy end of an arrow from the feathered end—and only two patrollers. And five fierce Karda. That last thought settled her tumultuous insides so they wobbled around a little less.

The pass was so narrow in places Jenna wondered how the big freight wagons could get through, or what happened when one wagon train met another. Twice she saw enormous rocks lying on the snow-drifted road where it wound around a steep slope. Fallen boulders were a constant problem in both the north and south passes. They flew over a work party clearing two horse-sized boulders from the half-frozen, half-muddy road, bounded on one side by a sheer drop into a deep canyon and on the other side by a steep cliff.

This was the place. Something in her middle pulled her toward it. The mountain would be responsive here. ChiChi and Mia circled around Mirjana, ChiChi pointing and waving at the ground and the cliff, standing as tall as her rigging straps would let her. It terrified Jenna.

She leaned in the saddle the way Dalys told her to guide her Karda, thinking hard at Mirjana, and they flew close enough to Dalys and Seralla to shout and signal for a landing. The five of them dropped down and flew over the work party to a wider place in the road, where they could land without wingtips shredding on the sheer sides of the pass.

For the first time since their trip started, her legs were steady when she dismounted. She was toughening up. What had happened to her that the idea that she was toughening up was a good thought, a proud thought? She didn't think she could pretend to be pretty and helpless anymore. Headed up the road to where they'd seen the workers, she had to stop walking to catch her breath, but there wasn't enough air. She leaned down, her hands on her knees, and sucked in as hard and as fast as she could. Gray fuzz closed in on the edges of her vision.

Dalys caught up with her. "Slow down, Jenna. You can't run a race at this altitude, and we've been flying even higher most of the day. Your body isn't used to the thin air. Don't fight it. Take long, slow breaths till you feel better."

"Why—why doesn't it affect you and ChiChi like this?" The words wheezed out of her.

"Chiara's been flying since she was four. And I've been on a couple of worlds with lower oxygen levels so I've learned how to deal with it. You've never flown this high or for this long. I don't know how you're still conscious."

Jenna heard a note of surprise hiding in Dalys's voice—and was there even a hint of respect? Respect she was grateful for? When had she started feeling gratitude for the respect of a Mi'hiru? When had she ever felt respect from a Mi'hiru? For the most part she hated them, sure they despised her for her cowardice around the Karda and disapproved of what they called her man-hunting behind her back. She picked up a small rock and threw it against the side of the hill, starting a little avalanche. Like the one in her defenses.

She put a hand on the Mi'hiru's shoulder. "Thanks, Dalys. I feel better." Her eyes slid sideways to Dalys's beautiful face surrounded by a halo of golden curls. She looked like a sweet young girl, not the fierce and competent Mi'hiru Jenna knew she was. "It's good to have someone to lean on when you need it." Something Jenna hadn't had since she was a small child. Except for ChiChi, and leaning on her wasn't fair.

"Did you see the size of the boulders those men are trying to move?"

"Oh. Yes." ChiChi danced around in front of them, walking backwards, looking up at the cliffside. "Oh, Jenna. This will be perfect."

Dalys looked at Jenna's determined face, then at ChiChi's excited one. "What are you talking about?"

"See the ridge on the other side of this canyon? Is there space for our Karda to land up there?"

Dalys got the looking-inward expression that meant she was talking to her Karda in her head, and Seralla and Mirjana took off. By the time the three girls—Patrollers Kory and Arron behind them, hands on their swords—reached the work party trying to pry the enormous boulders off the road and down the cliff, Dalys had an answer. "Seralla says yes. It might be a long walk for us to reach the ridge to look down at the road, but there is a place for them to land." She looked up at the steep cliff above them. "I don't think these men will be too happy about this."

And they weren't.

"No, ma'am. We can't leave these rocks here. We have orders to clear this pass by the time the mud dries."

"Holder Me'Bolyn knows what we're doing."

"Show us the orders."

She didn't have any, and they wouldn't be convinced.

Finally, her diplomatic abilities failing, Jenna put on her most arrogant, aristocratic, dictatorial airs. "I will not tolerate your obstinacy. If we have to fly back to get Me'Bolyn, the mercenaries will be on us before you can spit. Guardian Daryl is fighting a desperate war to save us. Would you stand in our way and cause his failure? ChiChi, go back and get the guards to arrest these men."

With that threat, the men retreated, and the five of them flew the short hop across the canyon, landed, and climbed to the top of the ridge across the river from the road. The workers were gone. The two boulders stayed where they were. The three girls settled themselves cross-legged on the ground in a line facing the cliff across from them, knees touching, with Jenna in the middle. Dalys's leg trembled against hers.

Jenna and Chichi had studied and worked with their talents since they learned to walk and talk. Dalys's talent was new. Two years ago she hadn't even known about talent. Then when she'd figured out there was some kind of elemental magic on this planet, and that she had it, she couldn't even ask for help. She wasn't from this planet, and she had to keep it secret. Even talking about it now, when so many knew who she was, was uncomfortable for her.

"I don't think I can do this, Jenna. I don't know how to help you. Using my Air talent is easy. All I use it for is flying and moving warm or cool air around the mews. I'm afraid to let it loose after I almost flipped Seralla and me upside down and into a hillside. And I have no idea about how to use Earth, let alone how to control it." Fierce, intrepid Dalys's eyes were wide, scanning back and forth at the cliff across the chasm. Her face matched the pale color of the limestone rocks they perched on.

On Jenna's other side, ChiChi's chatter stopped. Silent, stiff, and still, her hands stuffed in the pockets of her thick wool riding skirt, she was barely breathing, so tense Jenna felt the ground around her tremble.

What was she asking her to do? ChiChi was only ten. Almost

eleven was still ten and still a little girl. She was a powerful Earth talent but so young.

As if she sensed Jenna's thought, ChiChi turned her head to glare at Jenna. "Don't you dare tell me to go away. Don't you dare. You can't do this without me, Jenna. You know that."

Kory and Arron moved to stand behind them, each between two girls, hands on the shoulders in front of them. Arron was strong enough with Earth talent. Not as strong by far as ChiChi, or even Jenna, but strong enough to ground the three girls and keep them safe.

Arron stood between Jenna and Dalys. "I'm not a strong talent, but I will be able to monitor you and keep you grounded. Kory's Air is strong enough to make him excellent at monitoring and control. If we feel one of you drifting, we'll tap your shoulder and bring you back. Will that help?"

Jenna twisted her head to look up at him. "Yes, that will help. I was afraid I'd have to monitor, but we'll need the strength of all three of us to do this. This won't be easy."

She looked at the steep incline across from them, closed her eyes, took a deep breath and reached for the other two. Dalys was a cyclone next to her, and Jenna felt her fighting to ground. She felt her drifting and pulled her back, helping Arron anchor her in Earth. ChiChi was a rock. A rock half-embedded in her element and enjoying it, Jenna could tell. A rock with roots that reached deep, down through the ridge, under the swift water of the river below them, down and down until Jenna feared she'd get lost there and touched her knee to catch her attention.

ChiChi steadied and reached across the canyon, Dalys and Jenna right behind her—Dalys supporting and Jenna guiding. Jenna set a firm hold on the road. She didn't want the road to be completely gone, just blocked. Their talents linked, and they entered the mountain across from them. She could feel their combined talent fingers work through and between rocks, like fast-growing powerful tree roots, loosening, prying, separating. She pulled up water to soften the earth.

She felt Kory's hand grip her shoulder hard and she reached for

ChiChi. The child was moving too fast and too far. Jenna snagged every talent finger she could find, wrapped herself around them and pulled ChiChi back. At first she fought Jenna, then she slowed and spread out through the face of the mountain. Time passed in silent, pregnant moments until Jenna thought her ears would burst.

Finally Jenna felt ChiChi take a firm hold. Dalys was stretched as far as she could be, her Air widening spaces, loosening dirt and rock, her control thinning. Jenna tightened her hold on Chiara's hand and squeezed Dalys's. ChiChi dug in. All three of them opened their eyes, looked at each other, and jerked. Hard. The hillside sagged and slipped. Rocks loosened. Rumbling, grinding, sliding groaned from the cliffside. Small trees growing in shallow crevices lost their grip and fell. A slow slump started just above the road in the cliffside of rocks and dirt, then it moved faster and faster. Thunder boomed through the air, slamming against the five of them. A choking cloud of dust bloomed and billowed.

Arron coughed and touched Jenna's shoulder. "It's done. It's done."

Jenna pulled and pulled until she felt ChiChi return to her body and slump against her. She put her arm around her sister, fighting panic for a minute until she realized ChiChi was back, just tired. Then she put her hand on Dalys's knee, and the two of them moved the air. Wind moaned and roared up the pass. All five of them flattened themselves against the ground, scrunching their eyes shut against the dust and grit until the whirling wind swept it beyond them.

After several long minutes, Jenna sat up and opened her eyes. The air was clear. There was a long hollow space of bare rock across from her. A long scree of rocks covered the road and tumbled to the bottom of the ravine. The soft clink clink of rocks still moving was the only sound she could hear. What—how had they done that? She hadn't been sure they could do anything, and this was—her mouth was dry. If she found words to describe this, she couldn't have spoken them. She reached for her sister. "ChiChi?"

The almost-eleven-year-old sat up, leaning against Jenna, her body shaking, and stared at the great gap in the cliffside and the monster mound of dirt and rocks hiding the road. "We did that? Jenna? We did that?"

Jenna looked down at her, holding herself together. She couldn't let ChiChi know how much this had frightened her. "Yes, we did, ChiChi. You almost did it by yourself. Your control was close to perfect."

"Not perfect. You had to come get me, or I'd still be there, tearing that mountain apart." Her slow whisper was the whisper of a scared little girl. "I have a lot to learn."

Jenna put her arm around her and pulled her close. "You did great. See if you can feel the road? Is it still there? Not you, Dalys, You need to recover." It took effort to keep her voice calm and controlled.

Dalys was curled up on the ground, knees to her chest, shaking. "I couldn't anyway." Her voice was muffled and frightened.

ChiChi looked up at Jenna, eyes wide. "Will you stay with me? I don't want to get lost again, ever."

"We'll both do it. Kory and Arron can help us." She looked up at both patrollers. "Can't you?"

"Anytime, Miss Jenna." Both men looked awed and shaken, not the silent, hard-nosed patrollers they'd been, indulging the whims of three girls.

Jenna closed her eyes—she didn't want to, but she did—and felt for the road. Arron and Kory with their hands on her shoulders moved with her, side by side, and they reached with talent for the hard surface of the road. It was still there. Under tonnes of earth and rock, but still there. Jenna fell backward on the ground, pulling ChiChi with her. "Someone throw a saddle blanket over us and leave us here for about three days."

She covered her face with her hands and fought tears of relief. She now had time to find Daryl and warn him. He would have more time to prepare. It would take tendays to clear the road. Trade would be stopped for a long while, but war would be worse for the caravans of traders and freighters who traveled this pass. She shuddered to think the mercenaries might turn back and take their frustration out on Me'Bolyn Hold. But the holder's troops should be able to hold them in the pass. They had no Karda to fly out on. They had no choice but to clear the road of the fallen mountainside. It would take tendays, and then there'd be mud.

The mercenaries were locked in.

And the five of them had at least a tenday's flight to Restal Prime to report to Daryl what they'd done.

CHAPTER TEN

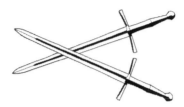

The day was darkening under heavy cloud cover when the returning Karda circled Ardencroft and landed, one after the other. Daryl landed first and watched the rest come in from Abala's back.

A tree was down along the other side of the runway meadow. Long since toppled, bare, stripped white, torn roots and all from the ground that supported it all its life, by the force of a storm it could not withstand. He stared at it between the landing Karda and riders, unable to look away. It was—or had been--a beech tree like the Fort Tree he, Krager, and Reader had played in when they were young. Reader's happy face. Reader's laughing face. Wooden swords and fierce fights. He'd broken his arm in one of those fights, or Reader had broken it for him. How upset his brother was. He was so upset he'd run to their father and confessed, asking for punishment. Which he never got.

Daryl shook his attention back to the field. Three Karda carried bodies strapped facedown across their saddles. Four wore empty rigging. Four more carried riders with a wounded patroller strapped in front of them. One or two stumbled as they loped to a stop, barely clearing the runway meadow for the next, and stood, heads down, chests heaving, riders drooping, sliding rather than climbing down. A few riders sat on the ground, leaning against their exhausted Karda, heads in their hands. One's shoulders were shaking.

Daryl dismounted, walked over to him, and gripped his shoulder for a moment, then went to unsaddle Abala and stow his rigging, forcing down thoughts of the day's battle. There were too many things to organize, too many responsibilities to worry about things past, things long out of his control. Why did the ring of psychics fail today? They were their most effective defense. He had to know why, and he had to find a solution.

The wounded were taken care of. He'd done what battlefield triage he could. Now other healers would take over. He ran his mind over the patrollers who'd stayed to guard Ardencroft. Three of them could heal when needed. In fact, he could see them coming with stretchers. Mireia was also a good healer, at need, and two were with the people who'd come to put the village in order for the refugees.

Would he need to bring refugees from other villages here as well as the settlers from the ship?

Daryl was brushing Abala when Galen, behind his gold Karda, Ket, walked into the overcrowded mews. He stood silent, staring at nothing, then said, "every one is exhausted, so I better wait till tomorrow to bury...the ones who didn't make it. Under an oak, don't you think? To honor their strength?" Galen stood for a moment, leaning with his head pressed into Ket's mane. "After all those villagers I just buried, I don't think I could do it again today anyway."

He was still for several minutes, then started coiling the straps of Ket's rigging. "And Ket says thank you again for taking care of the gouge above his hock." He lifted the saddle off Ket and found an empty saddle rack. "I think he learned his lesson. The black-hole-bedamned urbat can jump higher than he thought, which I've told him over and over." He slapped Ket's haunch. "Idiot."

If a creature with fierce eyes and a dangerous beak could look sheepish, Ket would have. Then he looked down his beak with his best arrogant, patrician look of superiority, and snorted air out his nares.

~Silly fledgling.~

Daryl glanced at Abala. Ket? A fledgling? If he grew much more, he would soon be the biggest Karda Daryl ever saw.

"I don't know who those four Karda are who so often show up when we're at our most desperate, but they look like you, Ket. If you talk to them, I hope you relay our gratitude." Daryl finished combing tangles out of Abala's mane and handed the comb to Galen. Ket's color—and that of the four mysterious Karda—was a stunning pale, gleaming gold no one had ever reported seeing before. Except Altan. The dead mother of the fledglings he'd rescued last summer was the same color.

"I have a tenday to spend here to see that things are as ready as they can be to accept refugees from the ship. I need to get to Restal Prime and go from there to meet Altan and his troops from Toldar." He leaned into Abala's shoulder with the brush. "He's set up his permanent base on Tessa's father's hold." Marta's ability to speak telepathically with Altan across distances was invaluable.

Galen was leaning against the wall with his eyes closed, mane comb forgotten in his hand. "I understand Marta's going with you, so Tessa and I will stay here in Ardencroft and help the ship ambassadors with what they need. And I have no deep desire to visit my father-in-law." He pushed away and followed Daryl into the feed room.

The two men filled buckets with hot grain mash the Mi'hiru kept warm on the magma stone stove. Daryl thunked his bucket against Galen's. "And let's hope you don't get any more calls about urbat attacks. I'll only take half a patrol wing, so you'll have plenty for defense. And Adalta help us, I hope they don't attack here."

Tessa stuck her head out of Kishar's stall. "Kishar says he needs to talk to us and Mireia about what happened to the psychic defense ring today."

Kishar's shining black head popped out over hers. ~If you would not mind staying and sending someone for Mireia.~

As always, the small-for-a-Karda Kishar awed Daryl. Built more like a nimble sparrow hawk than the other, bigger Karda, Kishar was ancient, the last of his kind. History buff Daryl didn't think

Tessa understood there were no more like Kishar because the others had died killing the Larrak five hundred years before. He didn't want to know either. Kishar had been too young to kill the Itza, the last Larrak, so it was locked in the pillars of the vast cavern under Restal Keep. Until Readen's attempt to take over Restal failed, and it escaped.

Daryl stopped a patroller heading out of the mews and sent him for Mireia, dropped down on a bale of hay, elbows on knees, head on hands, and closed his eyes, grateful for the brief respite, grateful to postpone the walk back to the village he wasn't sure he could make anyway. Behind him, Abala ate slowly, too slowly—as tired as Daryl.

His mother's voice called, "Here, Daryl. Stop for a while. You're wearing yourself out. Father, he's wearing you out, too. Put those practice swords down and come sit on the wall with me for a minute. Watch that trooper over there. See how he moves his feet, Daryl? See how he stays balanced? Doesn't let his opponent wear him down?"

~Wake, Daryl.~

Safe in his grandfather's hold in Anuma Quadrant. Safe. His mother alive. Daryl didn't want to open his eyes. And when he did, it wasn't in that long-away time and place of safety and rest. He woke to cold stone, the spicy smell of Karda, the sweet smell of hay, and the reality of three dead patrollers, too many dead villagers, and the figures of Mireia and Cedar silhouetted in the opening to the mews.

What was Cedar doing here? He hadn't sent for her. Heat flooded his neck and threatened to blow flame out his ears. He closed his eyes against the irrational anger. Why was he angry? He took a couple of deep breaths. He wasn't angry at her, he was angry because he feared he couldn't protect her. Angry because just being on his planet put her in danger. Angry because they'd been defeated today. He looked over their heads at the sky to the west.

Blood-red clouds decorated the hem of black sky above blacker mountains. He shook his head and stood. He couldn't afford this feeling, couldn't afford to let this loss defeat him, this defeat push him down. If he didn't figure out what happened today, the next village—and there would be a next village—could be worse. This wasn't a responsibility he wanted, but it was his nevertheless. What he wanted was to lose himself in a book and make the world go away.

"What did you do for Mireia during the fight?" His voice sounded like pounding sleet in a cold wind to his own ears. Why was he attacking her?

Halfway down the hallway, Cedar stopped, her fist pressed under her nose. She didn't speak until she got close in front of him. She leaned over, her voice so soft only he could hear. "You didn't fail, today, Daryl. You can't depend on this evil force to stand still for you. You learn, they learn, you learn more."

Astonished, he couldn't respond. She sat beside him on the hay bale, her shoulder against his, and Mireia asked, "What happened today, Daryl?"

The mews was so still his ears ached. He couldn't speak. He glanced at Cedar. Her eyes held the certainty that he needed, that he didn't have, that he wanted to accept.

Tessa spoke for him, her voice too quiet, too measured, as if they hurt coming out of her mouth. "There were too many of them, but the ring of Air talents was holding their own against the Itza Larrak's psychic terror attacks and making headway with disrupting his hold on the urbat." She looked at her boots.

Galen spoke. "The urbat lost all organization. We thought the ring had broken the Itza Larrak's hold."

"But it hadn't." Tessa spoke as if the words were too heavy, as if it required too much effort for just one person to speak all of them. "It dropped its control and aimed everything it had at the ring. I hope it was everything it had."

"Their deaths were quick," Galen finished. "They were sitting together, hands and knees touching as they'd practiced, then they fell as if a strong wind blew them over and died. Their mouths were open as if they screamed, but there was no sound."

Marta whispered, "The Karda heard. All of them. They came close to knocking Karda from the sky, those silent screams."

Mireia stared at them, looking back and forth, her mouth partly open; no words came. Then, "All of them dead? At one time?" Her whisper ricocheted off the stone walls of the mews until Daryl thought it would deafen him. And he wished it could.

Galen said, "The only thing that saved the village from a complete massacre was that Tessa and Kishar went after the Itza Larrak with such fury it retreated into thick woods where even Kishar couldn't follow. If it hadn't, I think they might have killed it this time."

~With the help of your fire bolts, Daryl.~ Kishar's voice was something between flame and cinder, flickering between anger and determination and deep sadness unflavored with hope.

It resonated with the desolation eating away inside Daryl. Cedar's shoulder pressed against his.

"None of you has the sole responsibility in this battle. It will be more efficient if you let go of that and start thinking about what we —we—can do next." Cedar stood, arms akimbo, and glared at Daryl.

Daryl glared back at her. "This isn't your problem, Cedar." Her glare poked at the abscess inside him he dared not touch. That he couldn't, wouldn't ever be enough.

"When I'm asking my people to leave what they see as the safety of the ship and come to a world besieged by killing monsters it is very much my problem. As for what I did to Mireia, I knew she needed help, so I grabbed her. I think. I don't remember."

"Oh, but I think it might be." Mireia looked as though someone lit a lamp inside her. "When she grabbed me, that was when her talent surged through her. It boosted the entire ring. If she hadn't done that, we'd have been killed like the ones who died today."

There was a long silence. Finally, Daryl broke it.

"There won't be a new talent surging through every ring in every village that's attacked. So how does that help us?" He stared at his hands cupped in front of him, the fingers splayed as if the bitter tasting words he spoke would flow right through to the seams between the stones and sizzle like acid.

After a moment, Mireia spoke again, her words slow, thoughtful, "I don't think we have to. We've been relying only on the strong Air talents, because we thought they were the best to combat a psychic attack and disrupt the psychic link between the urbat and the Larrak. But when Cedar grabbed me, what I felt wasn't Air talent. It was undifferentiated power straight from Adalta."

She started pacing back and forth in front of them. "Any strong talent can loan power. We need to make double rings, with back-up talents strong in anything to boost the Air's range and power when needed."

"So more people can be killed?" Daryl knew his despair was showing. He wanted to shove the words back in his mouth and swallow their bitterness, so it didn't infect anyone else. He looked at Cedar.

Cedar looked back at him, holding his eyes as if she knew something he didn't. "Trying and failing is a better death than waiting to be torn apart by urbat."

Several days later, after much talking, planning, and sending messengers, Karda patrollers and Mi'hiru both, to every village and hold within range of the urbat from the circle—and it was a broad range—Daryl was in the mews early to saddle Abala. He tossed his packs up behind the cantle and buckled them on. This was his last chance for a while to be alone with Abala. He missed this time. He needed this time. Especially since he'd become Restal's guardian, and his life's complications and responsibilities started growing and growing and growing.

Abala swung his haunch and shoved him. ~Are you feeling sorry for yourself?~

~I never feel sorry for myself. Are you? I don't know why. All you do is eat, sleep, and fly around in the sky chasing clouds.~ He shoved back. ~Stand still so I can reach that buckle.~

~How can I fly around and chase clouds with half a tonne of your stuff on my back?~

~Some of it's your food. In case we don't see anything on the way for you to hunt.~

~Hunt. Hunt. I remember hunting, I think. But the memory is blocked by the taste of dried meat and vegetables.~

Daryl looked at Abala's feed tray, empty and clean, and back at the big Karda. ~And hot mash. Don't forget I fixed hot mash for your breakfast. With molasses.~

~Ahhh.~

Their repartee was interrupted by the sound of voices. Several Mi'hiru arrived and behind them Marta—and Cedar. Both with packs slung over their shoulders and Cedar with a long staff. She was moving faster, less clumsy. It made him happy.

"Look what someone found for me. Isn't it beautiful?"

The staff was polished to a dark sheen, with iron bands on each end, knobs and curves sanded down, or worn down by age to a long, smooth sweep as tall as she was.

"That's a fighting staff." Daryl rubbed the back of his neck. "Who gave you a fighting staff? What are you going to do with a fighting staff?"

"Weeell. I'll start by leaning on it. Then I'll graduate to taking a few steps with it. Then I'll break into a walk, and next, I'll hit you over the head with it."

Marta's hand covered her mouth. "You might wait till I give you a few lessons. He's pretty fast. He'll just duck."

Daryl ignored her. "Why are you carrying someone's packs?"

"They're not someone's. They're mine."

"You are not going with us."

"Yes, I am. Marta will never introduce me to the delicious Altan, so I'm forcing her hand. If he's all she says, I'll take him away from her. Besides, Glenn wants me to go to Me'Cowyn Hold to visit with Tessa's father about settling some of our people there."

A breeze swept down the mews alleyway, ruffling the black curls around her bright face. Daryl couldn't move for a minute. He dropped his head to one hand, fingers massaging his eyes. "No. In the first place, we're not going straight to Altan's camp. I have to spend some time in the Prime." Altan and Marta were together for eternity. He knew that. Why did "I'll take him away from her" disturb him? He wasn't being rational. He was always rational.

"That's perfect. Glenn will want me to explore opportunities in Restal Prime. We didn't get to see much before we left for here. We need to know more about your people and the possibilities for *our* people. It will be good to see your Armsmaster Krager and Commander Kyle again."

"She'll ride with me and Sidhari. You'll hardly know she's there. I'll keep her quiet." Marta was going to have tooth marks in her lip from biting back snorts of laughter.

From the next stall, Sidhari's, Daryl heard the snort that meant the Karda was laughing.

"No, if she has to go, she'll ride with Abala and me." Why did he say that?

Cedar poked her head around the stall corner. "Good morning, Sidhari. Will your feelings be hurt if I ride with Abala?" She turned to Abala. "And good morning to you, too, Abala. You look all shiny and splendid. If I'm ordered to fly with you, I promise not to hit you over the head with my wonderful new staff. Isn't it lovely?" She swung it up for Abala to see.

Daryl ducked. "You'll have to leave that here."

"Does he have a brain or is it locked up somewhere safe where he keeps his sense of humor?" she asked Abala. And smiled such a lovely smile at Daryl his knees almost gave way.

He took her packs from her and flung them at Marta. "You carry these." It was a petty revenge, unsatisfying, but he didn't have time or thought for a better one.

He was saved from further embarrassment by the arrival of the four patrollers who were to accompany them and Captain Ethyn. He grabbed the captain by the elbow and led him down the mews.

"She's amazing, isn't she?" Ethyn said, looking back. "I was at the bootmaker's yesterday when she talked him into fitting a riding boot with tiny buckles down the side so it was easier to get on her bad leg. And I do mean talked. She never stopped. And she's funny. I've never seen anyone smile..." He looked back around at Daryl's unsmiling face. "Oh, yes. You have orders for me?"

"You're in charge while I'm gone."

"Not Galen? Or Tessa?"

"They'll be here, but they scout, constantly. New Mi'hiru arrive daily. I haven't time to discover if any of them path with their Karda. And Marta's going with us. So get with Philipa and find someone. "

Philipa, the lead Mi'hiru here, walked up. "But we have other means of communication. We'll be all right. You know all this. You need to stop worrying about things that are others' responsibilities. You have enough of your own. Go find Cedar's delicious Altan Me'Gerron."

Yes, he did. The problem was taking care of them. And what was so "delicious" about Altan?

Philipa looked down the mews alley at the Karda and riders rigging up to fly. "When we have to fight, we'll fight."

Daryl closed his eyes at the deep sadness and pain in her words. He gathered it up and added another layer to his resolve to stop the monsters from destroying his world, however inept and unprepared he might be. He glanced at Cedar again, and he didn't feel quite so inept. How did she do that?

Krager made his regular early evening walk through Restal Prime down the hill to the mews to brush Tarath, his bonded Karda. He expected Daryl any day, which he hoped was this day. He stopped to chat with a few people but never stayed long—a short greeting here, another there. Shopkeepers rolled up dripping awnings and rolled bins inside. A few stepped inside their doors when they saw him coming. Several people averted their faces when he passed.

A shopkeeper knocked his pipe against the stone of his building and glared at him. A cart man offered him the last sausage roll, murmuring two words as he handed it to him. A rough-dressed man walking fast through the crowd brushed against him, and Krager walked past three more shops before he put his hand in his pocket to feel the crumpled piece of paper. If people were risking passing him messages when he was the Arms-master, and not Payne, the sometime-mercenary, something was changing.

"Good evening, Armsmaster."

He was walking past small brick and stone houses now, many with people raking back mulch, clearing winter dead vegetation, readying their gardens for planting. A young guard strolled to the gate where his uniform jacket draped, trowel in one hand, a fistful of limp weeds in the other.

"Someone put you to work, Naden? Didn't even give you time to put your feet up after patrol, looks like."

"M'mother. Not much for idleness. She sees someone ready to sit down, and before their butt hits the chair, the next thing she needs done pops out of her mouth. Usually with *lazy scoundrel* attached." He tossed the weeds toward the pile behind him. "What news of Readen, sir?"

"Still in the west, inviting unsavory visitors. Might need to make a trip over there one day to see for myself soon as the weather warms a bit more." He wasn't about to announce when and was peeved at himself for saying anything at all. He was letting the tension get to him.

He walked on. A young boy, tall and stringy, appeared out of nowhere and danced backward in front of him.

"Greetings, Becca."

"Bek. Why can't you remember? It's Bek. You're gonna get me hurt."

"You're not going to be able to be a *Bek* much longer. That wrap around your—chest—has to be so tight I don't know how you take a full breath. What have you got for me?"

"That a sausage roll?"

"Amazing guess, Bek. What gave it away?"

Bek's eyes and nose followed the savory roll all the way to Krager's mouth before he saluted her with it. And she grabbed.

"You haven't eaten at all today, have you? I've told you before, and I'll keep telling you, until I see you at the keep working in the kitchens or gardens like I told you, this is too dangerous."

"Then who'd tell you what guard is passing messages for Samel? And who he reports to?"

"Becca, you're going to get yourself killed, and that will make me very angry with you."

She let him catch up and walked beside him, munching slow, taking tiny bites so the sausage roll would last longer, and told him. "You was just talking to him."

Naden. Angry that he should be surprised, Krager took ten steps on the rough cobblestones before he could ask the next question, and she beat him to it.

"He reports to one of Holder Me'Neve's men. Recognized him from when he was here when you kicked Readen out. Name's Derrick."

"Me'Neve wasn't here then."

"Yes, Krager, he was. He slipped out soon as Daryl made his move." She ate the last nibble of her sausage roll and disappeared in an alley three steps from the small gate to the mews.

Krager pushed it open and stood for a moment, soaking up the smell and the peace, wrestling down his fury. Me'Neve. Apparently he was leaning farther toward Readen's side of the fence he'd been straddling than Krager thought. He'd like to put the wriggling worm on a hook and dangle him in a pool of relentless nibbling fish with sharp teeth. Derrick was the man Mother Girt at the Bloody Talons told him about.

That made three powerful holders supporting Readen. Though Me'Neve hadn't made a move yet, Krager wasn't looking forward to telling Daryl. He needed to make some trips to other holders. He was making a mental list when incoming Karda came thundering down the runway, one at a time. Whatever information Daryl brought, he hoped it was good news. His quota of bad news overflowed.

CHAPTER ELEVEN

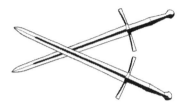

Abala's "kee kee kee" raised heads, and the Restal Prime landing meadow cleared of troopers practicing close formations. Something they hadn't used or known of before the illegal hi-tech akenguns had appeared, smuggled to Readen from the ship. Before a remorseful Galen found the shields to protect against them. Abala back-winged with a thunder and loped down the field to the mews.

Krager sighed and scrubbed at his face. There was a tiny figure glued behind Daryl. Marta and Sidhari followed, and too few troopers landed with them. Irritated that Daryl didn't protect himself better, Krager moved to help unsaddle and groom Abala. Daryl looked at Krager's face, and his shoulders straightened.

"Tell me. What's happened?"

Krager lifted the saddle to a saddle stand, and Daryl draped the sweaty saddle blanket over it to dry. Krager wanted to put his hand on Daryl's stiff shoulder and say "nothing," but he said, "Me'Neve."

There was a throat-clogging note of apprehension in Daryl's words. "His hold's been attacked?" He tripped over a dangling strap. An iron-bound staff just missed his head, and a small woman with a head of black curls grabbed his arm and didn't let go.

"Hello. I'm Cedar Evans, one of the ship's envoys, and you are Krager, Restal's Armsmaster."

Krager started to reach to grasp her forearm in greeting, but she kept hold of Daryl. "Greetings, Cedar Evans. How could I forget you? I watched you land in a spaceship. Something I'm not going to forget soon."

"Shuttle, not spaceship." She and Daryl spoke the words, he just a note behind her in their duet. Cedar's fingers tightened on Daryl's arm. "Another attack?"

Krager gave Daryl a question mark eyebrow raise.

"You might as well. She's not going away." He wasn't laughing, and his words should have carried a resigned there's-nothing-I-can-do-about-it tone, but they didn't.

He was busy not-looking at Cedar, so Krager looked to Marta, who said, "I thought I heard you say Me'Neve Hold. What's happened?"

Krager saw a fierce flash of don't-tell-him in Cedar's face. But it disappeared. What was going on there?

"Me'Neve has spies in Restal Prime and..." An equally fierce he-needs-to-know look on his face, Krager spoke directly at Cedar, not Daryl.

Daryl shook his head. "All the big holders have people in Restal Prime. Always have."

"But they're not all spreading revolt and gathering supporters for Readen's so-called rebellion against talent rule." His words hung in the air like ink-black icicles. Krager wished he could pull them back and melt their sharp points.

Daryl stood even straighter, shoulders tight, then he gently removed Cedar's hand from his sleeve and walked to Abala's side. He took a deep breath and let it out in a long, drawn-out blow. "How many?"

"Three squads. Me'Neve hasn't fallen completely off the fence, but his balance is precarious, and it doesn't look like he'll jump back our way. We need to do some accounting."

"That's why I'm here. I need to be at Altan's camp in a few days before Turin shows up with his troops, but I've been away from the

Prime too long. I need to show my face and try to look confident before the whole city panics."

One of the Mi'hiru said, "Who's this coming?"

Three small Karda with tiny riders on their backs approached the landing meadow. Two patrollers on larger Karda in colors Daryl didn't immediately recognize followed them.

"I have a feeling you're not going to like this. They won't tell me who they are," said Marta.

The first Karda, a small dark gray with wine-colored wings, came in for a landing, flipping back and forth the width of the runway—bright, joyful, wild but controlled aerobatics. She flared her wings at the last moment, then pranced down the meadow, stepping high, to stop in front of them, her rider trailing straps already unbuckled. The other two small Karda flew watchful circles above her until she touched down, then landed one after the other. Much more sedate landings—two patrollers in what Daryl remembered as Me'Bolyn colors landed behind them.

A little girl stood up on the saddle and jumped to the ground, feet running. "We did it. We did it." Her high voice rang and bounced off the mews' stone walls. "We closed the pass. Hi, I'm Chiara Me'Nowyk, and this is Mia. Where's Guardian Daryl? A Karda told us he was here, but I asked her not to tell we were coming so we could surprise him. We need to tell him we closed the pass."

She grabbed Krager's hand. "You must be the guardian. We closed the pass, sir. The mercenaries will be tendays getting through, and then—"

Krager heard Marta's low voice behind him. "Uh-oh."

A small, dark-haired beauty stepped from the knee of her Karda to the ground. She winced, and steadied herself by hanging on to the stirrup. Uh, Oh. The petite figure walking toward them, rubbing her butt had to be Jenna Me'Nowyk, the coastal holder's daughter and heir. He looked from her to Daryl, then to Cedar, who was looking at him, one hand over her nose, one hand holding a small jar, her eyes peering inside him. He and Marta exchanged a glance. Trouble.

Krager took ChiChi's hand and turned her around. "Chiara Me'Nowyk, may I present our guardian, Daryl Me'Vere? Guardian, I believe this flyer has something to tell you."

And he stepped back to watch. The thing he did best, except fighting. He'd make sure he left as soon as he could to make a round of holders. Holders he hoped were still loyal and willing to support Daryl with troops. He knew who the beauty was, and he knew who she'd come for. She was notorious in her ambitions, and she'd lost Altan to Marta. She'd refocused and now had Daryl in her sights. He didn't want to watch that. Protecting Daryl was his job, but this kind of fight was too fraught with danger for him.

"It's difficult to know how well the shields Galen brought from the ship will work since we don't have an akengun to test them with," Commander Kyle said. He handed a lumpy, heavy canvas bag to Daryl. "It wasn't easy to convince the troopers that they weren't just a piece of jewelry to pin on a baldric. I hate to let these go. Readen's going to attack here first, you know that. What do you intend to do with them?"

Daryl didn't answer. He wasn't sure he knew yet, but he was sure the plan forming in his head wouldn't be popular.

They'd been in Restal Prime eight, no, seven days and Daryl needed to be in Altan's camp to meet the other guardians in a couple of days. "I imagine it hasn't been easy getting the guard to work together in tight formation." Daryl's mind was on a million things, but he brought it back to the conversation with Kyle.

"No, it hasn't. But your lessons in ancient battle tactics were helpful. The descriptions from Marta and Galen about what the akenguns do to a body helped even more. It didn't take long for word to spread about the Karda brought down by the illegal weapons. The troops got better at working in close formation to protect each other. None of them wants to be hit by whatever it is those weapons fire." Kyle leaned forward in his chair. Daryl's study was warm, with sunlight gleaming through the tall mullioned windows and magma stones glowing in the grate of the fireplace, blackened where Daryl's father used to indulge himself with real wood fires.

"Guardian—"

Daryl stiffened. Kyle never called him by his title. Daryl heard the note of worry behind it.

"We're thin on troops here. I'm hoping when you get the troops from Anuma, Rashiba, Toldar, and Akhara deployed, you will be able to spare more troops to defend the Prime."

"Those girls closing the pass has given us a little more time. Marta says the Karda report the mercenaries from Akhara are nearing the block with Me'Bolyn's forces behind them, so they'd have to fight to get back to the coast. If they try to sail around to the closest of our northern ports, it will take a month. The ice has just begun breaking up there, and I'm not sure when they'd be able to disembark," said Daryl.

Kyle held up one finger. "First, they'd have to navigate the narrow channel between the reef and the edge of the mountain range where the currents and winds are chaotic, and sailing is risky." He held up a second finger. "Or go all the way around the reef which could take—maybe a month longer. They're not going to do either. From Jenna's description of what she left in the pass, the best estimate of the Earth talents I've talked to is three tendays for them to clear the pass. Then they have to fight their way—"

Daryl scrubbed at the stubble on his face. "No, they won't have to fight their way through the troops guarding the pass. That's where I stationed Me'Neve's guard. I'll send word to—" He pushed his glasses up and pinched the bridge of his nose. "Holder Me'Cowyn, I guess. He's the closest I can trust right now."

He looked up in time to see the concern Kyle tried to wipe from his face.

"Don't worry about us. Between Krager and myself, we can handle Readen long enough for you to get—" Kyle looked at Daryl, who'd raised his hand, palm out.

"I'm sending Krager to Eastern Restal and up the north corner. I need to know who to trust. Who might support Readen, who will fight the urbat but not Readen, who will support me..." He stared out the windows as if watching the rest of his words disappear. Then he put his hands on the arms of his chair and levered his body to standing.

"I'm to meet with the group of finders Mireia organized to travel up to the ship to prepare them for what they can expect when they arrive here. That many new talents..." He looked at Kyle, mouth quirked up. "Don't you wish you could go with them? To see the ship?" He blew out a long breath. "Just fly away?"

Kyle's face was a picture of I-do-not-ever-wish-to-be-that-far-from-the-ground.

"Well, Andra's waiting for me in the mews—she leaves today to join her wagon train. I'm hoping she'll tell me her planters are getting close to the circle. And I have to get to Altan's camp to meet with the other guardians and the holders—the holders left who will help, anyway. Keep practicing formations with those shields to deflect whatever it is the akenguns shoot. I hope it's just because I'm tired, but I don't have good feelings about leaving here. Let's hope Readen waits for his mercenaries, and I can somehow stop them reaching him. If he'd planned it, these urbat attacks couldn't have worked out better for Readen, keeping me spread out all over the north around the Itza Larrak's circle while he prepares to use those akenguns here in the Prime."

Kyle stared down at his hands and didn't look up.

Three days later, the sky was light, but the sun hadn't breached the horizon when Krager got to the mews, certain there'd be no one there, and he could leave unnoticed. But there was. In the second stall stood a small grey Karda, long, sweeping swallow-like wings nearly touching the ground, with a small, dark-haired figure clinging to her mane, shoulders shaking. There was straw in her hair. She must have spent the night tucked under her Karda's wing to keep warm.

He meant to walk on by, let her have her privacy, but his boot scuffed on a flagstone. She jumped and turned around, desolation drooped all over her, her face red and blotched.

He knew he'd be sorry if he did this. He stepped to the entrance of the stall. Now what was he going to say?

Jenna looked straight at him and wiped her reddened eyes. Her feet apart, arms hanging loose at her side, she pulled her shoulders up, and said, as if the words fell out of her, "I have nowhere."

It was difficult to believe this was the arrogant, flirtatious, patrician Jenna Me'Nowyk, sister to the bouncing ChiChi. "What is your Karda's name? She's beautiful." Could he find anything dumber to say?

"Mirjana." Jenna cleared her throat. "I'm told it means peace." She swiped at her blotchy face with the back of her hand.

"I thought you didn't like Karda."

"Mirjana changed all that." It looked like she tried to smile, but it was a quivering failure.

"I know it's none of my business, but why do you say you have nowhere?" His hands rubbed up and down the sides of his pants. His legs wouldn't move. "I'm sorry. It's none of my business."

"I left the hold without permission and against my father's orders. And I didn't take ChiChi home when she caught up to us. I can't go back." She hid her head in Mirjana's shoulder again. "As soon as I tell him I have no intention of 'chasing Daryl down,' as he put it, I'll be trapped there until I'm old and ugly."

Krager hadn't realized how much tension his shoulders were holding until it dropped away. "I have no intention of chasing Daryl down." He didn't know why those words sounded so sweet, but it didn't matter. She was beyond his reach, but it didn't matter, he wasn't reaching. Tarath walked up and butted him with his head, looked at him, at Jenna, and at Mirjana. Mirjana moved to the saddle stand and picked up her saddle blanket with her beak.

"I think they want you to go with me." How did those words bypass his brain and fall out of his mouth unfiltered?

Jenna's hands flew up, framing her face, and for a minute, her eyes shone. Then she bit her lip and turned back to her Karda. "I'd slow you down, and anyway I can't leave ChiChi."

Mirjana ran her beak through Jenna's hair over and over.

Krager looked down, looked at her, looked at Tarath, motioned his head toward Tarath's stall and walked away. His body moved, but his mind was stuck. When had he ever not known what to do? Ever? He half-turned back, then marched on to Tarath's stall and picked up the saddle blanket, threw it to the floor and stood, head down, seeing the red-splotched face, the messy dark hair with straw in it. His stomach was so tight, bending over to pick up the blanket gave him a cramp.

"Krager?" Daryl's voice rang down the alleyway; his boot steps slowed, then stopped. "Jenna? What are you doing here so early?"

Krager couldn't hear Jenna's answer. Then Daryl appeared at the doorway to the stall with the characteristic listening-to-my-Karda head tilt. He put a knuckle to his mouth and bit.

"What are you laughing about? What is Abala telling you?"

"That you are your usual dense and single-minded self, only more so." Daryl listened again. "I think that's an excellent idea."

Krager scratched his chest. His heart itched. He couldn't look at Daryl. "What's an excellent idea?" He tried willing his ears to close.

"I don't know Jenna well, but I do know, young as she is, she's said to have one of the sharpest political minds on Adalta. She'd be very helpful to you. Dalys and ChiChi speak with Seralla and Mia, so you'll know not to land if there are no Karda in a hold without more information. You'll be less threatening. You'll look like a family come to visit."

Krager glared at Daryl's smirking face. "You're enjoying this, aren't you?"

"In all the years I've known you, I've never seen you so flustered. Yes, I'm enjoying this. It may be the only bright spot I'll see this tenday."

"Except for the pretty dark-haired thing who keeps trying to knock you in the head with her staff." It was Krager's turn to smirk.

"She only came because we're on our way to meet Altan. And she's not used to this world. And she's an intuitive systems thinker, according to Mireia."

Abala snorted.

"Whatever that means, or whatever it has to do with why you're letting her trail you around," Krager said.

Daryl ignored that. "Let's talk to Jenna. I expect Dalys and ChiChi to be here any minute with packs and their two patrollers. I wonder how it will feel—the infamous inscrutable loner traveling with an entourage. Of females."

"Only half female." At least he seemed to have brought a little joy into Daryl's life. He pushed his hair back with both hands. He didn't know what the unfamiliar feeling filling his chest was or what to do with it. He suspected it was terror. Three females.

Readen stumbled on the bottom stair to the cells below his holding's hall. Sometimes his body felt like it didn't belong to him. His fingernails were stronger and darker, curved and pointed—more talons than nails. He wore gloves to hide them. Subtle changes to the scars on his arm and across his chest and belly were appearing. He no longer needed to shave. There was still hair on his head, but nowhere else. He couldn't decide whether to welcome the changes or fear them.

Often, especially when he was tired, it was as though another being's thoughts were in his head—familiar, and so much like his own thoughts he wasn't sure it was a different voice. But at night, in that hazy time just before he fell asleep, something alien rummaged through his mind. Rearranging it. Enough like a strange dream Readen could convince himself that was all it was.

He needed to contact the Itza Larrak. No longer could he call it to him. No longer did it dematerialize to reappear only when Readen chanted and smeared blood on the obsidian scars he'd carved into his body to call the Itza Larrak into a material being after he escaped from prison. Those rigid scars that were spreading, flattening, broadening on his arms and chest were now unreadable, unfamiliar.

The Larrak was entirely in the world now. Readen wondered how much, if any, of the human body it had borrowed to become solid, then discarded, was still part of it. He shivered. It had almost been his body.

He walked into the guard room, and Pol stood to greet him. Pol, who had been with Readen since childhood. It never occurred to him to wonder about Pol's age or his health. Pol was always there, where he was supposed to be, and always would be.

"Bring the woman to my table, Pol." Readen passed through the room, down the long passageway of broad shallow steps, to the small stone room, deep beneath the hall of his hold. His mind was on the Itza Larrak—where it was, what it was doing—not on the prisoner Pol would bring. No erotic thought of the pleasure he could take from her. No titillating thought of arousing her to the point of pain. No groin-pulsing thought of her fear when she saw the little silver knife. No thought of why those thoughts weren't there as if they had never been. As if they belonged to another person.

His scouts reported a landslide in the pass through the mountains had blocked the mercenaries. A trade caravan headed for the pass was turned back by soldiers from Restal Prime. If they were working from this end to help clear it, Daryl was the fool he thought he was. Readen had no Karda to fly over to see how bad the blockage was, no way to know when the mercenaries could clear it to get through. He was furious at the delay. A whole winter's planning ruined by Adalta. He pressed his sharp nails into the palm of his hand, damping the fury. When he and the Itza Larrak finally controlled the planet, he would rename it.

He needed to find the Itza Larrak. And to do that he needed power. Pol stepped through the doorway, a firm hold on a young woman's arm. Her jaw was so taut the muscles bunched. She was angry. Frightened and angry. This would be the third time he'd bled her. He looked at her white face, vaguely puzzled. He didn't bother to touch her. He didn't bother to cut her. He didn't bother to arouse her. There was no hot feeling in his groin, no shiver of anticipation at the pain he could bring to her, no hunger for her fear, for the power they would bring him. He didn't care. He didn't need it.

He didn't wonder why.

All he needed was her blood. No drugs contaminated it now.

Readen handed Pol the small silver bowl and the tiny silver knife. Dim light gleamed along its razor edge. He pulled off his gloves and removed his tunic, exposing the black scarred symbols on his arms and chest and stomach.

"Bleed her, then take her back. Feed both her and the man well. I may need his blood, too."

The woman no longer bothered to struggle. Pol never took enough to seriously harm her. In a day she would be fine, with one more red, swollen scar on her wrist or inside the bend of her elbow.

Burgundy blood flowed into the tiny silver bowl over Readen's fingers. He closed his eyes. The heat of power in her blood moved up through his arms and filled him, warmed him.

Pol pulled the woman away and put a pad over the small slice in her arm, binding it tight. His movements were automatic. Neither he nor the woman took their eyes off the dark fingers with curving, pointed, dark nails curled in silver bowl of warm blood.

Readen began to chant, rubbing blood on his morphing scars, his hand dripping back and forth between the silver bowl and the black scars.

"Dalla Itza Larrak Alka Ra.

"Dalla Itza Larrak Alka Ra."

He murmured the words over and over, eyes closed. Then he went silent and stood, head arched up, arms extended, blood dripping down his chest and belly. A shuffle and the click of the door closing interrupted the silence. Pol and the woman leaving. They'd stayed too long, watching him. He didn't care.

Readen circled around and around, then stopped, elated. He found a direction. He knew where the Itza Larrak was.

He found a clean cloth and the jug of water Pol left for him, wiped the blood away, and stared at the hard, obsidian scars. They'd changed even more. Spread out more. It was hard to tell where one ended and another began.

Early the next morning, he led his horse out of the stable, wearing the uniform of an ordinary patroller and a long cloak. He'd left Captain Paules with instructions and orders to keep working the troops and send messengers to the pass. Readen would be gone less than a tenday, and when he returned, he wanted to know exactly where his mercenaries were.

The watch was changing. No one would notice an extra trooper headed out, but he whispered a don't-look-here spell anyway. Readen didn't wonder about the source of the power he used. He hadn't tortured the man or the woman at all. He didn't even think about it. Except way back in a corner of his mind, where a tiny thought grew that the power coming through him wasn't from him. It screamed on, unheard.

Cold fog lay on the bare ground outside the hold walls. Much of the forest was cleared away for meters around. When he reached the trees, fog swirled around the winter black trunks and branches. His horse made no sound on the damp forest floor; no birds sang. A fine mist obscured the narrow road ahead in places. Part of his mind noticed. Noticed the lack of sound. Noticed the cold on his face. Noticed the crisp smell of the early spring morning.

Another part of his mind assessed these things, calculated the power in everything around it, adding the information to—to something Readen couldn't reach. Something hidden, frightening, and unfamiliar. His hands trembled on the reins, and his horse sidled beneath him. Then the something was gone, and there was nothing but the beginning of daylight blooming red in the east. He rode easier, his horse settled into its ground-eating lope, and he tried thinking about nothing. Nothing but reaching the Itza Larrak.

The hard edge of a scar, a spreading, flattening scar, snagged on the inside of his sleeve.

Readen ignored it.

CHAPTER TWELVE

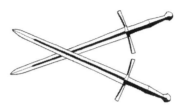

Cedar's Cue buzzed in the pocket of her skirt draped across the end of the bed. The curtains were open, and her room in Restal Keep glowed in the early morning light. The buzzing forced her out of the warm bed, and she shivered her way into her clothes. The magma stones in the small fireplace glowed with what passed for warmth on this cold planet. Mireia hadn't yet taught her the little twist she needed to heat them. That would be the first thing she'd ask next time she saw her.

It was Glenn Voigt on the Cue, calling from Ardencroft. "They need you up there, Cedar. Captain sent a heli-shuttle. I sent it on to you. Should be there soon. With Galen."

"Why?"

"Because you're not here. You're there."

She closed her eyes, blew out a breath, and humored him. "Why do they need me, Glenn? Is it Mother?"

"Tech problems, not mother problems." And he clicked off. She blew another, bigger breath. Glenn got great pleasure out of being cryptic—not even the guilty kind of pleasure.

She pulled on her boots and buckled the six small buckles down the outside of her left boot over her useless bionic block of a leg.

The foot Daryl kept looking at. Smelling of—not aversion, but the insatiable curiosity that was a big part of him. She wondered when he'd drop his relentless politeness and ask to examine it. And what he'd be able to sense. She grabbed her staff and went to breakfast, hoping she could find it in the maze of endless corridors.

"You look like you're thinking of something unpleasant." Marta sat beside her when she finally found the dining hall, bringing two hot mugs of tea.

"How long do you think it will take me to grow coffee here?" Cedar glared at the too-pale liquid. "Do you think I could get Galen to grow it really fast?"

"We'll gang up on him. Won't give him a choice."

Both of them looked up at the faint calls from dozens of Karda like harmonious, joyous bells. They looked out the window next to the magma fire Cedar was all but sitting in. Dozens of Karda flew a wide, wide circle over the landing fields just outside the walls. Cedar heard the whine of the shuttle rotors. She grabbed Marta's arm. "Tell them to be careful. They could get caught in the—"

Marta laughed. "If there's anything Karda know, it's air currents. They're having fun. And they're excited to see their first shuttle. They'll surround it when it touches down. We won't be able to get to it, so finish your breakfast."

When they did get there, Daryl and Abala right behind them, Galen stood at the open hatch surrounded by Karda, laughing.

"All this welcome for me?" Galen spread his arms wide. Abala pushed him aside and shoved his big head into the opening, one taloned foot on the ramp.

"I don't think you'll fit inside, Abala." Daryl took Cedar's arm and pulled her through the crowd of curious Karda to Galen. Pulled her up when she stumbled over her staff. Ducked when she aimed it at his head. Accidentally.

"I can walk by myself, Daryl." She jerked her arm. He ignored her and held on, but it felt like she was holding him up, like he'd fall if he let her go. Like he didn't want her to go. She stopped trying to pull away.

"What are you doing here, Galen? What's the shuttle doing

here? What's happened?" he asked when they reached the ramp, not without difficulty. They didn't get stepped on thanks to Daryl's loud voice and Marta's link with the giant creatures whose attention was fixated on the shuttle.

Galen looked at Cedar. "Sorry, Elf. They need us upstairs. I think your plants miss you. Or the ship needs you to give them a talking-to. Apparently, it can't wait. They didn't even alert us, just sent the shuttle and called Glenn."

Daryl's hand tightened on her arm till it hurt. His look at her when he let go and she boarded was so intense it almost hurt. She hesitated at the door and turned toward him. For a second, she thought he was going to come after her. Then he smiled his serious smile, waved at Galen, and turned away, taking the Karda with him.

Once on board, she propped her staff between her knees, buckled in, then held it in both hands so tight her fingers tingled from lack of blood. She leaned back and started breathing long, measured breaths, in and out, in and out. She didn't want to go back to the ship. It meant facing her doubts about the safety of the world they were fast moving away from. How was she going to tell people about the dangers without starting a panic and adding fuel to the doubters and deniers arguments?

Director of Security Sharon Chobra and Clare Taylon, Director of Engineering and Maintenance, were there when she walked out of the airlock, trying to control her hair. The medics sent air blasting through the lock to collect and isolate the organisms she carried on her body and breath. They swabbed her mouth but agreed to wait for the more invasive collections. No longer was this just for the ship's protection. Cedar knew they were working frantically on antibodies, vaccines, helpful bacteria for both ship personnel and the inhabitants of the planet. It was a massive project.

But that wasn't why she and Galen were there. "Galen and I have both read your reports. Let's wait for him to come out before you start adding to what we've read." She was glad she'd dabbed pine salve under her nose. Probably going to need the whole little wooden box Mireia had given her. Even through the strong sap smell and her tightened shields, the air carried the odor of bad news and worry soaking in a soup of scared.

Sharon pushed a stray blond hair back into place. "Let's get the important part over first. So, Cedar, have you ridden a Karda yet?"

"Yes."

"And? And?"

"It was a long, long way to the ground." She looked away. "I know you've seen pictures of those fierce heads with their vicious beaks."

"You're no fun."

"I don't want to take away from your first experience of Karda, Sharon." Cedar's voice lowered. She shuddered and looked away, her face a study of remembered fear and dread.

"Oh, no, it's that bad?" Sharon looked like someone had run over her favorite pair of shoes with a freight cart.

Cedar looked back at her and said, voice still serious, solemn, "You're so easy, Sharon."

Sharon hit her arm.

"Ouch."

Galen came stumbling out of the airlock. "I forget how awful that is every time. Do you think I block it from my memory?"

Sharon and Clare stared at Galen. At the leaf markings on his face, the root and tree markings on his hands, the tattoo-like bracelets around his wrists, curiosity falling out their open mouths. "What's that on your face?" Clare asked.

"And your hands?" Sharon said.

"He fell in love, and now he's a legendary hero come to life. Just ignore it. Please don't feed the ego." She now knew Galen's root and tree not-tattoos that replaced the horrific burn scars were a gift from Adalta when he became the Kern. The scars he got when he tried to save the akenguns he'd tried to illegally smuggle to Adalta from being destroyed by fire. They changed his life. Cedar had no idea why the roots and branches on his arms and the tripartite leaves on his face showed up now where his scars should be.

Galen hit Cedar on the arm and leaned against the wall, one hand flat on it as if listening.

"Why is every one hitting me?" She looked at Clare. "Show us the problems and tell us why you sent for us."

The happy-to-see-you teasing looks disappeared, and something slid across both faces like heavy curtains pulled shut. She so did not want to hear what they were going to say.

The two women looked at each other. "You go first, Clare."

"We've lost two more pods. One of them a living complex pod."

Cedar felt blood leave her head, sucked in a heavy breath, and steadied herself on Galen's arm. "Was anyone…?"

"Three children and two mothers were home when it broke loose."

Cedar stared at the two women. She walked away, down the unmoving walkway, the words a knell reverberating in her head. She stopped and stared ahead at nothing for a long time. There was no world outside the words she'd just heard. Only silence and those words: "Three children and two mothers."

Fifteen seconds. That's how long it takes to die unprotected in space. No more than fifteen seconds. Cedar counted slowly in her head. Fifteen seconds. A child reaching for her mother. A mother grabbing a child to save him, to hug him tight to expel the air from his lungs so they didn't explode. A long, long time to die, to watch your child die. To say goodbye.

She shouldn't have left. She shouldn't have left. She should have done…something. What?

She turned back to Galen and slumped to the floor, back curled against the wall where he sat, head on his shoulders. Sharon and Clare stood, heads down. "When did this happen? What happened to the fail-safes? The interior hatches?" Cedar made herself ask. "Where are they now? The pods? I need to see them."

Clare looked relieved to have a question she could answer. "The other pod was a warehouse pod. It's tethered—they both are. It was full of trade goods useless on this planet. We're dumping it out so we can move it down. The stuff in it will burn up in the atmosphere. Or become an orbiting cloud of junk. The living pod—nothing's been decided about that. Captain Kendra…." She didn't finish the sentence. "No one is sure yet why it broke loose. Or how."

"What else?" asked Galen. Cedar smelled his foreboding. And his shocked grief. It matched hers.

Sharon looked down at her locked fingers and cleared her throat. "I'm hearing—and I hate to repeat this—but I'm hearing a lot of rumors and panicked talk about the so-called aliens on the planet. In all the hundreds of years the trade ships have been traveling between the colonized planets, no one has ever run into another species in space. The rumor running the corridors is that the alien you call the Itza Larrak is attacking us to try to steal this ship and enslave us. Every rumor, of course, has its counter-rumors, and the most prevalent is that there is no alien—it is a myth, a scary story."

No one said anything. Disbelief hung in the air they walked through.

Finally Clare said, "So far, no life support problems, and other than your quarantine gro-pod no other pods gone, but half the walkways are now just that: walkways. They don't move. I'm surprised you haven't heard the frustrated and angry screams and complaints on the planet."

"Fortunately, so far, Medic is immune to what's happening. Probably because Arlan Garcia is such an—so asinine." Sharon didn't need to finish her sentence. every one knew what Arlan was.

"Nine shades of an ass is right," Galen muttered.

Clare interrupted. "It's full of people with panic attacks they're sure are heart seizures—some of them are, and he's dealing with those, too." She looked at Galen. "We hoped, with what we understand you can do now, you could do something. It's the plants. They're invading everywhere." She looked at Cedar. "You said before you left, when this started, that they looked like they were waiting. Well, they aren't waiting any longer. People are frightened."

Sharon looked around. "Let's go before someone recognizes you, and we get mobbed. My office. I made coffee. What is that for?" She waved a hand at Cedar's staff. "I know you don't fight with it. You can't fight."

Even the thought of coffee didn't cheer Cedar. "My leg doesn't work on planet, and so far it isn't working up here anymore either." Sharon's words registered. "Why would I get mobbed?"

"Oh, yeah. I forgot about your leg. Never thought…." Her words trailed off and her face flushed. She turned to Galen. "I think you better put that cloak on and pull up the hood. It will look strange, but you look more strange without it. No offense. They're beautiful, by the way. Whoever did your tattoos was an artist. They look so real."

Galen smiled and pulled on the cloak, hood up. "You have no idea."

She finally answered Cedar's question. "We can talk about that in my office."

That didn't bode well. Cedar gripped her staff tighter and wished it were Daryl's arm.

They encountered few people on their way to Sharon's office. Some were Cedar's bio-systems workers who looked like they wanted, needed, to talk to her, and there were more of Sharon's ship's patrol than Cedar expected to see—ever. Two of them fell in behind. And they were armed with tasers. Cedar had never seen the ship patrol armed before. Never. Truncheons, yes. Tasers? No.

The four of them settled into Sharon's office with their coffee. Cedar cradled her cup reverently in her hands, grateful for the warmth. She didn't think she'd ever be warm again. Cold invaded her bones, and it wasn't the temperature.

"We don't just have engineering and tech problems, Cedar. And what is that not-exactly-perfume I smell?"

"It's Cedar, and don't ask." Galen got up and poured his second cup of coffee. "Is that why we were surrounded by ship patrol the moment we docked?"

"We were?" Cedar's coffee sloshed.

"Pay attention, Cedar. All is not well on the good ship Lollipop."

"Is that what the plants were telling you?"

"I've known it for a while. When I came back from my last two planet assignments, I was mobbed by people who wanted to know what life was like off ship. How the people lived, how they were governed—every question you can think of, they asked. And they often asked when they were sure no one would hear them, cornering me one, two, three at a time, quietly. It stopped when they realized I was an asshole, and most of my stories were unbelievable. They were convinced that the struggles I related, about the primitive living conditions, about dissension, power struggles, failed tech, were lies I was told to tell."

"Why? Not why they realized you were an asshole. We all realized that before you were three years old. But why did they think you were lying?" Cedar asked.

Sharon leaned forward, elbows on her desk. "There is a faction, has been a faction—it started about fifty years after the trade consortium was organized with the people who didn't want to leave the Ark ships—that wants us to abandon this ship for life on a planet. They're never able to agree on which planet. You may not think they believed your so-called lies, Galen, but many of them did."

She shifted, leaned back so just her fingertips touched the desk. "They want pre-collapse Earth, and we've never found one. This planet they've rejected—the no-technology thing. They don't want to live on a planet where they can't continue the life they have on this ship, but with weather—and seasons. Though not one of them has ever been on a planet with a vicious winter as I have. 54Ayeshia had winter for three quarters of the year." She shivered. "They know the ship's old, and there are problems, but they're sure it will hold together for at least one more move with a little patch work."

"Tell them about the other factions, Sharon," said Clare. "Then we have to get to the tech stuff." She got up for the coffeepot. She refilled Cedar's cup, put her hand on her shoulder and held it there for a moment.

The momentary warmth was sucked up by the cold drifting over Cedar's heart. She kept her breath even. She kept her control balanced on its thin edge. She kept her hands wrapped around the heat of the coffee cup as if it held sanity.

"The other faction refuses to believe the ship is failing despite everything that's happening. They think you lost control of the plants and abandoned us. They blame you, Cedar, and some blame

you, Galen." Clare refilled his cup. "For bringing some strange—
something—that has infected the plants, changed their genetics so
they grow out of control. Some of them want to force you back
here, Cedar, so you'll start killing the out-of-control plants and, I
don't know, grow new ones that behave?"

Sharon pinched her nose, eyes closed, then finally looked up at
Cedar. "Three of your bio-systems workers have been beaten.
They're pretty tough, and two of them gave as good or better than
they got. But the third faced a lot more than he could handle. He's
in Medic. In a coma."

Cedar's hands gripped her hair so hard it stretched the skin on
her forehead. A wordless moan started in her chest and grew and
grew until it had to come out. She wrapped her arms across her
stomach and bent over, unable to control herself any longer. The
blow landed hard. Her people. Her wonderful, imperfect, irritating,
and loved people.

Galen grabbed her, arms so tight around her she couldn't move,
and stroked her hair. And she grieved. The mothers, the children,
her workers.

Then she got angry. It started with her ears. They got hot. The
heat spread to her face, down her throat, into her chest, and lit a fire
so hot it was as though she breathed fire. She struggled out of
Galen's grip. "I need to see them. And I need to get to my lab."

Sharon's immaculate blond hair was coming loose from her bun.
She shoved it back, her head down. She wiped a hand over her forehead. "Cedar." The tremble in her voice hooked Cedar's attention.
She'd never heard anything but strength from Sharon. "Cedar." She
looked up, one hand lifted toward Cedar, then it dropped to her
side. "Cedar, they trashed your lab. We've sealed it off. You have a
lot of stuff in there that can't get loose. The dangerous bacteria and
viruses are safe, according to your assistant, Mannik."

Cedar's head was inside a bell, an enormous bell where there
was nothing but silence and the harsh, hard words, "They trashed
your lab. Two mothers. Three children. Your people." Clanging,
clanging, bouncing off the sides of the inside of her skull.

She felt Galen's shoulder press against hers, but she was a rock again. An unmoving, unfeeling, unthinking rock with a clanging bell inside.

"In a coma." Clang.

"Your workers were beaten." Clang.

"They trashed your lab." Bang.

"Two mothers. Three children." Bang. Clang.

Now she knew why they'd called her back. She wished she hadn't come.

CHAPTER THIRTEEN

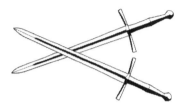

Daryl watched Krager's "little family" fly off, losing them in the mist under the low-lying clouds and headed back to saddle Abala for the flight to Altan's camp. He was uneasy about leaving Restal Prime without Krager there, but he needed to know where the smaller holders stood, and he had confidence in Commander Kyle.

The mews filled with his two wings of Karda Patrol and interrupted his heavy thoughts. Marta among them. He caught himself watching for Cedar, shut his eyes and shut off the thought that she was on the ship by now. But he couldn't shut off the thought of her. That left a vacuum he didn't understand and didn't need.

He mounted Abala, and his party took off for Altan's camp and the battles to come. They reached flying altitude, and he eased back in the saddle, pulling his hands through his hair. Abala's wings stilled, and they began a long glide toward another rising thermal. There was nothing but wind and silence and Abala's little adjusting maneuvers he barely noticed.

Responsibility. Responsibility for Restal had been only a distant possibility when his father was alive. He'd not thought about it much, not particularly wanted it, but he'd do his duty. It hadn't seemed so heavy then. He'd end his father's excesses, listen more to the villages and small holders, restart the planting, be a good guardian. Little adjusting maneuvers in the journey of Restal's ongoing history. Now? Now the journey was nothing but turbulence, his responsibilities weighed heavy, and they were all he thought about.

He did a skip and slide around thoughts of his brother, Readen. His release of the Itza Larrak was accidental. He'd been unconscious when the Larrak was last seen—and only by Marta, who'd been tortured and bled and, at the end, rendered unconscious. It was difficult, but Daryl had to acknowledge Readen had done that. But Daryl would not believe his brother could willingly side with the alien and its vicious monsters. He was its victim, not its ally. The death and destruction they brought were horrifying—to any human.

He stopped those thoughts and shifted to thoughts of strategy and tactics, troop placements and movements, the holders and guardians he'd be guiding. Always those last thoughts too heavily salted with the knowledge that, other than Anuma's Guardian Ballard, he was the youngest. He had the knowledge they needed. He'd read every book and paper he could find on strategy and tactics from the ancient Sun Tzu's *The Art of War* to the latest report from one of his field commanders. But, other than Ballard, he had the least experience.

Jerked out of his thoughts and plans by Abala's sudden tilt, he was surprised to see the cluster of white tents and the short landing field of Altan's camp below them already. Marta and Sidhari were arrowing in first, and Altan was at the edge of the field with, Daryl knew, his eyes locked on her. Marta could not only talk to any Karda, but she and Altan could talk telepathically over great distances. Another thing that came from legends past. But they'd been apart for too long.

He watched the rest of his fliers land, then Abala circled down and loped to a stop by the Karda carrying packs. He'd help unload and give Altan and Marta a little time.

When he finally walked into Altan's command tent, Altan started talking without giving him a chance to say hello. "I stopped by Readen's hold on the way here. Five days ago, there were only a few troops, relatively few anyway. He's clearing the trees away from his walls but hasn't gotten very far. He's vulnerable. Now's our chance to stop him, Daryl. Then we'd only have one battle to fight, not two."

Daryl stopped and didn't speak for a minute. Then, "Readen's not your problem, Altan. How willing will my holders be to follow me if I allow you, Guardian Heir of Toldar, to attack a Restal hold with me? Especially when too many don't understand much about what Readen did."

Altan leaned both hands on his camp desk and slumped over them.

"Besides, Readen has the akenguns." He wouldn't risk Karda and troopers when they were so badly needed in the fight against the Larrak.

"Yeah, I know. I know I can't attack him, but you can, and you have shields. Galen and Cedar found the shields for us."

And she probably risked her career to do it. Daryl closed his eyes. "Altan, we have no idea if the shields will cover a Karda wingtip to wingtip. Readen has spies all over Restal—he had years to set them up. It will take a tenday and a half to get troops with shields to his hold, and he'd know about it before they even left the Prime. We can't stop the battle against the Larrak and the Lines of Devastation to take on Readen."

~Prime Guardian Me'Rahl approaches.~

Daryl looked out the tent entrance at Abala's words. He saw Altan start. Kibrath must have told him, too.

"I can't risk it. I won't risk it. Let's go meet Hugh."

The sky was full of Karda whirling above them. One by one, four Karda and riders peeled off to land. Prime Guardian Hugh Me'Rahl loped down the field toward them. Twelve Karda and riders stayed aloft until the others landed, then turned as one like a flock of enormous starlings and headed back north and east.

Daryl could feel Altan's frustration. He had to have risked a lot to get close enough to Readen's hold to get his information. It was too risky for Karda to fly over it. The few who had were dead, killed by the akenguns. He hoped he was making the right decision.

The battles with the Itza Larrak and its urbat so far had been reactionary. Daryl knew they kept him and his troops on the move from one crisis to another, distracted from the Circles of Disorder and the Lines of Devastation growing from them. But they also distracted him from the threat of Readen, distracted from the threat of the akenguns. And Readen could take advantage of that. Once before, he took the Prime in Daryl's absence. What would it say about Daryl's leadership if it happened again, this time with forbidden weapons Daryl failed to capture and destroy?

Mounts unsaddled, rigging stowed, Karda fed and groomed, Hugh and Daryl sat at the rickety makeshift table in Altan's command tent, maps spread out three deep in front of them. One corner of all three maps curled up every time Daryl lifted his hand. He'd run out of heavy objects to hold the corners down.

He stood, stretched, rolled his shoulders and rubbed his face. If he stopped to think about how tired he was, he'd fall over. Stepping outside, he looked around for a rock.

Hugh stood beside him, hands on hips. Small pops sounded as he stretched back and forth. "Are you going to use that rock to hit yourself on the head and end all this? Hit me first if you are."

They watched a small, delicate brown Karda with pale blue head and flight feathers land, a tiny figure on her back. Philipa and Cystra loped straight to the command tent. The Mi'hiru didn't dismount. "Turin and his troops are a day and a half away from you. He has half a wing of Karda Patrol and one Mi'hiru with him. As you suggested, we asked several Karda to fly above them for the last tenday. He was moving toward the Prime when they showed up. But he was only heading for a village under attack. It was just a small group of urbat, and the Itza Larrak wasn't with them. When he finished there—they stayed long enough to help with the healing —he turned and headed this way. But he did send a small troop in the direction of Restal Prime. Scouts." She saluted, and Cystra headed toward the tent set up for the Karda and their rigging.

Daryl was uneasy about Turin and his troops passing so close to Restal Prime. And he didn't forget for a moment that the mercenaries now blocked in the pass were from Akhara, where Turin was guardian. Nor did he forget Turin knew about the akenguns smuggled to Readen from the spaceship—weapons banned by law on Adalta.

"He isn't going to ignore those akenguns," said Hugh.

"The weapons aren't in the Prime." Daryl went back inside the tent and fell into his chair, elbows propped, head dropped into his hands just for a moment. He sat straighter. "We have to turn the tables on the Itza Larrak. If we continue doing nothing but reacting to the urbat attacks, we lose. And I need to be back in Restal Hall soon. With Krager gone, I'll get fewer reliable reports from there. I can't lose the Hall again. If I do, I'll lose the whole Prime, and with the holders who've already aligned with Readen I'll be on the way to losing the whole quadrant. Taking it back will be hell. And if I get distracted by that, the Itza Larrak gets stronger. Readen shows no interest in fighting it, and some of the attacks have been close enough to his hold he should have. How many troops will I have left if things continue like this?"

He looked up at Hugh. "There's an ancient Earth philosopher who wrote, hell is other people. I think, in my case hell is my brother." He put his hand on the map so it covered Restal Prime. His voice soft, as though his next words were more thought than spoken, he said, "Isn't it interesting, that we no longer refer to a heaven, but we still have a hell?" He blinked and wished he had time for philosophical discussions again.

But he didn't.

Hugh was silent for several long seconds. "We discussed the strategy we used before, last fall. The more urbat we kill, the weaker the Itza Larrak will get. That was our working theory. There's no reason it won't still work. Keep it inside the circle. Don't let it get out. Eventually, we will be able to kill it."

"Master Planter Andra has wagon trains loaded with abelee tree sprouts and remedial plant seeds headed for the circle, one moving around the east half and one around the west. I assigned enough troops to protect them until they start deploying all around the edge. That's when we need to be there. The Itza Larrak will be forced to pull back its urbat, and the attacks on villages will stop. Or they should."

Abelee trees, a cross between Adalta's dalum tree and Earth's poplar, used too little and too late to heal the pollution on Earth, were a big part of the tangle of remedial plants that contained and shrank the Circles of Devastation. They were the beginnings of the forests that surrounded and shrank the circles.

Altan entered the tent. "Sorry I'm late. My Karda Wing watching Readen's hold just reported in. Something is happening. Or rather, nothing is happening, which means something is. Happening, I mean."

Hugh snorted. "I actually understood that."

"Tell me." Daryl felt his face tighten, his thoughtfulness leave. He didn't want to understand Altan, but he was afraid he did. And he didn't want to hear Altan's next words.

"I think Readen's gone. Probably during the night two days ago. The flyers have to stay so high to be out of range of the akenguns they can't tell who's in charge, but it's not Readen. Me'Kammin from the description. A round man who throws his hands in the air a lot and accomplishes nothing. It's not chaos down there. More like everything's slowed to a near stop."

He sounded like he was speaking through gritted teeth. Altan hated Readen, and with reason. He'd come close to killing Marta last summer when he captured her, tortured her, and called the Itza Larrak—who tried to use her body to materialize completely and reach into the heart of Adalta. Altan was on his way to rescue her when, with the help of Adalta, she rescued herself.

Everything stopped in the tent. Hugh and Altan looked at Daryl. Daryl looked away, out the tent opening. The field was busy with riders unsaddling Karda, troopers carrying packs, buckets of feed, bales of hay. A few Karda took off again, going hunting. He turned back, composing his face, and dropped his eyes to the maps, pulling the bottom-most one to the top. The map of the Circle of Disorder in the north, with penciled lines snaking out of it to the east, the west, and the south. With deliberate care, he pinned the edges down with his books and the rock. It seemed every time a patrol or a Mi'hiru reported in, he had to extend his pencil lines. Two of them were getting far too close to connecting. Finally, he looked up. "Let's hope this isn't the calm before the storm. I assume he's gone to garner support from what holders he can. How did he get past my watchers?"

Should he attack Readen's hold now while he was absent? No, he decided. He couldn't get distracted from the immediate danger. And he said it aloud, "We can't let him distract us. We'll stay here and force the Larrak to defend its circle."

He put his finger in the center of the darkness on the map and leaned forward. That one index finger might be all that held him up. "Andra's close, but the ground is thawing, and that means her wagons are struggling through mud to get there. The latest word I have from her is that they'll be moving in to start establishing camps within the next five to ten days."

Altan sat in a chair opposite Daryl, looking resigned. "Not only do we need to know how soon she's ready, but where she sends her planters. Last time we concentrated those we had in one area."

Hugh sat beside him. "It was a good strategy then, and it almost worked. But if we intend to finish this, if we intend to get rid of the Itza Larrak and the urbat for all time, we'll need a better one."

"Andra's establishing camps all around the circle. That's what we must be prepared to protect. Ballard is already spreading his troops around the northeast edge, backed up, I hope, by troops from holders in that area like Me'Kahn that Krager is contacting. My troops will be below them on the southeast arc. You, Hugh, will cover the south arc. Altan, Holders Me'Fiere and Me'Cowyn will spread around along the west and northwest."

He moved his finger to the north edge of the circle. "Turin will be here."

Hugh and Altan looked at him, at each other, apparently decided not to say anything, and looked back at the map. Daryl noted and discarded their obvious doubt. There was little choice.

"Each of you will defend the planters in about a fifty kilometer section. You'll have reinforcements from several holders in your sectors. The Itza Larrak will be trapped. If it tries with more urbat, you have only to call on one or the other, or both, on either side of you. Tessa and Galen are scouting, constantly. And I'm sure you've noticed the flocks of Karda watching from on high. They can't get near the circle, but when they're high enough they can see far inside it. Hopefully you'll have warning of attacks."

His finger traced the Line of Devastation getting too close to the line extending from the nearest circle to the southwest. "We have to do something about the growth of these Lines of Devastation before it becomes unstoppable."

Readen rode into the night, following the pull of the Itza Larrak. It took him directly to the Circle of Disorder north and east of his hold, though he needed to skirt several settlements. All of whose walls, he noticed, were higher and thicker. High enough the urbat would have difficulty flying over them, but urbat, with their long metal claws, could climb stone and shred wood.

In the light of pre-dawn, he noted evidence of urbat attacks in every village he passed near: fresh graves, damaged and scored walls, fewer people moving to the fields preparing for spring planting. And all of them protected, some with nothing but razor-sharp scythes and sharpened hoes—homegrown protection with few trained soldiers. His strategy was working. Daryl must be frustrated, trying to be everywhere at once. Readen knew his brother's weaknesses well. Daryl would be doubting himself, doubting every decision, calling for help, proving his inability to lead. Soon...soon Daryl would make the big mistake Readen waited for, and he could move.

He spurred his horse into a faster canter. When the sky glowed brighter pink beneath the cloud cover, and he'd moved far enough toward the center of the forest for the trees to be smaller, some barely a meter or two higher than his head, the horse sidled and balked. He was almost at the circle. A line of dead white trees appeared, some standing skeletons, some fallen, and not even spurs would make his mount go any farther. Readen rode back into the forest until it calmed enough it wouldn't break its tie and race back to the hold, leaving him stranded. He slipped the bit from its mouth, tied it with enough rope length to reach grass, and walked back to the wide band of dead trees close to the circle.

At first, it was only a tingle all over his body, but it grew and grew until his blood bubbled, effervescent with power that spread and spread until he felt he could contain no more. He walked closer to the circle and the place where he sensed the Itza Larrak waiting for him.

Then there it was—tall, black against the pink-and-grey sky, its wings moving incessantly, like a stiff cloak hanging from its shoulders and stirred by the wind. Readen neared, and the Itza Larrak turned, movements slow, deliberate, wings spreading and receding, spreading and receding. A dark menace defying the light of dawn.

"You are late."

Readen started. He'd forgotten the harsh, metallic, mechanical tone of its voice, somehow more terrifying than its appearance. But the power boiling in his blood lent iron to his bones, steel to his muscles, and built a wall in front of the fear he didn't dare show. The strange feeling of someone, or something, in his head grew, and he fought it, shoving it out. But part of it working into a shadow at the back of his mind stayed. The shadow grew. He was barely aware of it. An annoyance.

The Itza Larrak spoke again. "There are humans moving toward my circle with their digging tools and trees and seeds. They must be stopped. You must advance out of your hold to fight them."

The symbols Readen had carved into his body to free the Itza Larrak, to allow it to return to the world, burned with the pain he felt when he cut them and they blackened into hard, glittering, obsidian scars.

His whole body burned with pain and the power that bubbled in his veins. The Larrak stepped closer, and Readen wanted to move, to shift away, but he refused to let his feet move even to widen his stance. "I cannot. You know I cannot. If I send troops to support you, they will desert. Father." That last word was distinct, deliberate. He'd never said it aloud before.

Its voice rasping, metallic, slow and so soft Readen leaned closer to hear, the Larrak said, "Never forget, I created you as my vessel. You and your body belong to me."

A sharp surge of power shoved at Readen. He fought for balance, fought not to sway away.

With effort, Readen firmed his voice as he spoke back, his words deliberately soft and slow. "Never forget. If I die, you die. We are locked together."

If the insect-like face could smile, it would look as it did now. "Yessss. I have not forgotten."

The dark bubble in the back of Readen's mind pushed out a tiny, tentative tendril, no more than a little itch. He scratched his head but snapped his hand back to his side. He never slipped into an uncontrolled movement like that. He tightened his shield and didn't notice when the tiny tendril attached itself to it, like ivy invading, unnoticed, the mortar that held the stones of a building together.

After a few moments of forcing his feet to stay planted, Readen looked beyond the Itza Larrak at the circle behind it. "As soon as the mercenaries from Akhara get through the pass, I will attack Restal Prime."

"I cannot wait that long. You must strike now. You have the weapons. Use them."

"Remember, they can only be used for a short time before they fail. And you have not found a way to recharge them as you said you could."

Readen suddenly felt very small, like the young child he had been when the Larrak first appeared before him. The monster's wings spread wide, blocking everything behind him. Gusts flapped Readen's cloak against his legs. Strands of his hair blew out of its immaculate tail.

"You will attack now." And the Itza Larrak took to the air, flying east into the darkness of the circle. It wasn't out of sight before Readen collapsed, his head bursting with pain, his muscles slack, his physical strength icy water leaking away into the ground beneath him.

It was a long time before he recovered, stood, found and untied his horse, and rode straight back to his hold, not avoiding any villages this time. He settled a shroud of invisibility, not just a don't-look-here shield, over both him and his mount. He'd never been able to cast a spell that big before. And it didn't even begin to task the power he'd gained from the Line of Devastation and the Circle of Disorder—without the need and the thrill of pain and terror from a victim. Readen didn't even think about how that happened when it hadn't ever happened before—only about the strength of power available to him now. He fisted the hand not holding the reins. Curved, iron-hard nails pierced his palm through his black leather gloves.

Krager and Jenna flew into Me'Kahn Hold late in the afternoon after a long day in the air. This was their last hold to approach, and Jenna was glad after too many long and arduous flights. At Me'Pargit and Me'Teriaga Holds, both of medium size, they achieved qualified successes. Both holders were supporters of Daryl's guardianship, especially after he started a second council made up of the smaller holders. It wouldn't be an end to rule by strongest talent, but neither wanted that anyway. What they wanted was what Daryl intended to provide: official say in the affairs of the quadrant. Lucas Me'Kahn was not a small holder, but he knew his neighbors well. That was why Krager and Jenna were there.

Me'Kahn himself waited in the mews when they landed. As they'd agreed, Jenna took the lead. "Good evening, Holder Me'Kahn." She stretched out her arm to grasp his in greeting. "I hope you remember me. I'm Jenna Me'Nowyk from Toldar's Coastal Holding."

The tall, austere man with slightly sloping shoulders, a high fore-head, and a face that told her he remembered and didn't much care for the memory, said, "Yes, Jenna. I do remember you. I believe we met in Rashiba at the last assembly." He turned away and grasped

Krager's arm. "And how are you, Armsmaster? We have not seen you in a while, but I understand you have kept your sword busy."

Was she to be forever dismissed as a…she guessed he thought of her as a status hungry husband hunter? She dropped her head. Her eyes burned. Probably all he remembered of her was how hard she chased Altan Me'Gerron while she and her father were at Toldar Hall. She took such a deep breath her diaphragm shoved against her empty stomach. Fatigue drooped over her, pulling at her posture. Today's flight was the longest she'd ever made without a stop. Mirjana nudged her shoulder, and she leaned against her.

"Holder Me'Kahn, may I present Jenna's sister, Chiara Me'Nowyk and Mi'hiru Dalys," said Krager.

ChiChi pushed forward, and Me'Kahn shook her forearm. "Holder Me'Kahn, may I introduce our Karda, Mia, Mirjana, and Seralla. Mia says you know Tarath."

The holder bowed slightly to the four Karda, who inclined their heads to him.

ChiChi bounced up and down on her heels. "I hope they have permission to hunt on your hold. They're hungry. And I hope we can stay the night. We're tired. We've been flying for a long time. I never get tired of flying, but I almost did today."

His solemn face warmed with a smile. "Of course, Flyer Chiara. May our table provide you sustenance, may our land provide you work to suit your heart and hands, and may you find safety within our walls in your rest." He looked at the Karda. "And of course, you have permission to hunt. And when you return, even if you're successful, there will be grain and grass hay for you here in the mews."

To ChiChi he said, "Now, let's go to the hall and see what we can find for you to eat. My bonded is visiting her family, but we should be able to scrounge something." He looked at Jenna, then at Dalys, who was moving to start unsaddling the Karda, then at Krager. His face didn't lose its warmth, but his eyes narrowed just a little. "And perhaps you can tell me what I can do for you. Somehow I don't think this is a simple stop for the night on your way to some-where else."

Over a late supper, they discussed, in general terms, the situation in Restal—for the most part, the battles against the Larrak and urbat, avoiding any mention of Readen Me'Vere. Me'Kahn Hold was a long way from the Itza Larrak's Circle of Disorder and a longer way from where Readen sat, secluded in his hold.

Finally, Jenna put down her fork. "That was wonderful, Holder Me'Kahn. Please give your cook our thanks for providing us such a late supper."

"Please call me Lucas, all of you. Even you, Krager, and I'll call you Krager because I don't think you have another name I've ever heard."

If she didn't start it, she knew the conversation would be between the two men, and the holder would ignore her. Jenna gave Krager an I-hope-you-don't-mind glance and spoke. Krager didn't look back, but his face almost cracked a smile. "Holder—excuse me, Lucas—Guardian Daryl and Toldar's Guardian Heir Altan Me'Gerron have sent us on a—I guess you could call it a fact-finding journey. We're visiting all the holds we can to find out what is happening to the Circles of Disorder in their areas, what is being done to protect their people if the scourge of urbat reaches you, and if there have been any sightings of the Itza Larrak in your area."

Lucas looked at her, his head cocked. "I assume you are also interested in our political leanings. What has Toldar to do with the internal politics of Restal?"

Jenna expected Krager to jump in, but he sat, a mute statue, looking at her. She was sure a gleam of amusement hid somewhere in those dark eyes. Dishes pushed away, Jenna leaned forward, her hands folded, fingers laced, on the table. "The circles are a problem that affects all of Adalta. The Lines of Devastation pushing out of them are reaching to meet and connect all the circles. Kishar, who chose Tessa Me'Cowyn as the Austringer, informed us that if they are allowed to meet, the urbat cocooned in the other circles will probably be released. But that's not the bad part. If allowed to grow and connect they will form a network, a communication web the Itza Larrak will use to reach other Larrak. And they will return. That will destroy us, will destroy all life on

Adalta. They are like parasites who destroy their hosts and move on to destroy another."

She spread her hands flat on the table. "And what happens politically in Restal is of supreme interest to the guardian of Toldar, to the people of Toldar. The tension and animosity between the two quadrants are good for neither, and it's beginning to change for the better." Jenna stopped before she said the name Readen. She didn't like the impassive look on Me'Kahn's face. He didn't look away from her. She didn't like that either.

Silence held the table for several minutes until Krager spoke. "What Jenna is not saying, what she cannot say, is the greater danger to Toldar of Readen's attempt to depose Daryl as guardian and the end of any hope of good relations between the two quadrants will signal the end of hope for all Adalta. Readen has allied himself to the Itza Larrak."

"Readen is locked away in his holding, is he not? How is he a danger? He doesn't have talent. He's powerless."

Krager relaxed in his chair, as relaxed as Krager ever could be, leaning back, long legs crossed. "He's hired two troops of mercenaries from Akhara. They're presently trapped in the northern pass, thanks to Jenna, ChiChi, and Dalys, who brought a cliff down on the road."

Me'Kahn looked at the three of them—two small women and a ten-year-old girl—with a mixed expression of curiosity, suspicion, and a dawning of respect.

Krager went on, "He convinced a few of the large holders to support him with troops, and he's appealing to holders, the ones ruling holds smaller than yours, with the excuse that rule by strong talent must be overthrown, and he is the one to lead that revolt."

Me'Kahn's answering smile was grim. "But every one knows he has no talent. No one wants a guardian with no talent, no power. He'd be destroyed in the chaos that would follow, and Restal would suffer terrible damage. We're already suffering the damage his father did."

"There are several who do want it. And Readen has power. Lots of power. He has learned it from the Itza Larrak." Krager looked at

ChiChi, who was having difficulty keeping her eyes open. "I will explain it to you later…"

"No human would ally with such a monster."

Krager and Jenna were both silent, their eyes on the holder, their faces unmoving. Jenna folded her hands on the table to keep from reaching for Krager. Where did that urge come from? Had she gotten that needy?

"And you, Mi'hiru Dalys. Why are you here? Mi'hiru are neutral, sworn to Adalta and the Karda, not to any quadrant."

Dalys looked at him. The tiny Mi'hiru seemed to grow several inches. "Holder Me'Kahn, the bigger threat *is* to Adalta."

His eyes moved back and forth between the three adult's faces, finally settling on Chiara, who'd slipped down in her chair, eyes closed, clearly asleep and about to fall under the table.

Finally, he said, "We'll talk again in the morning after breakfast. Perhaps Chiara could be persuaded to check on your Karda then. I have a feeling there are some things you haven't said yet that I need to hear." He stood. "Not only is Aria gone, but she took the house-keeper with her, so I'll show you up to your rooms. I can promise they'll be clean and ready. She didn't leave me all alone and unprepared."

Krager carried ChiChi up to their rooms and settled her in one of the two beds. She shifted around and sprawled out to take up most of the bed. He whispered to Jenna. "I feel sorry for you. She hasn't left you any space."

"No need to whisper, she couldn't hear a medgeran roar. And I'm used to fighting her off." Jenna looked up at him and reached to touch his arm but pulled her hand back. "Thank you for supporting me down there. I apparently have a reputation to overcome."

He was silent. And when he spoke, it was to Dalys. "You might communicate with Seralla before our meeting in the morning."

"She's already told me she has information we need. I don't think the holder realizes ChiChi and I speak to our Karda. He doesn't have that ability."

Krager left with nod to Dalys and a soft "Goodnight" to Jenna.

She stood watching the closed door for a long time after he left.

CHAPTER FOURTEEN

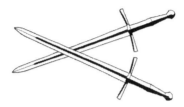

The familiar captain's conference room vibrated with tension, the wall of pristine white cabinets on one side an unsettling contrast to the enormous digital screen on the other. A wall screen covered with the image of the severed living quarters, workers in pressure suits swarming it, tugs and tethers holding it in place.

Sharon, the always immaculate chief of security, had a hair out of place, more than one, and her always-immaculate uniform was—not immaculate. It had wrinkles. That was as upsetting to Cedar as Sharon's words.

"So, here's the situation simplified in a couple of bytes. One faction wants to stay on the ship and find another planet accepting of technology. One faction wants to leave and erase any trace we were here for fear the Trade Federation sanctions on smuggling the akenguns to a world where they are illegal will destroy us. Both refuse to believe the ship is failing and insist we leave orbit right now, without delay. And, of course, there's the slim but loud majority, who accept the ship is failing, and we must abandon it immediately."

Cedar sat very still next to Captain Kendra Pathal, who smelled of anger, disapproval, disbelief, and a particularly unpleasant odor of helplessness. She concentrated on her tree filter and letting the ugliness flow through her, not stopping. And wondered if she should pull out her pine salve.

"There are those, among all three factions, who believe you, Galen, are a traitor, and all this is your fault, and those who believe you, Cedar, much as they love you, are too young to be Director of Bio-Systems and have lost control over it. And, of course, there are the ones who believe the alien you've warned us about is trying to take over the ship and enslave us all and the ones who believe it doesn't exist."

Captain Kendra turned her head away from the screen covering one wall where the floating pods hung suspended to stare at the tripartite leaf markings on his face where his scars should be. She didn't comment on them, just said to his cheek, "You say, Galen, that there is only the one alien. That seems unlikely and not much of a threat if it is true. Which it's not. It's a legend or something native their stories have turned into a space monster." She turned her face back to the screen. "In all the years the trade ships have traveled space, no one has ever encountered alien ships."

The silence that followed her words shouted disbelief and lasted too long for Cedar. No one was willing to disagree with the captain.

Finally, Clare, Director of Engineering and Maintenance, took up the litany of problems. "What we haven't told anyone is that the living pod didn't come loose because of out-of-control bio-system plants. Sharon's people and mine are still investigating the cause. The damage to the entry hatch is extensive, and the interior hatches and back-up life systems in all its smaller group pods failed. All of them. Within milliseconds of each other. That's impossible. Except, obviously the impossible wasn't."

Head of Medic Arlan Garcia, his white coat stained with blood and fluids Cedar didn't want to know about, came in and took a place with empty chairs between him and the others. "People are terrified. Medic is swamped. Anxiety is exacerbating existing health problems and creating new, sometimes imaginary ones. Having engineers swarming over everything both calms and agitates patients and staff. No one knows what to think or believe. The ship is approaching chaos." His index finger was raw where he constantly worried his cuticle. He, too, stared at Galen's face, clasped his hands together and hid them under the table. Cedar knew he despised Galen. She smelled anger and jealousy. Apparently he'd rather see ugly scars than a beautiful tattoo.

Cedar added leaves to her tree filter so a cubic micron couldn't get through, and still she detected his fear. It wasn't just Arlan's staff who were terrified. Her jar of pine salve wasn't going to last much longer. She'd have to find something as strong on the ship somehow without telling anyone why she needed it. They weren't ready for that conversation. She wasn't ready.

Through the whole conversation Captain Kendra stared at the display screen showing the severed pod without uttering a word—a petrified tree trembling on the edge of a precipice.

The discussion circled around the same problems over and over, finally fading to silence. The ship's officers looked back and forth between Galen and Cedar. Except for the captain, still staring at the suited workers scrambling over the living pod. Cedar thought she was as detached from the situation as the pod was from the ship, only there were no workers scurrying to fix what was broken in her.

She broke the silence. "Galen, tell them what we are facing on the planet."

Galen stepped up to the control panel beside the display and switched the view to the planet. Cedar saw the captain stir, then return to being a petrified tree.

He brought the planet into close focus. It was a rare clear day below them, and the whole of the enormous single continent came into view. White mountains to the west with the tiny strip of the Coastal Holdings between them and the island-dotted ocean. The bright turquoise gulf held between the arms of Akhara and Anuma glistened to the east. The focus moved close enough to see the sun glinting off the vast field of greenhouses in Rashiba Prime like crystals embedded in the land along precise rows.

Cedar heard Clare suck in a deep breath and let it out in a whisper. "It's so beautiful from here, with its circles of green forest set like emeralds in the vast seas of brown barrens. It will be an honor and a delight to help restore more life to Adalta."

Galen snorted. "Honor and a lot of hard, dirty work." He stood half-turned so he could see both the screen and the others. "The Cues are working better than they have for some time, so I know you have some information about what is happening down there. Assam has been in communication with his people, and he's reported to you, Captain, daily."

Kendra's eyes shifted from the screen to him. Her head dipped just enough to acknowledge him. Her eyes blinked and shifted back to the screen.

"There are a number of issues your settlers will face. It's important that the first people you send be accompanied by those able to fight. I don't know how many Ship Patrol you can spare, Sharon. It sounds like you need them here. But there are a few retired agents used to being on an uneasy planet." He looked at Sharon. "You'll need to start getting them up to fighting strength and use them to train others, not just to fight, but in how to adjust to problems on a new planet. If that pod hadn't been sabotaged and broken loose—"

Captain Kendra snapped and finally spoke, her voice hard with anger. "No one has mentioned sabotage."

"You're right, Captain. No one has mentioned the obvious, but it still has to be faced."

Galen and Kendra glared at each other until she turned her head back to the screen and became a rock again. Sharon and Clare looked at each other with relief. Clare ran her hands through her spiky red hair. Arlan's elbows were on the table, his head was down, propped in his hands, his shoulders slumped into his pudgy body. Cedar decided he looked like the top half of a melon across the table from her.

"If the pod hadn't broken loose as it did," continued Galen, "I would urge you to delay relocation until the issues down there could be resolved. But it looks like delay is impossible. Assam asked for spy drones and spy bots. He says some of them are working, and he has them reporting on the areas around the Circle of Devastation in the north of Restal, where there have been so many attacks. I think his people have reports for you, so you'll be somewhat prepared to meet what your people will need to defend against."

Cedar noticed that Galen used the pronouns *you* and *they*, not *we* and *us*. It seemed he no longer considered himself any part of this ship. He'd become Adaltan inside and out. She wondered if that could ever happen to her. She shifted her leg. There was no feeling, no sense of movement, even here on board the ship, where it should work at least a little.

She spoke, ignoring the bereft feeling that tightened her chest. "I suggest you stop trying to reattach the living pod to the ship and think about how you can get both it and the warehouse pod to the surface and settle them there. And how you can start moving other pods—living pods, warehouse pods, all the seed storage pods, embryo tanks—everything that can be detached and moved."

She looked directly at Kendra, willing the captain to face her. "There's a village called Ardencroft that's empty and perfect as headquarters for the relocation. A team of talent teachers is coming up here to prepare our people to adjust to what they will become—to teach them the basic principles of talent, to get used to the idea of elemental magic. There are others in the village whose sole job will be to help us learn about our individual talents. And others to help us find and train for work."

Clare looked from the screen image to Cedar. "How will they know who will have talents and who will not? I read the reports you, Glenn, and Assam sent about what happened to each of you. But it won't happen to every one, surely."

"There is only one person on Adalta who doesn't have talent, the only one in their history. So, yes, it will happen to every one."

Kendra didn't look away from the screen when she spoke. "And what of the people who refuse to leave?"

Neither Cedar nor Galen had an answer for her.

Cedar finally spoke into the long silence that trapped every one in the room like a bee in an acrylic cube. "That's a problem for the officers of the ship to deal with." She would figure out a way to deal with her mother. Later. Right now she didn't want to think about it.

"And you must start dealing with it. Now. There is no time to spare."

No time to spare, and yet no one would make the final, inevitable decision.

Jenna was in the mews early the morning after they arrived at Me'Kahn Hold, grooming Mirjana, thinking about nothing but the peace that radiated from her drowsy Karda. She couldn't speak with Mirjana, but her mind filled with images—images of tall white mountains, sides sheer and sharp, snowy tops hidden in snowy clouds. Images of winding valleys with snow cover pierced by green spears of spring grass and rivers roaring with cold snowmelt, cloudy with grit worn from the sides of the mountains. Images of steep cliffs riddled with large caves and nests that were piles of sticks with wide-eyed, downy beaked heads on fuzzy foal bodies peering out of them. Images of places no human had ever seen, no human had ever experienced.

"You are early, Jenna."

She jumped at the sound of Lucas's voice, and the images faded away like a vivid early morning dream that was there then suddenly it wasn't, and there was nothing left but an inexplicable sense of regret for a missed chance. "Good morning, sir."

A Mi'hiru walked in behind him headed for the feed room, looking closely at the strange Karda.

"And good morning to you, too, Mi'hiru. I'm Jenna Me'Cowyn, and this is Mirjana. Across there are Tarath, Mia, and Seralla." She reached out to grasp the Mi'hiru's forearm.

"I thought I recognized Tarath and Seralla. I assume Dalys is traveling with you. And the Restal armsmaster, too. I haven't seen Dalys since she finished her training in Rashiba and was sent to your hold on the coast. I'm Rayna, newly assigned here. Good morning to you, too, Holder." She looked back and forth between Mirjana and Jenna, who could see her curiosity hiding behind a polite smile.

"If you're finished here, Jenna, let's retire to the tack room where it's warm, or will be soon. It may be spring, but my bones argue it's still winter," said the holder.

Jenna started to ask him why, but he'd already turned away. "I've already fed our four Karda, but not those the troopers with us fly. Do you need my help, Rayna?" she asked.

But Rayna waved her on, looking like she'd like to be a mouse in the corner. A fierce mouse with a tiny sword.

Her reputation seemed to have spread everywhere. Rayna looked to Jenna like she wanted to protect the holder, who was old enough to be her uncle, if not her father. Heat burned the back of her neck, and she looked at the pitchfork hanging outside the tack room door with longing, undecided if she wanted to pitch hay with it or stab somebody. She took a deep breath and stepped inside. Me'Kahn heated the magma stones in the small iron stove and stood holding his hands out to the warmth. Jenna's face got hotter as if she'd fired a magma stone in her head. Being the target of judgment wasn't something she was used to or, she supposed, ever noticed.

"How did two young women, one who has always refused to fly a Karda, one a small child, close Revka Pass?" His eyes didn't narrow. His eyebrows weren't drawn into a frown. His mouth wasn't curled up in a smile, but neither was it drawn down by doubt or disbelief. It was bland. But his anger singed her like she was too close to the stove. He hadn't believed them. Didn't trust them. Or her. It was she he didn't trust. He probably thought she was here to entrap Restal's Armsmaster Krager because she hadn't trapped Altan or Daryl. It took effort not to scream at him.

"Holder Me'Kahn. I am a very strong talent in Air and Earth. Yes, ChiChi is very young, but her Earth talent could crack the substantial walls of your hold. Mi'hiru Dalys is new to her Air talent, but she could blow the dirt from under your foundations and your walls would crumble. I hope you have strong wards."

"What do you mean the Mi'hiru is new to her talent? We're born with it, how can it be new?"

"Dalys is one of the agents sent to gather information about

Adalta from the trade ship orbiting above us. As were Marta Me'Rowan and Galen Me'Cowyn, the Kern."

"Me'Rowan? Who gave her the title?"

"Guardian Stephan, after she blew up a magma stone. A sizable magma stone which she reduced to a pile of magma gravel. He embedded it in the front steps to his keep. They were free of ice the entire winter." She looked at him, trying not to let her anger and defiance leak through. Her face ached with the effort. Why now? Why was he so distrustful now when he'd been welcoming and friendly last night? Just because of her reputation? Had it been that bad? "Holder Me'Bolyn sent two of his strongest troopers with us. You can ask them."

"Me'Bolyn? Not your father?"

Jenna was silent.

"Your father didn't send you, did he?"

Jenna looked down at the floor of the tack room. At the stray wisps of hay. At the round dark spots of saddle oil on the flagstone. At the toes of her boots, scuffed and roughed with wear even though they were new. They needed to be cleaned and polished. Or, she guessed, she needed to clean and polish them. But she didn't know how. She sucked in a deep breath, turned her head to look at nothing, let it out and said, "My father got word of at least four ships of mercenaries passing our coast. He wasn't going to warn Me'Bolyn and probably wasn't going to send a report to either Toldar's guardian or your guardian."

"So you persuaded Mi'hiru Dalys to get you and your ten-year-old sister to Me'Bolyn Hold and then persuaded him to lend you two troopers and let you take your ten-year-old sister into the mountains. Where were you going?"

Jenna's head came up. "To warn Guardian Daryl about what was coming."

"And to try to close the pass—once again with your ten-year-old sister, her immense talent, and the control of a ten-year-old."

"She followed us, and I couldn't take her back. Father would have locked Dalys and I both up in the deepest dungeon of the keep after he had one dug. ChiChi would have left again, on her own, to warn Me'Bolyn. She's a very bright, very stubborn, very honest ten-year-old, and I've been teaching her control since she was three, as have her various tutors. That was after she reduced the hold gates to sawdust when Father tried to teach her a lesson about wandering away by locking her out."

"She's reckless. I watched her fly in. Her Karda was out of control, and so was she."

"Chiara has been flying since she snuck into the mews and bonded with Mia when she was four years old. As I tried to do, only she didn't fall off the first time she flew like I did. Her control is perfect. And I have to ask you, what right do you have to question me like this? I am of age. You are not my father. You are not the guardian of my quadrant. Not liking me, not approving of me, doesn't give you any right except the right to ask me to leave. Which I will do this morning. With ChiChi and Dalys."

A deep voice from the doorway said, "Do we have a problem here, Me'Kahn?" Krager's big form blocked the early morning light from the room.

Jenna didn't move. Didn't release Me'Kahn's gaze. "Do we?"

"You fell off a Karda when you were four?"

"She caught me."

"And you've been flying for how long? Tendays?"

"Something like that. I am bonded to Mirjana now."

"But I know you flew before that. I also know you hated it." Me'Kahn looked at her for a long time. Jenna didn't look away. "You are not the scatterbrained filly you appeared to be. In fact, you might be the alpha mare in your herd, and you are correct. I have no right to question you. Again, Jenna Me'Nowyk, welcome to my hold. I need to check with Mi'hiru Rayna. Perhaps we can meet over the breakfast table in, say, an hour? And discuss the state of things in my part of Restal Quadrant."

He looked at the hard, sober face of Krager. "I have a lot to tell you."

As soon as he was gone, Jenna collapsed against the wall. But by that time the mews was full with the other two Mi'hiru, troopers grooming and feeding Karda, and wheelbarrows of clean and dirty straw passing each other in the aisle. So she pulled herself together and helped ChiChi take care of Mia, and they headed for the hall, Krager and Dalys not far behind. Krager caught up to her, pointedly jerked his head at ChiChi, who dropped back to walk with Dalys.

"You were upset. What did he say to you?" His voice was rough—like he pushed it through his throat.

"It's fine. He just had some questions. I am from Toldar, after all. He was wondering why I was with you as a messenger from Daryl."

"You were angry. It was more than that."

Jenna stopped, hands on her hips. He was so close she was forced to tilt her head back to look at him. "I do not need a minder, Krager. I can look after myself."

He stared down at her, emotions flicking across his face so fast they confused her. He looked away. "Yes, you can." And he walked on, his long legs increasing the distance between them with every step.

The breakfast conversation was full of fits and starts. Jenna was upset. Upset with Me'Kahn, upset with Krager, but mostly upset with herself, upset that she had to defend herself against rumors and gossip she probably deserved. Finally Me'Kahn stood and paced in front of the fireplace with the large iron magma stone stove radiating welcome heat. "I know you have questions, Krager, Jenna. But first, let me tell you what I know and have done. Maybe I can give you answers before you need to ask. The circles. I've done what I could, but my people must be fed first, and without help from Restal Prime, the circles are growing. For the past year or more, the growth has increased by too much. And the two in this part of Restal are putting out lines, reaching toward each other and reaching in the direction of other circles. If those two circles haven't connected yet, they will soon."

He stopped pacing and looked at them. "I see you're not surprised. We're way up here in the far northeast section of Restal, about as far from the Prime as you can get. I'd hoped the problems besetting the west wouldn't reach here. But they have. In addition to the growing circles," he looked at Krager. "I understand Daryl has recognized the dilatory efforts his father made and is doing his best to rectify the problem. But now he's pulled his planters, most of them, away. That doesn't reassure me. Growing circles don't just affect the forest around them. The holdings nearest them had unsatisfactory harvests last fall, livestock born with defects, even a few children born with severe problems. Some died. Some will need care their whole lives."

His face got hard. "I caught four strangers preaching sedition in this area, and I know there are more. They're saying rule by strong talent no longer works, and there needs to be a change. Readen Me'Vere is mentioned often. This isn't the first time in our history on the planet that this issue has come up. All too often it led to spilled blood. I don't want that to happen here, so, following what Daryl was trying to do before this war, I've formed a council made up of people elected from my villages and small holds. Major decisions are still made by me, but they are discussed first in the council. Fewer people are listening to the idea of revolution against talent. The talk of revolt has faded, but it isn't gone."

Krager broke the long silence that followed Me'Kahn's speech. "I take it neither of your circles have produced urbat. Yet."

"No. All we have is stories about the attacks near the circle in the north not far from the mountains. I'd hoped the battle last fall finished them. Obviously, it didn't."

Me'Kahn stopped pacing and leaned on the table, his eyes sharp on Jenna. "And I must ask why Jenna from Toldar is here saying she comes from Guardian Daryl."

Krager started to get up, but she put a hand on his arm, and he sat back. "I did not say I came from Guardian Daryl. I was asked to accompany Armsmaster Krager by Daryl, Guardian Heir Altan of Toldar, and Prime Guardian Hugh Me'Rahl." Her voice was gentle.

She sat straight in her chair, hands folded on the table in front of her. "What is happening in Restal is of great concern to all Adalta. Readen is a threat to Restal, but also to Toldar. No one believes he will stop if he takes over this quadrant. There is no question that he has allied himself with the Itza Larrak." She didn't mention Daryl's stubborn, misplaced belief that he hadn't. "There is also little question that, contrary to Readen's belief, he does not control the Larrak. It controls him."

ChiChi could be still no longer. She was incandescent with impatience. "Kishar says—you know who Kishar is, don't you? The ancient Karda, the last Karda of his kind, who came from the mountains to choose Tessa as the Austringer and to kill the Itza Larrak, and he's the last of his kind because all the others like him were killed in the war with the Larrak five hundred years ago. He was to kill it when it came out again." She finally stopped to breathe. "I met him, and I got to talk to him. He's very nice. Not grumpy and crotchety like an old person." Jenna was more than grateful ChiChi stopped before she said, "Like you."

"Thank you, ChiChi." Jenna looked at the holder. "Kishar tells us that the lines extending from the circles will become a continent-wide antenna. Through it, the Itza Larrak will contact the others of its kind and call them back. They are space parasites. They will bleed Adalta dry, then leave for another planet to destroy."

She let the silence go on for several minutes, watching Me'Kahn's face as he processed her words. "It is Daryl's belief—and Kishar's—that Adalta will not let this happen." She waited again as the holder sat and leaned back in his chair. The relief on his face was that of a young boy who'd expected punishment and didn't get it. Adalta would save them.

Jenna's face was grim, but a quarter-smile turned up one corner of her mouth. Her voice was low, matter-of-fact, and relentless. "However, this is what we all know but no one will talk about. We will not survive. She will destroy life, destroy both the Larrak and us, and retreat to start again. Volcanoes will erupt, mountains will fall, rivers will dry up, the ocean will rise, and we will all be dead. So to answer your question about why I am here, why we are here—we ask, where do you stand? Who will have your support in the coming battles?"

Me'Kahn looked at her until she wanted to scream to shatter the silence. He looked at silent and stoic Krager. "Now, Krager, you tell me why I should believe her fantastic tale."

Jenna fought to sit straight, shoulders back, to breathe evenly. ChiChi looked about to jump out of her chair straight for Me'Kahn's throat. Jenna reached with one hand to grip her arm, the other grabbed Dalys's, holding all three of them fast in their chairs.

Fantastic tale? Fantastic tale?

That had to be verified by a man?

Jenna didn't turn toward Krager, but she could feel his eyes on her. He didn't speak. She sat, back straight, face straight, eyes straight on Me'Kahn's, and placed her hands on the table, one on top of the other with as much grace and control as she could muster while fire burned its way through the dark curls on top of her head and singed her hair.

"Holder Me'Kahn, I know, isolated though you are up here in the northeast, that you are more aware than you would have me believe. Guardian Merenya and her son Ballard Me'Kahryl must have passed through your hold with their troops on their way to the battle last fall. Ballard has called more troops, which probably passed through or close to your hold this spring. You did not choose to send any forces. You cannot say you are ignorant of that battle and the monsters. What I trust you are not aware of is that there have been some..."

Jenna glanced at Krager, whose long legs were crossed and stretched out in front of him, his chair pushed back from the table. He hadn't moved. His expression was as usual unreadable, inscrutable, sculpted from iron. He nodded slightly.

She leaned forward and looked at Me'Kahn. "There is little doubt that at least two, perhaps three major holders have defected to Readen. There is no doubt that Readen is allied with the Itza Larrak. That he has acquired forbidden high-tech weapons smuggled from the spaceship above us. There is no doubt whatsoever that what I've told you is not a fantasy. So the question becomes—in whose direction do your loyalty and support point?"

"It seems your reputation as a relentless husband-hunter is not the whole story. You are also a relentless ally—and would be a relentless antagonist." He was not smiling.

Jenna stood. "I am the heir to Toldar Coastal Holding. Cut off from the rest of the continent as we are, we have to be relentless— or be relegated to obscurity."

Dalys and ChiChi stood also. "I am certain you will do the right thing, Holder Me'Kahn. We will leave you to talk about what you can do to support your guardian with Armsmaster Krager."

"Man to man." Disgust and disappointment filled the high voice of little ChiChi. The stones of the floor shifted and groaned as she walked out.

CHAPTER FIFTEEN

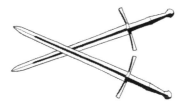

After two tendays of waiting, thinking, trying to formulate a plan—
in between emergency trips to counter urbat attacks, with mixed
results—Daryl stood at the front of his tent in Altan's camp
watching Captain Dalt get Guardian Turin's troops settled. He
wondered where the enormous man got a horse big enough to carry
him. Turin was possibly the largest man Daryl knew. *No wonder he
doesn't fly. Even Abala would have a hard time getting off the
ground with him.*

The big man clapped Captain Dalt on the shoulder and headed
toward him. Daryl laughed to himself. The cocky captain fought to
keep his balance and his ever-so-important cool composure. Turin
joined Daryl outside the tent and a few minutes later, a cacophony
of "kee kee kees" sounded from the sky. Troopers grabbed packs
and gear and horses and carts and cleared the landing field. An
enormous black Karda swooped low over the tops of the trees,
touched down with grace, and loped straight for Turin. Twenty-
seven flyers in Turin's colors landed one by one after him. Three
Karda Wings with a Mi'hiru each.

The looks that flashed across the big man's face were relief and a brief flicker of what Daryl could only call joy, maybe something more. But they were gone so fast he couldn't be certain. He was curious.

A tall young woman, her thick red hair coming loose from its braid, slid out of the saddle before her Karda stopped. She wore flying leathers that showed a tiny waist slung with a sword belt, an ample bosom, and shapely legs that spoke of hours of flying and perhaps fighting. There was a bow in a scabbard on her saddle and two full quivers.

Turin turned and slipped inside the tent, her right behind him. The big man's arms enveloped her, and he buried his face in her hair. Tall as she was, she almost disappeared. Daryl went to find something else to do. Turin. Who would ever dream?

He heard a closer "kee kee" and looked up in time to step back out of Kishar's way and cover his face against the dust and grass and twigs that whirled up when the black Karda landed next to him, Tessa on his back.

"Don't look so worried, Daryl. I left everything in good hands. There's hardly a person in Ardencroft right now who isn't a seasoned fighter, including Assam. Glenn talks on the Cue thing with Cedar and Galen all the time. I guess things are not going well up there. And you need me for this strategy session."

Daryl scrubbed his hands over his face, wishing he could scrub his worries away, hoping they didn't show. "Greetings to you, Tessa, and to you, Kishar. I'm glad you're here. We do need you. And it's not Ardencroft I'm worried about, or not too worried."

"Don't worry about Cedar. She'll be all right."

"Of course. Why would you think I'm worried about her?"

She looked at him. "I think, right now is when Galen would say something profound from his space vocabulary, like…*Duh.*"

Daryl aimed an I'm-the-guardian face toward her, and she found something else to talk about. "I see Turin has arrived."

"And a special surprise came in right behind him. Is he bonded?"

"I wouldn't know. Turin is one man my father never shoved at me. And he'd never left Akhara before he showed up in Toldar at the bonding ceremony last fall and got stuck here all winter. Why?"

He gestured at the field full of Karda riders in Turin's colors, and Tessa answered her own question, "Yes. This could be either very good or very very bad."

~I will try to find out which it is,~ pathed Kishar to both of them. ~Their Mi'hiru are still with them, so it isn't bad yet. They would have left. You must find out what you can from them, Tessa.~

Daryl stared at the chaos on the field and Altan storming through it toward him. He recognized the face Altan wore. He didn't trust Turin either and held up a hand before Altan could speak. "Turin is on his way up the west side of the circle. He'll only be here long enough for us to coordinate strategy."

"I hope you know what you're doing." Altan didn't look happy. "You're sending him too close to the Revka Pass and the Akhara mercenaries. I know he says they're not his troops, but…"

"He wants to be near the ocean so he can sail home. Do you want him trekking his men through Toldar again?" Daryl smothered a smirk at the look on Altan's face at that.

"When he leaves, you can hope he turns toward the northern edge of the circle, but he can also turn south toward Readen. No one knows much about him except he's strong. He's been guardian of Akhara for five years. Sometimes their guardians only last months."

"I know." Daryl, silent, tense, his jaw clenched, watched Turin's troops settling in at the edge of the landing meadow. He had no choice but to trust the guardian. Akhara quadrant was tumultuous at the best of times. Daryl wondered how Turin had been able to leave it for so long. Until he looked again at the wings of Karda Patrol the red-headed flier brought with her. He wished he had time, and maybe the nerve, to ask the formidable guardian how he'd tamed Akhara.

He put the thoughts away for another time and looked at Tessa. "Your father will be here anytime now, Tessa. Master Planter Andra will be here soon. Me'Fiere came in last night with Me'Neve." It was all he could do not to spit that last name. He needed to set someone to watch Me'Neve. Someone more observant and suspicious than he had been.

"Hugh Me'Rahl's troops are camped ten kilometers from the southeast edge of the circle, and Ballard Me'Kahrl set up in the northeast. They both flew in this afternoon so we can finalize our strategy and discuss the best tactics to protect the planters Andra sent to the circle. We need Galen. Did Glenn give you any idea of when he and—when he might return, Tessa?"

He ignored the look she shot at him and turned back to the field full of fliers and troops. It was beginning.

Cedar stomp-limped to the dais in the ship's large assembly room, following Captain Kendra Pathal. Galen, his scars back, followed right on her heels, to her irritation. "Are you going to mother hen me everywhere I go?"

"Cluck cluck"

"It's not necessary. No one's come close to threatening me in the last four days."

"Cluck cluck"

She stuck her bottom lip out and huffed a huff that blew her hair off her forehead—just in time to keep the top of her head from blowing off. "Stupid, stupid, stupid people. Are we sure your father didn't have any more akenguns stashed somewhere?"

"Sharon's ship patrol has been all over this ship again and again. And after you got hit with the taser, the captain locked the rest of those up with the other weapons in her gun locker. And counted them to be certain they were all turned in."

"I wasn't thinking about someone else having them, I was thinking about getting one myself to go hunting for idiots. It was just my hand. There's hardly a tingle left now."

"And a nasty burn." He nodded to Clare, and they took seats beside her at the table on the small dais—Sharon on the far side of the captain with pudgy Arlan Garcia, Director of Medic, and immaculate Mark Kelton, Director of Finance.

The huge amphitheater was crowded. Every one of the eighty-five hundred people who didn't have a critical duty or a sick child was required to be there. Half of them looked eager, half of them looked defiant, and a third half looked resigned and antsy with a mix of anger. Cedar hid a sigh. Three halves described the balance in this room perfectly. There were small groups within groups, each with its own agenda, its own fears, its own, probably false, idea about what was happening to the ship. But she had a hunch that if all those who accepted that the ship was actually failing and they would be forced to leave glowed blue she'd have a hard time picking them out.

The pine salve smeared under her nose and the dense leaves she added to her tree filter were not enough to block all the smells of anger, of fear, of distrust. All her life, she'd thought the ship community was cohesive with only a few unimportant little cracks. But the smell of the maelstrom of emotions separating them now was so overwhelming she fought not to throw up.

Would she make it through this assembly without embarrassing herself? Somehow, when they got back to Adalta, she and Mireia would have to find a solution to this problem. Otherwise being in a room full of people would always be a problem. She couldn't deal with that. She'd have to find a cave and become a hermit.

It took a while for the crowd to settle. It had been years since such an assembly had been necessary. That was enough to trigger the disquiet, the rumors, and the fighting factions. The odor of grief and fear underlay everything. Grief for those who were lost when the living pod blew away and grief for the home about to be lost. The ship had been home to this small community for more than five hundred years.

Captain Kendra finally stood and held up her hand, palm out. Immediately people started shouting questions at her.

"What happened to the pods?"

"Will my living pod be next?"

"What about the plants going wild?"

"Are we in danger of attack from some alien ship?"

"Call Glenn Voigt back to the ship. Cedar can't help. Her plants are destroying—"

The captain held up both hands, pumping them palms down several times in front of her, and the room quieted. Somewhat. "The Director of Engineering and Maintenance is the best person to answer your questions—with facts, not wild rumors." She motioned to Clare, and the short, broad woman stood. Her red-threaded-with-silver hair was cut so short it bristled.

Cedar saw the angry, disgusted flash she shot at the captain, and she realized the captain was a coward. She was not even trying to think of solutions, of organizing the evacuation. She wasn't thinking at all. It was as though she froze when the pods broke away, and she couldn't thaw out.

Clare spoke over the flurry of questions that rose. Her deep voice filled the room. "First, before you try to hang Cedar from one of her trees, the pods did not break away because of the plants. They did *not* interfere with the hatches or the life systems. We are still investigating what happened—and the possibility it was human-caused. The Director of Security also has her people investigating. Five people were killed. If it was someone on ship who caused this, it's murder."

The room went very still. Before it could erupt again, Clare went on, "Every hatch, all the mechanical life systems, every inch of this ship is being checked and rechecked. The only incursions by the plants are in non-life-support systems. It might be inconvenient not to have moving walkways, but think of it as encouraging healthy walking. I've even trimmed down a little myself."

There was a light sprinkle of laughter—nervous and scattered—but laughter Cedar was relieved to hear.

"And the plants have retreated."

Someone yelled, "Can you fix the walkways?"

"No, we cannot. The ship is failing. Bit by bit, faster and faster. Complete failure is inevitable. We are working on a time estimate, but planning for removal to the planet needs to be sped up."

The room erupted. Clare stood, erect, calm, and waited for the noise to subside. Finally it quieted enough for her to speak. "Those of you who do not believe this is possible and inevitable are invited to choose three representatives to join me in an inspection. You will need to select people who are familiar with the mechanics of the ship, people you can trust to tell you the truth." She looked at Captain Kendra, who, Cedar noted, was busy staring at her fingers.

"Director of Security Chobra wants to speak next. Sharon?" Clare sat.

Sharon gave the captain much the same look as Clare had, not obvious enough for the crowd to notice, but Cedar did. She smelled disappointment, anger, and frustration from both women and smeared pine salve in her nostrils.

Sharon stood, adjusting her uniform. "To plan for evacuation, we need representatives from every living pod in organizing the departure. Cedar and Galen will tell you what to expect when we land on Adalta and begin to educate us about life down there.

"every one on the ship over the age of thirteen and under the age of sixty will report, pod by pod, to the armory to be evaluated for arms training. Anyone trained in fighting that does not involve technical or projectile weapons will report to my office. I know you've all heard rumors of the battles on the surface. We need to be prepared to defend ourselves."

Several hands went up all over the room, and there were a few shouts asking why they couldn't take their own weapons to the surface.

"First," Sharon answered, "we must obey their laws, and they forbid it. Second, they simply will not work down there. This isn't the only world we've encountered that only allows primitive weapons. We are all taught the history of why the Ark ships left Earth from the time we are very young. No one wants a repeat of the results of uncontrolled technical advances. Now here's Cedar."

The crowd stirred again, but Cedar started talking before it could erupt. "I have a lot to tell you. Some of it is going to be difficult for you to believe, let alone accept. Some of it is about the dangers we will face. Soon there will be instructors from Adalta transported up here to help you adjust to the abilities they assure me will manifest in every one of you. Believe them. These abilities are a form of elemental magic of Earth, Air, and Water and have manifested in some way in every agent sent to the surface."

There was a long, whispering hush, then she told them the hard part. About the other alien species that had attacked the planet, about the resurgence of that war, about the attempt of the last of those aliens to communicate with its kind and bring them back.

There was, of course, question after question from the now chastened crowd. The first was, "What kind of magic do you have, Cedar? And what kind does Galen have?"

"For one thing," Cedar's smile was more an evil leer than a smile, "you won't ever be able to tell me a lie."

Galen went to the wall where plants grew from the planters that surrounded almost every space on the ship. Cedar was grateful his tattoos weren't manifesting. That would be creepy scary for too many people. He held a vine in his hand, and it grew, twined twice around his wrist, then reached to the closest person, a young girl, who watched with delight as it circled her arm and burst into flower. "Oh, Mama, look. I want to do this." She looked up at Galen and repeated. "I want to do this," her face bright and alive with awe and eagerness that lit her corner of the room. Galen clipped it loose, bent down and mock-whispered, "Put it in a pot of dirt as soon as you get back to your pod so it doesn't die. It will be with you for years that way."

Cedar glanced at the captain. Kendra was staring at nothing, and Cedar suspected she had mentally left the room.

Clare said, "The first thing we'll do is move the severed warehouse pod to the planet, then the living pod. The first one that broke loose is already down there, being made habitable for us. Galen tells me the first colonists were able to do this—he's seen the one's they salvaged—so surely we can, too. We transport large cargo pods all the time. We're going to salvage everything we can of this ship. So it's not just us who are moving—we're moving our home, too."

There was more discussion, more questions, especially for Cedar and Galen. There was hostility, disbelief, anger, curiosity. By the time the room cleared Cedar was close to a mental shutdown, or at least a nasal shutdown. No one hurried, no one laughed, some were solemn, some were—Cedar could smell their dismay, distrust, danger through her tightest shields. Too much of it directed at her. One more assault and the leaves would start to fall. She needed to leave. Glenn needed to take her place up here no matter how much fun he was having on planet. So long as everything worked, she'd been trusted to do her job. That was no longer true.

But one thing she could do. She could sit down and sort out the emotions she'd smelled, how organized the factions were, and get a better idea of the tenor of the ship. Who could be trusted. Who couldn't.

Maybe this weird talent could be useful. Though it meant she couldn't cover herself in pine salve, and she'd need to add more leaf filters and send down more roots so her tree didn't topple in the smelly wind. She shuddered. It was beginning. Finally beginning.

"This does not look good." Altan and Marta stood at the edge of the landing field full of the three Karda Wings from Akhara. He tilted his head toward the tent where the tall woman had disappeared with Turin. "Who is she, I wonder?"

"I'll ask." Marta wore the listening-to-my-Karda look for several minutes. Creases formed between her eyes, her body stiffened and her jaw muscles went tight. Finally she spoke. "They were unusually reluctant to talk to me, except for one of the Mi'hiru's Karda. She's his bonded."

Altan looked at her, looked at the Karda, looked at the tent. "You mean Turin's bonded? Someone actually bonded to Turin?"

"She's also leader of Akhara's Karda Patrol."

"I thought Karda kept their distance from Akhara. I thought Mi'hiru hated going there."

Marta was still in listening-to-Karda mode. "Her name's Rachyl."

The Karda Rachyl had flown in on raised his head and looked straight at Marta. He trotted over and stopped in front of her, head high, neck arched. His body, mane, and tail were a gleaming blue-black. His feathers, too, were raven-black except where the tips and the long ends of his flight feathers glimmered pale gold. He was spectacular. Altan thought he was as big as Kibrath and Sidhari, maybe bigger.

~I am Gishgal, bonded to Flight Leader Rachyl. Do you have questions?~

"I heard that." Altan stepped half a step back. "You can speak to me, not just Marta?"

The massive head with its proud predator's beak turned toward him. ~I speak with whomever I wish. Your bonded will tell you what I say—why should I not speak to you directly?~

"We were not aware that Guardian Turin was bonded. Nor were we aware that Akhara had such a large Karda Patrol." Altan would not let this Karda intimidate him. Or maybe it was let this Karda know he was intimidated.

~It is a quite recent event.~

Event? The bonding might be recent, but the Karda Patrol? Was he speaking of one or both? Altan said, "Perhaps you could introduce us, and Guardian Daryl, to your flight leader and the guardian's bonded."

~First, Guardian Heir Altan Me'Gerron, I must give you my thanks for rescuing my niece and nephew when my sister and her mate were killed. I owe you both a debt that must be repaid. When we have finished with this current problem, I will come for them.~ He turned, his regal head high, and walked back toward Rachyl and Turin, who were now talking with Daryl.

Altan felt Marta's hand reach for his, and he squeezed hers hard. Her words, "They can't even fly yet," were a wistful whisper of sorrow. They both missed the orphan Karda fledglings they'd rescued when their mother and father were killed by a sample akengun Readen had. They'd had so little time with them.

The Cue in Marta's pocket buzzed. Galen's fuzzy face appeared on the screen. "Where are you? Where is Tessa? We're on our way back."

"At Altan's camp. Tessa's here. As are Daryl and nearly every one of importance, including a few new arrivals."

"I've locked on to your coordinates. Is the landing field big enough?"

"Oh, yes. Maybe a bit crowded, but we'll clear it off," said Altan. "There is quite a welcoming party here for you."

Altan reached over and clicked her Cue off before Galen could ask a question.

CHAPTER SIXTEEN

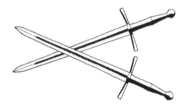

Cael was as near to panic as the seasoned spy could get without getting killed. He'd worked for Krager for years, ingratiating himself with Readen's forces, serving as a mercenary, passing on information whenever and however he could. He was the one who'd told Tessa about the children who'd been kidnapped to send to Readen. That put him in a precarious place with the man. Without the I'm-an-average-person-with-average-abilities shield spell Krager had taught him, he figured he'd be dead several times over.

This time Cael overstepped himself. Captain Paules of Readen's guard liked to spar, especially with guards who weren't that good. Which meant—in spite of sparring every day, sometimes several times a day—he wasn't much better than average. He challenged Cael, who always did his best to appear average. The captain taunted him and taunted him and taunted him.

Cael lost his temper. He made a mistake. The pressure he'd swallowed for so long, erupted. It was a simple quick parry and riposte, but he flipped Paules's sword out of his grip and narrowly avoided slicing the captain's hand.

It didn't matter that Cael stumbled and tried to make it look like a clumsy mistake that got lucky. The sudden narrowing of the captain's eye, the flared nostrils, the slow movements as he walked over to pick up his sword, the forced smile when he turned back told Cael his days as a spy were numbered, and the number was a low one. Hours, maybe days, but no longer, and Cael would be in the cell next to the two people Readen was bleeding.

"I can't believe I did that. That I *could* do that." He stuck out his chest, pulled off his practice helmet, scrabbled his hand through his hair. "Do you think I'm getting better, Captain? I'm not sure I know what I did, but maybe I am. Thank you for the workout, sir. You're a good teacher." He forced himself to stop talking. He was piling on too much of the ingratiating-fool act.

It was time to leave, and not just the practice arena. It was time to leave Readen's hold. He was tired. Tired of being hyper-alert, watching himself, watching everything around him, gleaning information, hiding what he knew, figuring out how to pass it back to Krager. He couldn't stay and make another mistake like today's.

Readen was gone, and Captain Paules was too intimidated to take any action by himself. But Readen would be back anytime now. On Cael's way to the barracks, he passed the beautiful Odalys, Readen's supposed mistress, though Cael knew she was his accomplice, not mistress. Readen's need for a mistress was long gone if indeed he'd ever felt such a need, and she was as cruel and vicious as he was. She was in the housekeeper's room and looked like she'd be there for a while. She wouldn't be in Readen's study—the only person Readen thought could get in there.

He slipped a few sheets of paper out of the guard post in the hall and walked up the stairs as if he belonged. No one saw him slide through Readen's wards and slip into the study, and it didn't take Cael long to find what he was looking for. Plans for the invasion of Restal Hall were in a neat stack on the desk. He flipped through them, memorizing what he could in the time he had, terrified at what he read.

Behind the desk stood a tall bookcase. On a low shelf, between some ancient history books, were a handful of thin leather-bound journals. He didn't hesitate, stuffed them inside his tunic, and turned to the three large chests stacked on one wall. This was the way his Water talent twisted. This was why he was such a good spy. There were spells on them—spells with Readen's unsettling magic. Cael's talent soaked, that was the only word to describe it, into the top chest and pooled around the lock, shifting the spell, loosening it, but not breaking it, like a stream loosened the rocks in its bed so tiny water creatures could slip under them. He lifted out two long, narrow bundles wrapped in oily cloth, closed the chest, and let his talent dissipate into mist. Readen would never notice. Until he needed the weapons.

Cael left for his quarters. He packed two packs, neither large enough to attract attention and carried one out to the stables with the two long bundles. He cleaned his horse's stall, piling fresh straw over them in a corner.

Three hours later, the light was going. The hold was quiet, and most were at dinner when he carried the other pack to the stables, kicking enough straw to hide it, too, and headed for the basement cells.

After the long years he'd spent with Readen, even before Readen's attempt to usurp Daryl as guardian, Cael was familiar to every one everywhere. The outer guard didn't even question him when he passed, handing him a bottle of wine. "If the captain asks, you never saw me."

"Hiding?"

"I accidentally knocked his sword out of his hand sparring this afternoon." Sometimes truth was the best lie.

The guard grinned and pulled the cork.

Pol was asleep on his cot when Cael knocked on his open door. He sat up when Cael waved the bottle in front of him.

"Thought you might be bored down here with Readen gone. I know I am." Cael picked up two dirty glasses from the table and filled them to the brim.

Pol shambled over, scrubbing his eyes. They fixed on the glasses and bottle. "Haven't seen you in a while, Cael. What are you doing here?"

"Hiding." He took a sip. Cael's Water talent cleared the wine in his glass of the sleep potion he'd put in the bottle, and he lifted his glass in a toast and told Pol what he'd done. "I don't know how I did it, but I'm staying least in sight for a while." No one wanted to be around Pol. No one would look for him here.

Pol's narrowed eyes opened. The single brow above his nose became two, and he laughed, or that was what Cael figured the odd sound coming from him was. He wondered if anyone else had ever heard the man laugh. The wine in Pol's glass was gone. Cael poured more. Twenty minutes later, he wished he'd brought two bottles. But Pol pulled another from a cabinet, and finally, the big man's eyes closed, and he slumped in his chair. Most of Cael's wine was under the table.

Cael helped him back to his cot, unclipped the keys from his belt, rolled him to face the wall, pulled a blanket over him and left. He'd done things he could never be proud of during his years with Readen, but, by Adalta, he wasn't going to leave without the two prisoners. He only hoped they were strong enough to keep up with him and smart enough to follow his lead.

He was down the long hall in minutes and searching for the right keys. "If you can follow my orders, I'll get you out of here. It won't be easy, and they'll come after us. If they catch us, we'll be dead. Or worse. But I need to go, and I don't want to leave you here." It was foolish and dangerous, but Cael was finished with sacrificing others to do his job. There'd been too many.

The woman began to cry and hiccuped her words out. "Anything. Anything. Just get us out of here."

The man took her hand through the bars. "Just tell us what to do." His voice shook.

Cael unlocked the side-by side-cells. "What are your names?"

"Darnela," said the woman, "and this is Poulter."

On their way out, Cael clipped the ring of keys back on Pol's belt.

Cael, Darnela and Poulter avoided the guard and slipped to the side of the stable. "You'll need warmer clothing. It's gonna be a cold, wet, muddy ride. I got what I could find. Put on everything you can wear and bundle up the rest. I hope the boots come close to fitting." Cael motioned the two shivering escapees between a stack of hay and the stone wall where he'd stashed the clothes. "Don't move from here till I'm back." He walked around the corner and stepped inside. The stable was empty of humans except for the guard at the double doors. One side was propped open a sliver, and the guard stood just inside out of the wind.

"Curse this wind." Cael shivered. "And curse the captain for sending me out in it tonight. He should be checking on the guards himself instead of—"

The guard laughed. "Instead of what, Cael? Sitting by a hot stove with a bottle of wine and his newest flirt? He's the captain, and you and I get to freeze in the dark." He shifted his feet and wrapped his arms over his stomach. "As long as you're here, I need to take a break. I must'a ate somethin' bad. Won't be long." And he left at a stumbling run. The few minutes Cael spent in the kitchens this afternoon was paying off. It didn't happen often, but the cooks weren't always careful about the way they kept the food. He'd just made sure it would happen tonight. He'd been preparing for this a long time.

He stepped to the side of the barn and signaled the other two inside. The only sounds were the shuffling of horse hooves on straw, the munching of horses eating hay and grain, and a soft whicker. He knew which horses he'd take. Small, not more than fourteen hands, big, healthy feet—they'd be traveling through mud and off trails— shabby, heavy coats, sturdy and with a gait they could maintain for kilometers.

There were trail packs and pack harnesses in the tack room as well as the saddles, bridles, halters, and ropes they'd need. Cael took down a bow from the wall and found two quivers of arrows. They couldn't carry enough food. He'd have to hunt.

"Cael?" All three froze. The guard was back, but his voice wobbled. Cael stuck his head out of the tack room. "Yeah? What do you need, Arnson?"

"I'm hoping you will take this watch for me." He shifted his feet. "I'll return the favor soon's I get over this."

"Yeah, I guess I can do that. But you'll owe me two shifts." He hadn't finished speaking before the guard left, walking fast.

"That was a lucky break." Darnela's voice was as shaky as the guard's—for entirely different reasons. "Will we be as lucky passing the guards at the gate?"

"Don't worry about that. Just get your horse saddled and the packs on, and rifle other trail packs for extra blankets and three more heavy cloaks. I'll fill the grain sacks. Poulter, can you fit the harness on the pack horse?"

Cael hoped the other two couldn't hear the worry behind his words. The two former prisoners were not as strong as they should be. But Readen had been gone for several days. He hoped they'd recovered enough from the blood loss and whatever else Readen had done to them. They had days of hard riding ahead of them.

He got a sword out of the armory for Poulter, but whether the man could use it was questionable. And Darnela double-wrapped a belt with a big knife around her waist. Both of them followed his instructions and only spoke a few necessary words. He hoped determination would be enough. They both had a lot of determination.

They mounted inside the stable, Poulter with the lead rope for the pack horse. "Whatever you do, Darnela, don't speak. Poulter, you speak only if you have to. We have orders from Readen to head out if he wasn't back by now."

Darnela's hand went to her mouth to stop a cry, her eyes so wide Cael could see the glitter of their whites even in the darkness.

"That's our excuse, Darnela. Calm down." Poulter reached out and grabbed her arm tight. She looked at him, jerked her head in a nod, and pulled her hood as far forward as would still let her see.

Cael tapped his horse's flank with his spurs, and they headed for the gates. His excuse—orders from Readen—worked. Readen's easy-going-friend-to-all facade slipped too often now. No one would question them because no one would claim an order from Readen unless it was true. He was no longer an easy master to serve, and the last few months had gotten worse.

The three riders passed the outside guards with no problem. Captain Paules always kept the tenday's password in the back of a drawer in his desk. Cael always knew it. As soon as they were out of view of the last guard, they slipped off the road and headed south and west. Now what they needed to worry about was Daryl's guards. But they were there to watch for troop movements, not to watch stray travelers.

They saw no one. It was too late for villagers to be in their fields or in the woods hunting, so they made decent time despite the mud. The trees were thinned out for a hundred fifty meters outside the walls, and the horses sank to their pasterns. It wasn't so bad when they got to the forest, but by the time dawn was pinking the sky, the tree cover was thinner, the sun was able to get through, and the mud got deeper. The going slowed, and the horses tired, so Cael called a halt before they rode out of the forest.

"We'll rest here till it gets lighter. The horses need it, and so do we. There'll be a ground cloth in the trail pack, so pull one out, would you, Darnela, and a couple of blankets, while Poulter and I check the horses' legs and feet. We don't need a crippled horse."

"I know more about horses than he does, so he can get the blankets." Darnela's voice was high, tired, and tremulous. "How far have we come, and what about the urbat? What if they attack us?"

Cael wondered if Darnela would ever feel safe again. "We're about fifteen kilometers south of the hold, and we don't need to worry about the urbat. We're too far from the Circle of Disorder in the north which is the only circle they come from. It's safe to turn east soon in as straight a line as we can manage to Restal Prime. Poulter, get those blankets and maybe find something for us to eat— not too much, we have a long way to go. Then you two can rest. I'll keep watch." He moved away, saying over his shoulder, "Oh, and there's saddle sore salve in each travel pack. You both probably need a liberal application."

At least they didn't fall off, Cael thought. Neither one had ridden much. Almost five hundred kilometers. At least a tenday and a half to Restal Prime. If the horses stayed sound. If Readen didn't return and send a troop after them. If Darnela and Poulter stayed strong enough. If a saddle girth didn't break. If his luck held. He'd held onto luck for years. Please Adalta, he could hold on for a bit longer. He tapped the leather pouch, slung over his shoulder and tucked under his arm, where Readen's journals rested. Please

Adalta, his luck lasted until he could get them to Krager, and Krager could get them to Daryl.

He hadn't looked at them since the first time he found them, several years before. He didn't want to look at them now. Just carrying them so close to his body sickened him.

Two days later, Readen rode through the gates of his hold, tired, more tired than he should be. The struggle going on in his head escalated to battle. He went straight to his rooms, telling the guard to have Captain Paules report to him in an hour. First, get rid of his filthy trail clothes, then a hot bath, then hear the report from the captain, then to the cellars.

He needed to understand what was happening to him. He must find the power that was his alone, uncontaminated by the Itza Larrak. He had to know if that was possible. Readen flicked that last thought away. It had to be possible. If he went back to the beginning of his lessons with the Itza Larrak, he'd find a way to isolate his power. Partner—the Itza Larrak was supposed to be his partner, his resource. The blood spell that linked them was to protect him, not provide a path into his mind.

Someone heated the magma stones under the roof cistern the minute he rode in, so his bath was hot. He pulled off the boots cramping his feet. The boot maker in Restal Prime would be one of his first visits when he took the Prime back. Ill-fitting boots were unacceptable. He looked at his feet and froze. His toes were longer, his toenails dark, pointed, and too long. Was the arch of his sole higher? A lot higher?

The rest of his clothes flew as he ripped them away. His left arm, the arm he'd carved with the symbols he'd studied from childhood, was covered with glistening obsidian armor. The symbols were gone. Gone from his arm, from his chest, from his belly. Where they'd been was now hard, flexible armor. He touched his chest, tapped it, tapped it harder. He tried to pull it off and stopped. That only hurt.

His body slickened with sweat. Strength ran out of his muscles. He vomited into the stone sink, retching even when there was nothing left to retch, and his stomach muscles burned. Arms braced on the edge of the sink, he looked at the face in the small mirror and caught himself before he slumped to the floor. His face was normal. Readen closed his eyes and dropped his head, turned on the faucets to rinse the sink and his mouth. When his head came back up, his eyes went back to the face in the mirror, to yellow eyes. Pale, brownish yellow eyes.

Readen stared for a long time, unwilling to think. The small, niggling pressure squirmed in the back of his mind, and he snapped back to fight it. To force it away, but it slipped into the dark bubble that hid just out of his reach. The pressure retreated. He took a long, deep breath, then another, then another. Finally, he stepped into the hot bath. He was alone in his head. For now.

Bathed and dressed, Readen stepped into his study, where Captain Paules waited.

"Good afternoon, sir. It is good to have you back. I assume Cael found you?"

"Cael? Why was Cael looking for me? Did you send him?"

The captain's mouth opened, but no words came out. He sidled away from the graveled menace in Readen's voice. Readen moved around to sit at his desk, hands flat in front of him. "Did you?"

"No—no, sir. The guards on the gate when the three of them left said he had orders to meet you. I didn't even know he'd gone until I read the guard reports for the day. I assumed..." His words trailed away into silence.

Readen's voice was low, quiet, calm. "Have I ever left such orders?"

The captain cleared his throat. Twice. "No, sir. You haven't, but..."

"Are you unable to finish a sentence, Captain Paules? But what?" He didn't question why the captain was so terrified when he hadn't been before. Not like this, anyway.

"I didn't question Cael's orders, sir. I understood they came from you, and I would never question your orders. Sir."

Readen was silent for several minutes. He looked at the man, whose shaking hands crossed in front of his privates, whose legs trembled so Readen wasn't sure how he was still standing. It pleased him. Then the thought that he wasn't harvesting the captain's terror floated up. For just a moment Readen felt a fear of his own. Fear that he was no longer *able* to harvest it. He deliberately pulled in a long, long breath of the captain's fear and felt power sift through his body. When did he stop doing this? He sat back in his chair and watched the captain relax a fraction.

"Give me your report now, Captain." He held the terse menace out of his voice.

The captain began to talk—too fast. "The daily reports are on your desk, sir, if you need more information. We've received little word from the scouts you sent to Revka pass, and no word from the mercenaries. The pass is guarded so well the scouts haven't been able to get close. And finally, word from Restal Prime says it is light on troops. There have been so many urbat attacks, Guardian Daryl needs all the troops that can be spared to guard villages and holds near the Circle of Disorder in the north."

"Send three squads with akenguns to attack the guards around the pass as soon as they hear the block has been cleared and to escort the mercenaries here. You are dismissed, Captain." Readen smiled. The captain saluted and left. Readen smiled again. Restal Prime was nearly unguarded. Daryl might believe the Karda would warn him in time if Readen were to start moving troops that way, but he was certain he had the power now to hide those troops from flying spies. Especially if they marched at night.

He headed for the basement cells. How had he not noticed he wasn't drawing power from the fear of others? Why had he stopped the torture that gave him not only power but so much pleasure for so many years? Since childhood. Since before the Itza Larrak. Even before he got to the guardroom, he sensed it, what he had been missing. He felt the fear and terror soaked into the walls contort his face into a smile.

Until he reached the guard room nearest the cells and found Pol, too drunk to stand, and crying. He didn't need to wait till Pol finished slurring his wet, unintelligible words. He knew the prisoners were gone. His world turned red. Readen pulled his gloves off finger by finger, laid them on the table, and drew his belt knife. Pol knelt, clung to Readen's leg, and sobbed. Readen put a finger under his chin and looked into the eyes of the man who had served him since he was a child. Pol looked up at him with a worshipful smile. Readen drew the knife deep across his neck and fed on the power from Pol's fading life and talent. Fed on his own anger, his disappointment and twisted grief for his servant. He cupped his hands beneath Pol's gushing throat, caught as much blood as he could before the man fell, and drank. The dark place in the back of his mind screamed frustration.

Readen shuddered with the power streaming through him. Finally, he went to the filthy sink in Pol's small bathroom and cleaned the blood from his hands and face. He drew his gloves back on with care and climbed up to his study. He felt nothing. He'd killed Pol. Pol, who'd been with him since he was a small child. He felt nothing and he didn't wonder about it. A small voice screamed in the back of his mind. Tendrils reached for it, and it stilled.

At his desk, he found a pen and reached for his latest journal at the bottom of the bookshelf behind him. His hand skimmed across the books, and he swiveled around. These were the wrong books. His journals, his precious, private journals, were gone. He stood, slamming the chair against the shelves, and took the stairs two at a time to the captain's office.

"Send three men immediately to Restal Prime to capture Cael. I want him brought back to me untouched. They are to bring everything he has—his packs, his clothes—everything, as fast as they can travel. They are to bring him back. Now. I don't care if they kill six horses doing it."

CHAPTER SEVENTEEN

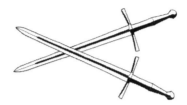

Finalizing maps for troop deployment and locations for planter camps absorbed Daryl. So many details. He loved it. Two troopers with drawing skills worked quietly behind him, copying. A small part of him listened to the sounds outside—the clash of sword against sword from the landing field where troops sparred, a whinny from the direction of the rope corral. And the scuff of a boot at the tent entrance.

"I'm afraid it's my fault, Daryl."

He glanced up from the map over the top of his glasses. Marta's hair looked as if she and Sidhari had been flying upside down in a gale.

She rubbed at the back of her neck. "Altan and I were talking—out loud—and didn't see Me'Neve."

Daryl laid his glasses down with meticulous care and leaned forward with his arms on the table as if he could transfer the weight on his shoulders to it. The two troopers slipped around them and left, and he watched them go. He never yelled at anyone, but right now, he wanted to—at them, at Marta, at himself. "I assume he's gone. How long?"

"Philipa told me he asked her for a Karda to take him back to his hold to attend to some business two days ago. She gave him an excuse as you asked, but I guess he didn't believe her. He's kilometers away by now, riding by night and keeping to the trees."

Daryl dropped his head. How had he been so stupid as to let Me'Neve sneak away? It was a detail he'd let slip. How many other details...? He didn't finish the thought.

"I checked with the horse handlers before I came here. He took three for himself and extras for the six troopers who were here with him. That's what's missing. The horse master thinks he bribed someone. He's pretty angry, so he'll find whoever it was. I'm so sorry, Daryl."

Tough, battle-hardened Marta looked like she wanted to cry. So did he. "It's more my fault than yours, Marta. I left him loose, hoping I could learn more about other Readen sympathizers. Somehow he slipped my watchers." His tone was even, his voice steady, controlled. "If you can find out from your eyes-in-the-sky how many troops he left there, it will help. Maybe we can stop them before they leave too. Even if he's called for them, his messenger won't reach them before the Karda can. And send someone for Captain Ethyn. I need to know how they let him slip."

"The man Ethyn had watching him is dead, Daryl." He heard the guilt strangling her voice. "They found him this morning."

The silence stretched until Daryl thought he would snap. Then, "I'll find troops to seize Me'Neve Hold. He forfeited it with murder and his clear intent of sedition."

Marta said softly, "Renewal," and added, not so softly, "Good."

He looked away from her so she couldn't see the self-doubt in his eyes. Renewal. Would there be renewal? If Krager came back with news that they'd already lost half the holders in the east, he wasn't sure they could win the fight for Restal. Not that and battle the Itza Larrak and its urbat, too. Readen's timing was impeccable. How long before he realized the weaknesses in the Prime's defenses?

"Sidhari and I will take enough troopers and go. Yours, if you'll tell me which wing to take. I can't take one of Altan's, not when this is a Restal problem." She stood for a minute as if to say sorry again, but he nodded, quirked up one side of his mouth in what he hoped she'd interpret as a smile, and she left.

He sank back into his chair, pulled his glasses from the top of his head to his nose and went back to his troop deployments before another messenger interrupted him. He couldn't afford to indulge in retrospective regret. Prime Guardian Hugh and Anuma's Guardian would leave today. He needed the finalized maps finished for them. Master Planter Andra was nearing the circle with her army of plants and planters. She was due here any day to start scouting the circumference of the circle with him, locating defensible sites for her planters. It was essential they be protected—more than protected. They were the bait to draw the urbat away from the villages and back to the circle. If it worked, he wouldn't be chasing urbat all over this part of Restal, and he could consolidate the allied troops.

And it would be the Itza Larrak's turn to have his urbat scattered kilometers apart trying to defend his circle. Now it would be Daryl and the planters choosing where to fight.

Daryl knew he needed to send more troops to Restal Prime. It was too light on defense, especially with both him and Krager gone and only Commander Kyle there. Too many of the Restal Guard were defending villages near the circle. The Prime was vulnerable. If the mercenaries got through the pass and through the troops he had there...

He needed to talk to Turin. Right now he was afraid his whole world turned on Turin—and that was an unintentional pun that was not the least bit funny. But then, glaciers didn't laugh, and glacier was what he needed to be right now, cold and deliberate.

An hour and a half later, after a long walk and talk with Turin, Daryl watched his troops finish packing to leave. Rachyl and her three Karda Patrol wings were already gone. Altan and Ballard headed toward Daryl's tent, both with faces like stones, like glowing magma stones. Hugh Me'Rahl stood at the tent entrance with Daryl, watching the tents go down and the packs go up on the pack-horses and wagons.

"I hope you know what you're doing, Daryl. He has several opportunities to betray you. He can veer off toward Readen's hold and either join him or take the akenguns from him. He could suborn the mercenaries and come back to attack the Prime himself, and I'll have to gather my troops and go with you to defend it. Or he can simply gather up the mercenaries and the guns and head to the north coast, wait for the ice to clear and sail off. He's been away from Akhara too long."

Daryl didn't say anything.

"If he does any of those things, we've lost. He's an enigma. We won't know until…"

Daryl wasn't sure he could trust the enigmatic Turin either. But he had little choice.

Every one looked up at a strange noise. Karda and riders scattered away from the landing meadow, more Karda formed a wide circle in the sky, and the whine of rotors sounded loud in the sudden quiet. The shuttle was back. Cedar was back.

Daryl rubbed a hand over his face to hide the grin he couldn't rub away and smoothed the hair he'd worried loose back into its leather tie. He couldn't look away from the noisy dot in the sky getting bigger and bigger. He glanced at Hugh, and realized the guardian was laughing at him, but he couldn't stop his feet from heading toward the field. "It will be good to have Galen back. We need him badly."

The big man laughed loud and clapped his hand on Daryl's shoulder. "Yes, and we need Cedar's strange talent right now. I suggest you introduce her to Turin. Here he comes, obviously eager to meet her too."

Daryl's steps stuttered, and he looked at Hugh. "You're laughing at me. She's just interesting, that's all, and Mireia tells me she's an intuitive systems thinker."

"Oh, well, then." His head cocked to one side. "What does that mean, exactly?"

Daryl ignored him, tried to control his grin, cool his face, and slow his walk. Tessa and Kishar landed in a cloud of dust and dried grass next to the two men, who coughed and glared at them both.

Hugh waved his hand in front of his face. "Kishar, you need to learn a new trick. I think you enjoy landing as close to people as you can so you can enjoy their sneezes."

~It's what I do. Old Karda don't like to learn new tricks,~ pathed the small, ancient black Karda.

Ignoring them, Tessa jumped down and ran toward the field. The heli-shuttle landed and the ramp extended, almost smashing Tessa's toes. Galen met her halfway down the ramp and whirled her round and around, his face buried in her shoulder.

Daryl didn't know how to interpret Cedar's reaction as she watched them. Was she jealous? He didn't like the way that made him feel. Then she found Daryl in the crowd, and he didn't know how to interpret that reaction either—his or hers. He wouldn't even try. Whatever it was he wouldn't think about it. His mind was getting crowded with all the things he didn't want to think about.

Turin caught up to them just as he and Hugh reached the ramp. "So this is the representative from the ship. Introduce me, Daryl. I have lots of questions for her, most of them from Rachyl, and no telling what she'll do to me if I don't get answers."

Cedar managed to get past Tessa and Galen, greeted Hugh, and made her way to Daryl's side carrying a large case. He took the case and almost dropped the heavy box. Cedar gasped. "Oh, be careful with that. It's the most precious thing I own." She smiled up at him and put her hand on his arm. It felt like the home he'd never had and didn't know he'd missed.

She didn't give Daryl a chance to introduce her. "Hello. I'm Cedar Evans, one of the trade ship's ambassadors. You must be Guardian Turin. I'd heard what a big man you are, and no one exaggerated." She reached to grasp Turin's arm in greeting, and Daryl managed to avoid getting conked by her staff.

Maybe he should just let her hit him on the head and put an end to this crazy need to be next to her, to protect her.

She looked around. "It looks like someone is packing to leave. A lot of someones. What's happening?"

"Guardian Turin was leaving when we heard you coming in," said Hugh. "It looks like you'll have to hurry to answer his questions."

She tightened her hand on Daryl's arm, which thawed his ice a little, and said, "And I have lots of questions for him, too, about Akhara Quadrant. If you'll excuse us, we'll have a nice ask and answer session, and would you have someone put my box in my tent? Carefully?"

She looked up at Turin. "After, if you'd like, I'll show you the heli-shuttle. Who's Rachyl?" And the two of them walked toward the cook's tent. "I brought some seedlings I'd like you to try, Guardian Turin." She waved a small, fragrant bag. "Because from the early scans we made, there are some areas in your quadrant where I believe this can be grown. And, if I'm to live on this planet, I'll need coffee in my future. "

Daryl watched her limp away, gesturing with her hands and too often with her staff. A trooper dodged out of her way laughing. He felt as if part of him had just reattached. He had no idea how to handle that. He took her precious box to her tent himself, and caught up with Galen and Tessa, wondering if there was any way to pry them apart and get a report from Galen. Probably not. He didn't know how to handle that feeling either. He'd go back to his maps. He knew how to handle them.

He hoped he also knew how to handle Turin better than he'd handled Me'Neve.

Readen paced the compound outside his keep, cape fastened around him so that little showed except his head. In the back of which a battle was raging unnoticed but for a slight tingle at the base of his skull.

Piles of travel gear, tents, bedrolls, bags and boxes of supplies for horses and people, cooking pots, grates—all the necessities for an army on the move—were slowly being loaded in wagons and on pack horses. He was tired of waiting for his mercenaries to clear the pass; he'd divert them to the Prime when they broke through. He could take the city on his own. The mercenaries would secure the rest of the quadrant.

He concentrated on holding a shield over the organized confusion. It must be invisible from the Karda constantly wheeling in the sky over Me'Vere Hold. Readen was ready to move on Restal Prime. And the Itza Larrak was unhappy. Though unhappy was not the right word. Unhappy was a human emotion, and what Readen felt from the Itza Larrak was not a human emotion. It was worse.

The insistent, impatient, imperative pull toward the circle to the north fought with the focus Readen needed to hold the veil over his troops. His jaw ached from clenching his teeth. His stiff shoulders shot pains up the back of his skull, trying to cleave it in half. The Itza Larrak was hundreds of kilometers away, guarding his circle from the army of planters preparing to surround it. How could it affect him so strongly, as if it were here, in his hold, inside his head?

He clenched his hands, and one long nail pierced the finger of his reinforced glove, stabbed through the leather and into his palm. The pain drove the pull from the Larrak back. Readen let out a long, relieved breath and rolled his shoulders. It was gone. He ignored that small space, that small bubble and its penetrating tendrils in the back of his mind. His head was whole again. He needed his full concentration on this expedition. He held the shield, certain he was becoming more powerful than the Itza Larrak, his father. It taught him well. Now it was his time.

He thought the laughter in his head was his own.

"Captain Paules," he called. The captain came so fast it was as though he transported himself across the compound.

"Sir, we are about an hour and a half from being loaded and ready to move. All I need is the location of the akengun cases and we can get them loaded. I'll separate them into three wagons, as you sug—as you ordered, so if one batch catches fire we won't lose all of them. You said that happened to the first weapons."

"Send a small patrol out now, no more than an ordinary scouting patrol. I know you have at least one trooper who can farsee. He can watch for their signals. I can hold the invisibility shield over us, but it will do no good if we run into one of Daryl's patrols."

"Yes, sir. He's not able to far-see for any great distance, but it will be enough, I think."

"If they get too far ahead of us, send a messenger dressed as a hunter to slow them down. One small patrol or a single rider won't raise alarms. Arm four of your best troopers with akenguns. If Daryl's spies get too close, they must kill them all. None must escape to warn Daryl or Commander Kyle that we are coming."

Captain Paules swallowed. "Yes, sir."

"You are to choose enough troopers to remain here so it appears we haven't left, including one in your uniform and one in a cloak like mine. They'll need to move around the courtyard constantly so they seem more than they are. We must fool the flying watchers for as long as possible. They won't be able to see my troops on the march, but they will know I've left if they see too few troopers here. Send me some stout troopers. I'll lead them to the akenguns. Have the wagons you want them loaded on pull up as close as possible to the side door." He clapped Captain Paules on the shoulder. "We're taking our own back, Captain. I hold no doubt."

Less than an hour later, Readen's army was on the move. Four hundred kilometers, one hundred troopers, each with three horses, four wagons with two team changes each, and mud on a road that was more trail than road. If they traveled into the night, left early each morning and rode hard, in less than two tendays, they would be at the gates of Restal Prime.

Cael held up a hand. Darnela and Poulter reined their horses in so sharply they took two steps back. The pack horse's ears swiveled forward and it started sidling. Cael pulled it up close enough to put his hand over the small horse's nose, and it calmed.

"Listen," he whispered.

Darnela made a soft, despairing mewling sound, and Poulter reached for her arm.

The noise of many horses' hooves moving through the darkness on the forest road came from ahead of them just above the arroyo where they stopped—jingling bridles, creaking saddles, an occasional cough or soft voice.

Cael kept his voice low. "That's too many to be just a patrol sent after us." Why couldn't he see anything? After a minute, he added, "Those sounds are too close, and there are too many of them for us not to be able to see them, even through this brush. A single patrol would have already passed us by, but they are still coming."

"Wait," whispered Darnela, and she slid from her saddle, her movements slow, deliberate, and silent. She squatted down and peered through the underbrush. Not for long. She stood and motioned the other two back down into the arroyo they'd just climbed out of.

The three of them pulled up behind a thick cluster of berry bushes beginning to show a few buds. "I could see their legs. The horses, I mean." Her voice shook, and her eyes gleamed white in the darkness. "Only from the knees and hocks down. Above that—nothing. There was nothing there even though I could hear them—riders I mean. How is that possible? I know there are strong Air talents who can put a don't-look-here spell on something as big as an army. But this wasn't like that. There was just nothing above the lower legs."

Cael, who'd used that kind of spell several times already on their six-day journey toward Restal Prime, said, "The only person, or rather thing, I've ever heard of that could do an invisibility shield over an army is the Itza Larrak."

Darnela's hands flew to her horrified face. Poulter's face was so pale it looked like a tiny moon low in the darkness.

"We've seen no signs of urbat, and they usually surround it, or are close by. We'd have smelled them, or seen tracks." Cael kept his tone casual, his words thoughtful. He didn't need the other two to panic. He dismounted, climbed up the side of the gully, and burrowed under a bush to listen. It was a full and tense thirty minutes before he climbed back down. "I don't know how many passed before we heard them, but a hundred and thirteen rode by while I counted. It's not just a few patrols. It's an army, and it's headed for Restal Prime. It can only be—"

"Readen." Poulter's words hissed out of his mouth.

"Headed for Restal Prime?" Darnela's words tilted up at the

end, but she wasn't asking a question. She knew. They all three knew.

Cael opened the packs behind his saddle. "We have to split up. It sounded like they were stopping to camp. I can get around them and travel the road again. It should take about a day and a half of straight hard riding for me to get to the Prime. But they won't be far behind me."

"I'm not going to the Prime. I'm not going to get caught by Readen again." Darnela's voice got shriller and louder until Poulter put his arm around her and pressed a finger against her mouth.

"No, we're not going there. I don't know where we'll go, but it won't be there."

Cael said, "I'll take as little of the foodstuff as I can get by with. You two head for Ardencroft. Find whoever is in charge there and tell them what we've seen. Wait until you're sure Readen's back trail is clear, then cross the road and head east and a bit north. I'll give you my map. If you ride as hard as the horses can bear, it should take you a little more than five days. You know how to pace them by now." He hoped.

He pulled the map out of his inside pocket and unfolded it on Poulter's saddle. "We're at the western edge of the forest that surrounds the Prime, so much of the time you'll be crossing unreclaimed barrens. When you're a day and a half away from the road, I don't think you'll need to worry about being seen. And if you get lucky enough to sight a Karda, even one without a rider, do your best to flag him down and tell him, or her, what we saw. They'll understand you, and relay the message."

He pushed his warm hat off his head and scrubbed at his scalp. "I'm counting on either Krager or Daryl being in the Prime. But they might not be, so you have to get word to them."

Darnela's hands shook as she sorted supplies and Poulter chewed at his lip until it bled, but they both looked as determined as they were scared. "We'll get there," Darnela said at the same time Poulter said, "We'll get the message to someone, and fast."

Most of Cael's saddlebags he loaded with grain for his horse. He'd be riding hard and not stopping often, but their need to travel constantly on the watch and dodging Readen's patrol meant they'd moved slow and with care. His horse was in good shape. Slow and with care was no longer an option.

He took off with a final wave and "Good luck" to the other two, riding through the woods to avoid Readen's scouts until he got to the last of the barrens before Restal Prime where he could move faster. With luck, a horse that stayed sound, and few stops, the hundred-and-twenty-kilometer ride to the Prime would take a day and a half. He settled in for a hard ride, wary and fighting fear.

CHAPTER EIGHTEEN

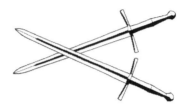

Cedar sat on a rock near the small creek in the clearing where she, Master Planter Andra, and Daryl landed after a long flight from Altan's now-deserted camp. Daryl worked at an efficient camp desk on his stack of papers. Every time he pulled one off the top, another probably materialized at the bottom. She rubbed first one leg, then the other, moving her Cue from hand to hand. Director of Engineering and Maintenance Clare's voice was scratchy with static.

"The first warehouse pod is now in Ardencroft. Glenn and Assam are working with the carpenters and metal workers to make it habitable. We're moving the severed living pod as soon as they get a foundation pad for it finished. Glenn tells me that will be tomorrow."

"This has to be a challenging job, Clare. Congratulations. I talked to Glenn yesterday, and he seems happy with the progress."

"Which means he was only a little grumpy."

Cedar laughed, switching the Cue to the other hand to rub the other thigh. Her first flight alone on a Karda had been terrifying, if exhilarating, and the result was aching legs and rear. Her neck ached like her head had tried to snap off several times. She shifted on the hard rock. Andra tapped her on the shoulder, motioned her to stand, and slipped a folded blanket under her. Cedar tapped a thank you on her heart.

"I know you think you should either be up here or in Arden-croft, but, Cedar, your visits to holders are essential. They have to be made, and going now, so we can tell people at least a little of what opportunities there are on planet, will help adjust them to the urgency of our situation."

Cedar looked at Clare's grainy face on her Cue. "Urgency. Just how much more urgent is it? I just left." She looked over at Daryl, whose maps were now spread out on the ground in front of him held down by rocks, and bit her lip. This war must be won and must be won soon.

"Systems are failing even faster, either completely or intermittently, and there is no pattern to it, so we can't predict what might fail next."

"Will the captain come down with the first group? To look things over?"

"I haven't been able to talk to her about it." The answer was terse, and Cedar knew someone was listening to their conversation.

"She doesn't have to stay. But it would do a lot to reassure people on the ship if she came down and reported back on all the effort being put in to make the transition as smooth as possible for every one."

"Yes, it would," was Clare's short reply.

Cedar knew she'd be getting a private message from Clare, and probably Sharon, too.

The conversation went on for another fifteen or twenty minutes, getting more technical. Cedar noticed that as it did, Daryl's head came up, his glasses slid down his nose, and he listened closely. He seemed to drink in new information like dry soil drank in rain.

Finally, Clare asked, "How safe is it down there? Rumors are rampant about the troubles, about the strange monsters and the alien that controls them. Some people are eager to help fight—they know we have to settle here. And of course deniers are making the most of the fears."

Cedar absorbed Clare's words. "So all is normal. Things

change, and nothing changes." She laughed, then she asked the question she didn't want to ask. "Clare, have you seen my mother?" She looked at the silent Cue, hoping she'd lost the connection and the silence wasn't because there was something wrong.

"Your mother is fine, Cedar, working in the gro-pods, not talking much. She seems calm. Although Amalie says she won't talk about having to leave the ship. Watches her endless vids of Old Earth and ignores anything associated with leaving, even when your people are packing up things around her."

Cedar squeezed her eyes tight as if that would help her not hear Clare's words. Amalie was the woman she'd asked to take care of her mother.

"I'm sorry, Cedar."

"Maybe I should come back."

"No, I asked Amalie if that would help. It wouldn't, and it might make things worse. You are needed where you are, Cedar. She's good. Amalie says she's had no anxiety attack, and I'm watching. I know it doesn't help to hear don't worry, but don't worry too much." And they signed off.

Cedar sat for a long time on her rock, seeing nothing. Then she sniffed, confused at what she was smelling before she realized it was a real smell, not a talent smell. It was comforting and at the same time, triggered a faint atavistic fear. Daryl and Andra squatted near a small fire of downed and dry wood. It was wood smoke. Another new smell. New smells that were actual smell smells, not emotion smells. How was she able to keep them straight in her head?

They were camped in a small clearing with barely enough room for the Karda to land. The greening grass was ankle-high, cotton-wood and abelee trees along the stream bore glistening new green leaves that chattered in the slight breeze. The space, surrounded by huge ancient trees, was comforting. Altan's camp had been on the edge of the barrens, and their wide, endless spaces made her uneasy. She'd heard stories from advance agents sent to other planets about agoraphobia that even experienced agents dealt with after a long trip on board the spaceship where the only view outside was a digital image on a large screen. Sometimes it caught her unaware, and she felt as if she was falling. Just one of the myriad problems the new settlers would face.

Wandering over to where Master Planter Andra and Daryl knelt, she put her hand on Daryl's shoulder and felt it tense, then relax. She peered over their shoulders at the map they studied. "What's the circumference of the Circle of Disorder? How far apart are these camps?"

After a slight hesitation, Daryl said, "Three hundred fourteen kilometers at the edge, with a Planter Corp site and someone's troops every forty or so kilometers."

No one said anything for a time. Cedar moved to sit beside Daryl so the map was between the three of them. "What is it you intend to accomplish with this deployment?" She ran a finger lightly around the circle, curious about what he would say. Something about it bothered her.

Daryl leaned away and turned his head to look at her, then at Andra. His words slow and clipped, he said, "We're keeping the Itza Larrak's forces, its urbat, scattered, forcing it to divide its attention and spread its control over the urbat around the entire circle. That's its power source. It has to defend against the new plantings. New saplings and sprouting seeds weaken it. Every attack they make, we kill more urbat. We're hoping if he has to raise—or create—more urbat, it will take power he could use to fight us. There are anywhere from one to three hundred troopers and Karda patrollers at every encampment. They are close enough to reinforce each other quickly when needed."

"If no one can enter the circle, what advance notice can you have of an attack?"

"Cedar…" Daryl drew out her name with an irritated why-are-you-asking-this-is-not-your-problem drawl.

She looked at him, eyes wide, and just as patiently waited for his answer. Her certainty that there was something wrong with his plan grew.

"I thought you knew Galen can walk in the circles, can sense urbat inside from a distance…"

"But—"

"And Tessa and Kishar can fly over it. Tessa also has a sense of when they are moving. They can fly sixty to seventy kilometers a day, less if they take Galen with them. Every five days, they make a round of the entire circle. The Itza Larrak can't sense them, so unless he sees them he doesn't know where they are. Or so we hope. The way the urbat are built, their armor makes it difficult for them to look up, so they don't."

"So, your strategy is one of attrition. You plan to wear his forces down with a siege." Her certainty was almost full grown now. How was she going to tell him this wouldn't work? And what plan could she offer in its place? She had no solution, nothing except a certainty that this was wrong, and a lack of knowledge about warfare and fighting and the Itza Larrak itself.

"And keep them separated, so they have to attack in smaller numbers, and so the team we take to cut the source of the Line of Devastation running south is safe. Although Altan and a team of his Earth talents cut a smaller line on their way from Toldar, and the Itza Larrak didn't notice until later, nor did it notice when Altan, Merenya—Ballard's mother—Marta, and Galen cut this one." He laid a finger on the line to the south. "We believe it will take time for it to detect these efforts if they are far enough from the edge of the circle. When it does, it has to work fast and quick to repair the damage, or create a new army of bots, as Galen calls them. It can't get to the damage in time to catch whoever is cutting it. All that takes more of its energy and attention, wearing it down more."

"Do you have a sense of how many urbat he has left? Or how many more he might be able to—I think the word Galen used was raise?"

"That's where he and Tessa have been for the past tenday, doing recon over the circle."

Andra was watching their faces, her head moving back and forth with fixed concentration. Then her gaze stopped, and Cedar looked down. The hands in her lap were twisting together, first one way then the other. She didn't want to say what she was thinking.

Cedar looked at the map for a long time, chewing on her lip. Absently, she said, "That strategy won't work," then wished with all she had that she hadn't. She looked at Daryl, sneezed and bolstered her filters.

His irritation seasoned with what-does-she-know didn't smell good at all. And she didn't have an answer. Not yet. Oh, dear. Where was a passing asteroid she could leap to and disappear forever?

It was late. The noises from the troops settling for their short night of rest irritated Readen. He was exhausted from holding the invisibility shield over them for days. Now that it was dark, he could let go of it, but he could do nothing about the noise. He'd given orders to Captain Paules to keep them quiet, and part of him knew they were doing the best they could, but he was still furious. He took a step toward the captain to berate him, then thought better of it and walked deeper into the forest.

They'd marched double-time across the barrens between the forests and were now just inside the great forest around the Prime. He pushed through the thick undergrowth until he reached a small clearing where he was out of sight from his troops. He leaned against a tree and took off his gloves. The claw-like nails weren't growing. His hands moved over his face. Without a mirror, he couldn't be certain, but it didn't feel the same. His forehead had lines, deep lines that felt like they created sections. He dropped his cloak to the ground and stretched out his left arm. The armor spreading from the scars he'd carved into his skin bulged the sleeve of his jacket. He took it off and stared at the ripped sleeve and front of his linen shirt. His right arm was still unchanged, but the armor completely covered his left arm and his chest now.

He was elated, heart pounding. He'd become more his father—the Larrak's son. He had its power now. His eyes closed, he tilted his face to the sky, wanting to roar. He flared his nostrils and sucked in the night air. Now, more than ever, he must be subtle about how he used his power. No one must see how much he had. The mercenaries from Akhara would arrive soon after he took the Prime. They must never suspect. No one must see what he was becoming. His immense power must seem to others as his natural talent that finally developed. He would never again be able to let go of the illusion on his face unless he was alone. He ached with the need to see it. To actually see what he was becoming.

His legs folded, almost collapsed under him, and he sank to the ground, wrapping his black cloak around him. Tension in his shoulders loosened, and he leaned back against the tree. Eyes closed, he forced his body to relax, his mind to calm. He could not fall into overconfidence. The bark of the tree was rough through his shirt. The thought of wings floated into his head. Would he—

He heard the high metallic ring of the Itza Larrak's wings, and an enormous blackness blocked out the stars above him. It was here. He shivered and stood. Its black stillness filled the clearing. There were no more rustlings in the undergrowth, no more insect song, only the faint ringing of the Itza Larrak's constantly moving metal wings.

"Welcome, Father. I did not—"

"Do not call me father. I did not father you. I molded you from the soft, pliable cells I found in your mother's womb. I molded you, and you are my creature, not my son."

"But—" A maelstrom of confused emotions inside wouldn't let him form words. A slow thought rose out of the storm. Then who was he? Where did all his new power come from? A vague memory of Pol, of all the rituals Pol assisted him with, all the victims Pol found for him floated into his head. His hands were cupped in front of him. He looked down and felt the hot blood spurting into them from Pol's throat. Sourness surged up his throat, and he swallowed again and again.

"—must move north and draw him from the circle."

The Itza Larrak's words finally broke through Readen's dazed shock. "Go north? Fight who?"

"Your brother is surrounding my circle with his men, his planters, and his allies. I am trapped. You must draw them away."

Readen swallowed. The Itza Larrak's words worked through his scrambled thoughts. He cleared his throat. He must not sound tentative, unsure, or frightened. "That is what I am doing here. I will take control of the Prime within a few days, and Daryl will have to react. He will have to divert forces from the circle. There are several holders who have promised their troops to me when I have control of the city and am ready to take over the rest of the quadrant."

Pain bored into his head. The Itza Larrak searched his mind, and Readen was helpless to prevent it. He dropped to his knees. The heels of his palms pressed his temples as if to prevent his head from cleaving in two. At the same time, he felt something expand inside his brain, sending tendrils all through it. If it took control, his mind would be *his* mind no longer.

Vaguely he heard the Itza Larrak's wings spread and the musical thunder of its flight fill the clearing. It left.

Readen lay on the damp ground for a long time, battle waging inside his head, realizations budding and growing from forgotten lessons, from misplaced trust in the one being he'd thought of as his real family—not his puling, indulgent father, not his brother with his Karda, his sword, and his nose in a book

He rolled up to sitting and began tearing at the growing armor on his left arm, tore until it bled around its edges, but it didn't come loose. It was part of him. The Itza Larrak was part of him. The power he'd thought was his, wasn't. He hadn't used a power source of his own since he'd killed Pol.

He closed his eyes and started breathing long, deep, even breaths, in through his nose and out through his mouth like his hated tutor, Malyk, had taught him and Daryl when they were young. Daryl, the hated Daryl *was* his brother. They shared a father. Jealousy and rage flooded his body. Its familiarity calmed him. His turmoil subsided. The struggle in his head went on.

The strange tentacles reached and grasped for control, trying to take over. He could feel them working like worms in his brain and fought back, searing them with anger born of fear for his life, for his survival. He shuddered and swallowed, queasy and dizzy. How could he get rid of this alien presence? Was it even real?

Then he remembered. He remembered when he first materialized the Itza Larrak. He remembered the human body the alien took over to be fully in this world. The body Readen prepared for him. He remembered the terrifying journey to the Circle of Disorder and the strange fiery chasm into which the deteriorating human body containing the Larrak had descended. He remembered the Larrak's return, the human body sloughed away, the enormous black-winged figure restored.

Was it possible it knew its new form would not last? Was it possible the Itza Larrak was preparing him, Readen, to be its host body on Adalta?

He focused on the sounds the creature made as it flew in and out of the clearing. He could remember little about its leaving, but he could almost hear again the slight unevenness of its wings in landing. Perhaps the damage it suffered in the battle last fall was not fully repaired. Readen had dismissed the reports that its wing was almost severed from its body, so certain was he that the Larrak was indestructible.

Perhaps it wasn't. Perhaps that was why it had created—created, not fathered—Readen. He wouldn't think about that particular pain, that particular possibility. He couldn't.

He paced the small clearing, now lit by the dim light of the second moon, for hours. When dawn began to light the surrounding wood, he walked slowly back to his troops. His horse was fed, saddled, and ready. The need to capture the Prime was more urgent than before. Readen needed power, power of his own—not borrowed from the Larrak—and the city was full of power sources he could harvest. He would not let the Itza Larrak take him over, become him, destroy him. That was unthinkable. He would use it to keep Daryl occupied until Readen consolidated his power. He would find a way to force it to work with him, as his ally. He would not disappear into the Itza Larrak, never to be himself again. He would not allow it to conquer him.

Cael rode through the gates of Restal Prime in the last pale light of a long, hard day. His horse was lathered, his hands on the reins shook, his thighs burned. His head reeled when the guard said Krager was gone. Neither of the guards knew where he'd gone or when he'd be back. Commander Kyle, they said, was making his rounds of the city and could be anywhere.

"I need to find him. Readen and his troops armed with the akenguns are not far behind me. I have to get word to him now."

Both gate guards stared at him, faces slack as if they didn't know whether to be frightened or to dismiss this man in sweaty leathers, who'd pushed his horse too hard, as crazy or an alarmist.

He clenched his jaw tight in his impatience and snarled. "Don't waste time trying to decide if I'm crazy or delusional. Find Commander Kyle and send him to Kurtan's stable. I need to take care of my horse before he falls dead right here in the middle of the gates." He dismounted and led the valiant little horse up the hill to the closest stable he could afford. It took most of an hour for him to walk it, brush it, water it a bit at a time, so it didn't founder. When he got it settled in a stall, he picked up his packs, took the stable master's recommendation of a tavern, and left word with him to tell the commander where he went when he arrived. He hadn't eaten in twenty-four hours, hadn't slept in thirty-six.

He was halfway through his second bowl of stew when a tall, slender boy slipped into the chair opposite him. "How did you find me so fast, Becca?"

"Bek. Why can't you and Krager remember to call me Bek? What are you doing here, Cael? Did Readen send you on another errand?" One of his errands had been as driver of a closed wagon carrying then twelve-year-old Becca and two smaller children to Readen. Cael had found Tessa Me'Cowyn in time to warn her, the children were rescued, and Cael was given a convincing wound and sent back to Readen. He'd served as Krager's spy in Readen's mercenary troops for years. He'd been back to the Prime several times since, and each time Becca managed to find him in a matter of hours.

"Maybe because you no longer look much like a Bek. It's time for you to get off the streets, *Bek.* Where's Krager? When will he be back?" Becca was the surest way to find Krager fast.

"Daryl sent him and some girls to the east to sound out the smaller holders there and talk to Me'Kahn about sending troops to the Circle of Disorder. They're planning a siege of the Itza Larrak to finally get rid of it."

Cael's spoon stopped midair. He set it down, rubbed the back of his neck. His head dropped, then he looked up. "A siege. Oh, no." His shoulders dropped, and he slumped down in his chair. He was so tired, so tired of it all. He caught himself before he fell off.

Becca's eyes widened and her face paled. "Something's wrong. What is it Cael? What's happened?"

Cael looked away from her, took three deep breaths, and said, his voice low and quiet, "Readen will be here in no more than three days, maybe less."

Becca curled into her chair, her body shaking with terror. "I gotta hide. I gotta hide right now. I won't be caught again." Her voice quivered, and she could hardly get the words out.

The big man reached across the table and took both her hands in his to stop the trembling. This too-thin girl was one of the bravest, toughest people he knew, and her hands were ice cold. "Daryl left enough troops here to defend the Prime. Commander Kyle is a smart man. His troops have shields to protect them from the akenguns—"

The girl didn't let him finish. "I don't have a shield, and neither does anyone I know. Only the troops. Do you think Readen will let troops with shields stop him? Do you think Readen is so honorable he'll only kill troops?" She pulled her hands back and tried to stand.

"Sit down, Becca." Her eyes were wide, her head, her whole body twisting back and forth as if she could find a place to hide in the small smoky room. She was ready to run. "I need your help. I stole something from Readen that he wants back. I have to stay and do what I can to help Commander Kyle. But if Readen sees me, I'm dead. I need you to find Krager or Daryl and give these to whoever you find first."

Her head shook back and forth. "What are they? They must be

important. And how do I find them? Where would I go?" She wrapped her arms around her. "I don't have a horse, and if I did, the first person I saw would steal it. I don't have a sword, and if I did, I wouldn't know how to use it. I don't have—"

"They are Readen's personal journals, and they must be taken to Daryl."

Both Becca's hands covered her mouth, and her eyes got even bigger.

"They are proof even Daryl can't deny that Readen is in league with the Itza Larrak." He returned her wide-eyed stare, hoping his eyes were full of confidence when inside he was as terrified as she was. "I'll tell you how to get to Ardencroft. It's a long walk, but Becca, no one will suspect a kid like you of carrying anything important. I'll outfit you with a pack and everything you'll need. If you have anything you want to take with you, get it and meet me at Kurtan's stable in fifteen minutes. You are the only person I can trust. No one can see these journals but Daryl. No one can know the true story of how horrible Readen is, or Daryl, as his brother, will never be allowed to rule Restal, and Restal needs Daryl."

He took her hand again. "I need to stay here and fight. I've waited for this day for years. I'm probably the first person Readen will kill when he gets here, but I'm good at hiding." He squeezed it hard. "Don't you dare cry for me, Becca. You're one of the strongest, most trustworthy people I've ever known. You won't fail."

He started and scooted his chair back into the shadow of a post.

"What's the matter? What just happened?"

"One of Readen's men just went by. Probably one of the ones sent to find me." He reached for his belt purse and handed it to her. "Go out the back. Get to the stables. Take a pack and what you need for the road. Buy what else you need and don't buy it all from one place." He stood and slipped the slim bag with the journals over her head, leaned down and kissed the top of her head. "If I had a daughter, I'd want her to be you." He pulled the knife from his boot and left.

Becca didn't hesitate. She was already gone.

CHAPTER NINETEEN

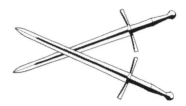

"Oh, good, Sharon." Cedar was sitting on another rock in another place by another little stream. Her tired shoulders straightened. "A hundred and fifty people? All comfortable with the idea of talent and most able to fight? That's galaxy great. It's finally starting."

Sharon's voice on Cedar's Cue was scratchy. "How are your meetings with the various leaders going? What do they say about letting our people settle in their jurisdictions?"

"We're at Holder Me'Cowyn's camp now and headed for Holder Me'Fiere's tomorrow."

Cedar stood and arched her back, bending side to side, hearing little pops. "The Karda say the living pod has landed, and Assam is satisfied with the foundation they built for it. Give Clare my congratulations. Will the captain be coming down with the next settlers? That would reassure the doubters on the ship—"

Sharon's words were terse and clipped. "She has no plans for that."

That meant she wasn't coming down the time after that, either. Cedar suspected Captain Kendra Pathal was one of the doubters —more than suspected, as every time she got near her Cedar smelled doubt, despair, and fear. Maybe she shouldn't judge the captain. Yes, she smelled her doubt, but what was the doubt about? How difficult it must be to have to leave the ship you have been on since you were born, to make it all the way to captain, and then have to order it taken apart, transported and scattered all over an alien continent, give the final abandon ship order and destroy what's left.

"Cedar." Sharon's words were in a pay-attention-you're-not-going-to-like-this tone. "The scanners are still working intermittently, and the last scan showed two of those lines, the ones you call Lines of Devastation, are within meters of touching."

"Wait, I need to get Daryl." Stiff from riding, she ran as best she could to the cook's tent where Daryl was talking to Me'Cowyn. "Daryl, you need to hear this. Tell me again, Sharon, so Daryl can hear." She squeezed between the two men at the table and sat. "This is Sharon Chobra, Director of Security on the ship. You both need to hear what she has to say. Go ahead, Sharon."

"Greetings from the sky, gentlemen. I look forward to meeting you. The ship's scanners are working intermittently, but today they showed clearly that the large Line of Devastation, as you call it, extending from the southernmost edge of your circle, is within meters of meeting another coming from a smaller circle to the south and west. It's in the middle of a barren area. The monitors detected a faint signal coming from that point. The alien is trying to send a message out. We scrambled the signal and blocked it, but we estimate that within a week—sorry—within seven days the lines will meet. We'll continue to block it and hope our sensors don't fail, but you need to prevent those lines from connecting."

Cedar looked back and forth between the men. Both Daryl's and Me'Cowyn's faces paled. Daryl's white fingers gripped the edge of the table. He looked to her as if for help, desolation and panic in his eyes, then they disappeared.

"Thank you, Sharon," he said with his usual calm. "We look forward to meeting you also. We will do our best to take care of this problem on the planet. As soon as you sense the signal getting stronger contact Cedar, if you would, please." The two men left the table. Me'Cowyn ran for the trooper's fire, and Daryl headed for the mews tent. His calm frightened Cedar far more than his look of panic.

Within minutes Cedar watched Philipa and Cystra lope up the landing field and take to the air, and she took to her feet to run—well, hobble quickly—to the mews. She'd have to talk hard and fast, but she wasn't going to be left behind. Not when the flaw in Daryl's strategy was flaring. She was beginning to figure out what to tell him, if she dared. If she could convince him—if she could convince herself—she knew enough to be right.

By evening of the next day, Daryl, Cedar, Tessa, Galen, and Connor Me'Cowyn were in the middle of a barrens midway between Altan's old camp and Readen's hold. Cedar unstrapped, slid out of Illyria's saddle to the Karda's extended knee and jumped to the ground. She wrapped a hand in Illyria's mane and hung on for a minute till her legs stopped quivering. "Thank you. Your flight is so smooth I hardly notice the ups and downs and side-to-sides anymore. And I didn't once feel sick."

She stroked the silver-gray shoulder. Illyria bent her head with its bright blue crest to be scratched. "This is only my second flight. Maybe by the fourth or fifth, I'll start feeling at home on your back. Now I have to learn to get your saddle rigging off without getting a hernia and tangling the straps so bad they are one big knot." She jumped to reach her packs, came down on her nonworking galaxy-damned leg, and landed flat on her back with the packs on top of her, looking up at an amused face. "Well, now I know what jokes smell like when they're on the other person. You're laughing at me, Daryl. You're laughing, and here I am, helpless on the ground beneath your feet." Those wrinkles at the corners of his eyes weren't from worry for a change.

He knelt down. "Thank you for bringing a bit of gaiety into my life today, Cedar. Would you like some help?"

"Yes, please. I'm sure your brain isn't accustomed to dealing with gaiety, and I don't want the top of your head to pop off."

He untangled her staff from the packs on top of her and set it down out of her reach.

"Hey, I need that."

"I'll give it back when I'm out of range." He motioned at Peele, the Karda patroller who'd come with them. "Take her packs to where Holder Me'Cowyn started setting up the tent and help him."

"My box! My box!" Cedar scrambled out from under the packs and dug through them, frantic.

"Here it is." Daryl pulled it out and rattled it. "Sounds like it's—"

"Oh, purple nebula, be careful. Let me have it."

He stood, reached down a hand and pulled her to her feet. She grabbed the box, sat awkwardly back down and unbuckled the straps to look inside. "Grateful galaxies. It's all right." She hugged the box to her chest, rested her head on it, and fought tears. After a moment, she looked up and said, "It's all I have left of what my life used to be."

She sat holding it for a long time, then Daryl took the box from her. "If it's what I think it is, it can be a connection to life here, too. One of them, anyway." Holding out his other hand, he pulled her up, picked up her staff and handed it to her, his eyes never leaving hers.

Thunder sounded above them. He grabbed her and pressed her face to his chest. "Clamp your eyes shut and hold your breath for a minute." Kishar and Tessa landed right next to them in a flurry of flying dust and debris.

When they could talk without inhaling dust, Daryl said, "You land closer to me every time. Next time I'll lie down, and you can land on top of me since that seems to be your goal, Kishar. Welcome, Tessa. Your father will be glad to see you. Where's—? Oh, there he is."

The shining golden Ket folded his wings and loped through the dust toward them, Galen on his back.

"How did you know to come here?" Daryl and Cedar asked in unison.

Tessa answered, "The KCN gets more efficient every day."

"The what?" Daryl looked at Galen.

"It's what she's decided to call our Karda messengers. The Karda Communication Network. She and Ket both practice saying,

'Alert the KCN. Alert the KCN,' till Kishar and I are ready to gag them."

"Me too," added Tessa's father, a broad man with hair as silver as Tessa's.

Galen scanned the intermittent black line that snaked across the barren countryside. "How did we miss this?"

"Let's help get the tent up. It's drizzling again. We should have more help by early tomorrow evening if the—what did you call it, the KCN?—has been efficient." Daryl slapped a hand over his mouth, which didn't stop a snort of laughter. Cedar knew he didn't realize he still had an arm around her, and she certainly wasn't going to remind him.

She inhaled another smell she'd not felt from Daryl before. The joy that came with loved companions. She ignored the ache from missing hers—and her mother. She couldn't think about her mother now.

Then she looked around. At barren ground. Kilometers of barren ground. Nothing but distance, empty distance as far as she could see. Her head spun. Daryl's arm tightened. His other arm grabbed her. The voices around her went distant and echoed, then —nothing.

As they flew toward Restal Prime, Krager saw ChiChi lean forward to talk to Mia, her Karda, then look up. Four Karda swooped from the clouds and circled them. Both she and Dalys signaled for Krager and Jenna to follow, and the Karda, one with a tiny rider on her back, headed straight for a small clearing in the trees and circled till they landed. Krager recognized the Mi'hiru and her Karda, Philipa and Cystra, usually with Daryl's forces.

"What is it Philipa? Why did you stop us?" Krager had a feeling like someone had tossed his last coins in the middle of a pond, and he was watching them slowly sink through clear water to jagged rocks on the bottom. Jenna took hold of his arm, her hand tight. He clamped it hard to his side and looked down at her. She looked up at him with a look on her face that said "Don't leave me," like she knew what Philipa was going to say would force them apart, and he knew he didn't want to. Philipa's words tore the moment away.

"I was carrying Daryl's messages to Commander Kyle and spotted a cloud of dust on the road a day, maybe a day and a half west of the Prime. These Karda joined me and forced me down into a small clearing nearby. I tried to get as close to the dust cloud as I could, but I could never see anything. I heard them, though. Troops. Lots of troops with some very good don't-look-here spell over the whole line of them. Readen's troops. I almost got caught by one of his outriders, but I climbed a tree—fast." She looked down at her uniform. "I got sap all over me. I knew you were coming in soon— Daryl sent messages for you too, so I've been watching for you. With their help." She gestured toward the other three Karda.

ChiChi and Mia were in the middle of the three, Mia relaying information back and forth. ChiChi ran up to Philipa. "They say they've been assigned as your guards, but they won't say who assigned them. Aren't they beautiful? I'm Chiara Me'Nowyk, this is my sister, Jenna, and you probably know Mi'hiru Dalys, but maybe not, because she's been in Me'Nowyk Hold with us since she landed from the spaceship. She actually lived on a spaceship. She was born on one. Can you imagine?"

Krager put out a long arm and pulled ChiChi close. "We call her ChiChi because she sounds like a flock of birds chattering all the time. Chee chee chee."

ChiChi glared at him, then pretended to stomp his foot. "I think he's teasing me, but he doesn't have a sense of humor, so—no."

Jenna reached out and clasped forearms with Philipa. "I'm Jenna Me'Nowyk. Thank you for coming to warn us."

Philipa's response was cool.

ChiChi shouldered herself between them and said, "She's different now that our father can't be after her to marry the most important man in the world all the time. So don't you dare judge her."

Philipa's face was the color of pink dawn, but Jenna's glowed red sky at morning, sailor take warning. She glared at ChiChi.

Krager pulled ChiChi away before Jenna strangled her. "You make life very interesting, ChiChi. But maybe now you could help Dalys unsaddle and brush down our Karda. They can rest while we decide what to do."

"I know what you're going to do, Krager. You're gonna send us home so you can fight. But we ran away, so we don't have any home now but the sky, so you can't." She stalked to the Karda and hid her face in Mia's mane, then straightened her shoulders and started unbuckling rigging, talking to her Karda the whole time, he could tell, but silently.

Philipa backed away and stumbled over a tuft of grass. "I need to get back to Daryl with this news as soon as possible."

Jenna and Krager watched her and her guard of Karda fly away. He wondered who assigned those Karda to her. Kishar? He'd not done that before that Krager knew of. He looked down. Jenna was trying so hard not to show her feelings on her face. Her chin quivered. A memory flashed of her standing in the mews at Restal Prime, crying into her Karda's mane.

She couldn't go with him to Restal Prime. Jenna wasn't a fighter, and she had her little sister to worry about. He'd never be able to hide them. Where could he send them? Certainly not back to Me'Nowyk Hold. She'd never go anyway. He kept his voice soft. "Go to Ardencroft, Jenna. You'll be safe there, and they can use your help acclimating the émigrés from the spaceship." When had this happened? When did she become so important to him? Again he remembered this small figure hiding her tears in her Karda's mane, looking at him, saying, "I have no place." Had she found her place in that moment?

Her head went down, her hands clasped tight in front of her, her shoulders slumped.

"Jenna, I'm a soldier. Soldiers have to go where the battles are. But every soldier needs somewhere—some*one* to come home to. Wherever you go, wherever you are, when this is over, I'll find you. Tarath and I will find you. If you want to be found."

Her eyes moved over his face for a long time, searching, then she unfolded from her tight hold on herself. Her arms went around

Krager's waist. Her head rested on his chest, his hand behind it, holding her close. He kissed her black curls and inhaled the smell of her deep into his being.

Cedar kept her head down, eyes on the ground, only glancing up to be sure she wouldn't run into someone. Everywhere else she'd been on the planet had been surrounded by trees—nothing like this...this openness. She grabbed Galen's arm with the hand not holding her staff. As long as there was someone to hold on to, she'd be okay. She'd get used to this. She'd have to. She'd have to convince a lot of people they'd get used to it too.

"You'll get used to it. It'll just take a while. Or you won't, and you'll have to stay in the middle of trees," Galen said.

She glanced up at him. The look on his face was what she'd call an evil grin. "How long did it take you?"

"I was so young the first time I was on a planet with Marta and her father, it didn't occur to me to be scared. Most people have this feeling at first. You've lived inside ship's walls most of your life, but Astarte15 was wide open like this."

Cedar shuddered and stumbled. That was a memory she didn't need now.

"Sorry. Didn't mean to remind you."

Astarte15 was where she'd lost her leg and her father. At six.

She knelt as close to the Line of Devastation as Galen would let her, unloaded her microscope from its padded box, smoothed a level place on the ground and set it up. The material was so close to the surface that shining black outcrops made a series of meandering dashes across the barren landscape like a natural formation. It wasn't surprising it hadn't seemed anything to worry about. There were no dead white skeletal trees here shouting "Something's wrong." Just occasional tufts of grass or a wiry bush or three.

Andra collected sample after sample from the soil. "What in the world are these bot things eating out here where nothing grows? I wish I could see into the line like Galen can." She spread a sample on one of Cedar's precious slides and handed it to her.

Galen stood even closer to the line, his concentration intense on the end of the outcrop of black mineral where it broke the surface. Tessa and her father were setting up a temporary camp.

Daryl stood close behind Cedar, who strengthened her filters. She could smell his worry about everything in the world, and on top of that his worry about her being so close to the line. And a faint floral scent of his confusion about why he worried more about her than the others. It made her smile inside.

"So, what's the major flaw you see in our strategy, Cedar?" asked Andra.

"This." Cedar waved her hand at the long, low ridges of black that extended as far as they could see back toward the Circle of Disorder. She blinked and looked down again before the dizziness came back.

Cedar slid the slide into the clips on the scope's stage, adjusted the mirror below to direct light through it, rotated the lens she wanted into place and put her eyes to the eyepieces. She was silent for several minutes, rotating from lens to lens, adjusting the mirror again. Finally, she looked up, squinted, pushed her hair back and looked into the scope again. "Where did you get this sample, Andra?"

Andra pointed to one of the small yellow flags stuck in the ground between them and the line. "That one. Galen gathered it. He wouldn't let me get closer."

Cedar put her face to the eyepieces. Her voice was muffled. "Bring me one from further away from the line, please." And went through the whole process again.

She sat back on her heels and called to Galen. "Galen, come look. Tell me if I'm losing my eyesight."

"I don't have to look. I know what you're seeing."

"What am I seeing, then?"

"Dirt."

"Well, duh."

"And nothing else."

They looked at each other.

"I knew the ground was barren, but not sterile like this. There are always places where microbes and worms and such can be found and a few things have started to grow. Here, there's nothing. Not even organic remnants from when this was forest or grassland or whatever it was before the Larrak war destroyed it. There usually is," said Galen. Then he called, "Tessa."

She looked up from the fire she was poking. "Do you have something useful for me to do, or can I just keep poking this fire? I'm about to persuade it to obey me."

"Find a small bag or cloth or something and ask Kishar to take you out about—" Galen looked at Cedar, who suggested, "A kilometer?"

"Yeah, a kilometer and bring us some dirt."

"Dirt? Oh, thank you, Adalta, now I have something important to do. Get a bag full of dirt."

"Just a little one, please. You can take some time off from feeling sorry for yourself. I know it's wearing you out."

Tessa ignored that, fished for a cloth and took off on Kishar with just a strap around his chest to hold on to.

Cedar shuddered. She knew she could never be that casual on a Karda. "Why would she feel sorry for herself?"

"She hates it when we need strong talents to do something. Hers is blocked. That's why she can fly inside the circles. I don't know why Kishar can. There are no other Karda like him. He's the last of his kind. All his relatives were killed in the last war with the Larrak five hundred years ago."

"He's over five hundred years old?" Cedar stared after them as they touched down, forgetting about the dizzying wide open space. "I wonder if that's why I can't tell what he smells of. He doesn't have any emotional smell at all."

"That must be very trying for you, Cedar—One-Who-Must-Know-All." He patted her on the head, and she elbowed him in the side.

When Tessa came back with her little bundle of dirt, Cedar and Galen looked at slide after slide. "There aren't many, but there are some microbes in this. There's none in the dirt near the line. None at all."

"Galen," said Tessa.

"I figured that," said Galen. "I could sense it through my feet. They don't start again for about twelve meters out from the line."

"You can feel it? Why am I doing all this work if you can simply feel it and tell us?"

"Galen," Tessa said again.

"You need to be kept busy." He ducked Cedar's staff. "And I wasn't sure."

"Oh, good grief." And Tessa stomped off toward Daryl, who was brushing Abala and carrying on a conversation about some obscure philosopher. "Daryl, there were about five urbat north of here headed this way until they saw Kishar and me, then they turned and ran like a deer with six wolves on its tail back toward the circle."

"Kishar just told me."

Kishar knelt, and Tessa tossed a saddle on his back and began buckling. "We'll track them as far as we can, but what are the odds that they're not going for reinforcements?"

~When have you ever seen them run from a fight?~ pathed Kishar.

Soon as she finished, they took off, and Daryl and Connor Me'Cowyn started thinking about defense.

Galen and Cedar never looked up from their work.

"This sample has some microbial life and isn't rich in organic material, but it's there. Dry and sparse, but there. How can it still be dry in such a wet climate?"

"It uses every bit of the moisture it gets just to stay alive. The nanobots are eating the few microbes there are and whatever organic material is left in this damaged soil to fuse the conduit they make when they die. Father told me the geo-guys think what they turn into, for lack of a better word, is an undiscovered allotrope of carbon. He was thrilled." Galen kicked at the small pile of dirt.

"How did he get the samples? You and Daryl won't even let me get close."

"After it almost killed me, he sent techs in full biohazard gear. They got sick and died anyway, but he got it analyzed. Very efficient, my father."

Cedar got a lesson in what bitterness smelled like.

"I wish we could find microbes that would eat *them*." For an instant, Galen looked like a lost little boy, and for an instant, Cedar was confused about what or who he meant when he said *them*— them or him.

"Galen." Her voice was thoughtful. "Tell me exactly what you see when they move to form more of the line—in as much detail as you can."

He moved back to the end of the line, closed his eyes for a long time, then stood staring at the line, his forehead drawn into a frown, for even longer. "It's as though they fuse their carapaces into tiny pieces of pure carbon held together by something that looks like— plastic. That's what burns when we fire it, and the carbon bits fall apart. Impossible as that is, that's what I see. And don't ask me to find you some to look at with your microscope. They're toxic, and I'm not going to test my immunity that far."

Cedar sat up on her knees. "Galen, I think...I think I might have something that can break them down. I have samples of microbes used to clean up slag piles from old coal mines, oil spills, landfills, chemical spills—all kinds of pollution and toxicity on Earth. My predecessors kept them dormant for years. We never destroy anything. The pure carbon itself can't be destroyed, but if the nanobots use the organic material from their bodies to fuse them together in this antenna line...maybe, just maybe..."

"How soon can we get a shuttle down here with them? How long before you could have enough to seed all the lines?"

"I'll call Clare right now. We can wake them and grow more down here—it's a simple process. I hope my staff has the lab put back together, and those samples weren't lost or destroyed when it got trashed." She pulled out her Cue.

Galen looked around him, then told Daryl and Me'Cowyn his bad news. "There's nothing in this soil I can use to grow a thorn fence. Nothing. I can move the dirt, but not enough to help. I can't stop the bots, or even slow them. I suggest we fire as much of the line as we can to slow it down and get out of here before they come back with a horde. I think Andra can do fire. How about Peele and Lange?" They were Daryl's troopers and constant guard.

Daryl pulled his hair back and twisted it into a small leather-wrapped tail so it would stay out of his face. "Some. But they'd be better used as talent boosters. Focused fire takes stronger talent than they have. Cedar can also boost—she doesn't have the knowledge yet to twist Earth and Air into fire."

He shot her a glance, and she made a face at him. He called to Peele, who'd started pulling down the tent they'd just gotten up. "Leave that until after. We might not have much time. Grab your packs and saddle your Karda, and I hope you've practiced running mounts. We might have to leave in a hurry."

They stood in a double half-circle—Daryl, then Andra, Galen, and Me'Cowyn inside, Peele and Lange on the outside with Cedar between them, their hands on the four strong talent's shoulders. She was scared, her mouth dry. The last time she did this, it knocked her out for days. That couldn't happen again. She wouldn't be a burden again.

"When we've done this before, it's taken more than the few hours we're likely to get. But the line is thinner, with so little organic material to fuel the nanobots, so we'll do as much damage as we can. The good news is, Cedar thinks she has some microbes on the ship that might be able to eliminate the problem, so we might not have to do this again," said Galen.

"Lange, you keep one eye out for Tessa and Kishar. When they get back, it will be time for us to get out of here. But we won't notice. This takes concentration," said Daryl. "Connor, I know you shoot lightning arrows, I assume you can also fire in blasts. Can you do a sustained stream?"

The holder shook his head. "But my blasts are powerful. Maybe, since Galen says this line is a kind of carbon, we can both kill the nanobots within reach and melt as much of the line as we can."

"You can't fire the carbon itself, only the substance that holds it together and the nanobots. If you do it in several places, won't that slow the recovery even more?" asked Cedar, keeping her voice steady.

Daryl studied her, eyes squinted. "You really can be useful at times."

"Better duck, Daryl," said Galen.

"It's a good idea. That's what we'll do. Let's get at it."

Three hours later, Lange sighted Tessa and Kishar flying fast toward them, and they ran for the saddled Karda. Thin lines of smoke wisped from four places along the line, and the air was full of an unpleasant odor every one could smell. Cedar also smelled grim satisfaction.

"What did you say, Abala?" Daryl spoke aloud to his Karda. He must have been startled. He got that looking-at-nothing expression that meant they were talking telepathically. He jerked the leather wrapping off the tail of his hair, and it fell loose around his shoulders. Cedar smelled irritation. Then he pulled his packs off and strapped them to the saddle on Illyria, the Karda Cedar rode.

"What's going on, Daryl?" The smell was getting so hot it singed her nose.

He took her staff from her and strapped it to the packs on Illyria. "Abala says we need to talk." His face held the warmth of a snowy mountain in the far north.

The hot smell was irritation peppered with doubt burning through ice. She rubbed her nose.

He boosted her up behind the saddle without asking, mounted and swung his right leg over the pommel and Abala's neck. "It's a good thing I left the extra straps on the rigging." When they were both buckled securely, Abala started his long lope toward takeoff.

Cedar grabbed Daryl around the waist, resisting the urge to pinch him or hit him over the head with her staff, which she couldn't reach anyway. Well, all right then. Thank you for asking, Daryl.

Abala smelled of amusement. Cedar so seldom smelled emotions from the Karda, she figured it was deliberate. Daryl's hair whipped her face. "Where is your leather tie? Your hair is blinding me. My eyeballs are probably already bleeding."

He dug in his pocket.

"Oh." She clutched him tighter around the waist. "Warn me when you're going to move like that."

He reached to tie his hair up, and she took the leather from him, gathered up the flying hair and wrapped it securely. "I wonder if you would mind telling me why I'm not flying on Illyria. Surely I wasn't so awkward she refused to carry me."

"Why won't the strategy work?"

She was silent and a little scared.

"If you don't start talking, we're going to land, and I'll get your staff and hit you over the head with it."

"What's the Itza Larrak's purpose? What's its main goal? What's its strategy for attaining it?"

"To protect its circle, its source of power."

"Why?"

"It needs that power to take over the planet."

"Why does it want to do that?"

"Kishar says it wants to bring its fellow creatures back."

"How?"

"You know—you've heard Kishar say it. By building an antenna for communication."

"How have you been fighting that?"

"By shrinking the circles. They are far, far smaller than they were when the colonists landed here. That's why it's fighting us. You know all this, Cedar."

Cedar knew better than to ask how the Itza Larrak had woken. He'd shut down so fast Abala would go into a spin. She'd fall off for sure then.

"So where's the flaw? I know it keeps our forces spread out, but trying to call it to one spot as we did last fall didn't work. True, Tessa and Kishar wounded it, but it healed itself over the winter. It's too easy for it to disappear back into the circle where only the two of them and Galen can follow. They can't kill it inside the circle with no supporting forces. It was scattering its attacks so it wouldn't get caught far from the circle again. Now we have it blocked in, our villages are safer, and it is weakening."

"But that could take years, Daryl. You know that's the big flaw. You know that. I'm not holding back some great tactical secret. All I see is this great hole you can all see, but you're ignoring it. It simply has to wait until its bots complete the antenna. Its purpose is not to protect its circles, it's to build that web of communication, call to its friends, and then they can come kill us all. Maybe my microbes will stop it, but maybe they'll only delay it. I don't have an answer, I just have questions. Probably because I'm new to this world and to this fight and don't know anything about fighting anyway. Now, can we enjoy this flight, the quiet, the rain that's starting, the cold I'm suffering because when you left my packs on Illyria, you not only took my staff, you left my rain gear. And yours are still with your packs too, I'd guess."

Now she knew what chagrin smelled like.

CHAPTER TWENTY

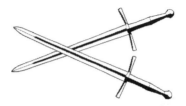

Krager watched Jenna and her companions until they were disappearing dots in the sky. Of course, they headed northwest, not northeast to Ardencroft. Why did he think they'd do what he told them to? Tarath butted him and broke him out of his reverie.

"Let's get my packs and your rigging off and hidden." He looked down at his clothes. "At least these are travel-worn almost to threads. And since it'll take me the rest of the day and half of tomorrow morning to get to the Prime, I'll have a good scruffy beard when I get there. This drizzle, which I sincerely hope doesn't turn to rain, is a good excuse to pull my cloak over my head. It would not do to be recognized."

Tarath snorted.

There was nothing in his packs that would identify him. His sword was in a worn, nondescript scabbard. He took off his flying boots and dug for the worn pair he wore in camp, wishing for his slouchy hat. He rolled a blanket, slung it across his back with a leather strap, piled his packs and Tarath's rig under the drooping branches of a spruce where it was dry, and covered it all with a pegged-down ground cloth he knew he'd regret leaving.

"Stay close. I don't know when or even whether I'll need you, but if I do, it will be quick and fast. I don't know how you know when I need you, but you always do." He laid his hand on Tarath's neck. "Don't stay so close you'll be recognized, and remember, Readen has those akenguns, so stay high. This is a good place for you to sleep, but be careful and scout before you land."

Tarath shoved at him with his shoulder.

"Yeah, I know. You aren't dumb. I just needed to say it. What's happened to me that being on my own again no longer feels so comfortable?"

He slapped Tarath's neck a couple of times and started walking, wishing the boots were a little less worn and a lot more waterproof.

He spent a few cold hours of the darkest part of the night rolled in his blanket under another spruce and reached Restal Prime early the next day. Drizzle did escalate into soft rain, so, hood pulled up, he managed to get through the gates unrecognized without using an illusion. The road was crowded with people leaving by foot, by horseback, by steam buggies, carts pulled by hand or mule, and two- and three-wheeled bicycles piled high. He assumed Readen—if it was him and not the Larrak—was no longer veiling his troops, as news of the approaching army had reached the city. Any of Daryl's supporters with a place of safety to get to were on their way.

He neared Bloody Talons tavern. The street was empty but for three men struggling to bind a third. It was Cael, the man who'd served for so many years as Krager's spy in Readen's guard. The men he recognized, too, three of Readen's troopers. Cael's knife caught one in the throat. Krager didn't hesitate. His sword pierced another's back in just the right place, and he fell. The third man started to run, but Cael caught him before Krager pulled his sword free. Then all three were dead. They dragged them into the alley, crossed the street and walked into the Bloody Talons.

Mother Girt sat on her usual stool at the end of the bar. Her one morning customer had been there long enough he could see nothing but what was in his glass. She refilled it and motioned Krager and Cael to a corner table and disappeared through the door to the kitchen. When she came back, she thunked a large pitcher of water on the table. "Go wash."

Krager stood. "Three dead in the alley across the way."

She nodded and disappeared again.

By the time the two men got as much blood as possible off themselves and returned to the table, she was back, and two tumblers of ale sat there.

Cael spoke the first words. "Thank you, Krager."

"You know Readen's on his way. You aren't safe here. You need to leave."

"I stole the bastard's journals. I need to stay and let him try to catch me till I'm sure they've gotten away and are on their way to Daryl. He has to read them. They're irrefutable proof Readen is in league with the Itza Larrak. I didn't read much, but enough to know Readen has saddled a horse too big for him to handle."

Krager put his head in his hands. Finally, proof Daryl could no longer deny. He wanted to weep. "I can take them to my Karda, Tarath. He's not that far away."

"They're already gone. And don't ask how or who." Cael put one fisted hand on the table. "I need to ask you a favor." The fist tightened until the knuckles were white. "I know he'll eventually catch me. I'm going to need protection. Not just because of the journals. I've witnessed too much. He's gotten some strange powers, strong powers. I don't want him to be able to control me with them."

"I'll strengthen the shields I put on you." Krager squinted. "They're still there and holding, but I can make them stronger."

"I've glimpsed a little of what he can do. That won't be enough, especially since he's going to know they're there. I need you to put a coercion on me. He can't use another if I'm already under yours."

Krager sat back, afraid of what he was going to hear next, afraid of the answer to the question he didn't want to ask.

"What kind of coercion?"

"He's used people for years with all kinds of torture to give him power. I don't want him to use me like that. I can't stop him using others, like we did for the children we saved, but I won't let him use me. I want to be able to kill myself, and I don't want him to be able to block it."

Krager watched Cael's face for a long time. He hated that this was what he had to do, that this was what Cael had to ask him. Then he placed his hand over Cael's fist. Cael looked down at it, then back up. Krager held his eyes. Neither blinked. "It's done. Don't get caught."

Cael's shoulders went up like he could grow wings and was light enough to fly. He leaned back in his chair, closed his eyes, and blew out a long breath. "I better get out of here before someone finds those bodies. You too. Leave word here if you need something from me. And if I hear anything you need to know, I'll do the same." He stood, reached across the table and grabbed Krager's forearm, gripping hard and holding on. Then he left.

Krager was glad he didn't look back. They'd known each other for a long time, since he was a boy idolizing a swordsman. He hadn't asked Cael to do what he'd been doing for so long. Cael volunteered. But it had destroyed any other life he could have lived. Krager hoped with a hope that started at his toes that Cael would still be alive when this was all over and could have a chance to live free again.

He pulled himself away from those thoughts, slipped onto the stool near Mother Girt, and dropped several coins on the bar.

She pushed them back at him. "Don't leave any more bodies on my front porch," she said and pulled a worn hat out from under the bar, slapping it in front of him. "You need a hat. Don't get caught," she added, echoing his words to Cael.

Three men pushed through the door, arguing about nothing.

"Go now. Come back early in the morning."

Krager left. He needed to find Commander Kyle. And he didn't need to be seen doing it.

He found him three streets away from the mews with a wing of Karda Patrol. Kyle stopped to speak to the guard stationed at the corner. The patrollers went on, and so did Kyle after a moment's instructions for the guard.

Krager pushed his slouchy hat back so Kyle could see his face and stepped up to walk beside him for a few steps. "Golden Stirrups

Inn," he said, head down, and turned and went in another direction.

At the next corner, he saw Kyle head down a street that didn't lead to the mews, and he hurried to the alleyway leading to the back of the inn. Five minutes later, Kyle stepped out the back door, and the two men went into a small storage shed half leaning against the back wall.

Kyle grasped Krager's forearm. "Thank Adalta, you're back. Readen is almost to the Prime. I don't know how he hid his troops all the way from his hold, but he did. None of the hall's far-seeing talents saw him. All they saw was occasional dust, and they discounted that." His eyes narrowed and so did his mouth. "As if there would be dust devils rising out of the mud. I'm flying out to take a look. Philipa didn't get a count. Then I'm sending for Daryl."

"Your guard, your patrol, and your Karda are wearing the shields Galen smuggled from the ship, right?"

"Of course. They're our best defense. Readen will be so angry he can't use his precious weapons, he'll lose his temper and forget whatever strategy he plans. A direct attack on the Prime won't work if the weapons don't work. He's too far from his hold, and whatever support he has there to start a siege." He pulled a palm-sized badge out of his pocket. "Here. Take this one. You'll need it."

Krager slipped the shield into the breast pocket of his jacket. He hadn't given a thought to personal risks until he felt a hole in his back close. "No need to send for Daryl. I'm sure he already knows or will very soon. The Karda will carry the news. What are you doing about the people leaving the Prime? They won't get far before he arrives. They'll be caught outside the walls."

"I've sent the Mounted Patrol to bring them back, then I'll close the gates." He looked at Krager's shabby clothes and stubbled face. "You need to get cleaned up and into your uniform. I'll need your help."

Krager half-turned, stood still and cocked his head. The faint thunder of fisted feet and broad wings sounded from the landing field outside the walls. He stepped to the doorway. "I think you're too late. Look." The noise went on and on, and the sky filled with Karda, many with riders.

"It sounds like they left without me. I doubt there's a single Karda left in the mews to carry me. I better get to the gates. Readen must be a lot closer than I expected him to be," said Kyle. "That was more than one wing of Karda Patrol taking off." He sounded like a kid left behind with the chores while his buddies went adventuring, instead of like a man who'd jumped into the middle of a brawl he didn't start. "Readen can't be allowed to take the guardianship from Daryl again."

Krager left him and made his way to the gates, with no intention of cleaning up and getting into uniform. The building tension in the muscles of his abdomen told him this wasn't going to be as simple as Kyle thought. It would be a Readen kind of battle, fought by Readen's kind of rules, which meant Krager would have to stay a mouse in the corner, or a cat in the alley—watch and learn. He knew what Kyle didn't. Daryl couldn't leave the battle with the Larrak. He wouldn't be coming, and he'd be agonizing about his decision not to attack Readen's hold like Altan urged him to tendays ago.

Three hours later, Krager settled high in a tree not far from the walls about sixty meters from the gates, watching people with hunted-deer faces move back through the outskirts of the Prime as if herded. Audible above the unnatural quiet of the people, hoofbeats and the sounds of creaking saddle leather, jangling tack, and a few shouted orders told him Readen and his forces were close behind.

Kyle's troops manned the walls on either side of the city gates. Seldom closed, now they were only half-open to let people through as fast as they could. It was apparent Kyle didn't want the gates open any wider so Readen could rush them. Two of Readen's squads moved to circle the terrified people and approached the gates from both sides. They halted just out of arrow range. People jammed the gates, trapped between Readen and the manned walls, unintentionally protecting Readen's forces.

Readen appeared, riding casually through the people, smiling, stopping occasionally to talk to a family, joking, even. Krager knew well this side of Readen. He'd used it for years to fool every one—holders, councilors, townspeople, troopers, and especially his father and his brother. Krager cursed to himself, cursed Daryl's dogged misplaced loyalty, which kept hidden and unacknowledged the ugly side of Readen. Too many people refused to believe what stories slipped out. Readen was a master manipulator.

Finally, Readen rode into arrow range in a wide circle empty of people. Krager heard Kyle's shout from the wall. "Fire."

An impossibly wide iridescent curtain appeared in front of Readen and his troops. Arrows bounced and slid off it and collected in a half circle around them.

Then he smiled, slowly raised his arm, an akengun in his grip. It slashed down to his side, the curtain flickered, and behind him, his mercenaries raised the strange weapons and fired. Blinding flashes raced along the wall behind Krager, lighting the dark underside of the leaves hiding him.

Not a trooper fell.

The shimmery curtain reappeared and a single soft laugh filled the shocked silence. Krager knew that laugh, and his shoulders tightened. Readen was angry, with his kind of patient, vicious, savage anger. Krager half started to climb down the tree, then stopped. He was helpless against whatever Readen would do next.

Then Readen spoke. His quiet voice filled the silent space like downy feathers filled the softest pillow, boosted by a power Krager knew he shouldn't have.

"Commander Kyle. Armsmaster Krager. I give you fifteen minutes to open the gates so these good people and my men may enter the city. At the end of those fifteen minutes, if you do not do as I say, I will kill three of these good people. Every fifteen minutes. Like this."

He beckoned a woman out of one of the horseless buggies. Krager recognized her—Minra Shreeve, Councilor Galel's bonded.

She stepped through the curtain and smiled at Readen with poise and courtesy. "Good afternoon, Readen." Even from where he hid, Krager saw white knuckles on the fingers of the hands clasped behind her back.

"Good afternoon to you, Minra. You are looking magnificent, as usual. Were you and the worthy councilor traveling somewhere?" Readen raised the akengun. There was no sound. She stood, perfectly still, for three seconds, three seconds that seemed to Krager to stretch into forever, with a large hole in her chest. Then she slid to the ground in a slow, silken slump, her smile still on her face. There was no blood.

Silence spread like a virulent plague of fear and held the crowd in its grip until Galel's voice rose in a tortured, high, disbelieving scream. "Nooooooo."

Becca fast-walked toward the gate. It had taken too long getting everything she needed for her long trek. She wasn't even sure how long a trek it was or if there was any place along the way to get more food. The canvas pack on her back was heavy. The slim leather satchel slung over her shoulder was clamped to her side. A walking staff would be helpful, but there were too few coins left in Cael's purse, and she needed to save them.

Tall for a young boy but small for her actual fifteen years, her chopped-at hair stuffed under a cap, too-big britches double-wrapped at her waist with a too-long belt, she walked close to the walls and didn't look up. A block away from the gate, the throng trying to leave stopped, people from behind pushing, creating a jam at the front. Then the noisy crowd went silent. A whispery snake of words started at the front and made its way back, person to person.

The crowd moved to back away. Becca stood, glued to the wall, afraid to move, afraid not to move.

She could see nothing, but then she heard a long Nooooo wail, and the screaming started.

People were running past her, and Becca flattened herself against the wall. Someone knocked against her, and she almost lost her pack.

Shouting started. "He killed her. Sat there on his horse and put a great hole in her with some awful talent weapon."

"He's gonna kill more. Every fifteen minutes."

"The city is lost. Where can we go?"

"Go home. Lock the doors. Don't come out until you have to."

She backed away. The marching sound of the commander's troops moving from the hall to the gates stopped. Kyle had surrendered the city. He'd had no choice. She turned a corner into an alley that twisted toward another street. Moving faster than an amble, but never too fast, Becca made her way through familiar alleys and back streets. She stopped in an alcove, hidden, she hoped, breathing hard, terrified, and watched one of the Restal Guard rip off his uniform shirt and stuff it in a rubbish bin. Where could she go? How could she get out of the city? Daryl must be told what was happening. He had to have these journals.

Her eyes closed tight, she slowed her breathing and tried to think—the Thieves' Gate. So few people knew it was even there it wouldn't be guarded. It was never guarded.

She slipped an arm out of the straps so her pack hung over one shoulder, and started walking, doing her best not to jump at every sound, not to shy away from the few people she passed. More than one was missing a shirt. One woman wore her uniform shirt wrong side out. No one gave the ragged "boy-child" a second glance.

The little Thieves' Gate hid where the long line of the city's greenhouses met the river. Overgrown by some kind of plant that made you itch, she struggled to get through. Becca rubbed her arm. If she started scratching her face, she wouldn't stop until it was raw and bleeding, which was how her insides felt.

At the first puddle she found, using her Water talent she pulled up enough clean water to scrub her arms and face, and the itching became tolerable. She slipped away from the road and hid from passing troops several times in the first hours. After that, traffic slowed. There was no one but her and the mud and the rain dripping through the overhanging trees.

Becca walked until the last light faded from the day, listening and watching every second for other travelers. The night was too dark without either moon in the sky, and she was too tired to go farther. Rolled in a blanket in a low spot overhung with bushes well away from the road, she figured she was as safe as she could be. Until the rain came down harder, and water started to trickle past her and seep under her. She managed to get up before everything was soaked and pulled her waterproof ground cloth around her. The first thing she checked was the satchel with the journals—still dry—and used her Water talent to wring the wet out of the blanket.

Becca started to cry. She cried for a long time. Readen would kill Cael. He would kill Krager. He'd find them. He'd torture them. Cael would never tell Readen who he'd given the journals to. Never. But he'd suffer. Finally, she fell asleep and didn't wake until the sun poked her in the eye with an early-to-rise sunbeam.

For three days she walked, trying not to think. She resorted to counting her steps so she wouldn't think about Cael, about the mercenary troops now in the city, about the terrified crowd, about whatever had caused that terrible wail of grief outside the walls. Just step step step step. Four hundred, four hundred thirty-five, six hundred—oops. Lost count again. Start over. Step one. Step two. Step….

Her pack was heavy on her back, and the leather bag slung across her bound chest was clamped so tight under the other arm it started to chafe.

Becca's battered boots splashed into another puddle she was too weary to walk around, her talent so depleted she couldn't dry a path through. It crossed the entire road, including the verge where she walked, slick with last year's dry brown grass and tiny points of green where spring pushed through. Tired as she was, she didn't dare stop, even if she could find a dry spot to rest in. But at least it finally stopped drizzling.

Thank Adalta, Becca knew where she was going. She hoped. Cael's directions to Ardencroft were clear. With every step, she begged the trees, the grass, the clouds dripping from the sky, to keep her on the right road. To keep her awake. To keep her walking. She begged Adalta to help her get there in time. Before Daryl left. Or Tessa. Or Galen. They'd been the ones to save her from being taken to Readen with two other children. They'd know who she was, who Cael was. She could—

Suddenly she was on her knees in the muddy muck. What had she tripped over? Slipping and sliding, she made it back to her feet and turned to see a long stick, about five centimeters thick and at least half a meter taller than her. Becca wiped the mud off it on a strip of dry grass, wishing she knew how to fight with a staff, and grateful for something to lean on.

Then she heard horse hooves moving up the road behind her. She'd stopped listening, and now she was about to be caught. There wasn't time to get off the road into the trees, but she tried.

Three of them pulled up; one circled around and stopped in front of her. Their horses were gaunt, their clothes worn with sloppy patches, their saddles much mended.

And she was alone. A smallish boy—at least, she hoped they thought she was a boy. She refused to think anything else. The ones behind forced her back to the middle of the road. Leaning hard on the stout stick, Becca crossed one leg over another, cocking it up on its toe, hoping she looked nonchalant, hoping they wouldn't notice her shaky legs. "Wat 'chu want wit me? I ain't got no money. Ain't got no food neither. And m'mam's waitin' fer me. She be sendin' m'brothers after me now."

All three of them laughed. "But yur'd be so handy in our work. And yer a little one. Yer'd be handy getting in places we can't, wouldn't 'chu?" It wasn't a question. The one who'd stayed in the middle of the road laughed.

Becca put both hands on her staff. Oh, how she wished she knew how to fight.

The man pulled his right foot out of the stirrup and leaned to dismount.

Then Becca heard thunder. Or it sounded like thunder. A huge shadow swooped down, snatched the rider from his saddle and disappeared over the top of the trees. All three horses went crazy. The riderless one disappeared back down the road, and the other two bucked and hopped and twisted, riders hanging on until they too disappeared.

She heard the thunder again, then hoofbeats, and loping toward her, splashing through the mud was a Karda. A pale gray Karda with red and white flight feathers. It was a good thing her stick was stout. Becca hung on it until her knees stopped shaking enough that she could stand.

The Karda slowed to a stop less than a meter from her. ~Hello. My name is Elleran, and you are Becca.~ He bent one knee and bowed his head. ~I am glad I found you.~

Becca found her breath. ~I'm glad too.~ Then she sat down, right in the mud. He'd talked to her. In her head. And she'd answered. With mind-talk. She wasn't even sure she believed mind-talk was anything more than another blown-up story about Karda. But she'd heard him. And she'd used it to speak to him.

He lowered his immense hawk head with its vicious predator's beak. ~Why did you sit down in the mud?~

Becca couldn't speak for a long, long time, unaware of time passing. Her eyes caught in his. Everything in her brain rearranged itself, whirling and swirling until it settled, and she came back to herself.

"Elleran." She said it out loud. Then she said it in her head. ~Elleran.~

He answered her. His voice brushed her mind like soft feathers. ~Becca. We are together now. Perhaps you have something in your little bag you can wipe yourself off with so you don't get my back all wet and muddy. That thing wound around your chest under your shirt you can fasten around my neck to wrap your legs around and hold on to.~

~I'm not a boy.~ Why had she said that?

~Of course you're not.~

~I have clean clothes.~

~That is a good thing. Do you wish me to turn my head away while you change?~

Becca laughed. She was so full of laughter her chest threatened to burst with it. She stood and reached up. Elleran dropped his head, and she put her arms around his neck, burying her face in his mane, breathing in his sharp, spicy smell. ~No. That's not necessary. But I do need to get off this muddy road. And I need to find Daryl Me'Vere.~

~I'll take you high above it. You don't belong on muddy roads anymore. And I'll take you to Daryl Me'Vere. But perhaps we'll have a riding lesson first. I don't want to lose you just when I found you. For you to fall off on our first flight would be embarrassing.~

Becca hoped the laughter would never leave her heart.

Krager slouched, head in his hands, a mostly empty mug of beer in front of him in the Bloody Talons. His beard was scruffier, his hair was dirtier and hung from under his hat in chopped-at locks. None of Readen's troops would know him as Krager. No one ever recognized him in this persona. He didn't think even Mother Girt knew who he was. Just another one of Krager's informants.

His head was down because he didn't want to see anything for a long while except Mother Girt's pitcher topping up his mug. The tavern was crowded but quiet. No one wanted to talk or listen to anyone else talk. Tomorrow every one would be talking about today. But tonight wasn't for talking. It was for disbelief, for shock, for grief, not for anger, not yet. That would come.

Krager sat until the crowd thinned. He sat until the tavern emptied. And still he sat. Mother Girt paused as she went past him to lock the door, but she didn't say anything. She took her cash box from under the bar and disappeared into the back. Some time later, she reappeared, laid a blanket on the table and left again.

He woke, stiff, sore, sad, and mad, on the floor beside the not-quite-warm magma stones in the stove, long legs tangled in his blanket. Thoughts skittered and scattered through his head. Where to start? Who to trust? How to stay hidden? A rumble sounded from the vicinity of his belly. Hunger was a good sign that despair wouldn't win. Blanket wrapped around his shoulders, he concentrated on the stones until they glowed red and moved to the table. Lists started forming in his head, and the first thing on the lists was to find a safe place to stay. Staying here much longer could compromise Mother Girt, and she was one of his best resources.

As that thought added itself to his who-to-trust list, she pushed through the door to the back with a steaming bowl of hot cereal. She'd added hot apples and nuts—even a hint of cinnamon. He was seeing a side of her that must be a recent transplant, or she wanted to be sure he was fed and happy and would leave. Probably both.

She sat down across from him. Krager looked at the bowl and back at her, twice.

"What?" she demanded.

"Just making sure it's still you in there." He wasn't sure, but he thought she might have a slight tinge of pink on her pale cheeks. He knew better than to smile.

"I've lived in Restal Prime all my life, my mother and her mother before me, all the way back to the beginning. I've lived through two generations of bad government, waiting for the promise that is Daryl Me'Vere. I've watched Readen Me'Vere since he was a young boy. If he wins the guardianship of Restal, I'm leaving. And I don't want to. My life is here, and I intend to fight to stay." She stood. "Now you eat that and leave. When you decide what you're going to do, don't tell me. Just let me know what you need. My eye is always open." She stepped behind the bar, and only the clatter of glasses and bottles and mugs betrayed how disturbed she was. Maybe she did know who he was.

Krager finished off the bowl of cereal and put the finishing touch on the final lists in his head and left. He had a lot to do.

CHAPTER TWENTY-ONE

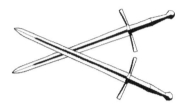

"What did you say?" Daryl half stood, leaning on the table as if without it, he'd fall and smash his face. He stared at Abala standing outside the tent entrance, the gray day's late spring sleet icing his back and mane. The brief, forlorn hope that he hadn't heard Abala right shredded. His legs started to shake, and he fumbled for the back of his chair to sit.

The others around the table in the communal tent at Me'Cowyn's camp stared at him. Then Tessa jumped to her feet. "No, Kishar. No. How?"

Galen paled and stood very still.

Abala pathed, ~Readen took the Prime. He killed Minra Shreeve with an akengun and threatened to kill three people every fifteen minutes until Commander Kyle and Armsmaster Krager gave him control.~

"When?" Somehow Daryl got the word out. Everything in the tent disappeared. All he saw was Abala.

~Yesterday. All the Karda left the city, and I just got the news. Some of their riders snuck back into the city, and some will be arriving any time. They're flying non-stop.~

He told Daryl the rest of the story. It swirled inside Daryl's head

—a maelstrom of horrible images, a mix of rage and despair and horror.

"Kishar says Krager is in the Prime wearing a disguise," whispered Tessa.

Daryl and Tessa stared at each other and Kishar. Connor was getting red in the face. "What are you talking about?"

Tessa told him.

"It's lost, then." Connor wouldn't look at Daryl, just sat and looked into the distance as if answers would fall out of the clouds with the rain.

Daryl knocked his chair back as he got up and headed out of the tent. Abala stood in his way and didn't move.

~We have to leave as soon as possible, Abala. Tarath can tell us how to find Krager. I can disguise myself as well as he can. I need to know how many troops Readen brought. Where are his Akhara mercenaries? Did they make it through the pass? We haven't heard from the troops we sent to guard the entrance. Why? We haven't heard from Turin. Why? Where is he? Did he join Readen like every one expected?~ On and on he went, listing what he needed to do, what he needed to know, blind to anything else. If he stopped planning, he'd implode, he'd shrivel to nothing. The wind would carry him away, a shower of cold, icy sleet that would melt and disappear into the ground.

Then Cedar was in front of him, poking him hard in the chest with the iron-shod end of her staff. "Go. Sit. Think." She took his arm and pulled him back to the table then stumbled against him.

He reached out and caught her automatically. She put a warm hand on either side of his face and pulled it down until his forehead rested on hers. "You'll handle this. You can handle this. Breathe."

He took a breath, then another, then another.

Galen cleared his throat. "I hate to interrupt, but we've got some serious thinking to do here."

Daryl jumped.

"Now, of course, you'll need a few moments to feel guilty, so we'll think while you brood for a bit." Cedar patted his cheeks and sat.

He sat next to her, his shoulder against hers as if she were his touchstone. "The first thing we must do is get word to the guardians and holders guarding the planters and keeping watch on the circle."

~Already done, Daryl,~ Kishar pathed just as Tessa said the same thing.

"I'll draft a letter to Hugh Me'Rahl. As Prime Guardian, he's the logical person to take control here while I——"

"No." "No." The no's rang around the table in a chorus.

Connor Me'Cowyn tapped a fist on the table. "Daryl, you cannot leave this battle. None of us can."

"I can't leave my people to Readen. Look at what he's done already. He's my brother, but even I know he's not fit to govern the Prime, let alone lead the quadrant, which will be his next step. He could well be successful before the end of planting season if I don't stop him." He clenched and spread his fingers as if trying to get a grip on the hilt of his sword.

Cedar put her hands over his and forced him to face her. "Daryl. If we lose to the Itza Larrak, if we are unable to stop it from constructing its antenna, it won't matter who rules Restal Quadrant, or Anuma or Toldar or Akhara. Your people and my people will be lost."

Galen pushed on his shoulder to force Daryl to face him and Tessa. Tessa said, "We won't be here. The Karda won't be here. There won't be any kurga, or medgeran, or birbir. Adalta will destroy herself before she lets the Larrak return to eat her alive."

"My hold is one of the closest to the Prime. It may be Readen's next target." Me'Cowyn stood next to them, feet wide, nostrils flared. "I understand what you are going through. But I agree. The Larrak. The Larrak must be our first priority. Then, I promise you, we will defeat Readen no matter what kind of weapon he has or what strange power he has developed."

Daryl scooted back and surveyed the group of them, including the ones huddled outside the tent in the cold—Kishar, Ket, and Abala.

He chewed his lip. He retied his hair. He stared at the spread fingers of his hands on the table for a moment. He stared into the wet mix of spring snow and sleet falling over the heads of the Karda blocking the cold wind at the open door of the tent.

He scratched his head, pulling hair loose again. "Yes. We need to figure out what the flaw in our strategy is. I need to stop looking at reports and take time to understand that. And I wish I knew where Turin is now. What he's done."

"Oh, fractured moons, why are you worrying about that?" All of them stared at Cedar. "You don't trust him?"

They still stared, wide-eyed and incredulous.

"Well. You could have just asked me. Turin smells of dependability. Complete dependability. Harsh, yes. Calculating, yes. But only so far. He smells of iron. He'll do what he said he'd do. Probably in his own way, but there is no smell of betrayal about him. None. Devious, yes. Disloyal, no." She smiled. "He's a very interesting man. I look forward to getting to know him. And Rachyl? Such subtle, complex smells."

She reached past Galen, pushed aside the reports and instructions Daryl intended to send to Commander Kyle and pulled over the map of the circle with all Daryl's notes and placements marked. "Now. What do we do next? Have you figured out what we need to do yet, or do I have to try to figure it out for you with my immense knowledge of strategy?" She looked around at them with the most ingenuous, innocent, and irritating wide-eyed look Daryl had ever seen. And he pushed back some very inappropriate-to-the-moment thoughts.

"Tell me again where we're going and why we're not heading back to Me'Bolyn Hold? You might be able to fight, but neither Chiara nor I know a thing beyond very basic self-defense." Jenna loaded her pack behind Mirjana's saddle.

"Every Karda we've seen in the sky has told Seralla we have to go to Daryl's camp now. Readen has taken the Prime." Dalys shifted her eyes to ChiChi, who was mending a strap on Mia's rig, her

SHERRILL NILSON

shoulders slumped, her eyes red, her hair a mess as if she were too tired to brush it. Which she was.

"ChiChi doesn't need to know the details. And she needs to stop long enough for a good rest. She's holding up for a ten-almost-eleven-year-old, but she's winding down too fast. I can't let her get sick."

"You're tired, too, Jenna. You've never flown this much in your life. You've never slept on the ground this many nights, or eaten so much camp food. Go sit on a rock by this pretty creek and let me help ChiChi get ready. Mirjana needs to finish eating anyway, all three of them do. What a kindness of those Karda to hunt for us this morning. Ours have been on dried meat and vegetables too long. I was getting concerned. Now we don't have to stop so they can hunt for themselves."

Jenna took two of the awful rock-hard travel biscuits and wandered to the creek. They'd camped in a small oasis, one of the many planted in the barrens by the First Planters as safe places for the planters who would follow in their efforts to re-establish life on Adalta. She looked out across the rocky landscape, still so vast, and wondered if it would ever be finished. Or if they'd be allowed to finish it. She shuddered.

At first she'd found it difficult to understand, when a passing Karda gave them the news, why Daryl didn't immediately head for Restal Prime to oust Readen. But he couldn't. If he took troops away from fighting the Itza Larrak, it wouldn't be long before the entire planet looked like these barrens, which it almost had before the other Larrak were killed when the first colonists arrived to join the fight.

The light slipped and slid through the greening leaves of the big sycamore across from her. The still pool threw its reflection at her. She couldn't see through the water to the rocky bottom of the shallow stream, as hidden to her as the future of life on this planet. For a moment, she imagined she saw Krager's tall form reflected there. She drew her knees up and wrapped her arms around them.

The sycamore leaned over the pool as if looking at its image. The immense mottled white and brown trunk met the stones at the water's edge and spread its thick roots over and under and around the jagged rocks, protecting them, holding them safe against the currents. When the flood came, they'd still be there, cradled in the big sycamore's hold, sharp edges and all. Like her.

Jenna jumped when Dalys called. All three Karda were rigged and ready, Dalys and ChiChi mounted. She smiled at the tree, at the opaque surface of the water that, however hard she looked, would only reflect the present. She cast an Air talent breeze across it, creating little silver ripples as a gift, and ran to mount Mirjana.

They made it to Daryl's camp by mid-afternoon, guided in by a Karda who spiraled down from the flock in the sky to show them the rough landing field. Right behind them came a fourth Karda, a small, ragged figure glued to its back, riding without a saddle.

Mi'hiru Tayla met them at the entrance to the big mews tent, its sides pulled down against the wind and the warm rain replacing the snow and sleet of the day before. "Greetings. The Karda told us to expect three someones, and we expected you'd be wet and cold, so we'll take care of your Karda. Grab your packs and I'll show you to your tent to change." Then she noticed the fourth Karda. "Who's this with you? I don't recognize the Karda or the boy on his back. Oh. Without a saddle."

The "boy" jumped down and ran between the other Karda to Tayla. "I have to see Guardian Daryl. Right now. Cael sent me from the Prime with something awful important. Cael was Krager's spy, and he said to get this to Guardian Daryl as fast as I could." She lifted her elbow to show the satchel. "Elleran found me on the road and rescued me. I have to see the guardian now." She looked back at her Karda and said, "Oh, and my name is Becca, and I'm not a boy."

"No, she's not," said ChiChi. "And Mia says what she has is real important."

Tayla reached for the leather bag. "I'll get this to Daryl. But first come in and get dry, you and your Karda—Elleran? You both look hungry, wet, and tired."

ChiChi, Dalys, and Becca all said "no," at the same time. Becca clamped her arm on the satchel. "I can't give them to anyone else. I have to give them to Daryl, only Daryl. Where can I find him?"

Jenna took her arm. "If you can walk without falling over, I'll take you to him. I may not be able to talk to Mirjana, my Karda, but these other two can. So this must be important. You're soaked. I'm sure you're so sore you can hardly walk, but we'll get there. My name is Jenna Me'Nowyk, Becca."

Looking startled at Jenna's name, Tayla gave up and unhooked a rain cloak from the rack by the door. "At least take this. Daryl's tent is that bigger one." She pointed through the rain, and Becca took off running, Jenna a step behind her.

Jenna could almost hear Becca's thoughts, so strong they were, battering against her Air talent—What am I going to say? Please let him see me. Please let him believe me—over and over as they splashed through the puddles.

Someone had erected an awning over the entrance to Daryl's tent, and the guard standing there made them wait. Becca was bouncing up and down on her feet, her face ivory pale, her eyes so wide they were almost all white, her whole body shaking from more than just the cold wind on her soaking clothes. Jenna saw her fight the fear and desperation she was almost too weary to bear. Becca grabbed Jenna's hand, holding it so tight Jenna's fingers cramped. She didn't think Becca was even aware of what she was doing.

Becca shook her head, and water dripped out of her clothes until she was dry. She looked at Jenna's clothes, and within a minute, Jenna was dry, too.

Before Jenna could thank her, the guard reappeared, held the door flap open, and motioned them inside.

His head down, Daryl sat writing at his paper-littered table surrounded by ledgers and boxes of more papers. Abala's saddle was propped on its pommel by the door, saddle blanket draped over it, a sword in a well-worn scabbard leaning against it. He finished what he was writing, folded it, dropped wax from a candle on it, stamped it with his ring and handed it to the guard. "For Me'Fiere." The guard left.

He looked up at Jenna. His face was thinner, with lines that hadn't been there before. "Welcome back, Jenna. Sorry to make you wait. I just got back from Me'Cowyn's camp and have a lot of catching up in front of me." His smile flickered as if it required more energy than was available. One arm lay on the table over the papers, the other stroked it up and down. Then his chin snapped up, and he looked at her, really looked this time. "You look exhausted. It would have been fine if you'd taken time to rest before you reported to me."

Becca stepped around Jenna and stood directly in front of him across the table. "It's me as has to give you something. Cael sent me with these, and he's probably going to die because of them, so you have to read them now."

Jenna put a hand on the girl's shoulders. They were tense and shaking so hard she had trouble pulling the strap of the satchel over her head. She held it out to him, her hands so tight on the leather he had to pull it from her.

Daryl smiled the kind of smile meant to reassure a child and never does. "Who is Cael, and why is he sending me this?"

"Cael is Krager's spy. He was with Readen for years." Becca was holding in so much emotion Jenna could hardly hear her words. She turned her head and looked at Jenna. Her mouth opened and closed twice, her eyes jerked from Jenna to Daryl to the opening flap.

"I'll wait outside for you, Becca. Then we'll find a place for you to clean up and rest."

Jenna leaned against one of the poles holding up the awning and dropped her head. She was so tired. So tired. Her shields—to her they looked like a wide windbreak of woven-together evergreens, some with thorns—wilted. She wasn't prepared for the blast of wild talent force that rocked her so she almost took the post down with her. Becca came out, white-faced and wobbly on her feet.

The guard returned, and Becca said, her voice hoarse, "He told me to say he wasn't to be disturbed until he called you. Not by anyone."

What had Jenna and ChiChi landed in?

Daryl stared at the open black leather-bound book on the paper-littered table in his command tent—the last book in the satchel Becca had brought. Someone scratched on the door flap. He didn't look up, and he didn't say anything. He couldn't. He stared at the side of the tent, seeing Readen's child face, at the Fort Tree, the tall beech with the crude wooden platform and the wooden ladder they'd cobbled together. Readen wore his laughing face and the wooden sword he broke Daryl's arm with.

Readen's laughing face on the side of the tent looked back at him, mocking Daryl with his happy laughter. How had Daryl seen love, not the mocking glee? How had he gotten it so wrong? How had he been so trusting, so blind?

There was another scratch, then a whack. He heard, but the sounds wouldn't register. Several seconds passed, then Cedar pushed the flap aside and peered in.

"Oh, Peele said you weren't to be bothered, but I…" Cedar sank to her knees beside Daryl, her hand tight over her nose. She whispered, "I couldn't leave. I couldn't leave with you alone in here with what I smelled."

The muscles around his tight eyes jumped and twitched. His fingers hovered over the pages of the last journal—he had read them all. He pushed it to the side of his desk, following it with his eyes as if he couldn't let go of it, but didn't want to touch it again lest it contaminate him further with the filth he'd never be able to rid himself of.

Cedar put her hands on his knees pulled him around to face her. He didn't resist. He let her move him because he couldn't move himself. She didn't let go, just waited. Then she reached to grasp his limp hands with hers.

He couldn't speak past the burning coal in the back of his throat.

They sat that way for a long while, her thumb rubbing the backs of his hands with slow, gentle movements that he could focus on and not think.

He knew Abala was trying to reach him, to talk to him, but he blocked the Karda from the ugliness in his mind. He couldn't spread this virulent, infectious disease. His brother. His brother did all those...those things. Was it in him, this disease? Had it been in his father? His grandfather?

His shoulders curved inward and his body curled over their joined hands. It was painful to speak. His voice was low and rough and echoed as if he heard it from a distance.

"I've been going through Readen's journals. Workbooks, he called them, detailing his 'experiments'." His stomach curdled. He almost gagged on his next words. "He discovered how to use the life force of others to build and enhance his power to make up for his lack of talent. Even as a child he was killing things and, as he put it, taking the power their 'insignificant lives' didn't need but he did. He fed on fear and death."

His fingers tightened on hers. "I had a dog, Baron. I loved Baron. Readen kept him alive for three days in the cavern under the hall, torturing him. He describes it all with glee! He relished it. And he fed on my worry and sadness. That's his expression. Fed. Every time I asked him if he'd seen Baron, he 'fed' from me. When my mother died, he went out to the gardens in the night and danced. He danced at my mother's death. Not because he hated her—he said he loved her, and loved her even more for dying because it hurt me. He fed from that, too, from my grief and confusion. Every time he thought I might be recovering, he reminded me with false sympathy so he could feed again."

Daryl drew in a shuddering breath and looked up at her. "That was all before he discovered the Itza Larrak. Before he started—" He closed his eyes and tried to swallow. His mouth was desert dry, mountainous desert dry, with rocks he struggled to speak around. "The Itza Larrak taught him how to use power from blood, sex, and death. How to convert the agony of others to his own use. It had had centuries to lurk and learn the lessons of human power, twisted power, and he twisted them further and taught Readen." His eyes held hers as if they could shelter him, as if they could tether him, as if without them he would dissolve. "When Marta's surge of talent knocked Readen unconscious, the Larrak disappeared. But Readen found a way to bring it back into the world, into its body."

He looked away. "I've been so wrong about him. I've been such a gullible fool. That's what he called me in his journals, over and over. And he was right. I'm a gullible fool. At best. He is my family. My brother. My *brother* did..."

He leaned back, pulled his hands away from hers, and was silent for a long time, looking over her head, lost in distance and memory. "I should have spent more time with the Guard, less with the Karda Patrol. I should have spent more time attending to political matters, more time paying attention to the complaints and problems of the Holders and the people of Restal Prime...." He dropped his head into his hands, elbows propped on the desk. "How could I have been so trusting, so blind? It's not just that I didn't see what Readen is. I made *excuses* for him. I felt responsible that I had talent and he didn't. He covered his anger and bitterness with a façade of wit and geniality, and I accepted that façade. I made excuses for my father's poor governance, too. As long as things went along smoothly on the surface, that's all I saw. All I wanted to see. I took care of the problems I found with the Karda Patrol and thought that's all I needed to do. I'm not fit to lead Restal."

Daryl's cheeks were cold, wet. His eyes moved back to her, the muscles of his face taut. "He is my brother, Cedar. Is there some of that in me? My father...my father.... is there a terrible taint infecting my family line? Can you smell a taint in me?"

Cedar put her hands on either side of his head and pulled it up to face her. "Never say that. Never even think it. You're nothing like that. Marta told me about Readen, about what he did to her. Tessa told me about the destroyed young girl she found wandering the halls when Readen finished with her. You are the antithesis of Readen. There's something twisted and broken in Readen. Maybe it came from his mother. Maybe something broke inside him when she died. Jealousy of your talent twisted him. I know you didn't want to see it, but, Daryl, he probably hated you from the day of your birth, and it just got worse as you got stronger."

Daryl was silent for a long time. If he could lose himself in the infinite depth of her eyes, he would. "I've let things get into an awful mess, haven't I? I've left my people to him. How can I ask them to trust me to be Guardian? When we destroy the Itza Larrak, how can I ask them to help me win the Prime back, win Restal back?"

He pulled back from her. She held his hands tighter and wouldn't let go.

"Daryl." Cedar leaned forward in her chair, her expression so intent and determined he couldn't look away. "You are still a young man. Young men can be forgiven mistakes if they learn from them, and you are. You are not the one who killed Minra Shreeve. You are not the one who threatened to kill even more innocent people unless the Prime surrendered to him. You are not the one who allied himself with the Itza Larrak."

Daryl winced.

"People know that. Readen is the one who did all that. You are the one who defeated and imprisoned Readen before. People know that. You are the one who worked all winter on strategy to defeat the Itza Larrak and the urbat. You are the one who led the fights all spring. People will understand, vicious as Readen is, that he is not the real threat to Restal, and you will take care of him when the Larrak threat is gone. Trust them. Trust yourself."

Anguish was a ball of nausea in his stomach, working its way up into his throat, and Daryl knew if he opened his mouth again it would come out in a scream of agony and despair.

"You don't have to believe what I say. But you do have to act as though you do—you have to be strong. You have to show you are in control. Smother your doubts with action. I'm sure if you asked any Guardian, or even Prime Guardian Hugh Me'Rahl, they would tell you they have those same doubts, and not only in the small hours of the night. Real leadership happens in spite of doubts. It's not a question of absence of doubt. That's megalomania, not leadership. That's Readen, not you."

Daryl looked away.

Cedar took his hands again, and sat with him, leaning against his knees. He wanted her to leave. He'd perish if she did.

CHAPTER TWENTY-TWO

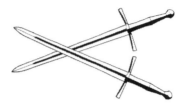

Becca sat in the grass outside the mews tent in Daryl's camp, leaning on Elleran's shoulder which towered over her even though he was lying down. ChiChi and Mia plopped down on her other side to relax in the rare warm sun. The ground was damp, but neither girls nor Karda cared. The sun was an infrequent visitor, and they were determined to capture every ray of it they could.

A wing of Karda Patrol loped down the field and took off with Mi'hiru Tayla, Tessa and Galen on Kishar and Ket in the lead. They'd just reported urbat headed for the planters along the circle in Daryl's assigned area and were off, to fight with the patrol and resume scouting the circle.

"I think they sleep in their saddles in the air," said ChiChi.

Becca was chewing on a slender stem of sweet grass—a new taste for the city girl. "Why do you say that?" She didn't take her eyes off the Karda taking to the sky. She didn't think she'd ever get bored with that. Elleran shifted his head, asking for a scratch under his chin, and Becca obliged him.

"I heard them talking to Daryl before they left. They scouted from Me'Fiere's area all the way across Me'Cowyn's and then to here in two days. And they had to stop and warn both of them about urbat."

"How far is that?" Becca was half-asleep in the warm sun, lying against the warm Karda. Then she sat up and looked at ChiChi. "What do you mean, you heard 'em talkin' to Daryl? They were inside his tent, and you wasn't. Weren't."

ChiChi didn't look up from braiding small rows in Mia's mane. "They must have flown most of a hundred and fifty kilometers in two days. Kishar and Tessa can fly across the circle, but Ket can't. He's really fast, though. I think he's one of the fastest Karda I've ever seen." Her tone was light as the breeze that ruffled the Karda's mane. She patted Mia's neck. "And the most beautiful. Next to you, of course." She laid her cheek against Mia and closed her eyes.

"You didn't answer my other question."

"Oh? What other question?" A more innocent looking child had never graced the planet.

She was saved by a thunder of incoming wings from a giant black Karda with gold-tipped wings, two Karda patrollers behind him. He loped to a stop, and a tall woman, red hair in a tight coiled braid, slid out of his saddle, jumped to the ground, and followed him into the mews tent with the patrollers.

ChiChi jumped up. "Come on. I'll show you. I think that's Rachyl, Guardian Turin's bonded. The patrollers couldn't stop talking about her. Isn't she beautiful? And that's Gishgal. Wow. He's gorgeous. They say he's the uncle of the fledglings Altan and Marta rescued. Hurry, she'll head straight for Daryl's tent."

She chattered on. Becca thought she could follow her without eyes, listening for the direction of chatter. But ChiChi went silent when they reached the end of the field and slipped into a thicket of bushes greening with tiny leaves. And thorns. "Ouch, ChiChi. Where—"

"Shhhh." ChiChi slipped to the ground, crawling along a trail she'd obviously crawled along before. Some of the long arching canes had been cut short to make a tunnel. The thorns caught Becca's short-chopped hair, but she followed, fighting her borrowed split skirt, worrying about the tears and snags in her borrowed jacket, wanting to slap ChiChi, wanting to slap herself for following her.

They reached the back side of the command tent. ChiChi lifted the bottom of the tent, where a peg was loose, enough for them to hear every word clearly. They'd almost beaten Rachyl there. She was greeting Daryl.

"I wouldn't have your job for any reward. Sometimes I think Turin's stacks of papers are going to topple over and bury him in a snowstorm."

Daryl laughed. "That would take a lot of paper."

Becca stiffened. There was something she hadn't heard before in Daryl's voice. She knew the sound of desperation. It was a sound too often heard in the poorer parts of Restal Prime where poverty ruled. She hadn't read the journals she'd carried to Daryl, but Cael had, and the tone of his voice when he'd told her about them was enough. She didn't ever want to read them. But Cael's anger was missing in Daryl.

"I assume you heard from the Karda that the mercenaries are through the pass. I'm not sure what else you've heard," Rachyl said.

"Tell me. What information I've gotten has been sketchy."

"We met a squad of Readen's men armed with those strange weapons, but the shields you gave Turin worked, and he killed them all. Gishgal and I took the two merc captains to a village he knew had been hit by the Itza Larrak and its urbat. That was all it took. They won't be joining Readen. By now they're setting up permanent camps, three camps, on the north arc of the circle, plus ours. On the way here, Gishgal and I stopped and informed the Planter Corps. They're moving in."

Daryl didn't speak for a moment. When he did, Becca heard the relief in his voice. "And the akenguns?"

"Don't know how much longer they will last. Two already failed. But the rest kill urbat faster than swords and arrows." Becca could almost hear Rachyl's evil-gleeful smile. "The circle is closed. The only way the monsters could get out now is to fly, and they can't fly high enough or long enough. They are trapped."

Daryl said, "The Itza Larrak can fly high enough and far

enough, so don't let your troops get cocky. I've told Turin about the force field of terror it can project. It can do that from behind you and still control the urbat."

"Between Turin and Gishgal, they have enough power to knock it on its weird ass when it tries. I know what it can do, Daryl, and we're prepared. Turin wants to know what you are doing about Restal Prime. Whether you're going to take some of your troops away from the circle to recapture Readen."

"Tell him not to worry. There won't be a weak spot in the circle. I have at least one or two sources of information inside the walls. It's hard for them to get word out—only one of them has a Karda, and he can't mind-talk with him. The problem of Readen has to wait until the Itza Larrak is gone. Its threat is bigger than Restal Prime. I know that only too well."

"The network of communication it's growing? Turin is also worried about that."

"I'm working on something to destroy the Lines of Devastation. If it works, we'll shout to every Karda in the sky. You'll know." The new voice belonged to Cedar.

Becca tapped ChiChi's shoulder and jerked her thumb toward the thorny tunnel. ChiChi shook her head. Becca yanked on her jacket, motioned with her thumb again and started back. She needed to talk to Elleran. There was something she needed to do, and she needed to do it soon.

ChiChi finally followed her out. "What are you in such a hurry about? They were still talking, and I wanted to hear."

"ChiChi, I have to go back." There was a long silence, void of ChiChi's chatter.

Then: "Go back? Back to the Prime? No, you can't, Becca. It's too dangerous."

The ground under Becca's feet trembled. "Stop that, ChiChi." The trembling stopped. "I'll be fine. I know how to stay out of sight. I have to go. There ain't no one in the Prime to get information to Daryl except Krager, and he has'ta slip out of the city and meet Tarath someplace far enough away they won't be seen. Every time he has'ta to do that, his risk of gettin' caught gits worse. I hav'ta go back."

They reached their two Karda, still half-asleep in the sun. Becca dropped down by Elleran's head. ~We have to go back.~

He blinked at her.

She looked down at her borrowed clothes. "Where are the clothes I was wearing, ChiChi? I saw you sneak them away."

"I—uh—I hid them." Her face pinked, and she wouldn't look at Becca. "I thought they might, you know, come in handy? Sometime?"

"And you thought you could pass as a street kid?"

"Weeeell."

Becca laughed. "I'm glad you saved 'em. I'm gonna need 'em."

Elleran and Mia both raised their heads at that.

~You want to go back? Into a Prime taken over by a madman? Who kills without a thought? Where I can't protect you?~ Elleran's pathed voice lifted with alarm at the end of each sentence.

"Mia says you can't. It's too dangerous." ChiChi wiped a spot of blood from her face where a thorn pricked her. "No one will let you go."

"I hav'ta. And you hav'ta help me. There ain't no one else can do this." Becca looked from Elleran to ChiChi to Mia. "And you have to swear you won't follow me. Mia, you can't let her follow me."

ChiChi looked down. Her toe scuffed at the new green shoots of grass. Mia, on the other hand, nodded her head up and down several times, her eyes on Becca with her promise.

"ChiChi?"

"Oh, all right, Becca. I promise."

"Promise what?"

"I swear not to follow you."

"Good, now, where are my clothes, and how are we gonna get enough food and stuff together in a pack and sneak it to the mews and not get caught?"

ChiChi grinned.

Two hours later, Becca lounged in the straw in Elleran's area of the mews tent, waiting. Finally the last patroller and Mi'hiru left, walking out together. The Mi'hiru, Philipa—Becca thought that was her name—glanced over and smiled. "You need to hang out with Elleran as much as you can, Becca. I'm glad to see you here." And she was gone. Becca jumped up, stripped out of her borrowed clothes, wrapped her chest in the bindings—now uncomfortably tight after days without them—grabbed Elleran's rigging, then the pack ChiChi managed to sneak in for her, saddled up and headed for the landing field.

Readen went up the stairs to his tower two at a time. Triumph added steel springs to his legs. He walked the two main rooms, his fingers trailing over chests, his desk, chairs, the bed in his bedroom. He opened a window wide, cold though it was, to chase the musty unoccupied smell out. A smell with a faint tinge of old blood that made him smile.

With a light tap on the door, Odalys, his cold, beautiful servant, entered, her arms full of firewood, her steps silent, as always, on the flagstone floor.

He smiled. A fire. A wood fire he could have someone light in his tower in Restal Hall, now all his. How Daryl would disapprove. His father would have forbidden it, though he indulged in wood fires for his own spaces.

"Should I move into the apartments of my father, Odalys?" he mused, almost to himself.

Odalys didn't answer. She never did. When she'd gotten the fire going, she started cleaning. Readen opened his mouth to tell her to leave, but she said, "Captain Paules waits in your office with his report."

Still smiling, he left. His office. He smiled all the way back down the tower stairs and up the steps to his father's old office, Daryl's former office. Captain Paules stood outside the door to one side, feet apart, hands behind his back, one eye twitching. Readen couldn't seem to stop smiling. Until he saw the office. It was a wreck.

Someone had gone through it in a hurry and, he was certain, removed every slip of paper of the least importance. Even most of Daryl's precious books were gone.

Rage blew through him, and a long, angry hiss snaked between rigid lips and bared teeth. His throat muscles tightened. Pressure inside his head built and built. Anger shoved the intruder in his mind to the back of his skull behind his seething thoughts, where it coiled, waiting.

He looked at Captain Paules standing in the doorway, brittle and tense. "Find the steward Lerys. Now. I want to know who is responsible for this."

The captain took three steps toward the stairs, but Readen stopped him. "Never mind. I need your report first." And he pulled Paules in. It was like pulling a mechanical toy soldier. "Then send Lerys to clean this up."

He moved behind the plain table that Daryl had changed for his father's massive ornate desk. He'd have to have that found and brought back. His father. More rage pulsed inside him. The vapid, self-indulgent, irresponsible Roland was his father after all, not the Itza Larrak. At the base of his skull, the waiting cold pushed more slow tendrils through his mind.

For a moment, when he looked at the captain, it was as though he looked at him through two sets of eyes. He realized he'd stood too long, staring at Paules. He reached down, righted a fallen chair, and sat, shoving papers to the floor. The elation filling him when he entered the Prime and Restal Hall so effortlessly was subsumed by his anger—fuel for its fire. "Report, Captain."

Paules held his arms in front of him, his hands folded over his crotch. He opened and closed his mouth, tried to swallow, and finally spoke.

"There are none of Guar...of Daryl's guards left in the hall. He must have dismissed a number of servants as there are only a few still here. The city is under our control, with half a squad of our men stationed at each major intersection, and two full squads in the town plaza. One in three men are armed with akenguns."

Readen stood and walked to the floor-to-ceiling small-paned

windows behind him and stared out over his father's precious gardens, now untidy, untrimmed, neglected.

"How many of Kyle's troops have you arrested?"

It took Paules too long to answer. Readen turned back. The muscles of his face contracted into a smile that wasn't a smile.

The captain swayed. "Fifty-seven."

Readen was silent, nostrils flared. The claw-like nails of his black-gloved hands bit into his palms. "I hope," he said, his voice quiet and smooth as a silken noose, "you are going to tell me there is a much larger number dead, and you have recovered whatever it was that shielded them from my weapons."

"No, sir." Captain Paules's too-high voice grated in Readen's ears, and the entity in the back of his mind growled.

"Commander Kyle?" The soft words sliced at Captain Paules.

"Gone, sir." Sounding as if the words ripped his throat raw, he added, "Before we got inside."

Readen closed his eyes. Killing Minra Shreeve had been gratifying. She'd always been one of Daryl's more vocal supporters, her distaste for Readen evident, even when they were children. But it might have been a miscalculation. His head filled with harsh mechanical laughter that was not his. He had to wait till it passed, but echoes of it lingered. He couldn't get rid of them.

"Find him. Find Krager. Find Cael."

Krager, Kyle, and Cael would be found even if there were more "miscalculations."

Paules left, and Readen stood still. Wind rattled a window, and a lone paper drifted off the table. Transfixed, he watched it fall, slipping side to side, until it settled on a lopsided tumble of other papers. He breathed. In and out. With long slow breaths, he battled the thing in his head until it shrank to a small dot and settled, thrumming at the base of his skull. A shock of current pulsed through his body twice. He breathed out a final long, slow breath, and power moved down his arms, through his trunk, and into his legs, filling him.

He moved to the window and stared through the tiny wavy panes until the garden faded into the last light of the day. His whole body thrummed in time with the small dot pulsing, faint and persistent, in his mind. Then he pulled his hood over his head, making certain nothing of his changed body showed, and walked toward the back halls of the building, down a narrow set of stairs out into the garden. The shrubs along the path he took were overgrown and snatched at his cloak. He didn't notice.

The night-black figure of the Itza Larrak waited for him, its wings unnaturally still and silent.

Sweat trickled down the side of Readen's face, but he didn't dare reach up to wipe it away. The Itza Larrak stood, an ominous black statue barely visible in the darkness at the end of the garden. It didn't speak until Readen was near enough to reach out and touch it. He didn't.

The glare from its hot yellow eyes reached into Readen's head and pulled out every thought, every secret, every wish, examined them, and shoved them back. Its implacable face showed nothing. "The mercenaries you hired have joined Guardian Turin on the north edge of the circle. The pitiful group of men you sent to meet them is dead. Every one of them—their akenguns lost to Turin." The Itza Larrak's musical mechanical voice was arctic.

Its words burned like hot ice as Readen slipped and slid to regain the senses the Itza Larrak scrambled in his head. When they finally began to clear, he felt only traces of the rage he should have felt. It was there, but smothering, cold, analytical rage against Turin and the loss of the guns. The loss of the men didn't register.

His head ached as if someone pounded fists against the walls of his skull. The thing in the back of his mind spread its tentacles, swelled and curled around the part that tried to scream its hot fury, that fought to regain its space, that fought for control. He bent over, hands braced on his knees, aware only of pain, while the battle raged in his head. The part that was Readen managed to throw up barriers and his mind split.

Readen straightened. His vision blurred—the Itza Larrak wavered in and out like it had when it first began to materialize. Then it turned, took two steps, spread its pierced metal wings, and took off into the darkness with an awkwardness Readen didn't note.

He headed back across the garden, his first steps staggering and awkward like a toddler's. It was hard to keep his balance.

Only the part of his mind fighting the tentacles wondered why the Itza Larrak had come and gone with no instructions or orders to deal with the loss of the guns and mercenaries. Only that part of his mind wondered at how his rage turned cold, devoid of emotion.

The rest of it relaxed and waited.

Now it would survive.

CHAPTER TWENTY-THREE

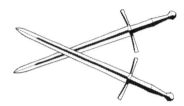

"If you need to get a message to me, tell a Karda to relay it to Abala. Mi'hiru Amanda can tell you how to signal one in the sky if you have to."

Daryl's voice was too tight, as it got every time Cedar left his sight. But, of course, he'd never admit it. Didn't even know he was doing it. Or why. It was alright. She'd wait. And she wouldn't tell him she might have to go back to the ship.

The mews was crowded with Karda patrollers and Mi'hiru throwing on saddles and buckling rigging as fast as they could. And they'd gotten good at being fast. This was the third alarm in two days. High flying Karda spotted urbat in the forty kilometer arc of the Circle of Disorder guarded by Daryl's troops. They couldn't actually see them, because they had to stay far away from the circle, but they watched for telltale dust clouds. They would hit the planters working at the circle's edge in fifteen minutes. There were patrollers with them, and Daryl and his men would be there in ten.

"I'm sorry, Cedar. I wish I could go with you." Daryl gave a yank to the last buckle.

This was the fourth, maybe the fifth time he'd said the same thing. They saw little of each other. Every time he came back from another urbat battle, she was taking off to talk to another holder or guardian about her settlers.

"Daryl, you are sending eight troopers with me like you do every time I leave. Troopers you need. And stop looking at my leg that way. There's nothing you can do to fix it." He was in love with the mystery of her leg. "I can walk. I can ride. I can even stumble into a sort-of run. True, I can't skip, but who feels like skipping now, anyway." She shook her staff at him.

"Don't hit me." He took it away from her and secured it under the stirrup leathers.

"Go. Fight. And don't let Abala get hurt."

"What about me?"

"A good knock on the head would help."

Abala sneezed a Karda laugh, and Cedar winked at him. It was good to see a little light in Daryl's eyes. It wasn't there very often now.

He moved to Abala, his back to her, and tightened a strap that didn't need tightening. "Will you go back to the ship?"

"Only if I need to. After these people get settled and I've got the microbes for you." Cedar tried to keep her distress, her worry about her mother out of her voice. He looked at her over his shoulder as he swung up on Abala. She smelled his worry, faint through the leaves of her tree filter.

"Come back." And he loped away.

Did he think she'd wait to fall to the ground in a smoking ball of broken ship? She stepped back beside Illyria, leaned against the wall with her good foot propped against the non-working leg, watched the troops move out, and watched him until he was a distant dot in the sky.

She cursed. Her black hole of a bionic leg ached, and she had to shift her weight to the other one. When would she learn it wouldn't hold her up? There was nothing she—or Daryl, however curious he was about it—could do.

He'd left Troopers Peele and Lange and six others, a full wing, plus Mi'hiru Amanda and Bettan, her Karda partner. Seven people just to fly with her to Ardencroft. People he needed here. All seven of them were staring after the two wings that just left. "Amanda," she said. "You know the two of us would be fine by ourselves. I know what to do to help with camp. We don't need a half a wing—"

A voice drawled behind her. "Lange, what do you think would happen if Daryl ever got good and angry?"

Another voice drawled, the words just as slow, "Being that he's got the talent of a Guardian, Peele, one of the strongest on the planet, I don't know as I want to be a charred cinder blowing in the wind."

Amanda sputtered, and Cedar turned to see the wing already mounted. She sighed and let the Mi'hiru help her up on Illyria. Amanda leaped into the saddle from Bettan's knee and led the way out of the mews. Illyria loped down the field behind them. Takeoffs were almost violent as the Karda's wings snapped out and grabbed the air again and again, lifting them away from the ground, but she was better at moving with Illyria, much better. She no longer felt like she had to hold on to her head, not all the time anyway.

Cedar grabbed the pommel handle and concentrated on moving with Illyria. Even so, she was sure her head would snap off before they evened out. She could look down, now, without a revolt from her stomach, and watch the forest slide by beneath her. The black branches, glistening in the drizzle, reached for the sky, pale with new leaves and burgeoning seeds in hazy pastel shades of green, pink, and pale orange. Occasional spots of brighter whites and reds shouted instead of hinted with their flowers.

This open space didn't bother her at all. Maybe Galen was right, and she'd get used to the barrens. Illyria tilted to change direction, and Cedar grabbed the pommel tighter. Maybe she'd even get used to this.

Two days later, the last of the red was disappearing from the western sky behind them, and they touched down in Ardencroft. A long, U-shaped stone wall marked one side of the field, a long line of wagons marked the other. One end of the U—the new still roof-less mews/stable—was draped with a tarp. Three people ran from the village to the other end, separated by a full wall and future tack and feed rooms, where horses were stabled. Now very nervous horses—Karda were apex predators. Horses were food. Forbidden food, but Cedar didn't think the horses knew that.

Short walls marked off spaces for stalls inside the mews end, and they draped their straps and saddles over them, blankets spread on top to dry. When they finished grooming and feeding the Karda, it was a short walk on a well-trodden path to the village. Cedar patted Illyria on the neck and whispered, "Thank you for the ride, Illyria. If you agree to keep carrying me, I'll try to get better at balancing with you instead of against you."

Illyria turned her head, winked at her, and went back to her food.

Assam greeted them at the village edge. "The little inn has room for you patrollers if you're willing to double up. There's no one else visiting at the moment. Welcome back, Cedar."

"This is Amanda, Assam, and squad leader Peele—" and Cedar rattled off the names of the other seven.

"I'm glad you're here," Assam said to the patrollers. "I've only fought the urbat once, and I'm sure you all have more experience with them than I ever want to have. Will you be able to stay a couple of days? There are fighters coming with this group of people from the ship, and your experience will be invaluable."

Peele nodded and reached out to grasp Assam's forearm. "Yes, sir. We'll be glad of the opportunity to help. And to see a space ship."

His voice was firm and sober, but Cedar sneezed. The smell of curiosity and the glee of a child expecting a big new toy filled her nostrils. If she weren't so tired, she'd laugh out loud.

Cedar and Amanda split off from the patrollers and headed through the dusk toward the small house she shared with Mireia and sometimes Marta. Everything about her ached. Riding was hard. "Slow down, Amanda. Your muscles are used to flying and mine aren't." She didn't add, "And my leg slows me down even more."

Amanda laughed. "Mireia will have some aspirtea, and you'll

sleep like a baby in a real bed with no little rocks that grow into boulders in the night."

And she did until a pounding on the door woke her, and she opened her eyes to rare sunlight and a crotchety, exasperated, gleefully wicked voice that could only be Glenn's yelled, "Well, wake her up. Come on, Cedar. Work to do. Time to get your hands dirty, unless you've been flying too high for dirt work since you left me here with that meteor-head Assam."

She struggled her stiff, sore body back into the few clothes she'd taken off last night. She needed a bath. And clean clothes. How good it was to hear the raspy voice yelling at her again. Just like home.

"Good morning, Glenn. I hope you told whoever's coming to bring coffee. It sounds like you need it." She hugged his too skinny shoulders, the ones that were always so broad and solid before.

He pulled away and grabbed her staff. "Here. We got things to do."

"Good morning, Cedar. I trust you rested well and are ready for some sustenance that doesn't taste of dirt and woodsmoke," Mireia said as if Glenn hadn't spoken, her voice calm and amused.

An urge to cry thickened Cedar's throat, and all she could do was nod. She missed the mother who used to be like this all the time, not just part of the time. She knew her mother wouldn't be coming with this transport—with any transport if given the choice. Cedar couldn't let her make that choice.

"Thank you, Mireia, and another cup of aspirtea would be welcome. I was so tired last night I'm certain I was rude."

"You are never rude, Cedar." Mireia put an arm around her and pulled her to the table where Amanda sat inhaling a sweet-smelling bowl of something with dried fruit. "You eat, too, Glenn, before I have to call a healer to bring you back to life when your brain explodes. You've done everything possible to get ready for our new people."

Our new people. New people sounded a lot better than refugees. And "our." She said "our."

Light saturated the air where Cedar and Glenn stood on crunchy, dry needles in the shelter of a…spruce? Amanda, Mireia, and the three other finders waited under a large tent set up at the edge of a pasture adjoining the village. The warehouse pod, Cedar's gro-pod, and the sections of the living pod that had separated from the ship were located there. Even to Cedar, they looked…alien. "Is this a spruce tree, Glenn?"

"Yup."

"How do you know?" It was like being in a green tent. A shedding tent. She dodged a few falling needles and stepped on one of its long, oval cones. Glenn caught her before she fell. "It's needles are dropping. Is it dying?"

"Does that in the spring."

"How do you know?"

He shoved his hands in his pockets and turned his head away. "Can't *not* know, Cedar."

Cedar smelled his irritation. She stretched a hand up and picked a few needles from above her. The sharp smell cleared her head. "It's not easy, is it, Glenn? It's not going to be easy for people to accept."

"Don't mean I don't like knowing things I shouldn't know, but… I asked one of the finders if I could turn it off. Or lose it. He'd never been asked that before and didn't know of anyone who'd tried." He looked at her. "It's going to be a lot harder to explain the alien and its minions."

Cedar's shoulders scrunched tight as if she could cover her ears with them.

Glenn took hold of her upper arm. "Assam told me about the attack, and I know the reason this village was empty. Something killed every person in it. All of them." He took a deep breath and blew it out. "It'll be easier to explain talent than to explain what we might have to fight and why no one was living here."

"I know."

He laughed. "At least nobody believes in ghosts. I hope."

They didn't speak again, and finally, the thunder of the approaching transport tugs sounded above them. Cedar took a deep breath. Who was coming? Who would be on the transport? She knew Sharon, Director of Security, would be. It wouldn't be her mother. She caught the sigh of relief before it escaped, but behind it pressed a big gust of guilt. She was glad she couldn't smell her own emotions—they'd probably make her throw up.

"Landing this transport will be a lot simpler than landing the living pod sections. It was a good thing it broke up. Getting air to circulate through an intact pod would have been a…bastard."

Cedar gave Glenn a smile with teeth. She'd broken him of the habit of using the other B word when she was twelve by asking, every time he said it, what it meant. Since there were no dogs on the ship except in books and vids, he had a hard time explaining.

They covered their heads with both arms. Debris started flying, and heat from the engines drove the drizzle away at least until they shut off and cooled, which seemed to take forever. The two of them walked toward the lowering ramp, and Assam joined them. Oh, galaxies. Cedar recognized the first three at the opening. Three of the biggest doubters on the ship. Meta, Head of Housekeeping under Clare, whom she Did Not Like. Jaden, who worked in accounting, and Javier—Cedar wasn't sure what he did—a teacher she thought. The ones who didn't want to leave. Who wanted to find another planet, certain the ship would last long enough to get them there.

The last one off was Sharon. She stopped at the top of the ramp, looked around, closed her eyes, and Cedar could tell she was breathing in the myriad smells of the new world. She spotted Cedar and ran to the ground, stumbled in unfamiliar grass, looked down, and knelt to run her fingers through the new green shoots.

Her eyes were wide, their pupils dark, and her brows headed for her hairline. "I know this isn't Earth, Cedar, but it looks just like the vids."

It was afternoon before every one was settled and Cedar found time to talk to Sharon alone. The mist finally blew off, and high clouds painted dancing shadows to run across the ground. They stood outside one of the living pod sections.

"I don't think I fully understood about the weather, Cedar," said Sharon. She wrapped her arms around her shoulders, and pulled her borrowed wool cloak tight. "The only other planet I've been on was hot and dry. Of course, I got almost this wet with sweat. I don't think I've ever been cold before. I've been in the seed banks on ship, and they're cold, sure, but I've always been in protective clothes, and I was in and out. I didn't have to stay there."

"It's actually warm today, Sharon. We're four tendays into spring." She turned and looked behind them at the pod. Or pods it was now. She shuddered. "I don't want to live in one of these."

"You're practically a native, then. Half of those who came this time may never step outside them again."

"The first time I saw the barrens, really saw them, I was terrified. So much space. You could see for kilometers. So many places for strange and dangerous things to hide and come at you. It's going to be hard for people to adjust to it. Add in the magic...? Is there anyone with this group who's been on a planet before?"

"Some of my people and a few others. They're still exploring the village—the one's complaining about how primitive everything they see is." Sharon's head never stopped moving. She never stopped looking—at everything. "I wish I could stay. I wish I could get on one of those horses and lose myself in these woods. I'd like to see the barrens and the green oases you talk about. I don't even know if I want to ride a Karda and fly over it all. I want to feel it, touch it, smell it, taste it."

They stood for several minutes. She took a deep breath, blew it out, and said, "I will, but not just now."

Cedar said, "Maybe you should just tell me what you don't want to tell me."

"Is there a place we can sit and talk without being interrupted?" She smirked and leaned close to whisper, "I brought coffee."

Cedar took off. "Follow me."

"Nice staff, by the way. If you hit somebody with that, they'd stay down."

"I'm a fighting fool."

Mireia and her finders were busy with the new people, and the house she and Cedar stayed in was empty. Cedar wasted no time getting there. The magma stones in the stove were glowing, and water was soon boiling.

"I know this is how to make tea. You should be able to make coffee like this too." She was right, even if they did have to strain it through their teeth.

They sat at the table in the small kitchen. "I still think I'm in the middle of a vid. This can't be real." She took a gulp of coffee and sputtered. "Ugh, Cedar. I think you need to experiment more. Coffee grounds in the teeth isn't pleasant." Sharon put the cup down. "First, Ahnna is fine. She's pretending nothing is changing, but she's fine. Your mother's not alone. There are too many like her, and I'm not sure what we will do about them. Most of them are old, some infirm, some are mothers with small children. I wish Kendra ignored that problem like she's ignoring everything else instead of making it worse. Every time Clare starts telling her about the latest disaster on the ship, she brushes her off. 'I was Director of Engineering and Maintenance before you were, Clare. I think I know this ship.' Then she'll poke her head out her door, glare at whoever's near, and ask when you're coming back. It's like she thinks all she has to do to make this problem go away is give you a good talking to when you come back from your little leave time."

She picked up her cup, looked in it, swirled it, and put it back down with a disgusted look. "I think she forgot she sent you three here as ambassadors to pave our way. When she does come out, she berates Clare about what she calls 'our maintenance problems,' then starts reassuring people. Everything is going to be all right. Nothing to worry about. She's sure the walkways will be working soon." She put both elbows on the table, her head in her hands. "She's supporting the doubters. Giving them ammunition, and nothing Clare or I or Arlan say penetrates the wall she's put up. Mark, of course, buries himself in his lists and doesn't look up. If we don't do something, Cedar, people are going to die up there, and I don't want to be one of them. I *won't* be one of them. But I don't want to cry mutiny, either."

Cedar took a careful sip of her coffee. The word was said, and Cedar didn't think Sharon would let it be unsaid. She didn't think she could either. "If you let the cup sit for a minute, the grounds settle down. But, somehow, I don't think letting Kendra sit for a minute is going to work. Do I need to go back up?"

There was a rap on the door, and Assam stuck his head in. "I smell coffee." Cedar waved her hand at the pot on the stove, and he poured himself a cup. "You two don't look happy, and I don't think I want to ask why."

"Did I bring you enough fighters to make you happy, Assam?" asked Sharon.

"I'm giving them a little time to absorb what I told them about the urbat. All of them have been on a planet and fought dangerous things before. They're deep in discussion with the Karda Patrol wing Cedar brought with her. Although I think they're talking more about flying than fighting. Thanks, Sharon. You picked well. And I'm glad you brought some of the ship's supply of akengun shields, because we got a strange message from Restal Prime you both need to hear. Glenn will be here in a minute to discuss what it means."

"From what Sharon has told me, I think there's more than one thing we need to discuss, Assam." Cedar didn't like hearing about a messenger from the Prime. Her shoulders tightened against the blow she feared was about to hit.

"It was from Daryl's brother, Readen. He's taken over the Prime and wants to send troops here to protect us from Daryl. I got the feeling his definition of protect is not the same as mine. His messenger carried an akengun."

Daryl sat on a camp stool under the awning of the cook's tent in the planter's camp and watched Galen work, moving a hill of dirt to bury dead and stinking urbat. Rain hung like shifting gauze curtains from the clouds, and Galen looked like he was melting.

Daryl had looked up after pulling his sword from the last monster to see him arrowing for the camp, ahead of the rain, with Tessa, Ket, and Kishar. Abala was now with their two Karda and a few un-partnered Karda, sheltered under the low, sweeping branches of a massive spruce. They couldn't fly in this. Which worried him.

Major flaw. What major flaw in our strategy was Cedar talking about? He supposed he could see it—a siege was a risky tactic and took time they might not have. But he wasn't sure what to do about it.

Tessa swung a stool down and sat beside him. "I'm glad I don't have to be out there with him in this. Does it make me a bad bond mate? That I'm happy to sit here in the dry and watch him work?"

"I don't think so."

"Nope, neither do I." She put her forearms on her knees and relaxed forward. "I'm tired, Daryl. Galen is tired. Ket is tired. And Kishar, Kishar is tired and sad."

There was no answer to that. So was he, so was every one— which she knew well. Finally, he said, "In spite of everything, it is good to see you happy, Tessa, even in the middle of all this."

She twisted her head around, looked at him, and back at Galen. "Yes."

There was another long silence. "I know the rain would have eventually cleared the stink away, but…."

"After how many years of rotting urbat corpse smell?" Tessa finished for him and stuck her finger in her open mouth. "Gag."

"Cedar says our strategy has a major flaw."

Tessa dropped her head for a minute and looked out at Galen again. "Kishar says the Larrak never needs to rest. It isn't like anything else in this world. I'd say it's like a machine, but that isn't right, either. It's…it's…alien is the right word, the only word. It's been gone, what? Thirty minutes."

"If that."

"And it's probably already attacking somewhere else right now."

It was Daryl's turn to drop his head. "Even urbat have a hard time, fighting in the mud."

"It doesn't care. I don't think 'care' is a word you could ever use about the Itza Larrak. I wonder if they were all like that, the others of its kind."

There was silence for a few seconds. Daryl's head jerked up. Others of its kind. Others of its kind. Faint bells rang in his mind, so far away they were just a hint. He sat up straight. Had Cedar seen this when he hadn't? "Others of its kind, Tessa. What's its main goal?"

"To destroy us."

"No. That's not it. It's not enough. It's *kind* could destroy us, but *it* can't. Not alone. It can devastate Restal, but it can't destroy Adalta. Not by itself. According to Kishar, there are no more in the other circles. And it's slowing. The urbat are slowing."

Tessa shook her head and started to speak.

"No, wait, Tessa. You know they are. It's not enough, but we've gained an edge we didn't have before. Why? Where are its efforts going? Where is its energy going?"

They looked at each other.

"Survival. It's fighting for its survival, and nothing else matters. Not us, not the urbat, nothing else. And where is its survival going to come from?"

"The lines," they both breathed it at the same time.

"Its communication lines. It's going to come from the Larrak it calls when the lines connect," whispered Daryl. "We're fighting a long, slow battle of attrition. How long can we hold this defense together? Months? Years? Until the other Guardians have to take their troops and go? I've known this, we all have, we just haven't wanted to know it. It can get at us, but we can't get at it." Daryl hesitated. "We *were* going to use the microbes on all the lines, and hope they would be enough to destroy them in time. But, Tessa, what if we concentrate on only one, the one right over there?" Daryl waved a hand toward the southwest of the circle. "The one that's almost connecting. What if we attack it with all the microbes Cedar can get for us, all at once."

"The Larrak will have to come out." Tessa's words were the barest whisper of sound, of hope. "And this time it won't be right next to the circle where it can retreat." She ran out through the curtains of rain to get Galen, who was standing, shoulders slumped, as if the downpour would wash his exhaustion away with its fat, heavy, pounding drops.

Daryl closed his eyes and smiled inside. Now he'd be forced to tell Cedar she was right.

CHAPTER TWENTY-FOUR

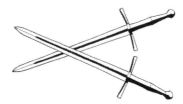

"Made a hole in her belly big as a melon with a strange stick he carried."

The quiet words Krager heard too often echoed in a sudden lull in the tavern noise. The man in the stained grocer's apron who uttered them looked like he wanted to be the chair he was sitting in. Just a piece of furniture. No one wanted to talk about the woman Readen killed at the gates to the Prime, and too many people of the Prime didn't see it and so didn't believe it. Possibly more than half.

The talk came back, subdued as it was too often now. Krager pulled his hat down further and lifted his mug of not very good ale. It didn't take much to slow the talk lately. No loud conversations except from those whose drunken haze never ended. Desultory fights. Half thrown insults often cut off in the middle. No one wanted the guard called. Too many of them carried the strange weapons that might not make melon-sized holes in your body but killed you anyway.

Beside him, a thinner, scruffier, hunch-shouldered Cael said, "He's sending messengers to holders and villages all around the Prime. Armed with akenguns. Two days ago, he sent one to Ardencroft."

Krager forced himself to breathe and came as close to panic as he'd ever been. Jenna was supposed to be in Ardencroft, though he suspected she still was visiting holders for Daryl to see who'd fight for him, or at least not fight against him when he was able to move against Readen. When he finished with the Itza Larrak. Krager didn't let himself think about any other possibility. He scratched his head with more vigor than usual. Hiding in the stews of the Prime carried its costs, and he was afraid he was carrying more than one. A bath and some pine soap needed to be moved up on his list of essential things to accomplish today. At least the constant itches distracted him from his panic.

"I hope the two you brought are well hidden."

Cael looked at him, unblinking, until the noise around them peaked for a second, then he said, "Old man Patel's loft. Southeast corner. Now there's three, and Readen has one less guard."

"That might have been foolish."

"Didn't have a choice." He didn't lift his head, but his eyes moved sideways to the filthy floor. "Thought he was a friend. Thought he'd be a good contact."

Krager knew better than to say he was sorry.

Cael moved his hand and flipped a tight wad of paper across the sticky table.

Krager palmed it with three fingers, lifted his mug to his mouth in the same motion, shifted his chair sideways, and leaned back, ankles crossed.

Cael's head was still down, and he spoke into his mug. "The roster of duty for the next tenday and names of the few contacts I'm certain of. None of them was issued a gun. When I say certain, I mean reasonably certain. Be careful."

"How'd you get the roster?"

"It took years to learn how to get around Readen's wards without leaving traces. Anyway, there's too many coming and going from the keep for them to be very strong 'cept on his study."

"Can you…?"

"Nope. It's a Water thing. Maybe I could teach someone, but it would take too long. Wasn't easy to develop. Like I said, it took years."

The silence stretched while the two men stared at each other, thinking about the possibilities this offered. Not smiling on the outside, only with their eyes. Krager fought the sudden lift of euphoria.

"Even more reason you must be careful. I hope you have a good hiding place." Cael might be the only chance they had to save the Prime. "Stay in it." Krager stood, nodded, knocked his knuckles on the table once, and left. Cael would revolt if Krager tied a leash on him.

His next stop was Mother Girt's Bloody Talons tavern by way of too many alleys. It would add to the lovely odor he carried with him. He pushed through the door of the tavern and did a dance to avoid a bucket of soapy water sloshing across the flagstones. One look at the boy with the bucket and his shoulders slumped, his temper spiked. It was not a boy. Becca avoided his eyes, hers on the movements of the mop in her hands as if it were the last thing she would ever see. Which it might be.

"What the bloody hell are you doing here?" The words hissed through his clenched teeth.

She glanced over at the two men arguing by the stove and back at him.

"Kitchen." His jaw was so tight it hurt to snarl the word. Becca went on mopping and refused to look up.

Krager joined Mother Girt at her usual place behind the end of the bar, her face set, eyes glaring and daring him to say anything. "She showed up a few days ago. What could I do, run her off?"

He put his head in his hands, rubbing at the itch from the sweat and grit on his face.

"You need a bath and some good strong pine sap soap. Don't need to ask where you've been sleeping. I can smell the alleys on you."

"You offerin'?"

"Hunnh."

"Didn't think so. Who do I need to talk to?"

Mother Girt spoke seldom and listened a lot—her hearing was sharp, and she could hone in on conversations that caught her attention despite the tavern's noise level. And any word about Readen caught her attention. She'd lost a little kitchen helper years before. The only reason Krager knew about it was she'd asked him to look for her. He'd never found her. It was years before he and she realized what happened to her. With one of her few sentences, she'd once told him she thought Readen used a "look at me: I'm handsome, charming, witty, and, oh, by the way, not evil" spell. Krager wasn't sure she was wrong.

He memorized the names she gave him, hit Becca with a pointed glare and jerked his thumb toward the kitchen. She wrung out the mop with great care and propped it by the door. Hefting the bucket, she opened the door and sloshed its contents over each step with fastidious care. Finally, she headed for the kitchen. Krager didn't think it was possible to walk that slow without falling over. By the time they faced each other over the long deal table, her expression had morphed from scared little girl to belligerent teen.

Krager lowered his head and forced the words between tight lips. "Why did you come back, and how did you get back here so fast? You didn't have time to get to Ardencroft, find Daryl, and return. He needs to see those journals."

"I went to his camp. That's where he was. And I gave him the journals. Then there wasn't anything for me to do, some I came back. You need me here."

"That's twice as far as Ardencroft. It's not possible." A pain built between his eyes.

"Oh, Krager." Her sudden smile was a bright magic ball of light. "A Karda found me. Some men tried ta stop me on the road, 'n Elleran swooped down outa nowhere and drove 'em off. He knew how ta find Daryl, so he took me there. He's beautiful and he says he'll be with me for as long as I live and when I'm old 'nough I can be a Mi'hiru if I want but he won't make me if I decide I wanna do somethin' else but he'll never leave." She stopped for a breath, but only one. "And he agreed with me that you need us here because we c'n talk to each other in our heads and there's no one else here who can and Daryl needs ta know what's happn'n and you need to be able to pass messages to him."

"Did this wonderful Karda show up with saddle and straps? How did you ride him?" Krager was still untangling her words.

The brightness faded from Becca's face. "You think I'm lying? What 'chu think I did, throw Cael's satchel away, turn round and come back with a big fat lie? His name's Elleran, and we used the straps from my pack and anythin' else I could find to tie around his neck. He was careful, told me what ta do 'n how ta move, and I didn't fall off. I'm not lying to ya, Krager. I don' think I could if I wanted to. You're too scary." Her head was down. Her fingers traced the grain of the wood in the table.

He didn't want her to look up, afraid there'd be tears.

Finally, he untangled enough of her words for them to register. "You talk with your Karda?" Oh, Adalta, some men found her. Cael should never have sent her. Krager should have gone after her and sent the journals with Tarath. Guilt was dirtier than the worst alley he'd been through. He'd never be able to wash it off.

She must have heard it in his voice. "I'm okay, Krager. Nothing happened to me, and now I have Elleran. I have somebody. I'm not alone anymore."

Now the guilt was heavy enough he didn't know if he'd be able to stand. "Did Daryl read them?" Daryl's over-developed sense of rightness could well have convinced him it would be an invasion into Readen's life and not ethical to read his brother's private journals.

Becca looked up, a little crease of worry on her dirty forehead. "He didn't come out of his tent for a long time. I think he wanted to come back here immediately, but Cedar talked to him. ChiChi said—"

The wide-eyed guilt on her face said if she could reach out and stuff those last two words back in her mouth, she would.

"ChiChi said...?" he growled. What had those two girls been doing?

Becca's attempt to laugh failed. "Someday she'll be a better spy than you or Cael."

A muscle popped in Krager's jaw. "Where's ChiChi and... where's ChiChi now?"

She looked at him, head tilted.

"Be careful, Becca. That smirk might not wash off your face with the dirt. If you ever get to wash your face."

"They're making a circuit of holders for Daryl, to see who's still with him. He sent troopers with them, and ChiChi said Jenna has a good idea of who not to trust from before when they went with you." She switched directions. "Do you have a message for Daryl for Elleran to relay?"

Krager forced himself to breathe again. Jenna was as safe as anyone could be in Restal now, and he couldn't afford to divide his concentration. "Yes. Tell him Cael can get through Readen's wards undetected. If he can stay alive long enough, we might have a chance to finish this without harming anyone but Readen. We have a hundred and forty troops in the city waiting for him to defeat the Itza Larrak, so tell him to hurry. I don't know how long we can keep them hidden. No pressure. And no, you don't need to know who *we* is."

He headed for the door out the back. "Keep your head down and your ears open. Nothing else. Do you hear me, Becca? Nothing. Else."

"Daryl sent word they need microbes for four sections of the Lines of Devastation, Mannik." Cedar and Mannik, her assistant, worked in a makeshift lab in a small outbuilding in Ardencroft propagating pollution-eating microbes he'd brought from the ship. "Send them as soon as you finish and remind Galen they need to be hungry when he distributes them."

She looked at the vivid scar on Mannik's forehead. "You're not going back up there. If the captain asks about you, I'll tell her you had a relapse and let her know I hold her responsible for what happened to the three of you and the lab. I'll be back as soon as I can."

"Where are you going? Back to your circuit of holders? I thought Assam was doing that, and you were going back to the ship."

Cedar rubbed her head with vigor and looked up at the ceiling as if she saw spiders or other crawlies there. "Sharon and I are taking Jaden, Meta, and Javier to see the produce gardens and fields outside the village to convince them this world is safe and livable without all the tech they're used to. We'll also show them how the living pods are set up. I hope seeing it and remembering why the pods are here will help convince them the ship is failing. Sharon says they're the three biggest naysayers on the ship. She worked hard to persuade them to come see for themselves."

"Meta." He grinned. "Better you than me. I wish I could have seen the pod get here. Glenn said it was amazing. Clare and her engineering crew looked like they'd done this many times. Tell her he said that, 'cause I know he didn't tell her before she left."

"The shock will prostrate her. Should I put Meta on a Karda first thing?"

She left Mannik laughing.

Meta was one of the most vocal people on the ship, and she'd been very vocal when Cedar was named Director of Bio-Systems at her too-young age. The three of them and Sharon waited for her in front of the village's Downy Feather Inn. If Meta pursed her lips any tighter, they'd fall off from lack of circulation. Jaden hunched his shoulders so tight it was probably slowing his heart. Only Javier was looking around with curiosity, pointing at things, and asking Sharon questions she couldn't answer. He didn't wait for them anyway.

"Meta says she wants to fly on one of those Karda *things*." Sharon's face was solemn, and her voice was so dry it made Cedar thirsty.

"Ah. We'll take a tour of the mews later. And, Meta, the Karda are not things, they are sentient beings who communicate tele-pathically."

Meta snorted. "Telepathic. Hunnh."

"How much of the village have you seen? The people Guardian

Daryl sent here have worked hard to get it ready for you." Cedar hid a sigh and ignored Meta's disbelief. The mews visit would be interesting.

"Not for me," Jaden muttered into his chest, his head down, his shoulders hunched.

"What was that strange stuff they fed us for dinner last night?" Meta unpursed her lips long enough to ask, her loud voice even louder than usual.

Sharon looked at Cedar. The muscles of her face were twitching with the effort not to laugh. "The innkeeper—that's what she's called, right?—said it was lamb stew."

Jaden's eyes widened. "Lamb. You killed a baby animal to eat? A baby animal?" His voice screeched against Cedar's ears, and she smelled incredulity with a hint of nausea. "I ate a baby animal?" That odor faded to make way for a strong smell of smug satisfaction. He found ammunition he could use.

Sharon exuded a smell of laughter. "And you remarked on the subtle flavoring and asked for a second bowl. You eat chicken and eggs, Jaden, and eggs are baby chickens. What's the difference? The only reason you haven't eaten baby animals lately is because they're too difficult to raise on the ship. We stock up on meat from every planet we visit."

Now Cedar smelled anger from all three representatives and wondered if her tree filter's leaves would burn up before the day was over. She reached deeper into Adalta for water to strengthen it. Under the anger, she smelled its origin—the strong scent of fear approaching panic. This was the first time on a planet for all three.

"Before we start our tour, I know someone from Medic talked to you about open space and your mind and body reaction to this new experience. You've all gotten a few hours of VR to help acclimate. But if at any time you begin to feel uncomfortable, let us know, and we'll stop until you feel safe."

"Humph," was Meta's response. "Let's get to it so we can report back to the ship about how unacceptably crude this world is. I've never been as cold as I was last night. I had to ask for more coverings for that decidedly uncomfortable bed."

"Oh, so did I," said Sharon. "It was wonderful to curl up in my warm cocoon with the cold air teasing my nose with all kinds of new and different smells." She linked her arm in Meta's. "Let's go see the gardens and the greenhouses. Did you know even the tiniest villages have greenhouses? Cedar can tell us what they're planting. Or Glenn. I understand he spends most of his time there."

Cedar swallowed a snort. Poor Glenn. He'd spent his life avoiding Meta, who would follow him everywhere if she could.

A small wagon with arched ribs over it and a canvas cover rolled to one side pulled up to the inn. None of the three was happy with their transport, but they climbed in. Glenn joined them when they toured the produce gardens at the edge of the town. They talked with some of the people planting and weeding—all chosen specially as the most friendly, light-hearted people Glenn could find. Then they visited the re-made living pods. Javier was captivated by the clockwork fans circulating air through the closed spaces. Jaden sniffed his nose at the tall water tower and the windmill that provided water, and Meta's lips got tighter, her comments more acerbic. She prided herself on knowing her own mind and never doubting it, but Cedar thought she was weakening. They passed by a pasture with sheep and goats and a field where horses pulled a seed drill planting wheat. Despite himself, Javier was fascinated by the "antique machinery."

They stopped for a lunch of sausage, bread, and apples by a small stream. Jadan's face dripped with nervous sweat. Meta was unusually silent, and Cedar smelled incipient panic. Although everywhere they'd been was surrounded by enormous trees, the trees were so tall and spread so wide you could see a long dark way into them. Even to her it was frightening, and she'd been on the planet for some time.

It wasn't what you could see, it was what you didn't see that might be lurking there that made it terrifying. So she and Sharon helped Bren pull the canvas cover over the wagon hoops. The others were quick to climb in, except Sharon who took in everything and wanted more. But she wore a sword.

Maybe that was what made the difference. Sharon knew she

could defend herself against most anything. Cedar wondered why she hadn't been overwhelmed. Her first and only other experience on a planet was not a good one. But she could remember loving it before their small caravan was attacked and every one killed but her and her mother.

Finally, Meta brought up the subject Cedar didn't want to talk about, although it was inevitable. She was surprised it took so long. "Ardencroft was empty until you decided we had to leave the ship, Cedar. So let me be frank."

She decided? And when had Meta ever not been frank? It was probably her second name.

"What happened here? What were the monsters that killed every living person in the town? What if they come back? How would we fight them? How do we know we won't wake up in the night to screams and blood with a monster at our throats?"

"First of all, Meta," Sharon's words were terse and quick and sharp as her sword, "there are five squads of Restal's troops here. Second, I brought thirty-six of our best, most experienced fighters with us—"

"And third, Meta," Cedar interrupted, "look above you. At every minute of the day or night, there are at least five Karda in the air keeping watch."

"What can they see at night, and can they see through trees?"

"They can see better at night than you can see during the day. And they fly high and can see for kilometers around."

"That didn't save the people who lived here. You want us to bring women and children, people who have no idea how to fight, to this place."

"Meta, before this attack, the urbat hadn't been seen or heard of in five hundred years. For the past several tendays they've been trapped in their circle, surrounded by troops from all over Adalta. This problem will be over soon. And now that we know there is another species capable of space travel, there is no guarantee of the ship's safety from monsters, either. The Karda and the people of Adalta defeated the Larrak before. There is only one left, and it will be defeated, too."

Just please, great gods of the galaxies, thought Cedar, don't let her find out Restal Prime has been taken over by a human who is as bad as the alien. Not yet, not yet.

Cedar started putting the lunch things back in the baskets, and Sharon stowed them under the wagon seats. "Now, let's go to the mews so you can meet the Karda of Adalta."

When they got there, Amanda was grooming Bettan in the alleyway. Illyria was watching and, Cedar suspected, gossiping. Meta, as usual, marched in the lead. She stopped at the entry, sucked in a breath, and took four steps back. All three of them stopped, mouths open, and stared at the enormous Karda.

Illyria lowered her head for Cedar to scratch. "Illyria, Amanda, Bettan, may I present the representatives from the ship—Meta, Jadan, and Javier. I hope you will welcome them to your planet. You've already met my friend, the ship's Director of Security Sharon Chobra. Representatives, this is Illyria, that is Bettan and on his other side, is his Mi'hiru and partner, Amanda."

Javier was the first to respond. He bowed and said, "Illyria, Bettan, we are honored to be here on your beautiful world."

Jadan looked terrified, as he had all day, but Meta snorted and stalked down the aisle, skittered to one side when a Karda poked her head out of her stall and four more heads popped up. "Don't be ridiculous, Javier. They can't understand what you say. You've been listening to their propaganda."

The alleyway got very crowded with Karda. Meta whirled to look behind her. "Who said that? Show yourself. That was rude."

Illyria turned around and made an even ruder sound from under her tail.

Oh, sucking black hole, Meta can hear the Karda, thought Cedar. She can hear them, and I can't. Life is just not fair.

CHAPTER TWENTY-FIVE

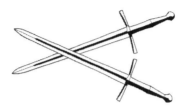

Cedar finished washing the microscope slides, stacked them in the holder to dry and picked up her packs.

"Cedar—"

"Don't look at me like that. I'll be fine." Mannik didn't look like he believed her, and she wasn't all that sure herself. "You are not going back with me. It isn't safe. You've already been attacked once, and that's enough."

"You're in more danger up there than I was, Cedar."

"I'll have guards. Besides, I have this." She shook her staff at him as she left the shed set up as their lab and headed for the transport. He wasn't convinced and she ignored him.

They'd delayed takeoff as long as they could. Captain Kendra sent increasingly terse messages to her, to Sharon, to Glenn, to Assam—who reported to Glenn by Cue that the reception in the villages and holds he'd visited so far ranged from enthusiastic to tepid, but never discouraging.

Sharon caught up to her. "This trip is not going to be a pleasant visit with old friends and long talks into the night over wine and cheese, or even coffee and cookies, Cedar." She gestured toward the transplanted pods. Javier, Meta, and Jaden chose to spend their last few nights there. Javier was looking around as if memorizing every-thing in sight. Jaden's shoulders were less hunched today, and his gaze was steady, not darting around like scared rabbit eyes, but steady on the ship as if it was salvation. Meta's jaw was clenched, her fists clenched, and her chest stuck out so far in front of her it looked like she was running to catch up with it. "We might have made one conquest with Javier, and I can't tell what has Meta so tight-assed. Whatever it is, she's determined to do it. Or not do it."

Cedar would be able to tell more about the three representatives when she got a little closer. Was she invading their privacy or being unethical by using the information she got from their smell? It was to save their lives, and it was a tool. Anyway, they were the ones putting out the pheromones, or whatever it was she smelled. Other people probably sensed emotions and used them, just not consciously. Why couldn't she have gotten something simple, like being able to move dirt or air or find water? Why did she have to have a talent with sticky ethical issues? She looked up and quickened her step. Or the ability to make it not rain for long enough to get aboard and not get wet. Again.

She stowed her staff in a locker and buckled in, Sharon in the seat next to her.

Cedar said, "It seems every one who came down with you—the ones staying—are settling in well. Mireia told me a few were coming into their talent, and no one panicked about it. None of the people who elected to stay in the pod were upset when Glenn told them it would be temporary. Some people were enthusiastic about exploring other places. They were all a pleasure to work with." She glanced at the three seated across the aisle and three rows ahead of them. "Most of them."

"Yeah, this group was easy. They were the most eager to come. It will get harder. A quarter of them were my people. People used to taking risks. It's not going to get easier."

The shuttle shuddered. There were, of course, no windows, but Cedar knew they were leaving the ground. Her breath wasn't there anymore; her chest was cold, her hands tight on the arms of her seat. The words "I don't want to leave. I can't leave. I have to go back. What will he do without me?" echoed in her head. Darkness feathered in from the edges of her vision.

Something bit her arm, and she jerked.

Sharon pinched her again. "Breathe, Cedar. Breathe. It's just a takeoff. We're okay. We're okay."

Air rushed back into her chest, and she was breathing again. She closed her eyes and leaned her head into the seat, letting the contoured headrest cradle it. She pictured Daryl in his tent, messengers going in and out, papers organized in a way only he could understand, looking up at her over the glasses on his nose. Her Daryl, oblivious Daryl, who looked at her so often with confusion, like he was missing something and didn't know what. "Come back," he'd said—before he'd flown off to fight monsters.

Be safe. Be safe. Be safe, Daryl.

"I'm okay, Sharon. It's not the flight, it's... I wish I could be sure this is the last trip I have to make."

"I know. Transport travel is a nasty cloud of radioactive space dust."

Cedar smiled and drifted into sleep. She woke when the grav-grab bumped but didn't open her eyes. Every memory, every thought, every interaction with Captain Kendra Pathal she could remember flipped through her head, loading her with information for developing strategy. Why couldn't it be Glenn who had to do this? He was older, respected, a director before Cedar was born. People would listen to him. She opened her eyes and unbuckled. Oh, yes, she remembered. He's irritable, impatient, and does not suffer fools at all. His solution would be drug them all and shove them on a transport. Would that work?

The procedure for disembarking was simpler now that so many people were traveling back and forth from the planet. No more decontamination ordeal. Whatever dangerous contaminant might transfer was a problem to be faced later. The first person she saw was Captain Kendra Pathal. The person she'd most like to see waving from an asteroid as the ship left.

"I suppose most of them came back with you." The I-knew-it expression faded when Cedar, Sharon, Meta, Javier, and Jaden came through the lock, and no one followed them. She frowned at the appearance of Cedar's guards, Peele and Lange and their swords.

"Actually, Captain," Javier's teeth flashed in his brown face, "I wanted to stay, but you sent us to report, so I didn't. It's beautiful, it's real. No VR experience could touch what it's like."

Meta glared at him. Cedar wondered if she even had another expression. "And it's unbelievably crude, inconvenient, and cold. Maybe the Karda are intelligent, but they are very rude and not friendly."

"In their defense, which they don't need, they mirrored your attitude, Meta," said Cedar.

No, Meta didn't have any other expression. "I'm going to my quarters to get warm and clean again."

"I'll hear your reports in my Meeting Room in two hours." Kendra's expression was almost gleeful as she left.

"I want to see my mother, Sharon. Give me a few minutes, and I'll meet you and Clare—where?"

"Coffee Clatch just down your corridor. We can't lose any time."

Cedar wished the walkways were still able to move. She took a shortcut through the empty assembly room and it still took twenty minutes to reach the quarters she shared with her mother. Her non-existent leg was on fire by the time she got there. Phantom pain was still pain, nothing phantom about it—pain she hadn't had for years. The room was a jungle of plants with a small clearing in the middle.

Amalie, the woman taking care of her mother, was sitting at the small desk, writing in a journal. "Oh, Cedar. It's good to see you again. Sit. Sit. I'll make coffee. Your mother is resting." She rubbed her hands up and down the sides of her trousers. "We..." She looked toward the bedroom, "I think we should talk before she wakes." She turned to the coffee machine, her back to Cedar, her movements slow and deliberate as she took down cups and fiddled with things Cedar knew didn't need fiddling with to make two cups of coffee. "Sugar?"

"No, thank you." She knew Cedar didn't take sugar. "What were you writing when I came in? I didn't know you kept a journal."

Cedar sat on the small couch, knees pressed together, her hands pressed hard on the cushion, fingers spread wide.

Amalie's hands stilled, then she carefully brought the coffee and set it on the table between the couch and the chair she sat in—on the edge. She looked like if she relaxed, she'd end up on the floor. "I started it a few days after you left." She shifted and reached over and touched Cedar's hand. Her eyebrows drew up, making small creases between her wide eyes that flicked over Cedar's face as if fearful of what she'd see there. Cedar realized she was holding her breath. She really, really didn't want to hear this.

"Don't be surprised by your mother's reaction to seeing you. She convinced herself you've not been gone, you are busy, you come home after she's asleep and leave before she's awake. Several times I've caught her coming out of your room in the night. She puts a finger to her lips and whispers, 'She's sleeping sound as a baby, Amalie. Don't wake her. She's tired.' So she won't be surprised to see you. You never left."

She picked up Cedar's limp hands in both of hers. "Sometimes a friend comes by, and she tells them all the things you've been doing. The rest of the time she takes care of the plants she's saving for you, or she sits and knits and watches vids of Old Earth, over and over and over. She's making you an afghan because you need it to keep warm. She knows what's happening—it's cold on the planet, not here. She can't—or maybe isn't ready to face it."

Cedar's face was frozen. If there were tears, they'd clink to the floor and splinter like ice. She could feel air moving in and out of her lungs, but she couldn't feel her heart beating. Amalie's voice was a distant, indistinct murmur. She felt warmth and looked down. Amalie pressed her hands around her coffee cup. She lifted it and took a big drink, let the scalding heat unfreeze her.

"Well, hello, Cedar." Her mother came out of the bedroom, every hair in place, in a soft blue sweater and pants, a large polished stone hanging from her neck. "It's nice to see you in daylight for a change, dear. Have you come to have dinner with us?"

There was no room to swallow anything past the lump in

Cedar's throat. How did she get so much worse? This was not her mother. Not her scared, damaged but sane mother.

"Oh, and the bean sprouts. They're ready to transplant into a garden pod. Can you send someone to pick them up? If you need me to help plant them, I'll be happy to."

"No, Mother. We've got it covered. I'll send someone in the morning with a cart. I can't stay long, but I'll come back for dinner. It seems like I never get to see you in the daylight."

Thirty minutes later, Cedar closed the door behind her and leaned her head against the wall. A sob hiccuped out, and a tear dripped into her hair. Her mother did smell of happiness and contentment, with an overlay of joy to see Cedar. But beneath it was a cloud of noxious terror and confusion. It seemed to breathe with her, receding only when she touched a plant, or held Cedar's hand. She'd bring her mother home with her this time. It would help. It had to help. Home. She swirled the word around, tasting it. Yes, home.

Clare and Sharon waved when she got to Coffee Clatch. "Sorry."

"I have four hundred people signed up to leave for Adalta as soon as possible. There are so many calls to the people already down there, it's hard to get through. They're doing our work for us." Clare smelled of relief and triumph. "And another warehouse pod broke loose. Since this one can't be pressurized, I'm getting all kinds of requests for space on it for personal items. Too many for my people to handle, so I gave the job to Mark. As Director of Finance, he doesn't have much to do with no trade going on, and it should be his anyway. He also has someone going through personnel files to look for skills that can be useful on the surface."

Sharon picked up their coffee at the counter and answered a small barrage of questions about her trip to the planet from the barista. "Your crew will fit right in since the major need they have is for people with experience in and love for plants." She set it on the table. "Cedar, like every one else, I had a meeting with a finder, Mireia, and she explained about the magic they call talent, but nothing's happened. As far as I know, nothing happened to anyone.

Has something—she called it manifesting—happened to you? every one I saw on the way here asked me what kind of magical powers I have."

There was a light scent of worry in the room. "Yes, but it didn't happen immediately, and I don't want to talk about it." She held up her hand. "No, no. It's not something horrible." Not exactly, anyway, if you didn't count all the throwing up. "It's just that I'm still adjusting—and trying to figure out the ethics of it. It would be easier if I could just shut it off, but I can only fine-tune filters." She closed her eyes and dropped her head. "I don't want to scare you, or for you to avoid me, but I can smell what you're feeling. Like right now, I'm smelling a hint of worry."

Clare laughed. "But, Cedar, you've always been able to tell what people are feeling. That's why you're so good with people."

"How very useful. Can you tell when someone's lying when they say they never saw whatever it is you know they stole?" Sharon leaned forward. "Can I use you in interrogations? Interviews? For my love life if I ever have one?"

"I have no wish to get close and personal with your love life—too much information. Let's go see the captain, and please don't tell anyone what I told you. Can you imagine what Meta would say if she knew I knew how she really feels about things?"

"How Meta feels about things is never a secret. But all right, we won't tell." Clare gathered the cups to put them in the tiny sink, and they left. No one said anything on the long walk to the Captain's Meeting Room, though Sharon snickered several times, probably thinking about ways to use Cedar's new skill. Cedar smacked her on the arm.

Mark and Arlan, the other two directors, were already in the room when they got there. For the first time, Cedar was uncomfortable in the white room, with its white cabinets and its massive vid screen with the image of the planet far below. Kendra fiddled with the focus, so Adalta appeared tiny and distant as if they were leaving it. The room was too sterile after the tendays she'd spent on planet. The air smelled like the filtered, recycled air it was. No tree smells. No fresh earthy scent. No smells of rain and wet clothes.

"Cedar." The captain's voice from the doorway was harsh and belligerent. "Would you tell me what you and Assam have been doing down there, going around and promising our people to the holders and villages? When we haven't even decided who's going or how many? And Clare, losing another warehouse pod is inexcusable. Mark, have you tallied our losses on this disastrous stop? What funds are left to start over somewhere else after this failure?"

Cedar dropped into a chair, and her hopes dropped to the floor. The captain was as delusional as her mother.

"Since we *will* have to start over after this failure."

At Captain Kendra's words, the room filled with a sharp scent of disbelief. Cedar held her breath and didn't move—and neither did anyone else. The captain pulled out a chair at the table and looked at Mark, waiting. But he was at a loss for words. His gaze went flitting all over the room. Looking for something to say, Cedar guessed.

Cedar pulled out her Cue and contacted Glenn. His greeting was abrupt; her voice was soft and clear and sad. "Glenn, I have you on speaker. Can you contact Assam and have him connect in? We are in the Captain's Meeting Room, and it will be helpful to have you both present."

Glenn didn't speak for two minutes, then, his tone crisp with no question mark in it, no grumpy, teasing tone, he said, "He's on, and I have asked dispatch to record this conversation."

Slowly the others took chairs. Except Sharon, who stood by the door, not quite standing at attention, but close. Cedar set her Cue on the table, and they each said their name, except the captain, so Cedar said it for her.

She was surprised Mark was the first to speak. He spoke to the Cue. "Mark here. Glenn and Assam, Captain Kendra has asked me about our finances. She wants to know where we stand for our next stop, since we lost so much money here." He looked up at the captain. "I have not calculated anything beyond my last report to you, Captain, because we are not leaving. We can't."

Having to deal with humans instead of numbers might make Mark human again. Almost before he finished, Clare said, "Another warehouse detached today. It's a pressurized pod, and will hold at least five hundred people with their immediate needs. When the tugs have it secure, we can connect it to a docking port to load it and send it down. That will take some pressure off the big transport shuttles. So far they are holding up with no problems, but moving another five hundred this way will help." She was directly across the table from the captain, but didn't look at her or ask permission. "I asked three more living pods to evacuate. They're gathering their essentials and moving to the assembly room and any other open room we can find. Their pods are unstable, and my crews are sealing them off from the rest of the ship."

Sharon opened her mouth, but before she could speak, Kendra held up her hand and said, "Clare, I was Director of Engineering and Maintenance for years before you. I'm afraid I'm going to have to overrule you. I'll inspect those pods myself immediately, but I'm afraid you're mistaken and have taken alarm where there is no need." She turned to Sharon, whose face was pink with suppressed fury. "Sharon, I'm afraid I need to ask you to accompany me with as many of your ship's patrollers as you think you will need to quell any panic Clare's actions have started."

Clare looked at her then, her mouth clamped. A muscle jumped in her tight jaw. Mark stared at the captain, anger wafted from him in a thick smelly wave. Sharon didn't move.

Cedar recognized the pungent odor of fear pulsing from the captain. I'm afraid. Kendra had repeated "I'm afraid" three times. Yes, she was afraid.

Kendra went on without a breath. "I've talked to Housekeeper Meta, and she tells me the situation is intolerable down there. The original inhabitants don't speak like we were told they did, their diction is crude, and they are definitely not friendly. She was both frightened and appalled. Jaden was terrified the entire time they were there. She reported Javier was useless. He was bewitched by the strange magic, if one could ever believe in magic, they are supposed to have there. We need to bring the hundred fifty people back we sent down, immediately, for their protection. She also told me there is a fight for the guardianship of the quadrant you, Cedar, decided we must use as our dispersal center. Which I was not informed of."

Was she serious? Cedar had reported it. Glenn and Assam had reported it. If Sharon hadn't yet, it was only because things were in such chaos, she hadn't found time. And their diction was crude? Crude diction was an obstacle?

The captain stood and stepped back from the table toward her office door. Glenn got half a word out before the captain interrupted him. "Sharon, I want you to put Clare under house arrest for dereliction of duty while I make my inspection. For her protection, of course. Leave your keys, Clare. I need access to your study."

She didn't even glance at Clare, who turned so pale her freckles were a dark pattern across her face. She looked sick, and Cedar was almost literally sick at the reek of emotions pervading the room. She was glad Glenn was only present by Cue—he must reek of volcano about to blow.

No one responded for a few seconds, then Assam's calm voice boomed from the Cue on the table into the dead silence. "It seems, Captain, you have a problem, and, as Director of Planetary Affairs, you need me there with you more than I'm needed here. One of the smaller transports is on the ground in Ardencroft now, and it's a short hop to where I am, so I'll be there as soon as possible with all the support needed."

Sharon's rigid stance by the door relaxed, but Cedar could only tell because a perfume of relief spritzed through the nose-biting smell of Sharon's fury.

"Good, Assam. In the meantime, I will begin my inspection tour of the ship. This meeting is closed until then." And Captain Kendra Pathal left the room.

Into the silence, Glenn's voice was calm, his words measured—a clear signal that he was in a tearing rage. "Dispatch, our meeting is over, you may stop recording now. The rest of this is me yelling at Cedar. You won't want to hear that."

The dispatcher laughed, sort of, and Cedar said, in an effort to calm him. "Glenn, if you can, you might need to come up too. The captain didn't say you couldn't—in fact she told us to return every one to the ship, so you can be the first. And we need you. People listen to you when they don't to me."

"I'm looking forward to the fight, Cedar. Don't anyone do anything you don't have to until we get there. Ending transmission now." But every one in the room heard his last words, "Never did think that woman should've been made captain. Never did think much of her."

There was silence until Sharon broke it with a laugh that smelled to Cedar like a bad case of nerves. "I sure hope dispatch stopped recording when he told her to. And has a faulty memory. Come on, Clare." She moved to touch Clare on the arm, breaking her out of her paralyzed incredulity. "She said house arrest, but she didn't say whose house. You're staying with me. We have plans to make."

Clare walked out with her, her teeth clenched so tight she couldn't speak if she wanted to, her back stiff, her shoulders back, her head up. The smoky scent surrounding her was her furious thoughts burning.

During the three days it took Glenn and Assam to get to the ship, Cedar went back to her regular work on the plants, Peele and Lange with her always. It took her to every part of the ship, and she talked to every one she encountered, answering questions, asking questions, cataloging smells. The two guards were almost hoarse by the end of each day, they'd been asked so many questions. The faction who didn't believe the ship was failing, or convinced themselves that the parts they'd lost made the ship more efficient and they could move on anytime they were ready was losing followers rapidly. There was anger about Clare's arrest.

Several times she ran across Meta talking to a small group. Meta went silent as soon as she saw Cedar. People looked from Meta's hostile glare to Cedar's open smile with confusion. Clare had made it clear for weeks the plants were not the cause of the pods breaking away. Even the ones openly hostile before were softening toward Cedar. But not all of them. Of course, Cedar knew Clare didn't mention things like walkways not working and com sats disappearing was the battle of tiny root versus tiny cable where the plants *had* invaded the systems.

Sharon and Cedar's own staff kept her surrounded by at least three or four guards at all times. She took at least one meal with her mother every day and tried to be there to wish her goodnight. And every minute they could—usually late at night—she, Sharon, and Clare met in Sharon's quarters to plan…something. They weren't sure what.

Mark proved to be invaluable. "I'm keeping lists of who is ready to leave the ship, who is resisting, who is rebelling, and I'm trying to note the ones I think might be more active in their rebellion. There is a small, quiet group who could try to take over the ship, if I read them right, and reading people is not my forte. I gave the list to Sharon if you need to see it. I didn't think I needed to make copies." Mark hadn't given up on his figures and lists, he'd just changed his focus—his still intense focus. He lowered his voice. Cedar leaned across the desk to hear him. "Give my…best to Clare. My support. And be careful."

During the days, she was too busy to think, but her nights were filled with uneasy thoughts and dreams. Once she woke Amalie with her screaming. Urbat were attacking their pod. She was armed with an immense sword she didn't know how to use and could hardly lift. Daryl lay in a lake of blood in a tangle of grass beside her saying, "I don't love you. I never did. Could I look at your leg?" in an incongruously strong voice, over and over, while she screamed and tried to cut off her other leg.

CHAPTER TWENTY-SIX

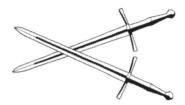

Daryl opened the latest messenger bag from Hugh Me'Rahl and looked for the tally of urbat engaged and killed right after he checked the tally of men Hugh lost. He always looked at that first. He leafed through for the report on interactions with the Itza Larrak in Hugh's sector of the circle, hoping to find more evidence of the Larrak's weakening. There wasn't much. Hugh thought one wing might be lower than the other, and sometimes it seemed to fly awkwardly, but the hints were small and might have been wishful thinking on the part of his patrollers. He didn't even mention Readen and the Prime, except a brief sentence at the end of his report. "Worry about the Prime when we're through here."

A report from Me'Cowyn on the other side of Daryl's section of the circle had much the same information. Altan's account came via Karda. Ballard's and Me'Kahn's came with Hugh's. He was missing statements from Turin and Me'Fiere, but he expected Tessa and Galen to show up with those any day. Me'Kahn reported the psychic rings in the planter's camps were experiencing a little less trouble interfering with the Larrak's control of the urbat but not enough to inspire hope in Daryl.

He tallied the number of urbat killed. It was sizable, but no one said there were fewer at the next attack. How many did it have? Was there an inexhaustible supply? He leaned back in his chair. Maybe they regenerated. Or reincarnated. And maybe he was losing his mind.

Someone scratched on the side of the tent opening. It was Tessa.

"I have reports from Turin, Altan, and Me'Fiere for you." There were bags under her eyes she could have carried the papers in. Her hair needed another shearing and flopped over her eyes. She dropped the pouch on Daryl's desk, rolled her shoulders, and stretched her head from side to side. Daryl heard her neck pop twice. She dropped into the chair across from him like she'd fallen from atop Kishar. "Kishar is eating and getting groomed in the mews. He asks that we come to him. He has a message from a young girl in the Prime for you. I know you'll hate leaving all this—I want to wave my hands over all the papers and make them go away, but I'm afraid you'd fade away to nothing without your reports. I'm hungry."

And so tired she couldn't sit straight, he noticed. "Beard," he called to the guard outside the tent. "Bring Tessa something to eat. Something hot and a large mug of tea."

"Thanks, Daryl. Soon as we eat and report, Kishar and I are going to sleep for days and days and days. Or an hour, whichever is longer."

He thought she'd fallen asleep, then she asked, "What young girl?"

And he asked at the same time, "Where's Galen?"

She sat straighter and rubbed her face with both hands. "Sitting in the circle."

She was trying to push her words with bravery and confidence, but it didn't work.

"What do you mean? Sitting in the circle?"

She rubbed her face again and moved her hands to her lap, then to grip the sides of her chair, then back to her lap. "Just that. Kishar and I dropped him in the circle not far enough from the opening where the Itza Larrak goes to regenerate—the strange opening Kishar says isn't supposed to be open. He managed to pull enough bushes out of the sick ground to cover himself. That's why we have to eat and rest in a hurry. He has water and food, and he's armed with his sword, a bow, a quiver full of arrows, and an akengun we talked Turin out of. But if he's spotted, it won't be enough. We're going straight back. We'll fly through the night, and since we can cross the circle and not go around, we should be there mid-morning."

Daryl could see sick worry in her eyes. And panic almost ready to bloom. He was amazed she'd left him—that the pull of duty was strong enough to make her.

Beard brought a tray in, and Daryl made a space on his table. At first Tessa looked at the food like it turned her stomach, but then she attacked it. Daryl looked through the reports she'd brought while she ate, but he couldn't concentrate. What in the world was the fool doing in the circle too close to the Itza Larrak's den? They couldn't lose Galen. They couldn't.

The walk to the mews tent was a short one. Kishar was dozing when they got there. "I hate to disturb him. Do you want to sleep now and call me when you're both awake?"

~I'm awake now.~ Kishar's pathed voice was tired. ~First, I have a message relayed from a very young Karda named Elleran who says he flies with the child Becca. She wants you to know she got inside the Prime safely, she found Krager, she's safe, and Krager wants you to know someone named Cael is able to get through Readen's wards undetected. Kyle's hidden a hundred and forty troops throughout the city, including a carefully segregated group of defectors from Readen, and there are more outside the walls avoiding patrols. They have at least three akenguns and are hoping for more.~

Daryl leaned against a tent pole and closed his eyes. Krager was safe. The child was safe. He took a deep breath and hoped they'd stay safe.

"You sent Becca—you sent a child into the Prime to spy on Readen?" Tessa growled like an outraged mother medgeran.

"No. I did not. She snuck off. She has an overdeveloped sense of responsibility." He looked at her like an insulted father medgeran.

323

An urge to laugh almost escaped her, but it didn't. "Turin says to tell you the akenguns dispose of urbat efficiently. He trained his troops to use short blasts, but he has no idea how long they will last. None have run out of whatever power keeps them working so far, but it could happen anytime."

"The glance I got at his report says he's lost fewer men and killed more urbat than anyone else, but the weapon doesn't penetrate the Larrak's shield. Altan told me about how it nearly killed itself trying to use it from inside its shield."

Kishar's head went up, and Abala announced to Daryl, ~One comes.~

Then they heard the thunder of wings as Bettan landed with Amanda.

"If she's bringing what I hope she is, you need to collect Galen and get back here as soon as you can. Abala, I need messengers. Alert who you can. She's bringing the microbes Cedar promised us." He reached for Tessa's hand at the same time she reached for his, and they gripped hard. Both wanted to feel relief and hope, but he didn't, and he didn't think she felt it either. The battle with the Itza Larrak had gone on too long to rely on hope.

"What do we need to do for the microbes until Galen and Tessa get back, Amanda?" Daryl brushed Abala's wing feathers with the light oil to help them shed water. It was an escape from the endless reports he received daily by Karda and Mi'hiru messengers. The Mi'hiru would do it, it was their job, but grooming Abala every day kept him sane. He'd done it every day since Abala found him when he was a boy. Right after Readen broke his arm as he didn't want to remember. The Karda's dry sense of humor and tendency to treat Daryl like he was still a foolish child kept his feet on the ground and his head from sinking under a sea of papers.

"Mannik, Cedar's assistant, said, or I deciphered from all the technical jargon he tried to impress me with, he'd propagated hundreds of each species they found. They were dormant, and they'll go dormant again with no food if we have to hold them for a while. But as soon as there's food, they'll wake up and go to work. They need to be hungry when we distribute them anyway. He didn't give us all of them, so there's a reserve if something happens to these." She patted the leather bag she carried over her shoulder and went back to grooming Bettan.

Daryl moved to Abala's other wing. "So, Cedar went back to the ship?"

Amanda's voice held so much suppressed laughter his face heated. "With Sharon and the three delegates who came to check things out for the captain. She's an amazing woman, Daryl. I know she's often in pain from her leg, but she hides it well. Sympathy makes her mad."

"She won't say what happened to it." This wasn't exactly a question, but....

"I asked her friend, Sharon. I didn't dare ask Cedar, but I'm nosy." She stopped, and Daryl waited. And waited. And waited. Was this his business? No. "Sharon said Cedar wouldn't tell me anyway."

Finally, he couldn't help it. "So what did she say?" Amanda was torturing him.

"She said she'll never talk about it." This time he didn't have to wait so long. "Her father was an advance agent like Galen and Marta. They were on a planet considered friendly. The ship traded there often, so he decided to take Cedar and her mother with him. Cedar was six. It was getting difficult for him and for them to leave his family for months at a time, sometimes longer. Other agents reported that although the political situation had changed, it was safe and the trade ship was welcome."

She moved to Bettan's other side. "But that's not what they found. Many of the food crops from the Ark Ship that brought the original colonists didn't survive. They had managed with what did and the domesticated and hybrid edible plants and animals they'd cultivated for hundreds of years. It was a precarious system with often unstable politics, and they depended on the trade ships for many of their goods. Then for two years in a row too many of their crops failed. There were few indigenous plants safe to eat, and too many bands of hungry people roaming. It was not an easy or welcoming planet. The colonists found no species they could communicate with, but lots that were dangerous. Cedar's little family with a wagon full of goods, including seeds, were headed for a large town. They had guards and should have been safe, but a large band hit them, killed the father, killed the guards, and stole the wagon. In the confusion, Cedar's mother pushed her into the bush, and crawled in after her. No one noticed. every one carried a Cue, even six-year-old Cedar, who had a deep cut in her calf."

Amanda put her brush in the tack box and walked around Abala to face Daryl. "Her mother was heroic. What food she salvaged, she gave most of to Cedar, and she kept them alive. When the rescue team found them, they were almost dead, surrounded by rotting bodies, and Cedar's leg was badly infected. It was a local bacterium the ship healers could find nothing to fight. So she lost her father, her leg, and, for all practical purposes, her mother, who never quite recovered. It was years before they could finally fit Cedar with a permanent bionic leg. Bionic means—"

"I know what it means, Amanda. Thank you." He didn't speak again, and held himself together until Amanda finally left. Bettan wandered back into his marked off area of the tent mews. Daryl leaned his head into Abala's neck and stayed there a long, long time, Abala crooning to him like when Daryl was a small, lonely child. He screamed inside. Angry at her parents, angry at their ship mates for letting that happen, angry at himself for intruding into Cedar's privacy. He grieved for that child, grieved for the mother who saved her but lost herself.

Finally, he moved to a far corner of the tent. Daryl pulled his glasses out of his pocket, sat on a bale of hay, and started going through more reports, turning down the corners of papers he wanted to return to. Abala stood, watching over him as he always had. He enjoyed the peace for thirty minutes or so, then a small Karda swooped over, and Abala relayed her message, ~Attack on planters two kilometers to the west.~

Daryl was ready for something to fight. He needed to hit something with his sword on the ground this time. So he looped the short, knotted drop-rope to the saddle handle, and when he and his Karda Patrol got to the site, Abala dropped him off near the rope corral for the horses, where the fight was most intense. He ignored the blood and the stink of urbat ichor, and fought, maneuvering to slice vulnerable necks and bellies, stepping over dead and wounded urbat without noticing. He chopped at unarmored feet and legs, flipped crippled urbat over, and sliced open bellies.

Finally the space around him cleared for a minute, and he looked around. He put a foot on the urbat he just killed, jerked out his sword, and glanced toward the circle. Low in the sky, he spotted a small, sleek black Karda with two riders arrowing toward them. Tessa and Galen were coming to join the fight. Kishar hovered out of reach of the urbat, and Daryl ran to guard while Galen climbed down his knotted drop-rope.

He fell to the ground on his hands and knees, head down. "Guard me for a minute, then I'll get up and take care of this little problem for you."

Daryl laughed and did just that until Galen looked up and started raising tough vines, entangling as many as three urbat at a time, piercing them with the long, wicked thorns. Then urbat seemed to lose their focus. They started milling in tight circles. Some simply stood still and almost invited someone to cut off their heads or kill them with thorns. The fight was over soon after. All of the urbat were dead but three who made a mad dash for the circle and escaped. Galen dropped flat to the ground, prone, arms stretched wide, fingers digging into the dirt.

He was exhausted. Daryl didn't know how long he'd been inside the circle, but it looked like it might have been a little too long. He watched for a minute as Galen reconnected with Adalta and began filling his immense reservoirs with talent power. Galen didn't have channels like others did. He had lakes inside him he could close off, which was why he was able to enter a Circle of Disorder and not die. Tessa's talent was blocked, and Kishar—well, Kishar was Kishar. Daryl headed for the main cook's tent, found a chair, and started cleaning his sword. He wasn't even tired. The fight gave him a surge of energy. It wouldn't last long, but he'd make the most of it while he could.

The leader of this camp's psychic defense ring, Masumi, dropped down next to him, so tired he almost missed the seat. "If the Itza Larrak was here, it's learned to hide from us. We couldn't sense it at all."

Daryl kept wiping his clean sword. "From the actions of the urbat, it's somewhere else. What did you do to them?"

"I found a link to one of them, and through it we were able to reach the others. It took us a while, but we used the link. We all sent confusing messages, different messages, through the links at the same time. We've been working on that for a while, and it finally worked. I don't know if it will work again, but I'll write up a detailed explanation of what we did. Enough for all the planter camps, and if you can ask the Karda to deliver them it might help. Attacks happen at numerous places around the circle at the same time, so the Larrak must be controlling them from a distance. We think—we hope—this will make it easier to disrupt its communications."

Daryl stopped over-polishing his sword and slipped it back in its scabbard. "Great work, Masumi. Tell your team thank you."

"Guardian, I don't really want to say this because it might well be nothing more than wishful thinking from a tired man, but all of us agree. We think the Larrak is weakening. Or not exactly weakening, but stretching itself too far. It's as if its energy, or concentration, shifts away, then back. That's how we were able to locate the link. The Larrak wasn't paying attention, and we slipped in while its attention was somewhere else."

Daryl stood and looked down at him, wondering if the battle energy was letting him make too much of this hope. "I trust none of you have mentioned this to anyone else?"

"No, and it won't be in the report I send either. We can't let up on our defenses. We can't get overconfident. It could mean disaster."

"Thank you again, Masumi, for your discretion. I'll speak to Abala, and he'll have messengers here for you as soon as possible. Now I need to help Galen with the wounded, if he's recovered, and talk to Tessa and Kishar about what you've discovered."

Already Galen had dispersed the inevitable stench from the camp, and four troopers were helping him pile urbat bodies so he could bury them. Healers were at work on the few wounded planters and troopers and didn't need Daryl's help. One of them told him if he didn't get some rest, he was going to need healing himself. "Tired people make mistakes and put not just themselves but others into danger. We can't afford for you to make mistakes because you're exhausted. Go lie down somewhere."

So he ended up with Tessa, Kishar, and Abala under a tree. Abala had no wounds or feather damage anywhere, although he told Daryl with a smug bird smile, ~I dropped five urbat to fertilize the trees in the forest.~

"It's a good thing they're not toxic like the circles they come from. Kishar, I have some news."

Kishar looked up, hay drooping out both sides of his vicious beak like a long mustache. Tessa and Daryl looked at each other, both trying not to laugh. They were exhausted, relieved at least this fight was over, and at the point where almost anything is hysterically funny.

~Good news, I hope. I am more than ready for good news,~ pathed Kishar.

"Good news." And he repeated what Masumi reported.

Kishar thought and chewed for a long time. ~Our history is oral, and although we're trained to be accurate, things still get lost. The humans in the last war were so busy working to feed themselves and find shelter, writing the history of the war was not a first priority. I was very young, but my uncle...~ His eyes opened and closed. ~I don't remember my uncle ever mentioning anything like this. It's true the Itza Larrak's wing did not heal properly, but it still flies, and that would not affect control of the urbat. I do not think it is something we can put much reliance on. For certain, this does not need to get out.~

His eyes closed again. ~Now, I must sleep. It was a long flight to retrieve Galen. And Tessa must sleep also.~

Daryl and Abala met Galen on the way to the landing meadow.

"They are asleep. Do you want to tell me what you learned watching the strange opening in the circle?"

They sat cross-legged at the edge of the field while Abala dug under the trees for tubers. Once, he pounced on an unwary and very stupid rabbit. It disappeared in seconds.

"The Itza Larrak returned to the opening three times while I was there hiding in a clump of scraggly bushes I managed to raise, hiding like that foolish rabbit. It never even looked my way. The opening is a long, rough split lit from the bottom with a fiery, wavering orange light. I was as far away from it as half again the length of this field, and I could still feel the heat. Twice from two to six urbat came with the Larrak. None of them came back out with it when it reappeared."

"Is it using them to help it regenerate?"

"That's my thought. It doesn't seem to need to eat. It's only partly organic, so I believe it gets energy some other way. I think it not only uses the urbat for defending the circle from us, but also as its energy reserve. I'm beginning to believe the circle is part of the Larrak, or the Larrak is part of the circle. Kishar agrees with me."

"I wish I could study it."

"No, you don't."

Daryl pulled a piece of grass from the ground and started tearing it in strips. "No, I don't."

They sat, silent and thinking or not thinking. Then Daryl said, "No ill effects from spending too much time near its lair?"

"Not so far, except talent depletion, which I'll make up for soon as we finish here. Where's Cedar, and what's going on with the ship?"

Daryl brought him up to date with what he knew, then added, "Readen sent a messenger to Ardencroft after she left offering his protection against me."

Galen laughed.

"The messenger carried an akengun."

Galen didn't laugh again.

CHAPTER TWENTY-SEVEN

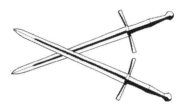

Readen pulled on his gloves, careful not to pull too tight. His claw-like nails had stopped growing, but they must stay hidden. He stared down at them, hating that they must be covered. Hating that they would grow no longer. His fingers curled in frustration, but he forced them to relax before they cut through the thin leather. Someone rapped twice on his study door, and Readen went to open it. Never again would he leave it unlocked and unwarded. Nor would he pass by anyone without searching for signs of illusion, signs they were not who they appeared to be.

"Have you found them yet?" But he knew before Captain Paules answered.

"No, sir." Paules didn't visibly cringe as he stepped into the darkened room. "We're not sure they are still here."

Readen moved behind the ornate desk, windows to his back, and waited.

"Two of the messengers you sent to holders returned. They reported someone was there before them, acting for Daryl."

Readen stood statue-still and waited, his face in shadow.

Paules stood, feet apart, hands curled against his legs. "They didn't identify them, just that they were from Daryl. It could have been Krager. That might be why we can't find him. He's not here."

Readen looked at him sharply. The captain was repeating himself. He'd have to be more careful about the way he acted toward him. He made himself relax and turned to look out the windows, his back to the captain as a signal of trust. "I sent the messengers with akenguns. Did they demonstrate?"

"Yes, sir. On animals, as you said."

"And?" There was impatient movement in the back of Readen's head, pulling at his control. He turned back around and smiled. It took an effort.

Captain Paules's face was still a pantomime of fear, uncertainty, a wish to be gone, and the fight not to show any of it. "It angered them."

There was silence. Tendrils from the thing in his head gained territory. This time Readen didn't notice. "Perhaps we should send our messengers with full squads."

Paules shifted again and folded his hands in front of his most vulnerable body part. "It might not be wise to remove so many of your guard from the city. Sir."

The air around Readen darkened, and Paules's shoulders hunched forward. Readen waited.

"My troopers tell me the last two people you executed for…treason. They say people are more angry and less fearful. We've lost four more men." Paules's voice was thick, as though his next words were stuck to his tongue and didn't want to come out. "And two weapons."

Readen didn't say anything. He was so angry and the tendrils so agitated it was difficult to think. He was losing his balance. Finally, he made a brusque motion with his hand. Captain Paules's exit was faster than immediate.

Readen dropped into his chair, body stiff and awkward. The words, "Daryl. Daryl. Daryl must be stopped. We must get free. We must call," banged around and around the room as if they came from both inside and outside his head. They made no sense. Except for the name. Daryl.

For a long time, he sat. It felt as if he were absent from his body, from his mind, until the words stopped, and he was himself and able to think.

Hope. That's where the resistance came from. Daryl was still alive and fighting. So long as they knew that, the people of Restal would wait. Readen held to the illusion of geniality he'd built around himself, and the propaganda he'd spread for years about the inequality of rule by strong talent. That would bring enough people to his side. That he'd made a mistake killing Minra Galel, or executing the traitors, or using the akenguns never occurred to him.

He needed the Itza Larrak. The thought wasn't even finished before his head again filled with cold words that weren't his. "Trapped, we are trapped. Our tools destroyed one by one by one. We are in our lake of fire, breathing it in, breathing it in, swelling with power, but it isn't enough. It isn't enough. We are failing. We can't fail. Our people? Where are our people? Why don't they come? Have they found another home? Have we failed them? Are they lost? We must try harder. We must call."

They made no sense and his head hit the desk. His chest burned. When he was able to sit up, double vision distorted the room. He got to his feet. His body was unfamiliar; his movements uncoordinated. He stood for a long time. For the first time in his life, he didn't know what to do. Cold filled the room, leaching heat from his body, and he shivered. He moved to the crackling wood fire and held his hands to it until he warmed, his head cleared, and he could think again.

He wasn't trapped. He wasn't encircled. He had weapons. He had control. The city was his, and when the Itza Larrak killed Daryl, the quadrant would be his, the world would be his.

He could wait. He wasn't trapped. Where did this panic come from? Not him. He had no panic.

"We can wait. Wait. Hide. Wait. Try to get more guns. But, Cael, you're not safe here. I've been doing this for so many years, that with a little illusion, people know me as Payne. I'm familiar. You're not." Krager wiped the blood from his knife and watched Cael wrap the wound on his arm. He held it out for Krager to tie the ends.

"I'm not always going to be there when you're attacked. You need to leave."

The two men were in the kitchen of the Bloody Talons, washing off too much blood. A long, wrapped bundle—an akengun—lay on the floor under the table.

"I have to wait for Daryl. I'm the only one who can get close to Readen without him knowing it. He sets wards everywhere. He killed a housekeeper with one, so he isn't making them lethal anymore, but the guards are frustrated. They have to respond to every breach."

"I can get you to Daryl."

"That's a lot of territory to cover, even if I can get a horse. With who knows how many of his men out there."

"Tarath can take you."

Cael cocked his head and squinted at Krager. "Who?"

"My Karda."

Silence. Eyes mere slits, head cocked to the other side, Cael repeated, "Your Karda."

"Why, Cael, I believe your face is a little pale. Are you well? Did you lose too much blood with that scratch?"

"I thought a bonded Karda would only carry the one he or she bonded to."

"An untrue but useful fact to spread. Otherwise, they'd be hounded to death."

"I can saddle a horse, but I've never been closer to a Karda than…than…"

"Do you need to go lie down somewhere? Are you ill?" Krager was having difficulty keeping his infamous dead-eye-tough-guy look on his face.

"Can you talk to Tarath from here?" There was a lot of hope-not in his question.

"No, he can't. But I can. Sort of." Becca sloshed through the

335

back door with a bucket and a brush. "What do you need to tell him? I'll tell Elleran."

She set the bucket on the floor and sat herself at the table. "You better get rid of that—bundle—quick-like. How many do you have now?"

The men looked at her, an identical "leave now" glare on both faces.

"Do what you have to for Mother Girt in a hurry and get back here and out of sight. You look less like a boy every day. I'll talk to you later." Krager's words carried enough growl in them Becca almost ran to the front of the tavern to make another futile effort to clean the floor.

He looked back at Cael and waited. Cael leaned back in his chair, crossed his legs, and closed his eyes. About the time Krager started wondering if he'd fallen asleep, he said, eyes still closed, "I'm tired, I'm scared, and you had to rescue me this time because I'm getting sloppy. I'll go. I'll give you the names of the people in Readen's guard you can watch. Don't trust any of them. Don't trust any of the women. There's only a few. They're tough. They're mean. They're loyal to money, not Readen, but as long as he's paying them, they're his. They're also honest. You can't buy them away. They'd go to him first, and he'd kill them. They've learned the hard way not to trust anyone but themselves, and I'm not sure they even go that far."

Krager listened hard, pressing each name in his memory. By the time Becca got back with her bucket of dirty water, they were finished, it was full dark outside, and Cael was gone, taking the akengun to stash it with the few others they'd acquired, gather his few things and leave.

She dumped the bucket outside, went to Mother Girt's cupboard, and brought out a small ham, bread, cheese, and an apple to split. "I don't know where or how she gets this. Not many of the farmers nearby will come into the city anymore. They're eating a lot better than we are."

"She knows a lot of smugglers, and the vines and bushes concealing Thieves' Gate are getting a little worn."

Becca stared at him, her eyes and mouth open wide, then her words fell out, "You know about Thieves' Gate?"

Krager didn't answer.

"Of course you do." She was talking around a mouthful of ham and bread. "Now, what do I need to tell Elleran?"

"Don't talk with your mouth full, and I see your grammar is getting better."

She ducked her head and swallowed. "ChiChi didn't talk ignorant like I do, and someday I want to find her again. She's the first real friend I ever had. I don't want Jenna or her to think I'm dumb. And I been listening careful to you. Carefully to you."

Krager couldn't talk for a minute. He finished his meal, made sure she ate what she needed, and left the rest for Mother. "Can you see through Elleran's eyes?"

"Wow, is that possible? How do you do that? Can I learn? Can you teach me? Can Elleran teach me?"

Krager propped his elbows on the table and pinched hard between his eyebrows. "When will I learn? I should never have asked. You and Elleran will have to experiment with it, some can, some can't, but here's what to ask him to tell Tarath—"

Daryl glanced up from the hot cup cradled in his hand he which couldn't force himself to drink from. Tessa and Galen were dashing from their tent to the cook's tent through curtains of rain.

"Oh, meteors of gold, is that coffee I smell?" Galen's first words of the day sounded like he was talking past a frog in his throat. "Where did you get coffee?"

"The last messenger from Ardencroft flew it in. He handled it like it was more important than the messages. It came with instructions from Cedar."

"Oh, no. Cedar couldn't cook boiled water. I better go see the cooks."

Tessa sat across the table from Daryl, her spiky hair leaning and flat.

"You need a haircut, Tessa. Why don't you let——"

"Oh, no. No one touches my hair but me."

"I see. And with your sword you're so very good at it."

"What are you drinking? It smells delicious."

"I'm trying to see what it is Cedar likes about this. I'm not succeeding."

Neither of them spoke again, just watched the curtains of rain blowing in the wind, until Galen came back with a fresh pot of coffee and a mug of tea for Tessa. He dumped Daryl's mug out and poured him another. "Put honey in it, that helps. And don't smile, you have coffee grounds in your teeth."

Daryl pushed his glasses up on his nose and spread a long, narrow map on the table. "Now that we have our beverages the way every one likes," he sipped, and his mouth puckered, "can we get to the situation at hand?" He smoothed his hand down the long Line of Devastation. "We'd planned to use the microbes on all the lines coming from this circle, but that won't help our situation. It will distract the Itza Larrak, but it will also stretch our forces too thin. What we're going to do— Can you relay this discussion to Kishar, Tessa? I know he doesn't want to stand outside in the pouring rain to be part of this. What we'll do is concentrate on this one line. The last message I got from Glenn on the ship said the line repaired itself and the signal started again. It's distorted and weak, and they can still block it, but if we don't do something more than what we've already tried, in a tenday or less, it will reach the line from the other circle, and the signal might get too strong to block."

Tessa dropped her head in her hands, and Galen put his arm around her and slid her closer. "Kishar says we cannot let that happen." Her voice was muffled and thick.

"We aren't going to, Tessa. Here's my plan, carefully thought out while I drank my bitter cup."

Galen snorted. "You can't think that fast, Daryl."

"I guess my attempt at levity didn't work." He put the full cup at the top of the map, which curled in the damp air. "Here, here, here, and here." He pointed at the small Xs where he'd marked it. "A concerted attack on this one line."

Tessa closed her eyes and ran her hand down the line. Galen frowned at each spot as if he could see through it to the actual place.

It was as detailed as Daryl's cartographer could make it after countless flights and reports from Karda and patrollers. The four places were selected for concealing troops and Karda, where his forces would hold the high ground, where there was enough vegetation for Galen to use to build blinds, where there was water near if they had to wait long. They were close enough for troops to move easily and quickly between them. Daryl had spent long days and nights working on this, as had Abala, relaying reports and descriptions from Karda.

"This is going to take a good number of troops away from the fight around the circle," said Galen. "That's a lot of kilometers to guard."

"Right now, Readen is holding the Prime by fear and intimidation. There is still resistance, but how long will it be before people start protecting themselves by reporting suspicious activities by their neighbors? What if he decides to take citizens as hostages? What if he decides to kill someone every day until I surrender? My troops are worried about their families. What if Readen decides to take families hostage and force my people to surrender, to join him?"

A server brought their breakfast, juggling plates. Galen rescued one and started eating like he hadn't eaten for days, which he probably hadn't.

Daryl pushed his hair back with both hands. He did it so often he'd be bald before much longer. "I don't have a long track record as Guardian. I've worked hard at making amends, at repairing relationships, but I'm untested as their leader. How long can I stay here, repelling the Larrak's attacks, unable to attack it, before my people get tired, or have to withdraw their troops to defend themselves? How long before someone makes a connection between the beginning of my rule, Readen's arrest, and the appearance of the Itza Larrak, and comes to the wrong conclusion?"

Neither of the other two said anything for a long time. Daryl wondered if summer would be there before they spoke. Then Galen leaned over one of the Xs on the map and said, "I might be able to create blinds here and here and here big enough to hide ground troops, even from the air. If the Larrak sends urbat, we'll have plenty of warning. If it comes by itself, which it probably won't do —it never has—we might be able to overwhelm it. I didn't get close enough to it to find out what would happen if I made the ground attack it last fall. I'd relish the chance. I didn't like being a rabbit hiding in the bush. This time I'd like to be the fox."

"Kishar says at the very least it will make the Larrak take to flight. We'll need people who can fight from the air as well as the ground," said Tessa, spooning honey over her bowl of oatmeal.

"The Karda Patrol out now is due back any minute, and the next one will be leaving any minute. Let's eat and think and meet in the mews tent as soon as it's empty. There's no point in waiting." Daryl looked at his food. Or would have looked at it if it were still there. He didn't remember eating it. The tiredness that never seemed to leave him was gone. Inside there was a growing mixture of hope and sadness. What friends, how many of his troops, would he lose with this last gamble? He walked outside. The rain was a soft drizzle now. He tilted his head up at the clouds, wishing he could see through them to the ship above.

Mi'hiru Amanda was saddling Bettan when Daryl got to the mews tent with her messenger packet. "Abala told us to get ready to deliver some messages, fast. Philipa will be back any minute from Ballard's camp. If we push it, we can each reach three camps a day, so every one will have your message in no more than three days. I'll go east, she'll go west."

"Be careful crossing the lines."

"We always cross them high and fast. But they don't bother us in the air. Safe flight, Daryl." She pulled the messenger bag over her shoulder, stepped from Bettan's knee to the saddle, and they loped down the field. She waved at Philipa as she and Cystra passed them in the air, their Karda playing chicken and flipping to vertical at the last minute. The Mi'hirus' laughter echoed back down the field.

"I think they have better sonar than bats." Galen arrived carrying saddlebags over his arm. He stopped in front of where his

Karda, Ket, was supposed to be, put his hands on his hips, let his head fall back, and closed his eyes. "Why do I always think he'll be here when I want him? Why couldn't I have a Karda who would bond with me? Why do I have a Karda who has his own ideas about where he needs to be and when? Tell me, oh great gods of the galaxies, why? Why? Why do I always think he'll be there when I need him?"

Kishar snorted. ~You do not need to complain. It is I who must carry you, not you who must carry me.~

"True. Now I'm much happier."

Tessa arrived, out of breath. "Sorry, I hope I'm not late. Where's Ket?"

"Wherever his young fancy took him. If he were a human boy I'd guess he was chasing girls." Galen heaved Kishar's rigging from the saddle stand.

~He said he needed to talk to someone. Tessa, would you brush my back before Galen puts the rigging on? I'm itchy.~

It was Abala's turn to snort. ~If you didn't insist on popping out of the sky right on top of people, you wouldn't get dust and grass bits all over you. Serves you right.~

Daryl finished grooming Abala. He knew the banter from both human and Karda was before-the-battle humor. No one knew if what they were doing would end in victory or disaster. "Do you have the microbes, Galen?"

Galen slapped the saddlebags he carried. "I think if Mannik knew I put these down to sleep, he'd go running to Cedar, and she'd be coming down by parachute right now and ripping me to pieces—so, yes, I do."

Daryl dropped his head and stepped around Abala to check a buckle. He heard Tessa's words, which were uttered in a stage whisper that probably carried across the whole camp.

"I think he's hiding a smile, Galen. I wonder what he's smiling about."

"Not possible. Daryl doesn't know how to smile, and anyway, he hasn't discovered girls yet, unlike the absent Ket must have. Let's go. I want this over with so I can sleep again. For a year."

CHAPTER TWENTY-EIGHT

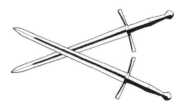

Glenn and Assam stepped through the containment hatch a few minutes after the small transport shuttle clamped to the ship. The captivating smells of the planet came through with them, along with the scent of confidence. Four of Daryl's troopers stepped out right behind them, anachronistic in their simple leather armor with swords strapped to their sides on a spaceship.

Cedar wanted to hug Glenn, but he hated that, so she took his arm, and he dodged her staff.

"Daryl sent Mi'hiru Philipa to check on us half a day after Readen's armed messenger left. She said he said for me to tell you to be careful. So, be careful."

"He didn't tell me to be careful. I don't think he cares about me, Cedar." Assam walked on her other side, face straight, eyes on Sharon, also there to meet them.

Cedar tried to trip him with her staff, but he jumped it.

The worry on Sharon's face eased. "Good move, bringing these four with you." She reached out and grasped the first trooper's forearm. "I'm Director of Security Sharon Chobra, and I believe you are Wingman Arden." She nodded to the female trooper. "I'm afraid I don't know your name."

"I'm Onevra, ma'am. I was on patrol when you were there."

"Welcome to the ship, all of you."

Cedar twisted to look behind them. "I see you are all there is. No returning settlers, Glenn? Like the captain ordered?"

"We did ask if anyone wanted to come. They decided the captain no longer has authority over them and refused to return." His grin was lopsided. "I didn't argue. They're right."

Sharon smoothed an errant hair behind her ear. "She's going to be furious."

"Why isn't she here to meet us?"

Cedar shuddered. "She's either busy with her laser, destroying roots everywhere she finds them, or she's telling another group everything's under control, everything's safe, and all's right with the ship, because she's in control of the systems now, not Clare." She pulled out her Cue. "I'll inform her you are here."

every one heard the captain's screamed response when Cedar told her none of the settlers had returned with Glenn and Assam. "In my Meeting Room, immediately."

Sharon took off, calling over her shoulder, "I'll collect Clare. We need her there. Call when you're close."

The others took every detour they could, and every one they met had questions. They engaged with them all. Cedar let the others answer questions about the planet, about those who'd stayed, about the village of Ardencroft—which formed the center of conversation everywhere—about the dangers, the revolt, the strange urbat, the alien. There were questions about fighting and especially what's it like to fly with a Karda. The wingmen in their flight leathers, swords at their belts, were the stars. It took an hour and a half to reach the Captain's Meeting Room. Sharon and Clare walked in behind them with four of Sharon's Ship Patrol.

The other two directors, Mark and Arlan, were already there. Cedar noted their "watch out" expressions. Captain Kendra stood at the head of the table, her face white with fury, her mouth a tight slash, her words gritted out between clamped teeth. "Is this what immediately means to you?"

The four wingmen from the planet stepped through the door

and stood to one side, feet apart, one hand on their sword pommels, and nodded politely to her.

She stepped back. "Who are these people? They're wearing swords. Why are they here with you?" She turned to Sharon. "And why is it necessary to have Ship Patrol here? Why is Clare here? I told you to confine her to quarters."

Sharon didn't answer, and Clare's eyes were tight. A vein pulsed in her temple. Mark moved to her side. Cedar stayed at the door. She wanted to be as far away from the captain as possible and still be in the room. Every time Kendra saw her it triggered more anger, and they didn't need that. Cedar didn't need that. Her own temper was losing its elasticity.

Glenn moved to the chair next to the captain, pulled it out and sat, one leg propped on the other knee, casual, relaxed. "They're representatives from Guardian Daryl of Restal, here to reassure you and others of safety on the planet, and to answer questions about what life on Adalta is like. They were each raised in a different village or holding in Restal Quadrant." He introduced them, his voice calm, matter-of-fact.

Kendra glared at Cedar, then focused on Assam. "Why did I have to wait for Meta to tell me about the dissension on the planet? About the revolt?"

There was silence, and Cedar's sinuses filled with thick odors of disbelief. Finally, Assam spoke, the strain of holding back his anger the smell of burning paper. "It was in all my reports. It was in all Glenn's reports; it has been in every copy I've gotten of Cedar's reports, and if Sharon hasn't reported it, it's because she hasn't finished hers yet."

"Yes, I have. And it was filed two days ago."

Kendra went on as if she heard nothing. "I have appointed Meta Director of Engineering and Maintenance. She should have been chosen over Clare in the first place."

By now Cedar knew she would recognize the smell of open-mouth disbelief in her sleep in the middle of a compost-sorting pod. It radiated, almost visible, from every director. Clare started forward, but Mark and Sharon each grabbed an arm, pulling her back.

Glenn was the first to speak, his voice low, resilient, tempered steel. "Kendra, even apart from the fact Meta knows little about the ship's systems, you cannot appoint a new director. This is not an autocracy. The departments choose their leaders with the consent of all other directors, including directors emeritus." He tapped his chest. "Your position depends on the will of the directors. Clare is still Director of Engineering and Maintenance. Your order to put her under house arrest was illegal."

Kendra's arms flew, one sweeping to point a shaking finger at Clare. "I've been all over this ship in the last two days. It's a mess. There are problems everywhere. She's been negligent and delinquent in her duties."

"Captain." Assam unfolded from his seat. "We've been telling you about the problems on the ship for months."

"Sit down." Her face was flushed. Her breathing hard and fast, and her voice neared a scream. "Sit down. I'm not finished. I can dismiss you too. Why are you here and not on the planet where you belong? You're Director of Planetary Affairs. Go back to the planet and take these...these...soldiers with you. Swords on a spaceship. Swords on a spaceship. This is insane."

Glenn stood and took hold of her arm. She jerked away. "Don't touch me."

"Captain..." Cedar tried to keep her voice calm and unthreatening, "Why don't we...?"

"You! It's all your fault." Her face twisted into a macabre parody of glee. "I've killed hundreds of your plants. I cut their roots, tore them out of every junction where they didn't belong. It's your plants trying to kill my ship." She stumbled backward toward her office. "*My* ship. This is *my* ship. This is my ship." Her words faded.

Glenn took her arm again, and she raised her face to him, her voice trembling with rage, her words close to incoherent. "This is my ship, Glenn. You understand you understand you understand..."

"Yes, Kendra, I understand. Let's go into your office and talk about these problems."

345

Cedar was glad her mother had filled their living space with so many plants. Without their peace, she would fall apart like the captain.

"They've told us we have to leave right now, Cedar. Where am I to go? They said we have to evacuate this pod. I've lived here all my life. You lived here all your life. Where are we to go?" Ahnna chewed on her lip and twisted strands of hair around her fingers. "Captain Kendra was just here yesterday. She said we were safe. What's wrong?"

"Mother, we're fine. I've found us a place on a transport. They are safe—self-contained with redundant systems. I'll be with you and Amalie."

"But our things, your father's picture." She dashed to a small sideboard, grabbed the holograph of Cedar's father, and clutched it to her chest.

Cedar bit her lip. She couldn't cry. Not now. Not in front of her mother. The holograph would not last on the planet. She closed her eyes, impressing his image in her memory. "There are special crews packing up everything, Mother. For when we are settled." She did not add "on the planet."

Amalie picked up Ahnna's knitting basket, a pack over her shoulder. With her on one side of her mother and Cedar on the other with another pack, they moved out the door. Then Cedar's Cue buzzed.

Clare's voice said, "Cedar, get out of there now. Now," and she cut off.

Cedar dropped the pack and pushed her mother out the door. The hall was crowded with people abandoning bundles and boxes and running for the pod entrance. The evacuation klaxons blared their piercing alarms alternating with the mechanical words, "Evacuate the pod immediately. Separation imminent," over and over.

Ahnna shook loose of Cedar's arm, grabbed her and started shoving through, pulling Cedar behind her. It was all Cedar could do to fight the thick odors of fear and panic. She was hanging on her staff, all but helpless. If her mother let go of her arm, she didn't know if she'd make it. They ran. "I won't lose you, Cedar." A woman with three small, terrified children in front of them struggled to herd them along. Ahnna scooped up one child without letting go of Cedar. "I won't let anyone hurt you." Then Amalie grabbed her other arm, and they both pulled her through the entrance. They ran until they found a place to huddle against a wall.

Cedar finally managed to clear her head enough to think. She stared at her mother, who still held Cedar's arm, her expression watchful, determined. Maybe the cage she'd been living in hadn't been entirely her own creation. Maybe she'd been sheltered too much. Even as a child, Cedar had tried to shelter her mother. It had been her distraction from the agony of her leg. Maybe Cedar had helped her build her cage.

When they'd caught their breath, she told her mother, "Warehouse pod nine. I've reserved our space." She shoved a paper into Ahnna's hand. "Don't lose this, and don't let anyone take it from you. It's our reservation." Her mother's eyes widened. "Thank you, Mother." She swallowed. Her throat was thick, and she could hardly get the words out. "You got me out of there, you and Amalie. You saved me again." Ahnna straightened, and her head came up. Her voice was the calm, steady one Cedar hadn't heard much of lately, and the words she said were her father's from long ago. "We'll make it, Muffin." Cedar blinked hard.

She watched them leave for the transport pod, then walked in the opposite direction, headed for Clare's department. She wanted to say goodbye to every plant she passed. The people could be saved —these plants could not. She felt as if she were betraying them, abandoning them. The seed bank pods were already on the ground with those of Cedar's experimental plants, including her precious coffee bushes. Glenn, who was adapting to life on the planet like he'd been born there, had brought people with the right talent ability to the ship to put the embryonic life forms that needed it into stasis. The systems that had kept them viable for centuries wouldn't work on the planet. She hoped this would.

The pod was nearly emptied, and the hallway was far less

SHERRILL NILSON

crowded. The threatened panic didn't manifest. She passed a small girl with a potted plant clasped firmly in one arm, her other hand firmly in her mother's. Cedar smiled and leaned down. "Thank you for saving your plant," she whispered, and the girl nodded, jaw firm, lips tight, chin high. Cedar took a full breath, her first in too long, at what this young girl with this young plant represented.

A huge boom reverberated through the hall, and the great hatch to the living pod slammed shut. She staggered, sucked for air in vain. She slid down the wall to the floor, dizzy until the emergency systems came on, and there was air to breathe again.

Stunned, she sat for a long time. The pod was not yet empty, she knew. How many hadn't made it out? How many believed the captain when she told them the pod was safe, when she told them Clare was wrong, and the pod was safe. Cedar stared at her hands, fingers interlocked tight, clenched. A drop of liquid shone on one, then another, and she realized they were tears. Her tears. She allowed them a few more minutes to fall, watching them slip between her fingers. Then she pulled out her Cue and thumbed off the visual.

"Sharon, what do you need me to do?"

"Clare has all but four of the big transports fitted for passengers and has crews working on those four. Glenn took control, organizing the transport, assigning tugs, doing the captain's job. Mark is assigning passengers, Arlan is packing up everything left in Medic he thinks can be of possible use. Assam is helping my crew calm people down. This is one pod. Everything else is stable."

Cedar knew Mannik had already packed what he'd salvaged from her lab, and it was probably on the ground.

"Assam will be on this transport, and Glenn insists you be on it too. This isn't orderly, but we're keeping the chaos under control. Thank the stars, we've been running more evacuation drills than usual. We'll speed everything up. Some of the transports Clare's fitting for passengers are ready, and the others are close. Our two shuttles will be making trips as fast as they can, which means the transports carrying four hundred per trip will only have to make two trips each. A few more trips, that's all we need. I'm sending some of

348

my Ship's Patrol with each transport to help you keep order. Maybe I should start calling them Ground Patrol. Clare and I will be on the last shuttle after…."

After they dismantled the ship and made certain what remained would fall into the ocean or on a barren. Cedar knew what Sharon didn't want to say.

"I wish we could save more of your plants, Cedar, but we can't, so you're not needed up here now. Get down there. You and Assam will have a lot to do to get ready for this influx. Four hundred people a trip is going to make Ardencroft a very busy and crowded place."

"Where's the captain?"

"Don't know, don't care." Sharon's voice tightened, and Cedar was glad she'd thumbed video off. "She told them they were safe. We lost twenty-five people, Cedar." There was a long silence. "Twenty-five people, too many of them children." Her words were choked. "Leave, Cedar. And find me a good horse, a good map, and a tent. I'll see you as soon as possible. Oh, wait. And someone to teach me to ride the horse."

Cedar had to sit for a while before she called Clare. Again she left the video off.

"Clare here."

"I know you're too busy to talk, but I needed to check in with you before I leave. Glenn is kicking me downstairs."

"Oh, Cedar. Sorry, I barely check to see who's calling me since it's always a problem I have to solve." There was a moment of silence, then, "Your mother all right?"

"We made it out, Clare. In fact, she got me out. We're fine, and she's on the next transport down, as I will be."

"The captain's gone, Cedar. She found an unguarded one-person shuttle, took it out and opened the hatches. She's gone."

Cedar dropped her head and pinched between her eyes. "Will you try to recover her body?"

"No, Glenn and I decided bringing her back to bury her on the planet she didn't want to go to would be cruel, if one can be cruel to a dead person. Once upon a time she was a good enough captain.

She's where she wants to be. Eventually, she'll become a falling star."

Neither said anything more. There wasn't anything more to say.

Finally Clare said, "Find me a friendly Karda to fly, Cedar. Be careful, take care of your mother and all the other people. Not too big a job for you. You can do it in your sleep. Don't kill Meta unless you have to, and I'll see you soon." She clicked off.

The trip down was far calmer than Cedar expected. Ahnna sat, strapped in, and knitted, her forehead creased in concentration, stopping occasionally to look around, her eyes narrowed. Cedar hadn't seen her this composed since the ship started failing. Since they'd escaped with their lives when their quarantine gro-pod blew away. Emergencies shook her out of her fog.

This emergency had blown a fog around Cedar. She'd been paralyzed by the terror and panic. She was so ashamed, so disappointed in herself. She was crippled by more than her leg—she was crippled by this awful, unpredictable talent. The thoughts ran around and around in her head and didn't stop until the sound of the rotors deploying shook her loose from them. She'd been worried about the ethics of it. Now she was worried about being overcome by it. When the transport bumped the ground it took fifteen minutes for the ramp to deploy. She pulled herself together. She had to.

Someone, she suspected Assam, had had the foresight to erect a long tent corridor to the largest section of the living pod on the ground so people weren't immediately subjected to unending open space and sky. That pod had a communal area large enough to serve as a dispersal point for the almost three thousand people yet to come, as long as they could be moved through quickly.

Most kept their heads down and hurried down the ramp to the makeshift tunnel after one glance around at what seemed limitless space when one has always lived in limited space. But Ahnna, walking down the ramp between Amalie and Cedar, had her head up, looking around. She took in several long, deep breaths and said, her voice breathy with awe, "I've always wondered what trees smell like. And grass. It's so green. And listen, Cedar, listen." A bird sang four notes over and over. "Is that—could that sound be a bird?"

350

Cedar wanted to cry. Something blew out of her on a long breath, a tension held since she'd first known she had to bring her mother to the planet. She felt so light it seemed her feet barely touched the ground, even her black hole of a fake foot.

Then she heard Meta's loud voice behind her. "Now, I'll be setting up my station right inside so I can start assigning quarters." And Cedar thunked back to reality.

"No, Meta, you are not in charge here, and you don't even know what arrangements have been made." Cedar heard Assam's voice override Meta. "Come along, and I'll explain to you and every one what's going on."

"But the captain—"

Cedar dropped her mother's arm and waited for Meta. Unlike Assam, she kept her voice low. "Let every one get inside first, Meta." She took Meta's arm, Assam took the other, and they pulled her around the crowd and under a tree a short distance away from the pod and the transport.

"What are you doing? I have work to do. I have to set up some kind of organization, assign housing, assign duties. The captain is depending on me."

"It's already done, Meta," Cedar began.

Assam put his hand on her shoulder and stopped her. "Meta," he said, "I am sorry you weren't told this in the confusion of leaving. First, the captain had no authority to make you responsible for the settlement here. Cedar and I are responsible. Second—and I know this will be upsetting to you, you were friends—Captain Kendra is dead."

Meta jerked around and started toward Cedar. "You're lying. You're both lying. It's not possible. Oh, someone killed her. She was murdered. Did you do it, Cedar? Was it Clare in revenge for putting me in charge of Engineering and Maintenance?" She was in Cedar's face, spittle and arms flying.

Ahnna pulled away from Amalie and ran across the grass to the tree. "Are you calling my daughter a liar? A murderer? Shame on you, Meta. Shame on you. Come on. They're going to need our help." She linked her arm with Meta's and pulled her away.

And Cedar found her mother again. The mother who'd saved her as a child. The mother who hid them both from the raiders who killed her father. The mother who covered Cedar's screams, who covered Cedar's eyes against the horrible scene, who witnessed her own husband's grisly death, who kept both of them alive for days until they were found by the searching shuttle on Astarte 15.

She might not ever be all the way back, but part way was good. It was good. Cedar heard the bird sing its four notes and watched her mother as this fierce little woman set Meta straight.

The halls of Restal Keep emptied at last light. No one was about except those on watch at the doors and gate. No one but Readen. With his hood pulled up and his cloak pulled tight, he identified himself to the guard and walked out into the town. Out of sight, he let his hood fall back. His hair was loose and blew across his face, but he didn't pull it back into a tail. He could no longer do that. If he did, the odd changes on his forehead were too apparent. No one could miss noticing the segmenting lines, or the small openings in his cheeks at the hinges of his jaws, hinges that were part bone, part tiny metal gears.

The intense battle inside his head sent him out tonight in search of blood. The streets were empty. Captain Paules had caught two more deserters today. And hung them. Publicly. Fewer and fewer people came out during the day, almost no one after it was truly dark. The lamplighters did their work before dark, and if a lamp sputtered out in the night, it wasn't relit.

Every time he used the strange power inside him, the entity in the back of his mind grew stronger. Tonight he would feed his own power. He would not lose control. He could not lose control. He could not lose himself, let himself be trapped inside his own head. He needed blood.

Why was the Itza Larrak doing this to him? The changes in his body, the strange changes in the sides of his head, the hard, fibrous armor covering his left arm and spreading across his shoulders, chest, and stomach, made him appear inhuman. It severely limited his ability to move around the keep and the Prime. He could no longer appear without completely covering himself or using an illusion, which meant using the strange power he didn't want to use. Readen feared Captain Paules had noticed. His reports were as brief as possible, and he escaped from Readen's study with such haste Readen barely had time to issue orders.

His mercenaries disappeared with alarming frequency, and Readen didn't know whether they were deserting or were dead. Two nights ago, someone piled three in front of the gates, dead and stripped of their weapons. Five more akenguns were lost. Paules informed him of rumors spreading that he was running short of coin. Mercenaries' loyalty was to coin, not to him.

If he started killing citizens to force control as he'd threatened, he'd lose and he knew it. Minra Shreeve might have been a mistake, and people would only be pushed so far before they rebelled and ended his rebellion. He had to become their protector. That's how he'd always presented himself. He had to remember that.

The entity in the back of his mind was furious—berating him for losing control, for losing the weapons, for not going after Daryl. The pressure was constant and growing. At times his vision doubled, and he saw colors he had no names for, objects ghosting where none should be. It dizzied him; he stumbled often. What he'd pushed away, ignored, dismissed as hallucination, now was ever-present.

He had power he didn't understand. Seductive power he didn't need to raise for himself. The temptation to use the power was strong, but every time he did, part of his mind screamed danger at him, screamed resist, resist. And the part not him exulted, grew stronger.

He heard the loud tramp of boots on cobblestones. Four of his guard marched down the middle of the street toward him. He couldn't hide; it was too late. He couldn't uncover his head, and there wasn't time to fashion an illusion. He touched the alien power, slipped into invisibility, and satisfaction spread tendrils through his body and his limbs. Impotent despair coiled and writhed in the back of his mind.

The patrol passed, their footsteps faded and the invisibility shield shimmered away. Down deserted streets, through empty alleys, past closed doors and gates, Readen wandered through the city he considered his—the empty city. The despair grew stronger, his vision cleared, his step firmed.

Finally, he found what he needed. A rough bundle of blankets in a corner of an alley where it was out of the wind. It stirred slightly. Readen pulled the blanket away from the shaggy head of a man—a drunk to unconsciousness man. He stood staring down at him for a long time and managed to shut off the conflict inside his head. What bloomed in its place was faint pity, barely detectable compassion, and disgust at the filthy stench. What he saw was a human who'd lost control of his life. He'd not felt emotions like this since he was a child. Physically shaking, he turned his head and managed not to vomit.

The man stirred, and Readen reached down, grasped the oily hair, pulled the head back, and pierced the carotid artery at the side of his neck with his small silver knife. Holding a wide-mouth pottery jar to the wound, he caught the steaming gush of blood, capped it, and wiped his knife on the dirty blanket. He pulled it back over the figure's head and left. The man never moved. The warmth of the jar cupped in his hands eased the despair in the part of his mind that was Readen, and he walked, his steps swift and loud in the silent streets, back to the keep, back to his tower.

CHAPTER TWENTY-NINE

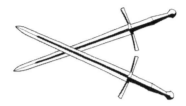

Daryl stepped out from under a massive elm. Its branches and those of its neighbors spread wide enough to cover the fifty tents going up like even rows of pointy mushrooms under the forest canopy. Ballard, Guardian of Anuma Quadrant, stood beside him, watching the small dots circling above. He and his Karda Patrol had arrived late in the night. Eager to avenge the death of his mother and her Karda, killed by the Itza Larrak in last fall's battle, he'd flown through the darkness.

"There was enough moonlight when we came in to see you've chosen the battleground well. The Line of Devastation snakes through thick forest then breaks out into the barrens often enough they—" he circled a hand above his head "—will be able to see anything that crawls or flies in time for us to get there before the Larrak and its urbat."

Ballard shoved his hands in his jacket pockets. The morning was cold, with clear turquoise sky visible through the trees. "Prime Guardian Hugh will be here probably mid-afternoon. He's organizing the ground troops we left behind, mine and his, to coordinate with Me'Kahn, who'll oversee our arc of the circle. What do you hear from the others? Who's coming, and who's staying to guard the other side of the circle?" He shifted from foot to foot. He was like a young hawk in yarak, so eager to fight he vibrated.

"Altan and Marta are on their way with five Karda wings," Daryl answered. "He hasn't heard from Turin, nor have I." His voice was hoarse with irritation, with the strain of waiting. He tempered it. "Who knows what he will do? He doesn't fly, so he won't be here, but I'm hoping Rachyl comes with several wings of their Karda Patrol. Holder Me'Fiere is spreading out to cover their arc with Me'Cowyn's men. Me'Cowyn should be here any moment. He's not bringing troops, but he's a fearsome fighter on his own—as you know—and has his own grudge against the Larrak."

"Being knocked off your Karda in mid-air would give me a grudge too." Ballard shivered. "I still don't know how Galen and Ket caught him."

Ballard's face was closed, and Daryl knew he was remembering the death of his mother and her Karda. She'd refused to leave her bonded, and they'd fallen to their deaths when the Itza Larrak had severed the Karda's wing.

"Me'Fiere..." Daryl stared far into the darkness beneath the trees and was silent. Then he took a breath and stepped around to face Ballard. "On my orders, Me'Fiere took several of his men a tenday ago and burned Readen's Hold to the ground. The villagers smashed anything left to rubble. They're already carting off stones to use elsewhere."

Ballard said nothing. He didn't have to. The grim satisfaction on his face and the sharp nod of his head said it for him. He raised a hand to shade his eyes and surveyed the moonlit sky. "Who's that?"

Daryl's heart plummeted to his toes and bounced back up to block his throat. He choked the words out. "That's Tarath." Why would Krager come here now? It would be something dire, or he wouldn't have left the Prime. Maybe Readen discovered him, and he was forced to get out. The rider was awkward in the saddle. Was he injured?

"Whoever Tarath's bringing is not an experienced rider," Ballard commented.

They came closer, and Daryl braced himself against the flood of relief that it wasn't Krager, that Krager wasn't injured, that he hadn't gotten caught or Tarath wouldn't be carrying someone else, he'd probably be dead too. ~Abala, who's riding Tarath? And what's happened to Krager?~

~Tarath tells me the man's name is Cael, and he is carrying him away from Readen before he is killed. Something about him as a spy. This is important for you, but Tarath does not know why. It was relayed from a young girl through a young Karda, and he did not get the whole story.~

Daryl waited while the two Karda talked. Becca made it back to the Prime and was safe. Another piece of lead hooked itself to the permanent yoke weighing down his shoulders. He hadn't given a thought to Becca since he discovered she'd snuck away.

~Tarath says you must not worry about Krager. He is working hard, and your worry will do nothing but distract him.~

Daryl rubbed his face. Tarath and Krager were a perfect match. Any other time he would have laughed.

Behind Tarath, two big Karda popped over the treetops as if they'd been skimming the forest, with several Karda wings in formation behind them. Altan, Kibrath, Marta, and Sidhari arrived. Getting that many Karda and troopers under the trees and out of sight created enough fuss and confusion that Daryl forgot about Tarath's passenger until he finally got back to his tent. The man, Cael, stood there, waiting.

Marta and Altan were right behind Daryl. Altan shouldered past him, his sword half-drawn, his voice rough and angry. "I know you. I know your face. I saw you at Readen's Hold."

Daryl pulled Altan back. "He's safe, Altan. He arrived on Krager's Tarath."

"How do you know he didn't kill Krager?"

Marta jerked at his arm and pushed his sword hand down. "Because Tarath would have killed him, not carried him, Altan." Her face looked like it was an effort not to add, "Idiot." Her temper was getting short too.

"You have a message for me, Cael? Tarath said you have important information," Daryl asked, his voice too harsh in his own ears.

He moved his head from side to side to relieve some of his tension. The waiting was getting to every one. He couldn't afford to let his show.

"You can talk to Tarath?"

"No, but Abala, my Karda, can, or you'd have gotten a more interesting welcome when you landed. What is it you have to tell me?"

Cael's eyes flicked to Altan, to Marta, and back to Daryl.

"Perhaps you'll be more comfortable if I tell you this is Altan Me'Gerron and Marta Me'Rowan."

Cael's eyes switched from narrowed to wide. "Marta? Readen hates you more than he hates Daryl or me."

Daryl winced.

"Could we talk inside, sir? And can we be certain no one listens in?"

Daryl nodded, tilted his head in talking-to-Karda mode, pushed aside the tent flap and ushered the three inside. "Abala will be here in a minute. He will tell me if anyone nears."

Cael glanced at the back side of the tent.

"Yes, from any direction," Daryl assured him.

Two minutes later, Abala announced, ~I am here. No one else is near. I am wearing my fiercest face.~

Marta laughed, and Abala said, ~I forget you can hear me, Marta Me'Rowan. It is disconcerting. I must watch my words.~

Daryl ignored them. "So tell me, Cael. What is so vital Krager sent Tarath with you?"

Cael's voice was low. Daryl strained to hear it. "I served for many years in the Restal Mounted Guard under Readen. He was a harsh but fair leader, kept us well supplied, busy, in good order—until the last few years. Things changed. Units were rearranged, men moved to special patrols for no purpose I could discern, except they were always the cruelest, harshest, least honest guards."

Altan shifted impatiently, but Cael went on in his quiet voice. "I knew Krager in his...as the tough, disreputable character he seems when he roams the taverns of the Prime. We weren't friends, especially, but behind his reputation, I sensed someone I could trust. I talked to him about leaving the mounted guard, and he asked me to stay. When Readen was imprisoned," Cael glanced sideways at Marta, "Krager told me who he really was and asked me to drift with the mercenaries toward Readen's Hold. I've been feeding him information since, as often as I could."

"You're the guard who told him about the children who were kidnapped," interjected Daryl. "Krager never told me your name. I should have recognized you."

Cael pushed his hair back from his forehead, scanned their faces, and finally said, "I'm also the one who stole Readen's journals."

Daryl abruptly stepped to the tent opening, pulled the flap open and stood, staring out, his stiff back to the others. The silence behind him was so taut, he thought if he tossed a coin behind him it would probably bounce back. Then he went back to his desk and rested one hand on a stack of reports. They steadied him. "That explains why you left the Prime, but why did Krager send you here on Tarath? More to the point, why did Tarath agree to leave Krager and bring you here?"

"He rescued me from Readen's guards one too many times. And I want to fight the monster that made Readen what he's becoming." He bit his lip, then went on, his voice still low. "But, I'm here because Krager wants you to know I am able to get through Readen's wards, from the simplest to the most complex, undetected, and he didn't want me killed before you got there. Readen hunts me, harder even than he hunts Krager."

Daryl's fist contracted, crumpling the topmost papers. Undetected. Cael could get through Readen's wards undetected. Ideas flashed through his head faster than he could catch them. He filed them. The problem of Readen had to wait. The battle that was here and now required all his attention. But Cael's words knocked a small weight from his shoulder yoke.

And he wanted the problem of Readen to go away. He wanted Readen to become his old self when the Itza Larrak died, and its influence was gone. He wanted the smart, witty Readen back, even if he was...

He stopped himself. He'd read the journals. What he wanted back was never there to begin with. He stood, unable to move while his mind whirled and tumbled.

Marta watched Daryl, her head tilted, waiting for him to speak. Finally, she gave an impatient snort and said to Cael, "You were right. No one...no one can know about this now. You carry yourself like a fighter, and you're certainly a survivor, but make sure you survive this coming battle. You're too important to lose. Come with us. We'll find you a place to sleep." She took his arm, grabbed Altan's hand, and they left. Her words trailed after them, "There's the cook's tent. Easy to find since it's the biggest thing around. Altan's forces are setting up under...."

Daryl and Abala walked further into the woods, out of sight from the growing camp. He pulled his sword and started his forms, slow at first. Gradually his movements grew faster and faster until his sword was a shifting, shining blur in the dimpled sunlight under the tree. Finally, Abala pathed, ~Enough. Enough. You are no longer practicing. You are fighting yourself again. Enough.~

His lungs strained for breath, and he stopped, bent over, hands on his knees, sucking in air.

Through the trees, Daryl heard the thunder of a landing Karda. He straightened and pulled himself back to the world he wasn't at all sure he wanted to be in.

It was Ket, back from his mysterious journey, with Galen on his back. Daryl met them in the trees at the end of their run. Galen didn't even get a leg slung over to dismount before Daryl asked, "Is it working? Are the microbes attacking the line?"

Galen slid down Ket's side. "Four of the strains are happily eating away at whatever's binding the carbon together. The other three died, or maybe went dormant. Either it isn't the kind of food that could sustain them, or the toxicity killed them. I couldn't be certain. But it doesn't matter because, yes. It's working, Daryl. It's working. Cedar gets to wear her 'I told you so' hat. She contacted me by Cue, by the way, maybe the last time they'll work. She's back in Ardencroft." He and Ket started toward the trees where the Karda made their quarters.

Daryl stood still for a moment. A small bit of the tension wracking him dried away like the sweat from his workout. The microbes worked. And Cedar was on the ground again. He wouldn't think about what Cael could do or about Readen. Not yet.

Then he remembered Cael's words. "What Readen is becoming." No. Not yet.

Four days later, stepping out of his tent for another futile scan of the sky, Daryl wondered if any of Turin's flyers would show up at all. Three Karda had landed in the last thirty minutes to report to Abala and Marta. No sightings of urbat, Itza Larrak, or Turin's Karda Patrol. Ket was pacing the short landing meadow, and Abala reminded him to keep under the trees out of sight from the air. Ket gave a sharp retort Daryl almost heard.

~Can he do what Kishar can? Make himself heard by anyone he chooses?~ he asked Abala.

~Not yet,~ was all the answer he got. What did that enigmatic response mean?

Galen and Ket carried on a verbal battle, loud on Galen's part, silent on Ket's, and Galen took off with Tessa on Kishar to check the lines and the work of the microbes again. Ket refused to leave the field, pacing back and forth under the trees out of sight from the air. His head raised, he watched the sky.

Daryl went back to his tent to redraw the battle plans, plans he knew wouldn't survive the first five minutes after the Itza Larrak arrived, to make allowances for the lack of Turin's troops. Every time he heard the loud whoosh of a landing Karda, he jumped up and went to see who it was. As did almost every one in the camp, except a few older fighters. The pre-battle tension gripping every one didn't seem to have a hold on them.

~You'd think,~ he pathed to Abala, who'd parked himself outside the tent to doze in the little sun filtering through the leaves and high-flying clouds, ~after two seasons of fighting, I'd have gotten used to this. Maybe it's because I'm still young and relatively inexperienced.~

Abala opened one eye. ~Don't be ridiculous. You fought bandits and raiders for years. You've fought almost every other day this spring. You are falling into your responsible-for-the-world-and-everything-in-it habits again. Leave your enormous mountain of papers, and let's find Galen and Tessa. Captain Ethyn can handle anything that comes up here, and you're wearing yourself out with worry.~ He closed his eye again

Clouds were piling up in the west, soft, mounded white mountains with dark, heavy bases, foretelling an end to the three days of clear skies. As soon as it started pouring down in blinding fury, the monster would arrive, and they'd be fighting it, rain, and probably gusting winds throwing them around in the air like dry leaves in a storm, thought Daryl. One of the troopers stationed at the tent with all the Karda rigging handed Abala's out to him. "Thanks, Chincho, you are well organized here."

"Yes, sir. If the captain hadn't stationed us here—well, let's just say, flyers are not always neat with their gear. And no one needs to waste time searching for it when it's needed, tossing everything everywhere and fighting each other's straps and stirrups."

Daryl laughed, the sound strange to his ears, and saddled Abala. The big Karda's feet fisted into ground mode, and he loped toward the small open space in the trees. By the time they reached it, he was at a gallop, and they lifted into the air, working hard to miss the trees at the other end, throwing Daryl back and forth in the saddle, even as experienced a flyer as he was. The bigger Karda like Abala and Kibrath had the most trouble with the small space.

They circled high for a time. A riderless Karda flew alongside for a few minutes then sheared off, but it wasn't three minutes before another took her place. ~They tell me someone is coming, following the line toward us, but too far away to tell. It isn't one flyer, though. It seems to be many. The message has been relayed too many times for an exact report, so I can't tell you how soon they'll be here.~

~How high from the ground do they fly?~

~Too high to be urbat. They're coming fast, several kilometers high, hitching a ride on a current.~

~Rachyl. It has to be Rachyl with Turin's patrollers.~ Weight fell away from him so fast, he was surprised Abala didn't shoot straight up without moving his wings.

~Let's check with Galen, Tessa, and Kishar, then get back to camp. I don't like being away too long.~

~Yes, of course. Everything will fall into one of Galen's famous black holes if you are not there every minute.~

Daryl never understood how a pathed voice could sound so dry and sarcastic in his head, but Abala was a master at it. ~Fly, don't lecture.~

They found Kishar and the other two at the farthest point on the line where they'd seeded Cedar's microbes. Galen stood, his toes almost touching a small hump of black rock breaking through the soil, staring at it, so still and intent Daryl wasn't certain he even noticed them land.

"Oh, bless Adalta, someone to talk to." Tessa bounded over to them before they even came to a stop, like a puppy chasing a ball. "Galen stares at the ground. I stare at the sky, and Kishar communes with—with himself, I guess. Nothing happens but the occasional Karda skimming by, waggling her wings and flying off again. I assume it would be more than a wing waggle if something were happening somewhere. Anywhere. Surely something is happening somewhere." She rubbed the back of her neck and glared off to the north as if she could manifest the Itza Larrak herself. "You'll have to poke Galen in the back with something sharp like your sword if you want him to come out of his trance." One hand shoveled through her spiky silver hair. "Please say something so I can be sure I haven't lost the use of my ears."

"You still have your mouth, though." Galen walked up behind her and attempted to smooth her hair.

"I see a copse of trees appeared since I was here last." Daryl swept his gaze around. A wide stand of trees was across the line from them, about fifty meters away. Thick clumps of bushes ranged in a rough circle around the line, tall and broad enough to hide a squad of men in each. "And the landscape is different, considerably. Where did you get the water? Or will they die when we leave? Seems a waste."

"I managed to pull up a spring. Well, not much more than a seep, but sufficient for the trees. The scrub bushes will last. I brought enough microbial matter to sustain them both and hopefully they will flourish. This will be an oasis in a few years." He gazed around the barren landscape. "All three sites will be if we don't destroy them in the battle."

"Cedar's microbes?" Daryl asked. He adjusted his sword and walked toward the line until Galen said, "Stop, you idiot." He walked back. If he didn't move his muscles would freeze up, and he'd start going over and over the plans they'd made in his head, tweaking and making changes until they devolved into a confused mess.

"The microbes are working away, flourishing, multiplying. In two of the places we seeded, they're breaking the links holding the carbon, and this one is starting to weaken. The breaks are still small. The Larrak might not be able to detect them yet, but it will soon. The other good news is, only the substance from the defunct nanobots is toxic and dangerous. That's what they're eating, and what's left might well be a resource for us. We'll need every resource you can find to rebuild Restal, so when it's safe, you'll need to send some Earth miners to bring up enough for your scholars to study."

"Maybe someone from the ship can help," said Tessa.

No one said, "If we win," or "When you defeat Readen," Daryl noted. Not even him.

~Abala tells me there is a large group of flyers less than a day out,~ Kishar said to all three of them. ~How long do you estimate it will be before the Itza Larrak detects the breaks in the line, Galen? ~

"I wish I could tell you. I contacted Clare on the ship. It's about empty, but she had three of her people watching for the signal, and it's disappeared. That's the last report I'll get from her. Almost every one is off the ship but her and a few of her crew. They're dismantling it as fast as they can, sending as much of it down as they can, and breaking the rest up into smaller chunks she hopes will burn up in the atmosphere on entry. Over the ocean."

He tilted his head up as if he could see it, shadows crossing his face like clouds before the sun.

Tessa watched him. Then Kishar broke the silence. ~It begins.~ And the same shadows flicked across Tessa's expression, but she was looking at Kishar with sorrow, resignation, and anticipation of great grief.

Then Daryl broke the mood. "It's time." His hand on Abala's neck, he repeated, "It's time. Let's get ready." He stepped on the big Karda's extended knee, grabbed the pommel handle and pulled himself up into the saddle. "I'll see you in camp—when?"

"This evening before dark. I want to watch a little longer." Galen went back to the line.

Tessa went back to watching the sky.

Kishar went back to communing with who knew what.

Daryl and Abala leaped into the air and felt the first tiny spits of rain from the black clouds moving fast between them and the sun.

CHAPTER THIRTY

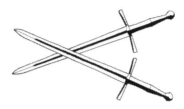

It was first light, the sun not even a red glow below the clouds to the east, when a giant black and gold Karda and its rider circled once above the battle camp, then headed back north, skimming the treetops.

Daryl stepped out from under the trees where he practiced his sword forms, wiped his face, dripping with half rain, half sweat, and stared after the Karda. Rachyl, commander of Akhara Karda Patrol, had arrived. Relief almost bent him double. He stripped off his sweaty shirt and ran for his tent, detouring past Mi'hiru Philipa's to shout, "Akhara is arriving any minute. Get ready for them, Philipa."

He sluiced himself down with icy water from a pitcher, donned his flight leathers, strapped his sword back on, and ran for the small landing field. How many fighters were with her? And did she bring the eight akenguns Turin had taken from Readen's men?

Ballard Me'Kahrl and Hugh Me'Rahl were there before him. Altan and Marta, her hair hastily twisted up with hair sticks, weren't far behind. "No one warned me. I didn't hear from a single Karda they were coming. They've never failed to warn me someone was coming before." Early morning grumps—or maybe pre-battle tension—sharpened her words.

"I think Kishar knew, but he didn't tell me either." Bleary-eyed Tessa, her hair sticking up on one side and matted on the other, stumbled up, Galen right behind her. He pulled her around, tamed one side of her hair, and fluffed out the other. She grimaced and scrubbed her hands through his hair. Which, of course, fell in perfect order around his half-beautiful, half-scarred face. He touched his nose to hers. Daryl had to look away. He refused to put a name to the pang he felt.

The sun, still behind the trees, threw long shadows across the field, and glinted off an enormous gold Karda that skimmed the treetops and dropped to a landing, back-winging so hard it tore leaves from the trees. He loped into the trees, snapping his wings in close before they got clipped. Daryl had never seen such an enormous Karda. It shone bright gold even in the shadows of the trees. A big man slid from the saddle and dropped to the ground with his saddlebags. Even for such a mountain of a man, the ground was a long way down.

"Blessed Adalta," exclaimed Hugh. "That's Turin."

"And it's one of the gold Karda we saw in the battle last fall. But I thought they disappeared."

Rachyl and the black and gold Karda circled above as Karda after Karda landed, all of them carrying double. Four wings of the Karda Patrol, Daryl estimated. Altogether sixty-four men. Sixty-four more fighters and half of them were ground fighters.

"Nine of them have akenguns," breathed Galen.

Finally, Rachyl and the black and gold Karda landed, loped to a stop in the trees, and Rachyl dismounted right next to Turin, but with grace. Turin shook his head over and over until Rachyl, laughing, took his face between her hands and brushed his mouth with hers. Then she went to the gold, stripped off his saddle rig, spoke to him for a moment, and bent from the waist in a bow. She glared at Turin until he did the same, only not quite so low.

Gishgal, Rachyl's Karda, and the gold looked at each other for several intent minutes, then Gishgal nodded, inclined his head, and the gold loped toward the field.

Karda lined the sides, heads dipped, all but small black Kishar's. The majestic gold loped out of the forest, paused and dipped his head to Kishar, aimed a wing swipe at Ket, and took off in a near-vertical climb.

"Galloping galaxies, Daryl. Isn't that a little unusual?" asked Galen in an I-don't-expect-an-answer tone.

No one said anything, and then the field was chaos again, until Mi'hirus Philipa, Amanda, Lili, and Marta gradually brought order, showing riders where to stow the saddles, pointing Karda toward the area in the trees reserved for them, and the fighters toward their area.

Turin walked out of the forest with Rachyl clamped to his side. She pulled loose and said, "I must take care of my Wings and Gishgal. You organize your ground troops and try to explain how you got here. I wish I could listen to that." She trotted to the field, issuing orders, separating riders and passengers, checking her orders and instructions with the Mi'hiru.

Turin planted himself in front of Daryl, arms akimbo, face in a fierce scowl. "I am never getting on a Karda again if I have to walk all the way back to Akhara."

Altan looked like he was about to explode with curiosity. "Where did...?"

"Best not to ask something I can't answer, Altan." He said to Daryl, "I brought four wings of Karda Patrol and thirty-two ground troops. These are the men your brother tried to hire to defeat you. I hope you don't have a problem with that. I also have nine akenguns, still with some charge. Not as full as they were when we got them—they work well on urbat. Don't know enough about them to be able to tell how much charge they have left."

"Welcome, Guardian." Daryl reached for Turin's forearm and took it firmly. "You are more than welcome—and your extra troops. They'll free more of our wingmen to fight from the air. Galen and Marta are both familiar with the akenguns. They'll check them out for us." He looked over Turin's broad shoulder.

"Captain Ethyn is on his way here to take you to the area for your troops."

Hugh grasped Turin's forearm, and his other hand patted Turin's shoulder. "It's good to see you, Turin." His grin was so wide Daryl could almost see his back teeth. "And congratulations on your inaugural flight on a Karda."

"And my last. Never been so scared in my long, scary life. Wasn't going to miss this fight." He looked around at the others. "Ballard, Altan, Tessa, Galen, good to see you again, especially seeing I'm on the ground and not as a bloody blot in the mud."

Daryl managed to quirk up a smile at the thought of Turin ever being scared of anything. "Get your men settled, then you and Rachyl join us in the cook's tent so we can bring you up to date and show you our battle plan. Please pick holes in it so we can patch it now instead of at the height of the fight." The relief he'd felt when Turin's forces flashed into the skies faded, and the constant dread curdling his gut was back. No plan survived the first few minutes of the battle. And this was their last chance. If this failed...

Turin started to meet Captain Ethyn, then stopped and asked Galen, "And your little bugs? Do they work?"

"Happily eating away at the line. It won't be more than a day or so before the Larrak notices, and all the fun starts."

The fun started three days later. Daryl woke up to Abala announcing in his head, ~The Larrak comes.~ Kishar was in his head with the same message, and Marta yelled it as she flipped the tent flap away and stuck her head inside. "Every Karda within my range is telling me the Itza Larrak is on its way."

"How many urbat?"

"Still getting counts. Some say three hundred, some say more."

His body tensed at those numbers, and his hand clenched as if it grasped his sword. "Where are they, and how fast are they moving?"

She was quiet for several minutes. "Me'Fiere let them through yesterday. They were shielded, so no one saw them, but one of the psychic ring people in the nearest village sensed them and flagged down a Karda. The scouts Me'Fiere sent were able to tell where they were."

He waited, and she listened.

"They'd traveled about seventy-five kilometers as of daylight."

He waited again.

"The Larrak drops the shield when they're in forested areas and puts it back in the barrens. But it can't shield the dust and the tracks. And Karda are sharp-eyed." She listened again. "They haven't stopped at all." Her head still cocked in listening-to-Karda mode, she added, "I'm almost happy." She didn't sound happy. "The interminable wait is over. We were about to start killing each other."

"Don't do anything today but monitor your Karda spy eyes and keep me informed." He sat up and threw the blankets off, almost happy himself for a short second before the doubt in its home in the lump in his belly woke up.

"Nice bod, Daryl. Cedar's almost as lucky as I am." She disappeared fast and didn't see the "nice bod" turn bright red. Or get hit by the boot he threw. Which landed in the wet, wet dew. But she did laugh and yell back, "As soon as you admit you're caught."

The atmosphere in the cook's tent was a mixture of jubilation and trepidation. A big horse was saddled outside, a trooper holding its reins. It looked like someone jury-rigged one of the smallest of the extra Karda saddles to fit the gelding.

Galen bent over the big map, telling Turin where he was to go. Turin was staring at him as if he couldn't believe what Galen was saying. "I raised a double line of trees here and here, on either side of the line. Your ground troops—and you—will be concealed even if it sends urbat wide to scout, and I don't think they're smart enough to be useful for that."

"They're not stupid unless the Larrak loses control of them. But we'll stay low and quiet and kill anything that comes close enough to see us."

Daryl interrupted. "Don't kill anything unless you have to, or the Larrak will know you're there. I depend on you to close the trap behind him." He looked at Galen. "The guns. Did you and Marta determine how much charge they have left? I know you didn't get back until late last night."

"We just did. Two have about fifteen short blasts left, three have a little more, and the other four are at three-quarters, less than forty. A lot depends on how they're fired. The shorter the blasts, the longer they last." Galen pulled the tie from his hair, gathered it back and tied it again. He was covered with dirt and mud and looked like something a farmer's plow turned up. "Turin, I'm sure you know what it takes to kill an urbat."

Daryl put a hand on his shoulder. "Galen, if you don't go lie on the ground somewhere, recharge and rest, you'll be useless in the fight. If you try to get up too soon, I'll have you staked to the ground. I'll finish briefing Turin and Rachyl. I know what you've done almost as well as you do."

Galen looked from Daryl to Turin and back. "Someday I'd like to sleep in a real bed, or even a real bedroll instead of on the bare ground. At least I'll be in a tent with a blanket over me and not the mud with my bare ass showing this time."

Daryl watched him walk off at more of a rambling stumble than a walk. He'd grown a small forest of trees and scrub in only a few days.

Altan joined them at the table, with Me'Rahl, Ballard, Me'Cowyn, and Tessa. Their Karda were lined up outside the tent close enough to hear. Marta sat at the far end of a table, scribbling notes, poking her hair with her pencil, and listening, listening, listening.

"As soon as Marta has a clear idea of how fast the monster is moving its army, we'll be able to deploy. So far it seems it is not stopping for rest, but that doesn't necessarily mean they'll be exhausted when they get here. They're not human, nor any animal we are familiar with. They're machines. They don't rest, they don't eat, they don't even shit," said Daryl.

"Thank Adalta for that," said Altan. "I don't want to think about what it would smell like."

"One last time." Daryl glanced at him as if the quip was puzzling, not funny. Nothing was funny. "We'll go over the strategy.

Turin and his ground troops will let them pass, wait until they have time to reach the first break in the line, then close in behind them. Galen seeded that spot with the most microbes. It's no longer toxic, so we aren't hampered by not being able to get close to it. He marked the boundaries of the safe area with piles of stones this morning. Stay aware. They don't need to stay out of the toxic areas, but we do. Impress that on your troops."

Marta got up and closed her notebook, marking her place with a finger. "The Larrak's traveling at the rate of more than a hundred kilometers in a day and a night. And it's less than eighty kilometers from us. That puts it here by tomorrow afternoon at the latest."

"Did you get a better idea of how many urbat are with it?" asked Daryl.

"Best guess is four hundred." Marta looked at him, both of them mentally calculating their odds. Marta bit her lip. "I guess any hope it would come alone was vain hope." Altan came up behind her, wrapping her in his arms. She leaned her head back against his shoulder.

Daryl heard her whisper, "Don't get killed." And Altan's response, "Stay safe. The only thing that could kill me is if you die."

Daryl glanced to the east for a few seconds wanting to whisper "Stay safe" into the breeze, then announced, "Let's move. Fly low. We don't want it to be able to see too many Karda in the air over its line." Daryl rolled up the map and dropped it in its leather tube. "Sorry—telling you things you already know. But if you have questions or concerns, let's hear them now. It's time to test Galen's hunting blinds. And, Turin, you'd best start moving your troops today. I hope they're good at covering their tracks."

Turin moved stiffly toward the big horse. "It'll be nice to be back on a horse. My fighters have to walk, but I don't think I could. Karda are a lot wider than horses."

Rachyl covered her mouth, but she couldn't hide the laugh lines around her eyes. Daryl hoped she'd still be able to laugh after the next few days.

Readen dressed with care. His high collared tunic was buttoned to his chin, black as night with silver buttons like stars marching down his chest. The tailor fussed about making it larger without measuring, but it needed to cover the armor on his arms and across his chest and upper abdomen that he couldn't let anyone see. His gloves fit his fingers, loose at the end, so the sharp nails didn't break through. The cloak he wore was black with silver bullion twisting around the edge of the hood pulled over his head, along the front edges, and around the hem. It closed with silver frogs.

His last appearance in the great hall was five days ago. Too long. There were three more holders here to talk to him. Here to *talk*, not to affirm their support, not to offer troops. Just to *talk*. He glanced at the small pot on the mantel surrounded by the light glitter of his preservation spell. Half the blood from the old man in the alley had suffused him with power. He didn't have to force himself to remember how to be the genial, witty, but firm leader. The power that belonged to him was full, and the other power faded as if something pulled at it. But it wasn't gone, and he could no longer be unaware of it, ever.

He'd apologized to Captain Paules for his "bad humor," blaming it on his anger at Daryl, on his worries for Restal, on whatever he could think of to appease the man and his troops. It was hard to remember why he'd been so driven. Why he'd been so careless with his anger. It had held at little more than a hidden simmer for years. Why it was breaking through now, he couldn't understand. He hadn't been himself for tendays. He had a lot of repair and reparation to do.

He pushed the hood back, stood in front of the small mirror on the wall, and pulled on the new blood power. The changes to his face, the segmented forehead, the small openings and gears at his jaw hinges, were slow to fade from view. But finally, his own face looked back at him. A small gesture with his fingers locked the illusion into place. He stared into the mirror, frowning as a realization grew. He could do this. Daryl could do this. Who else could do this? Krager?

Eyes closed, a deep breath filled his chest. He would need to scrutinize every one he met. Watch for small telltales that hinted they weren't who they appeared to be. He could trust no one. No one. He opened his eyes and tested a smile—the face smiling back was the genial, lightly mocking, slightly intense face he'd always worn. Until lately. He couldn't afford to let this illusion slip.

The hall was dim. Too dim, cold, unwelcoming. Readen motioned to Lerys, the old steward. "Lerys, get the rest of the torches lit, brighten things up in here. And throw a few juniper chips on the big braziers. You always make it smell so clean and fresh in here. And thank you for getting rid of the dais. No one needs to lord it over anyone anymore in Restal."

The old man blinked. The dais was the first thing Daryl got rid of when he took the keep back from Readen before, and the first thing Lerys had ordered put back when Readen arrived, but he beamed and bustled to do what Readen asked.

The first person in the room was Captain Paules. Readen beckoned him over and laid a hand on his shoulder. He sensed a tiny flinch and gave him a pat, holding his eyes and smiling a small, sad smile. "Captain, I want you to know I appreciate your loyalty and patience. I've been angry so long." He willed sadness into his face for a flash, straightened his shoulders, and went on. "Since I was...imprisoned. Often at you, as if I blamed you for something you had no control over. You have been steadfast and loyal in spite of my sometimes out-of-control moods. You deserve more than I can say, but I can say—*Commander* Paules."

The man's shoulders straightened. Readen could see the tension ease in his body. "Thank you, sir. I serve at your pleasure and with your guidance, gladly."

"Now, open the doors. They've been closed too long."

He paused to examine the room—the bright torches in gleaming bronze holders, the glint off silver and crystal on the tables. He sniffed the light, clean smell of juniper burning in the braziers, and smiled. It couldn't be more inviting.

Anson Me'Mattik was the first person through. Others were close behind him. Many were the usual court followers, people who'd found favor with his father, and taken as many favors as they could gather. Favors lost or threatened when Daryl was Guardian. Readen examined every face. Illusions left no telltales. It was only when behavior matched appearance that he could be satisfied they were who they appeared.

Holder Me'Neve was also there. Readen invited the two holders to his table, and before his bottom hit the chair, Me'Mattik said, "My hold, Readen. Your brother confiscated my hold and left troops there to guard it. When will you get it back for me? My troops are with yours..." he blinked at Readen's face and finished with, "and they will be until you don't need them any longer, but I can't take the hold back without them."

Readen laid a hand on Me'Mattik's arm, a light touch, but before he could speak, Holder Me'Koenig interrupted. He hadn't sat. Hands on a chair back, he leaned forward. "Minra Shreeve. Why kill Minra Shreeve? And that weapon you used. It's forbidden by law and by custom, and yet your men carry them on patrol through the city. I would like an explanation before I commit to supporting you, Readen. You've always been a tough commander of the Mounted Guard, and we need a tough Guardian, but this goes beyond tough."

Readen's anger seethed, but distant anger, as if part of him was preoccupied someplace else. But it marked Me'Koenig, and for a flash the man glowed dark, sick red to Readen's eyes. He put his gloved hands, fingers spread wide, on the table, and leaned toward Me'Koenig, holding his eyes. In a soft voice, filled with such regret and sadness it almost trembled, he said, "Sit, please, Holder, if you will."

The holder pulled the chair around and sat, arms crossed, back straight.

"I admit, those weapons I found are illegal here."

"Found? Where did you find them?" Me'Koenig's voice didn't soften.

Readen turned his head away. "I'm ashamed to say Daryl hid them. Hid them where I would never have thought to look, even if I'd had an inkling they even existed. A small village not far from my hold. They'd still be there waiting for him, but one of the villagers got suspicious. He came to me." He shook his head and scrubbed a hand hard over the lower part of his face. "I wouldn't have believed they were Daryl's except his guard here was armed with some kind of shield against them. Someone from the ship smuggled them, shields and weapons, to him. I know they're illegal, and as soon as this crisis passes and Restal is peaceful again, they'll be destroyed."

The table was still. The others looked back and forth between the two men. Me'Koenig, his arms crossed over his chest, didn't move. "Why is it he didn't take them to kill the urbat and the Itza Larrak that threaten us all?"

Readen waited a moment, head down, then looked up, eyes on Me'Koenig, voice soft and sad. "Me. He saved them to use against me."

A weak answer and he knew it. He'd need every bit of his ability to manipulate this man. Or kill him and blame it on Krager. A stronger answer.

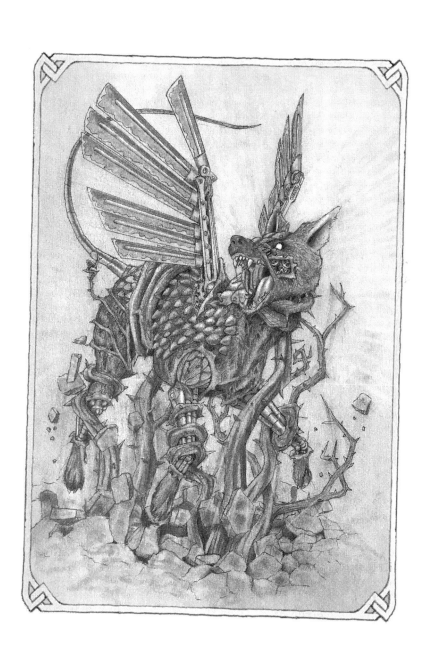

CHAPTER THIRTY-ONE

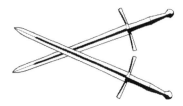

At first light Daryl and Galen flew to what they fervently hoped would be the battle site at the first break the microbes made in the Line of Devastation. Ballard, Altan and Me'Cowyn went with him. The Itza Larrak, with its horde of urbat, was a half-day away, and their troops were moving into place. Turin and his ground troops hid behind trees and clumps of tangled bush a hundred and twenty-five meters ahead of the first break in the line. Rachyl and Gishgal hid with him. As soon as the big gold and black Karda rose, the concealed Karda Patrols would rise in minutes. Ground troops hid in the trees and bushes Galen labored so hard to raise.

They checked all three breaks in the line, and Daryl was glad to move the rock cairns marking the boundaries of toxicity farther apart along the line. The microbes worked faster than Galen expected.

Daryl looked at the small visible humps of black lumps. "Time to get in place." Before they all exploded from waiting, waiting, waiting.

"Yes, it is." Altan walked to his side, holding Marta's arm. She wore the distant air that said she was listening to her Karda spotters, now so high they were mere dots in the sky. He kept hold of her, or she'd stumble and fall.

"Thirty kilometers."

Daryl signaled the others, and they mounted and took off in a flurry to join their troops.

Kishar and Tessa hunkered down in the small depression Galen scooped out for the four of them. Tessa leaned against his shoulder, and from the little popping breaths she made, he knew she was asleep. He moved his wing and covered her as best he could. Galen was flat on the ground, prone, his shirt off, staying in contact with Adalta as long as he could, packing his reservoirs to the brim with talent.

Kishar spoke to Ket in the range humans couldn't hear. ~You've done well, Ket. Persuading your father to carry Turin to this battle was a formidable job, I know. I do believe you are growing up. You will be a great ruler when your father is gone.~

The big, but not the biggest, gold Karda moved his head slightly. ~That you say this to me is the greatest honor I will ever receive, Kishar. When it is my time, I will try—not to be a great ruler but a good and just one. And an open one. It is long past the time we made more of ourselves known to the humans of this world. They are now as much a part of Adalta as we are after centuries of being born here, centuries of working to restore life here. Even if it is life from another planet, it is now part of Adalta, made of its soil and water as we are. And they have changed us as we have changed them. We understand more of the way they think now. We speak in their language—our language they must learn so they better understand the way we think. I don't know if this is a good or bad thing. I know humans and Karda are co-dominant species here, and to fulfill our responsibilities to Adalta it is essential we understand each other.~

Kishar mind-chuckled. ~Yes, you are growing up.~ He was silent for a while, listening, scenting the drifting changes in the air, watching the clouds darken above them. ~This will be a difficult fight. It will rain soon and make it even more difficult.~

Ket didn't speak. Then he lifted his head to look at Kishar. ~If we win this fight, if this is the last fight, you will not live, will you Kishar?~ It was more statement than question.

Kishar bent his neck around to look at the sleeping Tessa with one eye. ~You will watch out for her?~

~As long as she lives, there will be Karda to watch after her, to love her. I will carry her with Galen as long as my father rules, until other duties call me away. But I will not leave either of them alone. If there is one who will bond with her or one who will bond with Galen, they will find them. But they'll never be left alone. And if something happens to Sidhari or Kibrath, Gishgal and I will make certain Marta and Altan are not alone either. They saved my cousins. Anyway, I do not think either of the youngsters will leave them. They may be the first humans to be bonded to two Karda. I pity them.~

He stretched his head down along his forelegs. ~I sleep now. And Galen is with Adalta.~

Kishar waited for some time, then stirred enough to wake Tessa. He felt her small hand stroke his neck.

~I am afraid, Kishar.~ She spoke in the human range, a lower frequency. ~As if something worse than this battle is about to happen.~ She twisted around to sit cross-legged so she could see his eyes.

Kishar knew if she tried to speak aloud, in human speech, she wouldn't be able to. Even her pathed voice was choked.

~You said, when you found me and named me Austringer— the hunter, we would not be together forever. That you would leave when we finished our work.~ She paused and rubbed her eyes. ~You're going to die, aren't you?~ She looked deliberately into his eyes, first one, then the other. The muscles in her jaw clenched, but Kishar knew she wouldn't flinch away from the answer.

~If we are successful, yes, Tessa, I will die. It is the reason I have lived so long alone, the last of my kind. There were never many of us. Over the centuries of this war the others died and took a Larrak with them. It is the only way to kill it. I am the only way to kill it.~

Tessa scooted closer, and she laid her cheek against his head, her spiky hair soft against his feathers. They sat together for a long, long time.

Then Kishar said, ~You have your powers back now, Tessa.~

She raised her head and brushed her hands down her body. ~I don't feel any different, and it doesn't make me feel any better. I got used to not having them.~

~And you learned to be strong and powerful without them. But they are another tool, Tessa, like your sword and your bow.~

She cocked her head. There was a hint of panic in her voice. ~I won't lose those skills, will I? I'm going to need them today.~ Her fingers brushed the pommel of her sword, and her hand gripped the hilt. Her eyes were wide, on the verge of frightened.

~You've always possessed those abilities, and you will keep them. You will always be a hunter, but now you can be a healer too.~

~What will I do without you? You've been my best friend, my mentor, my teacher, my guide, my...~

~You have Galen now.~

~Yes, yes, I do, but...~

~And Ket will stay with you for as long as he can.~

~What does that mean—as long as he can? Is he going to die, too?~ Even a pathed voice could be shrill and frightened.

Kishar thought for a moment, then pathed, ~I know you've wondered about the gold Karda, about his color. Ket is heir to the — ~ He said a word with too many unpronounceable syllables. ~of the Karda. When his father begins to fail, which should be a long time away, he will have to leave. But I do not believe he will leave you and Galen entirely. You have a further task, you and Galen and Ket. The urbat will not die with the Itza Larrak, and they will be loose and without control. The circles will not be refuge or resource for them. That power dies with the last Larrak, and they will eventually die, but for some time still they will be a danger that must be faced. And the land in the circles will need to be healed. Your strength and returned talents will be vital to those tasks.~

381

He closed his eyes. ~Now, I must rest. Rest and think, until we are called.~

Daryl didn't take his eyes from the trees to the north where Rachyl and Gishgal hid until he was forced to close them against the dry burn and take several deep breaths to steady himself. As soon as he did Captain Ethyn grabbed his arm and shouted, "There they go, sir. There they go." And the black and gold Karda with its tiny rider burst into the air. Turin's forces broke cover on either side of the line behind the Itza Larrak.

It whirled, and in the instant, its iridescent bubble shield formed, and the urbat gathered in close ranks around it. They moved away from Turin's troops as a body, running at an easy gait. The first two rows behind it pivoted and headed for Turin. Even from a distance, Daryl could see the flash of his teeth when he drew his two big swords, whirled them in a complicated pattern, and walked toward the monsters like he was taking his morning stroll.

Daryl waited. When the Larrak passed the first cairn of rocks marking the safe part of the Line of Devastation, he and Abala stood. He jumped for the saddle, pumped one fist high to signal. Karda with and without riders burst like coveys of quail from Galen's new trees and bushes. Ground troops spread, four deep across the Larrak's path. It was surrounded.

Its clawed hands spread in front of its chest. It shoved as if to push its way through. Half the troops dropped to their knees or tried to run when the psychic wall of terror hit them. Several Karda faltered and lost altitude. Around it urbat fell, shriveled husks kicked aside by the others.

Daryl shoved back, sensed the immense power of Prime Guardian Hugh Me'Rahl join his. Ballard shoved a wall so powerful and angry it was almost visible. Resistance came from every flyer with strong enough talent to throw shields, and the terror dissipated, but Daryl could see fallen soldiers on the ground, urbat tearing at them. Too many. Even one fallen trooper was too many. Three

Karda hit the ground but managed to save themselves injury, and climbed back into the air, one of them limping as he loped to take off.

Three more of the urbat nearest the Itza Larrak fell over. ~He uses the urbat as a power source. Did you see that, Abala?~

~Yes, the effort took its toll. But he will try again.~

Tessa and Kishar flashed past them to circle the bubble shield— four quivers fastened to Kishar's saddle, two others slung across her back. Tessa was the fastest and most brilliant archer Daryl or anyone had ever seen. Kishar flew a tight circle around the Itza Larrak, his wings vertical, and Tessa didn't have to time her shots with his wing beats. She hit the Larrak's shield with a barrage of arrows. Some stuck, too many glanced away, but they left furrows and dark marks, and she didn't stop.

Me'Cowyn, her father, was firing his lethal lightning arrows, swooping in and out, though Arib wasn't as agile and quick as Kishar. The Itza Larrak was surrounded by the five guardians, the strongest talents on Adalta, plus Tessa and Me'Cowyn, all of them bombarding its shield with arrows, lightning arrows, and powerful firebolts. Altan and Kibrath rose up past Daryl and Abala so close their wings almost brushed, but neither missed a beat. The Karda flew as a flock, wheeling in synchrony that amazed Daryl, putting each rider in position to fire his or her weapon, get out of the way of the next, and come back for more.

~I need to go up, Abala. For an overview.~ He and Abala left the flock and flew wide around the battleground. Marta stayed high in the air, giving a running account from the other Karda to Abala, who relayed it to Daryl.

Karda, with and without riders, attacked the edges of the urbat formation. One would swoop close, an urbat would jump to try to catch it, then the Karda close behind grabbed it with long, sharp talons and flew high and away to drop it. Nothing survived that. The urbat's wings beat in a useless whir until they smashed on the ground.

The urbat held close protective rank around the Itza Larrak. The men and women of the allied troops fought in twos and threes, attacking over and over, dragging their wounded away so the healers could reach them and returning to the fight. There were hundreds of urbat, far more than human and Karda fighters. But the trap closed tighter and tighter.

Seven Karda and riders, picked for their psychic talents, flew in a close ring high above the monster at the middle of the pack. Its wings spread and closed, spread and closed. Every time it threw its arms in a psychic attack, shoving a force field of terror, the psychic ring of Karda and riders counteracted it.

Daryl watched Turin's forces close from the north. He tore into them, slicing urbat as if they were paper. His massive arms each wielded a heavy sword, and he used them with perfect precision, never wasting a stroke. Rachyl and Gishgal flew close above him. Every time he had a break, he bellowed at her to fly higher, and she darted down and snatched another urbat. Four men to one side of him and four women to the other, armed with the akenguns. It took two or three short blasts, sometimes more, to take down one urbat. The weapons weren't going to last long.

The Itza Larrak gestured toward Turin, and fifty more urbat rushed to attack. Daryl watched a trooper slip and fall in the blood and ichor on the ground smothered by snarling urbat Daryl heard even from high above. He and Abala dove, but they didn't reach him in time. Abala snatched two snarling monsters in his talons, and they flew high to drop them in the middle of other urbat, but that didn't erase the sight of the trooper he lost and the sounds of the urbat. Those would find a place in his nightmares.

On the south side, Galen pushed waves of dirt and thick vines with vicious thorns, pulling urbat down and burying them sometimes six or more at a time, or holding them for troopers to kill. Altan's troops flanked him on one side, Hugh's on the other. Daryl's troops and Ballard's closed the circle from east and west.

~Marta says, look above,~ said Abala. Dropping out of the bottom of the clouds were tiny gold dots. Four Karda in tight formation grew larger as they slowly circled down. They were joined by Ket.

Daryl saw Kishar and Tessa break away from the flock barraging the Itza Larrak and land behind Galen.

~Kishar says it's time. We must land.~

~Time? Time for what?~ Daryl asked. He didn't want to stop fighting. There were too many urbat to stop.

Abala didn't answer. He made a tight circle and landed, loping to where Tessa was taking the saddle off Kishar. Tears streamed down her face. She was shaking so hard her fingers fumbled on the buckles.

Galen stopped burying urbat and signaled to troopers on either side to fill the gap as he backed away.

"Why did you land? Tessa's not out of arrows. One of her quivers is still full. Are you hurt, Tessa? Is Kishar hurt? You're crying. Why are you crying? Why are you unsaddling Kishar?" Then his eyes went from Karda to girl and back again. He pushed Tessa's hands away, unbuckled Kishar's rigging, and dropped it to the ground.

Daryl watched the pain grow on his face. Galen gathered Tessa tight to him.

Kishar's feathers quivered. He shifted from foot to foot, like a hawk on a falconer's wrist, ready, eager to hunt and kill, a hawk, no, a fierce and dangerous Karda in yarak.

Kishar spoke. ~You must call the fighters away from the Larrak, Daryl. All must leave the sky.~

Daryl jerked and started to object or ask why. Then he nodded. The authority in Kishar's pathed voice was fierce. Gone was the sometimes funny, sometimes gentle, always wise Karda. This was the killer, the predator, the one, he realized, on whom everything depended. The one who knew he was going to die.

~Kishar,~ he said, his words slow, reluctant. ~I will sorely miss you. But when I need guidance, I will remember. I will remember Kishar, the last of his kind, my friend.~ He tried not to let what he knew show on his face. Tessa already knew, but his sympathy wouldn't help her now.

Kishar turned his head to Galen. ~It is time, Galen. It is time to use your fullest power. With Tessa it will be whole.~

"What do you mean, Kishar? I'm using it now. Or I was until you landed. And Tessa..." He didn't finish. every one knew Tessa's power was blocked. He stared at Kishar. Sudden joy flashed on his face, joy for her. Her talent was unblocked. Then Daryl saw realization hit him, and the joy snuffed out. Galen drew Tessa closer.

~The ground beneath the Itza Larrak. Tessa will lend you power. You must reach for it. You must move it. Force him into the air. As soon as you see it start to move, Daryl, call the others away. Clear the sky.~ The small black Karda butted Tessa gently with his head. She scratched it for a second, then he turned, spread his wings and took off straight up. High above, the four gold Karda hovered to strike.

"He took off without me." Tessa's mouth quivered. Galen took her into his arms, and Daryl heard his choked whisper, "We'll cry later. He gave us a job. The last job we'll do for him. Let's do it."

Daryl watched Kishar, watched him rise almost straight into the air, knowing never again would Kishar land beside him, throwing up dust and grass and making him sneeze. He blinked several times, forced himself to postpone his grief, and called six of his troops over. "Stand guard over these two. Don't let anything get near them. Anything." And he watched the glimmering bubble shield around the Itza Larrak, now marred with scorch marks, arrows stuck halfway through it, the monster inside gesturing, ordering his urbat to strike where he guided. Never taking his eyes from it, afraid to hope, terrified for Kishar, for himself, for his people, for his planet.

Kishar circled overhead.

The ground under the Itza Larrak's shield shifted, loosened. Its feet started sinking. It stepped away, but the same thing happened. Its clawed feet sank several inches into the dirt. Three more urbat near it faltered and collapsed, shrunken and dead, and the enormous figure of the Larrak, the Itza, the last Larrak, spread its wings and lifted from the ground into flight. Its flight was slightly unbalanced, but only slightly.

~Now, Abala, clear the sky. Marta, it is time to clear the sky.~ Within minutes it was clear, every rider watching from the ground, from their saddles wanting to be in the air. Every Karda head up, wings mantled, trembling, wanting to join Kishar's fight. Their riders baled off to join the fight against the urbat on the ground. Nothing was over yet.

The four magnificent, screaming golden Karda arrowed from the sky, one after the other, they smashed past the Larrak's shield, slashing with their talons, leaving great, gaping gouges.

Kishar dove straight through the tattered shield and locked onto the Itza Larrak's back. Round and round they whirled, dropping fast for the ground, the Larrak's sharp metal wings tore at Kishar. It reached back with its claws, tore at Kishar's wings, his body, anything it could reach. It screamed a high, piercing scream. The urbat on the ground leaped at the sky toward it in frenzied, futile leaps. More and more collapsed into shrunken heaps on the ground as the Larrak sucked strength from them.

Kishar held tight, wings bleeding. His talons pierced the armor and sank deep into the Larrak's body. He reached for the monster's spine with his terrible beak and tore the Larrak's head half off. Bright orange fluid sprayed, mingling with Kishar's scarlet blood. They burst into an enormous red fireball and fell in slow circles to the ground in the middle of the urbat.

The urbat, locked in place—frozen statues sitting on their haunches, muzzles raised as if they still watched the battle in the sky —scattered and ran.

The troops on the ground tore into them, chopping heads, legs, wings, but too many escaped.

The promised rain started falling. No one left. All watched to the last glowing coal of Kishar's pyre.

Daryl dropped to his knees, unable to feel relief, unable to feel satisfaction, unable to celebrate victory. He grieved Kishar, whose long life was over, whose long-delayed duty was finished. He grieved for Tessa, who'd lost him. He grieved for the fighters he'd lost and might still lose. He grieved for what he must do next.

Nothing. For a long time, there was nothing. Then warmth. A strange weight of warmth. It had experienced warmth, but it had never *been* warm before. Then a strange perception of something it knew. It had caused it, dealt it out, but never experienced it. Fear. Fear that didn't belong to it, yet it was all around him wherever he was. Where was he?

He. A limiting human word delineating an individual.

Alone. He, it, was alone. Was he an individual? Separate? Apart? Nothing to draw strength from. Where were they, his creatures? He reached out and there was nothing.

His ocular apparatuses tried to open. It took a long time, and he was distracted by the thing surrounding him. The thing that was warmth.

He started to check his organizational structure. Something must have gone wrong. There was nothing there. Nothing but a strange creature clawing at him, trying to push him out of the warmth.

Finally, he got his oculars open. There was definitely something awry with them. Only a few colors registered—everything blurred, indistinct, pale.

Something approached. A small man, stooped and weak—humans lived such short lives. The man showed little fear. It spoke at him, but the sounds didn't register. Not for a long time. Then they did.

"Readen, sir. Do you wish the hall opened for a session this afternoon?" A long pause. "Sir? Readen? Are you well?"

A strange suffusion lifted him. Success. He succeeded. He transferred. He lived.

Then there was a violent shove, and he was pushed to one side, forced to watch, unable to act, even to move a talon, or one ocular sphere. He settled in a small space. "I will watch and learn," he said to himself. Himself. He was a he. An I.

CHAPTER THIRTY-TWO

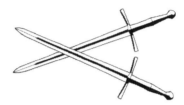

Readen finished dressing and walked back into his bathing room. A glance in the mirror showed his illusion was falling in place, layered over a face he barely recognized. The segmented lines in his face were deeper, his eyes glowed faintly yellow-green, his nose flattened, his mouth thinner. He stared at the image, appalled, and pressed his hands hard to his belly as if to hold back fear. Then his image solidified, smoothed into the illusion of the face he was born with.

A hard core inside him was cold—the cold of metal that froze to your skin and burned where it touched. His vision blurred, then sharpened. When his eyes roamed around the room, he saw details, even objects he'd never seen before. Colors he'd never known before faded in and out. Dust motes formed patterns in air currents he'd never seen before. He stood, unmoving, a terrified, petrified, granite statue.

Part of him exulted. One hand lifted to touch his head, fingers exploring. In his head floated alien thoughts, thoughts that didn't belong to him. "I, I, I will never fly again, but I am alive. I am an I. I am an I." An immense emptiness of loss threatened, and he grabbed for the warmth he floated in.

Warmth he floated in?

Horror turned his body cold. There was something, someone else in his head, invading his thoughts. Confused, petrified, a tiny mouse caught in a corner by an enormous cat, the words "I am trapped. I am trapped" and "I am Readen Me'Vere" ricocheted inside his skull, unable to find a place to attach, batted around by the something else, by the enormous hungry cat-like thing stalking around in his head.

The Larrak took three steps, but Readen forced his body to stop. The words "I must get to my circle. I must get to my circle," whirled around and around in his brain, trying to shove Readen aside, to move him forward. This wasn't imagination. This was real. Readen shook all over. His knees went weak, but the Larrak held him up.

He grasped his left forearm, felt the hard armor like the exoskeleton of an insect covering it. The paralyzing realization of what he'd done to himself spread through him. He remembered as if it were happening now, the pain when the small sliver of bone carved the first symbol from the Larrak's cavern prison into his flesh. He could see the blood dripping, see the bright crimson lines form. He remembered the searing pain, the exultation, the sense of freedom—whose freedom? Whose freedom?

Time stopped and the battle started. His body convulsed, and vomit forced its way up, burning through his throat, his mouth, burning his nose. Inside his head was incoherence and pain, searing pain, screaming pain, forever pain.

An atavistic grasp for survival woke inside Readen. Self-awareness crept back, and he fought harder. Terror started a slow morph into anger, anger at his own foolish, duped self, anger at the Larrak. Anger grew into rage. Readen stopped it before it reached incoherence again. He couldn't afford that. He couldn't make that mistake.

The small thing inside his head was small no longer. Its tentacles pulsed. Without his volition, his body tried to move, and he fought with every twitch of muscle for control. He stripped off his stinking clothes, mopped the floor with them and shoved them into a corner. A clear thought formed. He'd burn them later. Cold contempt that wasn't his followed it, and he fought on. Movements jerky, uncoordinated, he turned on hot water and managed to fold his fingers around a small towel. The touch of the scalding, dripping cloth woke sensitive nerves in his skin, his human skin. The Larrak part of him shrank away from it, but he kept on, washing every inch of himself, gaining strength with each swipe of the warm, sopping cloth over his skin.

Naked, he forced himself back to the bedroom. With both hands, he reached for the jar still half-full of the blood from the old man in the alley. One damp finger smeared a drip of flaky blood below the sealed cap, and he was able to open it. He fought to get it to his mouth, fought to force his throat to swallow, fought not to regurgitate it. Strength spread first inside his mouth, on his tongue, down, down, spreading through his body. His own power, Readen's power.

The pulses of alien strength weakened, but the part of him that was Readen didn't forget again. He could never forget again.

Putting on fresh clothes was not simple. The buttons were torture. He looked at his hands, fingers spread. The claw-like nails were the same—they had not grown. A deep breath filled his lungs. The relief from this one small thing lent him strength, but the Larrak inside grew colder, angrier.

Fully dressed, he faced the mirror again. Someone rapped on the door, light, timid raps. The Larrak receded enough for Readen to answer, and the image in the mirror solidified as Readen's face.

That would be Lerys, his steward. The thought was normal. It was his thought.

Readen strode to the door, made complicated gestures with his fingers, oddly stiff fingers, and threw it open. Could he trust his voice? What would it sound like? Human? Or the Larrak's mechanical, ringing tones like gears thrashing?

"Yes, Lerys. What is it?"

"Holder Me'Koenig wishes to speak with you, sir." Lerys tilted his head to one side. "Are you well, sir?" His words were untinged with the wariness his body couldn't hide.

Readen wished he could smile, but he couldn't force the muscles of his face to contract. If he tried harder, he didn't know what expression would result. He noted the steward's wariness. The

Larrak didn't care, didn't notice. Lerys could have been an uninteresting bug.

Readen stepped out and closed the door, setting the wards behind him. The simple presence of Lerys, of another human, increased his clarity. The separation between Readen and the Larrak widened by the breadth of a cat's whisker, a mouse's whisker. He didn't want to think of mouse and cat. He put a hand on Lerys's shoulder, partly to steady himself—his body's movements were too jerky—and wondered.

When was the last time he'd touched a human and not killed it? It? When did he start to think of other humans as It? When he found the Larrak in its cavern prison, or had he always? Chaos threatened his mind again, and he broke off the thought. He couldn't afford self-doubt. It was new, something he'd not felt for years, if ever. It weakened him. Or did it strengthen him? That human thought.

Me'Koenig waited outside Readen's study and watched him approach. Readen couldn't use the small gestures to break the spell that locked the door. Me'Koenig would see and wonder. Readen wasn't supposed to have such abilities. "Lerys, I'll take the holder to my mother's solarium. The sun shines today, and it will be a more pleasant place than my dark study full of work."

Lerys's eyes widened. Readen never went to her solarium, hadn't for years. Not since he'd grown into manhood.

"You're a little stiff today, Readen," said Me'Koenig.

"Difficult workout this morning. I haven't done enough sparring lately, and it shows."

Would he even be able to sit? He'd never seen the Larrak sit.

"Your body is my body now. It will do what is necessary," whispered inside his head.

No, no, no.

He sat in a chair close to a large plant spilling over the sides of its pot, wanting to be close to something alive. A blurred memory of his mother sitting in the same chair stirred and smiled at him. How could a memory smile?

He gestured Me'Koenig to a chair on the other side and moved a hand to finger the leaves of the vine. The effort it required stole his breath. Even through the gloves, the touch on the plant calmed him enough for this conversation. Why did he need that so badly? A sharp pain cramped his stomach.

The holder shifted his chair around to face him. "I'm leaving today, Readen. I've always liked you, your intelligence, your wit, and admired your leadership of the Mounted Patrol when your father was alive. Daryl is young and far less experienced in governing. A good fighter, though, as his defense against the Itza Larrak and its creatures showed."

The Larrak surged, and Readen stopped himself from leaping to his feet. "Kill him. Kill him." The voice in his head rang and echoed. "Kill him." His fingers dug into the arms of the chair to keep from reaching for his sword. The vine in his other hand snapped, and his fist clenched, piercing the palm with his nails. The muscles in his arms strained and bulged.

Me'Koenig noticed nothing. "But, frankly, I want to wait to see if you can rule Restal without talent. My men and I have noticed fear rules the streets here."

Readen forced calm over the seething inside him. "Yes, Captain Paules has reported the same thing to me. People are frightened about what Daryl will do. And they know his troops razed my hold to the ground. They fear for Restal, for their homes and families. But I have control of the prime and the ability to hold it. Those fears will fade."

"That's another thing. Those weapons."

Years of practice at hiding his real self allowed Readen to temper anger so he hoped only irritation showed on the illusion of his face. "I have assured you they will be destroyed when this crisis is over."

"Kill him. Kill him," Readen thought. It wasn't his thought.

Pressure to force him to the Larrak's Circle of Disorder shoved at him. He kept his boots welded to the floor, resisting, resisting.

It took four days for Daryl's camp to clear. Hugh Me'Rahl was the first. "If I could stay, Daryl, I would." The tension in his voice was palpable. "Whatever assistance I can give you unofficially, I will. But our laws are clear. Internal politics are out of bounds for other guardians, and the prime guardian especially must remain neutral whatever his personal inclinations." He stared across the landing field where Bren's crew was taking the big cook's tent down and loading the wagons. "I doubt Readen has ever seen Bren, or if he has, he won't remember just another trader. He'll stay as long as you need him."

Daryl said, "Marta tells me there have been a few reports of urbat sightings, but the creatures are disorganized and confused—though still dangerous killers. Tessa and Galen have gone to the Larrak's Circle of Disorder, but I've heard nothing from them yet. Since Ket can't fly over the circle until we're certain it's dead, Galen is on his own and on his own two feet." He looked down. "And Tessa needs time."

Hugh squinted at the western sky. "It will take more than time for her to stop missing Kishar. I doubt she ever will."

Daryl kicked a rock. "As do I."

"All of us. Soon as I find someone who can design something appropriate, there will be a monument in Rashiba to him."

"He'd hate that. But soon as I get the prime back, there'll be one there, too." He shifted so Hugh couldn't see his face. The older man put a hand on his upper arm and grasped his forearm with the other. "Goodbye, Daryl. Go slow, be smart, and stay safe." And he stepped up on Nereya's knee and swung into the saddle. His mouth opened as if to say something else, then closed. Hugh held Daryl's eye for an instant, then bent toward him from the waist in a gesture of respect. "You did well, Daryl." Nereya swung around, and they loped to a takeoff.

Ballard was the next scheduled to leave. He walked up to Daryl with Harani, his Karda, beside him, and they watched Hugh and his Karda Wings, with fewer riders and Karda than when they'd arrived, disappear to the east.

"I know you don't want to believe your brother had a part in this..." He paused.

Daryl, his eyes still following Hugh's flyers, and his voice tighter than the hide on a drumhead, said, "It has become too difficult not to believe."

Ballard shoved at his hair. "I have a wing of flyers who were at one time mercenaries."

Daryl stared at him. "Mercenaries the Karda agreed to carry?" That bit of astounding information released a little tension.

"They are paying recompense for past acts—to my mother, not me. They tell me they would like to be released to serve you."

"How many times did you have to hit them with the flat of your sword before they asked you?"

Ballard laughed one of his rare half-laughs, then his face morphed back to granite. "I can't legally help you, but Readen is as much responsible for my mother's and Pagra's deaths as the monster Kishar killed for us. One of those mercenaries might resemble me enough to be my twin. He might even share my middle name, Anatol. Don't laugh. They call him Tall, because he's tall like me."

Daryl looked at him long and hard.

"They won't accept pay. This is for my mother. It—we—will finish what they owe her."

For half a second there was a grieving, begging little boy in Ballard's eyes. Daryl nodded and reached for Ballard's forearm. "I accept their offer, but they—all—must agree to follow my orders."

The younger man shook Daryl's forearm, and a few harsh lines of bitter grief in his face evened out. "I better see if the rest of my men are ready to go. It's a long flight back to Anuma Prime, but they're missing the ocean, I think, as am I." He strode off, shoulders back, head up.

Daryl watched Rachyl and Gishgal organize her flyers. Daryl suspected Akhara Quadrant would soon become a quieter, safer place. If it wasn't already. Otherwise how could Turin have spent so much time away from his restive quadrant?

Turin left earlier that morning, headed with his mercenaries for the northern pass over the mountains—some grumbling about the long walk, others, like Turin, grateful not to be on a Karda again. Rachyl's messenger left the day before to get Me'Bolyn's permission to cross his hold to the coast. "Permission is less costly than a fight. I'm never tired of fighting, but the thought of a long slog over the mountains to the coast, then a stomach-heaving boat ride to Akhara, tempers my enthusiasm for it." He'd glared at Daryl and added, "And I'm never getting on a Karda again if I have to walk all the way." His troops might be walking, but he wouldn't. He'd struck a bargain with Bren for the big horse. He was happy, Bren was happy, and Daryl was happy he was leaving as a friend, or as close to a friend as Turin could ever be.

Altan walked up behind him, jumping him out of his thoughts. Marta was in the air somewhere with a small flock of Karda keeping watch for roving urbat. Galen reported no more nanobots working the Line of Devastation, but it was still toxic, and the microbes were still eating the toxicity. It would be a long time before they were safe. Every group that left carried batches of the minuscule bugs in whatever containers Galen found to carry them.

"If this is the say-goodbye-and-take-off place, I'll need to move away. Marta and I have been appointed ambassadors to Restal from Toldar, so leaving would be a dereliction of our duty."

"You've been appointed, or you appointed yourself?"

"Is there a difference? Where do we go from here? Before I take you home to Restal Keep and tuck you in safe where you belong."

"We have a lot of thinking and planning to do. This isn't going to be easy. He's holding the entire city hostage with the akenguns. What we did last time won't work."

"How about Ardencroft? Cedar is good at thinking problems through, considering stuff we'll probably never even think of. And you'll get to see her again."

"I don't know why you and Marta keep saying things like that. Even if she were interested, I don't have time for the romantic— whatever—you two have. Even if I defeat Readen, I have a quadrant to put back together, people from the ship to settle somewhere...." His voice faded away at the laughter Altan's face pointedly directed at him. "But Ardencroft makes sense, and

Me'Mattik's hold is empty except for a few of my troops, so your troops can stay there. Ask Marta to send a Karda with word for Tessa and Galen to meet us in the village as soon as Galen decides the circle is safe or decides what it needs to be made safe. It will take planters, and he'll be more than happy to find some among his stranded shipmates."

He stopped, gazing into the distance as if that was where the dead were. His voice was low as he said, "To replace the brave ones we lost who can never be replaced."

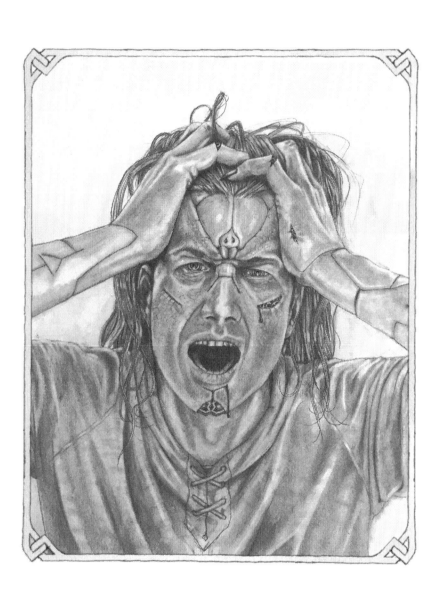

CHAPTER THIRTY-THREE

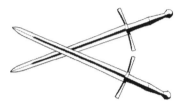

Becca ducked her head to the carrots she chopped in the kitchen of Restal Keep. Lerys shuffled in. His round, pale face developed new lines almost every day even in the short time she'd been working there. Krager finally agreed she could, though he didn't believe it was safe. But there'd been no unexplained attacks or disappearances of young people since Readen returned. The kitchen was alive with gossip, soft, tense, quiet, a constant shooshing sound of waves on a sandy beach. The only words she heard spoken in a normal tone were, "Chop more carrots," or whatever she was peeling or chopping at the moment.

The sounds intensified every time Lerys shuffled through the kitchen door. He was an inveterate gossip, and she harvested every word he spoke, gleaning information about Readen and about the guards' schedules and routines. The guards ate in a room off the kitchen, but Cook wouldn't let her serve them. She could hear, though, and they were loud. Plus, she was a Water talent, and there were large pitchers of water on every table. Water carried sound well. She harvested even more from their casual, incautious conversation.

"He looked tired today. Must have had a restless night.

Me'Koenig is leaving, but he didn't promise any help to the Guardian." Lerys was old, garrulous, and careless with his talk.

Becca cringed every time she heard someone call Readen the Guardian. Her shoulders straightened too much at his next words, and she forced them to slump into bored-with-chopping.

"He peers at every face he passes, at anyone who approaches, like he doesn't see very well, except I know he does. It's like he bores into your eyes to see inside you."

Becca's hands stilled, the knife poised over the carrots. Cook's glare fell on her, and her knife flashed through the carrots again. Illusions, she thought. He's checking for anyone wearing an illusion. She chopped faster. The sooner dinner was finished and served, in the guard's room as well as the hall, she could leave and report to Krager.

Elleran's voice popped into her head. ~It's dead. The Itza Larrak is dead, Becca. I just got the message. It's dead. Finally, it's dead.~

She went still, then started chopping with a frenzy as if she were chopping the Itza Larrak's body into small pieces. Her breath came fast and hard through her nose. Her mouth clamped tight, holding onto the words she wanted to scream and shout. Cook's voice brought her back to the kitchen and reality. "Careful with that knife, Becca. I don't want to serve stew with pieces of your finger instead of carrots."

Becca sat very still, then started on the carrots again, fighting not to show her relief and elation on her face. Should she announce it? Wait, no one would believe her, and she couldn't tell them how she knew. ~Oh, Elleran. Daryl will be coming here as soon as he can. I can't talk now. I have to listen even closer. He'll need everything Krager and I can find out.~

"You'll have to help me serve the guards tonight, Becca," said Cook. "Manni left. Said his ma needed him home." Her voice lowered, and Becca strained to hear. "I think she wanted him out of here."

"Nonsense," snapped Lerys. "Things are getting better every

day. He was entitled to a little anger after being imprisoned. Even after he escaped, he was virtually locked away in his hold."

every one in the kitchen stopped what they were doing and stared at him.

"Here's the guard's schedule for the next tenday. There's little change so you can continue to serve on the schedule you've been using." He passed two papers to the cook.

Becca watched her lay them on the table, spread them apart and study them for a minute. She shuffled them to the center of the table closer to Becca, without looking at her, then reached for a large basket of beans and a bowl and started snapping them.

"You've chopped enough carrots, now, Becca. Move over here and help me snap beans. At least you can't chop a finger off snapping beans." Halfway through the basket, Becca held the schedule so tight in her memory she didn't think she'd ever forget it, in spite of wanting to run out into the streets and start yelling, "It's dead. The Itza Larrak is dead!" until she went hoarse. She sucked her lips in and locked the words with her teeth until it hurt.

Cook moved the pot full of snapped beans to the sink for water and set it on the stove. "Go to the storeroom where the uniforms are and find a pair of trousers to fit. Loose. And a bigger shirt. It's nearly time to start serving the second shift guards." She directed her eyes at Becca's chest. "No point in advertising in there."

Becca also found a wide sash to use as a tight breast band. She couldn't pass as a boy any longer, and Krager had finally put his foot down about her staying with Mother Girt and agreed it was safer to work here in the kitchens since Becca refused to leave. But she didn't need to, as Cook put it, advertise.

When she carried two large baskets of bread into the guard's eating hall, the last of the early morning street shift left as the house guard filed in, rubbing eyes, adjusting uniforms and swords, and grumbling. She went to the sideboard and poured more glasses of water than she knew they'd drink. The water carried their voices to her as she went back and forth from the kitchen. If she relied on mugs of ale, their words were cloudy.

"He roams the halls almost every night. Every time he passes, he peers at you like he's memorizing your face. Again."

"Yeah, I've been with him a long time, and he's never acted that way before. He usually doesn't even notice you." The guard scratched his backside vigorously, and Becca made a note to throw away any leftovers from the basket he grabbed from her.

One of the street guards said, "He's puttin' more of us on the street with those weapons. Makes me nervous. My partner had to use one last night, and both of us threw up after."

"Careful with your words, man. You don't want Paules to hear."

"He won't carry one. He can barely stand to touch 'em to hand 'em out." The words were grumbled and low. Becca almost missed them.

"For a silver I'd be outta here."

"Don't wanna get hung, so I'm stayin'. I didn't hear that, an' you better hope no one else did either."

Becca helped serve three more guard changes. It seemed no one knew about the Itza Larrak. Cook kept her close, and she hardly got a glance from anyone. Not sure what she thought about that, she kept her head down, worked, and waited impatiently for Cook to say she was done for the day. Outside the gate from the kitchen gardens, Krager waited, hidden where the brick fence made a crook around a tree stump. He started off immediately and didn't let her speak until they reached the back door to Bloody Talons.

The small kitchen was empty, but the stove was warm and smelled of mystery stew and bread. Noise from the front of the tavern was considerable, but she was bouncing in her seat when he finally dished himself some stew and cut two thick slices of bread from the cloth-covered loaf on the table. He nodded, and words burst out of her, low and fast.

"It's dead, Krager. They've killed it. They've killed the Itza Larrak. A Karda named Kishar killed it. Daryl will be here soon. I've got the guards schedule for the next tenday, and Readen is acting strange. He studies every face he passes, close and hard. I think he's looking for someone wearing an illusion to get past the guards."

She stopped for a breath. "Tell me what to tell Elleran for Daryl. Oh, and he's looked grim and angry all day, according to the guards and Lerys. Lerys would hardly leave the kitchen, he was so nervous. I think he knows. Readen, I mean. About the Itza Larrak."

She cocked her head for a minute in the listening-to-Karda position. "Elleran says Daryl is going to Ardencroft with most of his troops and the others are going to Me'Mattik's old hold. Who's Me'Mattik? Oh, wait, he's one of the holders who supports Readen, and he's here. And why doesn't he come straight here? Daryl, I mean, not Me'Mattik. What do I tell Elleran? Are you going to leave? Are you going to bring all the troops out of hiding? Will there be an attack? Oh. Oh. What about the akenguns? What if he attacks, and Readen uses the akenguns?"

She stopped. Her face flushed pink. She was babbling. Across from her, Krager sat like a breathing statue—his eyes closed—for a very long time. Then he started in on her. He grilled her for an hour, question after question, sometimes the same questions over and over. She recited the guard's schedule, and he copied it in a small book from his breast pocket. Then he made her go over it again and again to be certain it was exactly right.

He pulled information about Readen out of her she didn't even know she had—pieced together from conversations she'd overheard from the house guards and from servants escaping for a few minutes to the kitchen, their safe haven. How Readen walked the halls of the keep all day muttering to himself, stumbling, sometimes almost falling, staring hard at every face he saw, pulling himself together and glaring anytime someone offered assistance or asked if something was wrong. His behavior wasn't normal until late in the afternoon. By the evening meal, Lerys reported he was smiling and exchanging barbs with Me'Neve and Me'Mattik, the two holders left in the hall.

Then he made her memorize what to ask Elleran to relay to Tarath and Abala, repeat it back to him, and even made her repeat every word she pathed to her Karda aloud.

When she was so tired her head drooped and almost hit the tabletop, he sent her to her cubbyhole to sleep. But first, he put his hand on her arm, patted it, and squeezed.

Never once did he mention the Itza Larrak.
Never once did he smile.

Daryl and Abala were both exhausted when they touched down on the landing field at Ardencroft and stumbled through driving rain to a stop, Ballard, Altan, and Marta right behind them with a reluctant Cael on a Karda again. They'd slept only a few hours a night since they left the Line of Devastation. Once in a small, isolated village barn to wait out a lightning storm. With a detour to Me'Mattik's confiscated hold, to leave troops and Captain Ethyn, they'd flown on.

Grateful for the stone walls and tiled roof of the new Ardencroft mews, they stripped wet saddles, toweled off wet manes and tails and hair, and stood back to get even wetter when all five Karda shook and fluffed out wet feathers. At the same time.

"You did that on purpose," Marta yelled, wiping her eyes with a not-so-clean corner of a dirty towel.

Mi'hiru Amanda lugged a bucket of hot mash to the stall Sidhari would share with Kibrath. "Do you want me to make them wait till this is cold?" Her Karda, Bettan, gave an owl-like hoot of laughter.

Altan lugged Kibrath's rigging to a saddle rack, took Sidhari's from Marta and slung it over another. Marta hung both wet saddle blankets on the low stall partition.

"They deserve a little fun after that flight. They have to be twice as tired as we are. We didn't have to flap our wings through the rain. They were looking pretty bedraggled when we landed." Abala butted Daryl with his head. Daryl almost dropped his saddle. He wished he had—he could lay his head on it, pull the wet saddle blanket over him, and sleep for a day right there on the cold brick floor of the alleyway. Instead, he threw it on the rack, hung the blanket to dry, and went to fetch two buckets of hot mash. Abala and Harani, Ballard's Karda, each had their own stall, and Ballard was already pitching hay down from the loft into their mangers.

Another Mi'hiru, Nyla, helped Cael groom the Karda who carried him.

Mi'hiru Tayla dashed in, pulling wide the big doors. "There are two troopers behind me to get your saddlebags, and Ket touched down with Galen and Tessa. She needs help. She's barely hanging on to Galen, who's strapped in like he's injured."

All three men ran toward the door as Ket appeared, stepped in far enough to be out of the rain, and stood with his head down, blowing hard.

"Where is he hurt?" asked Daryl, fingers flying on the buckles, Altan on the other side of the heaving Karda doing the same.

"Not hurt—tired, exhausted, drained. Idiot. Idiot. Idiot." Tessa's voice was full of fiercely held back tears.

"Tell us what you think, Tessa. Don't be shy." Altan hurried around, and the two of them managed to get the big man off Ket. Daryl looked up in time to catch Tessa before she fell.

She looked just as exhausted. "Get his wet clothes off and lay him facedown on the floor where he won't get stepped on. He can reach through the bricks. Hello, Tayla. Can you find some blankets to cover him?"

Daryl figured she was afraid that if she stopped, she'd collapse. She went to start pulling Ket's rigging off, but Ballard was already carrying them to the last empty stall, Ket following behind like a big, big golden puppy, staggering, wings drooped.

Tessa dropped down, legs straight out in front of her, leaning against the wall at Galen's head. Tayla wrapped a blanket around her shoulders and tucked another around her legs.

Daryl squatted down beside her. "What happened, Tessa? Why couldn't you stop and let him recharge?"

"We did. A couple of times. But he kept saying he'd gotten enough, and we needed to get here as fast as we could. Ket and I were stupid enough to believe him. We both lent him power for the last three hours to keep him alive." She closed her eyes and leaned her head back against the wall.

Daryl thought she'd fallen asleep. But she took a deep breath and blew it out from puffed cheeks between pursed lips. "Oh, great mother Adalta, I don't want to tell you this." She closed her eyes again. "Galen, the stupid man, walked into the circle as far as the strange opening Kishar and I discovered. The one glowing with weird orange light. The one the Larrak disappeared into when we wounded it last fall."

She opened her eyes, and the skin on the back of Daryl's neck tightened, his hair prickled. He didn't want to hear this. He really didn't want to hear this. His knees ached from squatting, and he wanted nothing more than to jump back on Abala, find an oasis in the middle of the broadest, emptiest barren he could find and live the rest of his life there.

Then Cedar came through the door, and some of Daryl's exhaustion faded. How did she do that?

"It's still there." Cedar's words were flat—not a question mark in them anywhere.

Tessa's eyes closed against the fat tears falling. She whispered, "Please tell me Kishar didn't die for nothing. Please tell me he didn't, Daryl. Please." Tayla brought another blanket to cover her shaking body.

Daryl went cold inside. Tessa's words came from a long way, as if they fought through her exhaustion, through his exhaustion, and couldn't find a place to fix themselves in his hearing, in his mind. A sudden urge to laugh ballooned up from his belly. Then he felt Cedar's small hand on his shoulder, he reached up and touched it, and the inappropriate balloon lost all its air.

He took both Tessa's hands in his and told her with the firmest words he could find it in himself to utter, "No. He did not die for nothing. We all witnessed the creature falling to the earth in flames. We watched the ashes blow away. Kishar killed it. We'll find out why its Circle of Devastation is not dead with it and kill that, too." He held her eyes until she nodded and curled herself into Galen.

He heard Cedar walk away, but in a few moments, she came back with a parade of troopers and Mi'hiru behind her lugging bales of hay, which they stacked around Tessa and Galen. Cael settled a closed iron pot, lid slightly askew, away from the straw with a glowing magma stone inside. Daryl dropped Tessa's hands and backed out. Cael stayed. Someone drew a ground cloth over the space to hold in the warmth. Tessa was already asleep. Daryl knew Cael might close his eyes, but he wouldn't sleep. His responsibility for her hadn't ended when her father threw him out of his hold when he got caught teaching her the sword.

Marta and Altan finished grooming their Karda—they'd taken care of Abala, too. Daryl walked behind the other three with Cedar still at his side. She smelled of the clean air of a mountainside covered with pines. "You smell like pine trees."

She stepped away a little. "Oh, I'm sorry. I'm learning to handle smells, but I figured emotions would be pretty high, so I might have over-done the pine salve."

"I like the smell of pine trees." How dumb could he get. Smooth he was not.

"Oh." She dropped her head, so all he could see was its black curls. "Come, I'll walk with you to the village. We've put you, Cael, and Ballard, I mean Tall, in the big house with Glenn and Assam. You can join the bickering. Marta and Altan will share a house with Tessa and Galen when he's strong enough to get there."

"Where do you stay?"

"I'm still with Mireia. She works with me on my—why is it so hard to say talent?—for two hours a day."

"Two hours?"

"There are ethical issues with what I am able to sense about people. Things someone with a more normal sense of empathy—I can't believe I can say anything to do with talent is normal—don't have to deal with, or learned when they were young, and it's become instinctive. Plus, I'm still working on effective filters."

She looked up at him, laughing. "I can almost guarantee I won't throw up on you again."

"I'll take all the good news I can get right now, and that's defi-nitely good news. I've run out of clean clothes. And you haven't tried to hit me with your staff yet either." Banter felt good. He felt lighter.

She bumped his shoulder hard with hers and didn't move away. He looked down, watching their feet splash through the wet grass and muddy spots, her steps almost even. But she still needed the black oak staff.

"Sharon is helping me learn to fight with this and not fall down."

He said nothing, but, at the thought of Cedar needing to learn to fight, the sense of peace building in him collapsed. They walked in silence for a few steps, then he said, "I need to hear from you three—you, Glenn, and Assam about the resettlement. And I'll meet with Miriea to see what problems and progress there's been with the talent issue, and what reeducation programs we need to focus on."

They walked a little farther, almost to the house. Her hand slipped into his before he opened his mouth again. He stopped and looked at her, at the questions on her face—too serious quirky smile, raised eyebrow, tilted head.

"Yes, and then there are plans you have to make." Her hand tightened on his as if he tried to get loose. "I need to be part of those plans." He knew she wasn't talking about the reeducation of the settlers from the ship.

He stopped, pulled his hand from hers.

She walked on, not limping—much. Her back straight, defiant. Her hand gripped the iron-tipped staff exactly where he would have if he were preparing for a fight.

CHAPTER THIRTY-FOUR

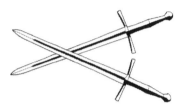

Krager held out an oiled packet of papers. "I want you out of here today, Becca, and...."

Becca stood up, the piece of firewood she'd intended to stuff in Mother Girt's kitchen stove in her hand like a weapon. "No. No. You need me here. And you promised. You promised we'd find ChiChi and Jenna when this was over. You can't send me away now."

"Take this packet to Daryl. And there's a note to Mireia. I want you to stay with her. You said you wanted to learn proper speech, and you need talent training. You're not using yours to the fullest. I'll be in Ardencroft to get you as soon as I can leave. I keep my promises, Becca."

She bent, shoved the wood in the stove, slammed the door to the firebox, and stirred the pot of cereal, her stiff back to him. Krager breathed a sigh of relief. She'd fight leaving, but not too hard. He knew better than to utter the word *safe*. That would plant her feet like nothing else. "Sit down and eat now. We're leaving as soon as we finish."

"We?"

"I'll get you to the Thieves' Gate. Then you run as hard and as fast as you can to Elleran and Tarath." He looked away, in the direction of the small meadow where he'd left Tarath, who must be very bored by now. "Check Tarath out as well as you can. He's been alone too long, and I'm worried about him. Elleran can tell him you're coming if he's off hunting."

"It's daylight. If we're on the streets, you'll get caught."

"I've checked. There are enough people out spreading the news about the death of the Itza Larrak, we won't be so noticeable." He took her bowl and his to the sink and dropped them in. "And look, Becca." He raised the illusion on his face. "No one will recognize me as Krager, and no one is looking for a thug like Payne. Let's go."

Becca ran to her cubbyhole, reached under her pallet and pulled out a small, dirty bundle. Krager looked away. It was all she had. One small, dirty bundle.

He was right—there were more people on the streets than he'd seen in tendays. The mood was lighter, less furtive. That worried him. It hadn't been the Itza Larrak that threatened them here in the prime. Not before now.

They used the alleys more than the streets, and he got her to Thieves' Gate without getting stopped once. She could have gotten there herself, but he wanted to see her through them. He wanted to know she was safe.

Krager stood for a minute after she disappeared into the brambles, fighting an unacountable sense of loss, a hole in his chest. He was so tired, tired of never-ending aloneness. He shook it off. He was getting soft.

Standing still too long made him noticeable, so he walked back up the row of greenhouses behind a small cart of vegetable seedlings and offered to carry the planter's precariously balanced tools.

He hit every tavern in the prime in the persona of Payne, which was becoming more real to him than his identity as Krager. He had his copy of Becca's list of the guard's rotation—he'd sent one to Daryl with her. He checked on every hidden guard, on the hidden akenguns, on the hidden shields. There was always one on his chest beneath his clothes. He finally went to ground in the run-down warehouse where Commander Kyle had his makeshift headquarters.

He reported every rumor, every piece of information he'd gleaned in the three days since he'd last been there, and handed Kyle the guard's schedule Becca had gotten.

"Do you need a copy, Krager?" asked Kyle. "How'd you get this? How accurate is it?"

Krager tapped his forehead. "It's in here. I had someone in the hall kitchen. She got lucky."

"Had?"

"She's safely gone."

Kyle frowned. "Why did you let her go? This is invaluable. We need more."

"She was a child. And Daryl will be here within days."

"Yes, he will." Kyle's broad face lost a few lines of tension, then gained them back with added lines of despair. "Let me know immediately when he tells you what he's planning. Then Readen will start killing our people until Daryl gives up. This is not a fight to be fought with an army."

Krager didn't answer.

Daryl told Glenn and Assam about the holds he'd confiscated from the holders supporting Readen. Me'Mattik's was the closest, and wagons were already organized to take the settlers they decided were most ready. People streamed in and out, and the house he shared with the two men devolved into chaos. Then another transport thundered in, and things got worse.

After lunch, he and Cael took the papers a tired and dejected Becca had flown in with back to the room he'd made his office. Daryl stationed Peele and Lange to keep people from intruding, but their efforts to keep Cedar away were useless. Becca was with her, rubbing her eyes, as was Tessa, demanding to know what Daryl was going to do about the Circle of Disorder.

Daryl glared at the three of them. He was tired. He was overwhelmed by the chaos. He was thinking coming to Ardencroft might have been a mistake. Then Cedar put a hand on Tessa's arm to stop her, and said to him, "You have to hear what Becca told Mireia."

"I do?" The question was a flat non-question fueled by I'm-busy-here.

"Tell him what you told us, Becca."

The girl was frightened and unsure, and Daryl erased the glare from his face. "I didn't have a chance to ask you when you came in —you almost fell out of the saddle asleep. How is Krager?"

She relaxed a little. "Grumpy, and he made me leave. I didn't want to. I'd be more help to you there than here. Can you order me to go back?"

"If he's grumpy, he's good. If you'd said he was cheerful, I'd be worried. And Abala has told Elleran not to take you back."

She got the talking-to-Karda expression on her face. Her eyes narrowed, and she bounced a fist twice on the table. Her lips were tight, but she said, "Cedar and Mireia said to tell you what I know, and what I think I saw. Readen roams the halls all night, and, till about a tenday ago, he was covered up with his cloak over 'is head so no one could see 'is face, even inside. Then, some of the guards said he were lookin' normal, no more coverin' his face. But—I'm not sure 'xacly what day the Itza Larrak was killed—" She flinched when Tessa stood and walked to the doorway, her back to them. "Well, it musta been soon after that happened, he got real strange. Stranger than ever."

She bit her lip and glanced at Daryl. Her face flushed as if she just remembered she was talking about his brother, but she went on. "A few guards started talkin' about how 'e don't move right. Like he can't move right—all clumsy 'n jumpy. 'E stares right in the face of ever'one 'e passes. They said it's like 'e tries to look through you."

She stopped, her head moving back and forth between Cedar and Daryl. "This is the weird thing. I only saw him once. Real early in the mornin', almost 'fore daylight. I had to go to the back hall to...." Her cheeks pinked. "And he came through. Anyways, he didn't see me cause I was peekin' through the door waitin' for 'im to go on. This is what Mireia said I need to tell you. First, I'm to say my talent's Water. Then I'm to tell you 'is face looked all...watery, kinda. Wavy, like you was lookin' at yourself in a still fountain, only not 'xacly, cause for a minute it was like seein' two people. Only one a 'em weren't like a real man, more like a man in a scary mask. Mireia said you'd know what I saw? She didn't want to tell me, cause it might change what I remembered. What did I see?"

Daryl dropped his head and rubbed his face with both hands. "An illusion. You saw him using an illusion, Becca." His answer was mechanical, flat. He saw Tessa, who'd turned back, her eyes wide, her nostrils flaring with each fast breath. They stared at each other for a long time. Her eyes angry. His eyes bleak, washed, hopeless, helpless, heavy in his head. Without taking his gaze from Tessa, he said, "Thank you, Becca. You've been a great help."

He hardly knew what words he said, and he couldn't look at the girl until she turned to leave.

Tessa ran from the tent, presumably to get Galen, and Cael walked out with Becca, leaning down, his body tight, asking something and listening to her answer. He closed the door behind them.

"I have to go alone. I have to take Cael and go alone." Daryl's voice was flat, toneless.

Two deep lines appeared between Cedar's brows. "I'm confused. I've missed something important."

He took her hand, holding it so tight her fingers turned white. He stared at them. She didn't move. Finally, she laid her other hand on his, and he loosened his grip. "You believe the Larrak didn't die. That it is inside Readen somehow."

"If it hasn't taken him over completely, if he's struggling with it, maybe I can exorcise it. Maybe I can save him."

Cedar turned her palm over, so both hands held his. It was the only place on his body that felt warm. She moved her face closer to his. Her voice was soft, low, not a whisper, and there was metal in it that pierced him like a sword tip. "You have to kill him, Daryl." Her eyes held him for a long time. She wouldn't look away, wouldn't let him twist away from the words she said.

Then she moved closer, took him in her arms, and he cried, soft, silent, body wracking grief—grief for Readen, grief for Readen's betrayal, grief and guilt for his long refusal to face who Readen was.

It seemed he would never be able to stop until Cael knocked and walked back in. Daryl pulled himself together, embarrassed, and they went to the mews and Abala. Cael glanced once at his face and didn't look again.

Daryl filled a bucket and splashed his face several times with cold water. ~The Larrak isn't dead, Abala.~

~Do you think I didn't feel it when the little girl told you? We have to kill Readen. Kill it. Again.~

Daryl leaned his head back in the hollow where Abala's neck met his shoulders. ~Do you think Kishar knew of this possibility?~

~No.~ There was no hesitation, no doubt in Abala's one word.

Cedar stopped to say hello to Illyria, the Karda who carried her when she needed to fly. Cael was right behind her, leaning on the stall opening.

"It's such a relief to come here, away from all the people and their smells," she said. "This is such an emotional time for every one here, both natives and new settlers, it tasks my filters. Mireia says it's good for me. I'm learning. I am also experimenting with soothing anxieties. She says there's no ethical problem so long as I'm not soothing someone into welcoming a mad mother medgeran. Apparently, I have the power to do that. And the sense to stay out of the way if I do, because soothing animals is *not* one of my abilities. Hello, Abala."

The big Karda lowered his head, and she scratched the top of it with vigor. He reached around and picked a loose feather off the stall floor with his big beak and managed to stick it in her hair. Daryl stared at him, surprised, and Abala winked back.

Cedar tried to secure the pale red feather in her curls. Finally, she gave up and tucked it over her ear. "Thank you, Abala. It sticks out so far in front of me I'm blind in one eye, but it's beautiful. I'm going with you."

Her words didn't register for a minute, then Daryl said, "No, you're not. It's too dangerous."

"I need to. I—"

"It's too dangerous, and you'll slow us down." That was a mistake, but he wasn't able to suck the words back in his mouth, so he blundered on. "Only Cael and I are going." He looked up into five more-than-irritated faces arranged in a half-circle around them in the alley.

"No, I'm going." The cords in Tessa's neck were taut cables, her chin was high, and her narrowed eyes glinted.

"You'll be recognized the minute you arrive." Altan leaned against the wall, arms folded across his chest.

"And you think *you* wouldn't be?" Daryl shot the words back and glared at each of them in turn. "Every one of you wears a well-known face. And I know if you can't do an illusion yourself, Altan can do it for you, but do you think Readen hasn't thought of that? No one knows exactly what he can do, but don't you think he might have given his guards a little illusion-breaking spell?"

"He has." Cael's words caught all of them by surprise. He leaned against one side of the opening, arms crossed. It was the first time he'd spoken. "A long time ago. It's sometimes a helpful thing to have."

"Cael," said Tessa, her voice soft. "I haven't even said hello to you. I apologize. When this is over, will you come back to Me'Cowyn hold with us? My father told me to ask you."

He smiled at her as if she were still the awkward girl with the too-big sword begging him to teach her how to use it. "Might."

"Daryl," said Galen, "trying to do this yourself is suicide. You'll be caught before you even step a foot inside the hall."

"No, he won't." Ballard's eyes narrowed on him. "He's lived in the prime and the hall for all his life. And if he's like me, he explored every inch of it for years. He knows it like no one else. Probably better than Readen. He'll know how to get in and around without being seen. If it were me in Anuma Hall, I could be there for days before I got caught. There'll be more guards, but he has the schedule. And Krager."

"No one is going with him but Cael, Becca, and me," said Cedar.

"And why you and Becca?" Daryl tried not to make his words mocking. The expression she wore told him he didn't succeed.

So she told him.

Cedar's head itched. Krager was a genius with disguises, but ash in dirty hair itched. The kitchen was empty but for Becca and Cook.

"He started sticking his head in here every few days not long after you left, Becca. Keep your head down. Stand where I tell you with your hands folded behind your back. You—" She narrowed her eyes at Cedar. "Your sister got pregnant by one of the guards, and I won't have that in my kitchen so you took her place. You're on probation while I decide if you're a good girl or not."

Cedar couldn't help grinning and cocking a hip.

"Don't grin. Don't act saucy. Keep your head down, your face dirty, and do what I told Becca."

Cedar flinched, calmed her nerves. She couldn't afford silliness. Her filters were tuned too fine. Even with the intense hours, days, Mireia had spent to prepare her for this, she missed the fear in Cook. Then the smell of it swamped her with nausea. Switching back and forth from nothing to nausea could get both of them killed. Maybe Daryl was right. She was inexperienced; she couldn't do this.

Becca pinched her arm with enough force to paralyze it, and Cook said, "Take her to the potato cellar. Bring up a basketful, and make sure enough potato dirt gets on her face and hands."

The clean, clear smell of the garden dirt clinging to the potatoes settled her, allowed her to tune and thicken the leaves on her shield tree. They might be in this kitchen for several days before Readen came.

The work was hard, tedious, mindless—just what Cedar needed. She kept a potato in her apron pocket. When the tension got to her, she pulled it out and held it to her nose. She had one other job, and it was constant. Every time she got close enough to a guard, she sniffed, using every trick Mireia helped her develop in the intense days and hours she'd spent with her before she left Ardencroft. People's emotions told stories, some she didn't want to know, but she kept at it, going deeper all the time. Gradually a narrative emerged. She tested and tested it with each person she was near.

The Readen these men followed, had followed loyally for years, was not the same Readen who roamed the hall night and day. He'd not been the same since he'd escaped from the prison at Ardencroft. The witty, often genial, slap-you-on-the-back Readen who'd not only led his men but taken care of them, of their families, wasn't there. Now they were frightened for those families. Some of them were frightened for themselves, a fear hidden from others, and often hidden from themselves. Their loyalty to him was fraying. His loyalty to them—loyalty they'd never questioned—was now in question.

Every time Cedar got a strong enough whiff of discontent or doubt from one of them, she pushed it, and Becca put his name on a list. Every night Becca took the list to Krager. Sometimes she came back with particular names, and Cedar sniffed for whatever she could glean. Becca put the results on her list. She never stayed nights. Cedar slept on a pallet in Cook's room and tore little strips of cloth to wad in her ears. Cook snored prodigiously.

Half a tenday after she got there, Lerys was gossiping and complaining, although he now kept his voice so low it was difficult to hear over the kitchen noises, and it was more old man rambling than gossip.

The door slammed back, and Readen stood in the opening. Cook grabbed Cedar's arm and pushed her back beside Becca, then took her stance in front, not quite hiding them.

Cedar stood very still. Readen scanned the room and took several steps inside, examining every face. His movements were smooth and normal, except every few minutes, some part of his body jerked or twitched, and he stilled it. Like he suffered sudden, sharp muscle spasms.

His smell was human—an odorous swamp of evil, fear, doubt, exhaustion, anger. She almost missed a faint drifting perfume of sadness and remorse that came and went. And the anger was a confusing bouquet of betrayer and betrayed.

Mixed into his complex, discordant symphony of odors, sometimes overlaying them, was a single smell with tiny hooks that would not let go. A cold—biting cold—sharp, permeating odor of a not-human, not-animal, life-but-not-life fighting to escape annihilation. And Cedar feared it was succeeding.

Head down, eyes closed tight, she breathed deep breaths, absorbing, sorting, categorizing, memorizing the tiniest hints of his complex, multitudinous scents. Her muscles slackened. Her knees threatened to give way. Becca moved close, hooked her arm, and pushed her against the big cupboard next to the stove. She didn't fall.

Finally, he left. He never asked who either of them was. He never said a word.

Cedar fell into a chair the minute the door closed, arms crossed on the tabletop, resting her head in their cradle. Becca sat close beside her, an arm around her, and Cook put a cup of hot broth in front of her.

She tried to form what she'd scented into words. Then she told Becca, "Ask Elleran to relay this to Daryl. Readen is still Readen, but he is riddled with despair and desperate, because he is also something else, something not human, with a powerful will to survive. Something he's fighting, and, I think, losing. We have a week."

"What's a week? What's it for?"

"Sorry. I mean seven days. No more."

CHAPTER THIRTY-FIVE

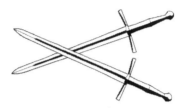

Daryl and Abala followed Elleran, with Cael on his back, to the small meadow where Krager's frustrated Tarath waited not very patiently.

~He's a little grumpy, so don't be surprised if he tries to ignore us,~ said Daryl.

~Like rider, like Karda,~ pathed Abala. ~I can't see your face but I know you're hiding a grin.~

Daryl put his hands on the pommel handle of the saddle and braced for landing. Abala was right. He'd be glad to see Krager again—to know he was safe. Abala dropped so fast his stomach did a little flip. They slowed to a stop under the tree where Tarath lay, Elleran and Cael almost too close behind them. Tarath opened one eye.

~He says it's about time. He's getting tired of hunting by himself, and rabbits aren't very filling,~ said Abala.

~Why is he eating rabbits? He must be starving.~

~He's eaten or run off everything bigger, and he won't leave long enough to range farther. I'll hunt for him now.~

Daryl unloaded his small pack and pulled Abala's rigging off, stuffing it under the tarp that covered Tarath's. Cael did the same and said thank you to Elleran, who took off to take up his endless circling of the prime again, to listen for Becca.

Abala told Daryl, ~Don't do anything stupid,~ and took off to hunt.

Daryl scratched Tarath's head. "It won't be long now, Tarath. One way or another, it won't be long." He and Cael took off through the woods for the Fort Tree where he and Krager had fought countless imaginary battles for years, often against Readen. An image of ten-year-old Readen laughing and wrestling eight-year-old Daryl to the ground flashed. "You're dead now, brother." There'd been rough love—brother love—in his face, without the mocking sarcasm he'd seen later. That he'd believed was still love right up until a bare year ago when he'd heard the words of the assassin who'd tried to garrote him. The words that finally convinced him that it was Readen who was trying to kill him.

He blinked and thumbed off the loop that held his sword in its sheath while he flew, making sure it would slip out easily if he needed it. There was no chance Readen had left the tree unguarded, thought it was well outside the walls. But Elleran assured Daryl the guard would be, maybe not friendly, but not hostile. The uneasy loyalty of Readen's troops was drifting away from him.

A slender man stepped from behind the tree and squinted his eyes at Cael. Daryl recognized him. He stopped a couple of meters away. "Good morning, Chen. I'm not surprised to see you here."

"Some lessons are harder to learn than others. Some loyalties are harder to hold to than others. Your brother crossed a river he should never have crossed." He looked at Cael for a minute. "You are a braver and wiser man than I."

"Or maybe just more scared."

None of the three offered a forearm in greeting.

"We need to move, sir. There are patrols through here often, and they don't always hold to their schedule."

They slipped through the woods Daryl knew so well to the far side of the prime, where a rocky finger of the hillside behind it cast a dark shadow on the wall surrounding Restal Hall. Two minutes after they got there, a knotted rope uncurled down the outside of the wall. Before the end of the rope reached them, Daryl had his cloak out of the small pack, swung over his shoulders, and tucked around his sword so it wouldn't bang the wall. Daryl watched Cael climb the rope first, then his gaze dropped to the solid rock wall in front of him. The wall between him and what he had to do.

And on the other side of this wall was Cedar. Was she safe? Daryl had to close off that question. If he thought about it...if he thought about her inside those walls with Readen...he couldn't. He closed it off.

Cael stopped about three feet from the top of the wall, wrapped both legs and one arm tight in the rope and made a series of small gestures with his fingers. He looked down, nodded and disappeared over the parapet in a second.

"Climb fast, sir. And good luck." Chen stood straight and saluted Daryl. "I'm gone until you call."

Halfway up, a gust of wind slammed Daryl against the rock and ripped at the cloak. Thank Adalta, that wasn't his sword arm. It hurt. Like blazes. He hung still until it passed, then climbed faster, past the pain. Four hands reached over, grabbed him and pulled him up the last meter. One face belonging to the hands was familiar, the other wasn't, but Daryl had to trust him anyway. Neither spoke.

One guard in front, one behind, they ran the short distance to a set of stairs down the inside of the wall. The man with the unfamiliar face stepped inside the guard hut at the bottom. The other pulled Daryl's arm when he hesitated, and they ran on, keeping close to the wall until they reached the kitchen garden fence, breathing like blown horses and trying to keep it quiet. In a matter of minutes, he'd see Cedar, he'd know she was safe. Or not. Close the door on that thought. Again. But he couldn't think further. If he did his thoughts would run into Readen and what he had to do. If he could.

The guard slipped four boards from the fence and shoved Daryl and Cael through. The boards were back in place, and the guard was gone in less than a minute. Cook stood at the kitchen door, her big hat off, wiping at her face with a towel. Daryl heard voices, and he and Cael flattened themselves between two rows of beans, waiting for her signal. So much depended on Cael, this man who was with Readen for years. Krager trusted him, but what kind of changes could happen to a man who'd been with a leader like Readen for so long? Then Daryl remembered the journals. Cael was the one who had stolen Readen's journals and sent them to him. What kind of courage had that taken?

When he heard Cook holler, "I'm coming, I'm coming," he ran down the row, across a tiny courtyard and into the garden shed. He leaned against the wall and sucked air into his starving lungs as if he hadn't taken a breath since he started up the rope. Maybe before that. Cael was right behind him, hands on his knees, breathing hard.

"Take this basket and get me more beans for lunchtime. The boy didn't bring in enough before." Cook's voice from the kitchen door was a little too loud.

Daryl slid around stacks of garden tools to the back of the shed. The boards gaped enough that he could see Cedar limp to the bean rows, lay her staff down and start picking. She stood up once, stared straight at the shed for too long, then put a hand to the small of her back, leaning one way, then the other, stretching.

He heard a guard step through the gate across from the shed. But the steps didn't stop at the shed door where they should have. They headed straight for Cedar instead. She leaned back and raised her arms to smooth back her hair, straining the front of her shirt. She stooped and picked up her staff as if to lean on it, but Daryl could see she wasn't. Her hands were placed where he would place his if he were going to strike.

"What are you doing?" The rough note in the guard's voice raised hairs on the back of Daryl's neck.

"Picking beans. Cook told me to pick beans." Her voice was dull, her face slack.

"Why don't I help you? Let's go in the shed and get another basket."

Daryl pushed his cloak behind his shoulders and slid his sword out. His hand was slippery with sweat. She was going to do something stupid. He backed toward the door, and Cael grabbed his arm. Before he could jerk away, Cedar's staff flashed up and whacked the side of the guard's head in less time than it took to blink twice. The man collapsed, and she whacked the other side.

Daryl slid to a stop in front of her. He wanted to grab her up and carry her outside the walls, put her someplace safe.

"I just wanted to make sure. He smelled of...he didn't smell right. I think he's dead. Is he dead?" Her brows drew together, two stark lines between them, and her mouth stretched into something sideways that was not a smile, something more like dread and sorrow.

A second guard half-stumbled through the gate. "I'm sorry. I'm sorry. He saw you, ma'am, and hit me over the head before I realized what he was doing. I know him. I should have known what was on his mind."

Cook and Becca ran out of the kitchen. Becca kicked the guard on the ground. "He's not dead. He twitched."

"Get out of here, all of you, Guardian," ordered Cook. "We'll take care of him. You need to keep moving."

Cedar stripped out of her dirty smock. Under it she wore a simple gown of fine pale blue silk. No jewelry. She steadied herself with her staff. Daryl could see her pull up her courage like pulling on boots. He wanted to throw her over his shoulder and run as far away as they could get. "Are you all right to take us?" she asked the guard.

"Us?" said Daryl.

"Yes, ma'am."

"Then let's go." She gave the man on the ground a jab between the legs with her staff. "I should have started there," she said and grabbed Daryl's arm.

"You can't—"

"I have to. No one but I can tell who is uppermost in Readen's body, him or the alien. You need to know who you're fighting. You know that, why do you keep acting like you forget?"

"Hurry," the guard said. "We're behind schedule, and there's not enough slack in it for that."

"Let me check first." Cook moved as fast as she could—not very—and stuck her head inside the kitchen. "Clear, but hurry."

They were through the kitchen, out the small door beside the pantry, and down Cook's private hall to her rooms before Daryl could object again. Krager was inside.

The two men stared at each other. Then they embraced, arms hard around each other. Daryl said, "I think you've gotten soft, Armsmaster Krager. Hugging me like this."

Krager laughed and stepped back. "It won't happen again, Guardian Daryl. It never happened. It was your secret wish." Then he looked around him at Cedar, trying to hide behind Cael, not easy in the tiny room over-stuffed with three large men. "It's too dangerous for her."

"I know." Fear piled up in his gut again. He didn't want her to get anywhere near Readen.

Cael spoke up. "Her argument is more than convincing. I suspect the Itza Larrak was pushing its way inside Readen's head long before this. This is not a sudden thing. I saw the signs before I left his hold. I just didn't know what they meant. *You* will not be able to tell which is in control. Not fast enough to know which you are fighting from one moment to the next. *She* can."

Both the other men were silent. Daryl closed his eyes and rubbed a hand over his forehead. He narrowed his eyes at Krager. "My job is to kill Readen." He didn't hesitate on the word *kill*. "Your job is to protect her." He turned to Cael. "Your primary job is to get us to Readen when he is alone—unseen and undetected. Your second primary job is to protect her. Cedar, your primary job is to stay out of the way of all the swords. And don't hit anybody with your stick."

"My, Daryl." She cocked her head. "Was that a sense of humor peeking through your words?" Her words might have been light, but Daryl could hear the tremor in her voice.

"Not so," said Krager. "Neither of us has a sense of humor. Do any of you have any idea how we can all sit in this very small room while we wait for our next guide?"

Cedar sat mouse-still on the bed, mashed between Daryl and Krager, thinking about the emotions of the guards she'd explored for the past several days, gleaning what she could with the tools Mireia spent hour after long hour helping her develop before she left Ardencroft.

Most of the guards considered themselves, and were, men of moderate, often minimal talent. In Readen's guard they'd found a home, comrades, a leader they could look up to who never gave in to despair despite having no talent at all, never gave up, never gave in to the temptation to become a spoiled dilettante like his father. It would have been easy for him. Instead, Readen had worked hard, fought hard to build up the guard.

What had changed? What had changed the man they followed into a man who could blow a hole in an unarmed woman—a respected woman whom he'd known most of his life? What changed him into the man who could flout the most basic maxim of this planet—the law against technology—any weapons beyond sword or bow—with such casual cruelty?

Even the toughest, most hardened guardsmen—Readen's Restal Guard was all men—who never consciously thought about such things had a scent of unease weaving its tentative fragrance through their core odor.

She sat on the edge of Cook's bed, elbows on her knees, and put her head in her hands, massaging her temples. She let her mind empty of everything but the miasma of emotions she'd been absorbing for days. She let them play against the background of what Daryl had told her about Readen, the Readen he remembered before he read the journals and after. Her thoughts were a dense cloud of scents, pregnant with possibilities that sparked like small lightnings. She let them play, watching, waiting, and by the time the expected knock sounded on the door, she had firmed her story—a story with holes, a story without an ending, but a story she could work with.

"There were no wards at all after we got through the ones on the wall. None in the garden and none in the kitchen."

Cael's words, spoken into the tense silence of waiting, startled Daryl.

"That luck won't last. Do not get in front of me at any time. There will be wards everywhere. Just because a guard can pass through them, don't assume you can, any of you. They'll be tuned to the guards and the servants, except for those on Readen's private spaces. Those are tuned to him and only him."

Someone rapped a simple pattern on the door.

"Time to go to work, then." Krager went to open the door.

Cael stopped him. "Like I just said, don't get in front of me." He stood in the threshold and held one hand up, palm out, to the nervous corporal outside and stood still. He cocked his head and made a series of complex gestures with his fingers. Then he did the same thing to each of the others. "Let's go. I've just made us invisible to the hall wards. All of them, I hope."

"Now all we have to worry about is someone seeing us who shouldn't. Which means anyone walking through the halls, coming out of a doorway, anyone going anywhere," said Krager. He nodded to the guard. "Thanks, Bemus."

"The halls are as safe as we could manage, sir. I've dismissed anyone not on the list your girl gave me. But you only have fifteen minutes before change of guard, and the halls will be full again."

"Thank you, Corporal. Where is he?" asked Daryl.

"He's in his study, uh—your study, sir. He'll probably be there for thirty more minutes, unless he comes out for the change of guards."

Daryl managed a small grin, took hold of Cedar's arm, and Cael led the way, following Daryl's quiet directions to back halls and seldom used corridors. The corporal was efficient. They saw no one.

Cael stopped them at every corner, twice repeating the series of gestures over them. "He's gotten more cautious. Usually there's only one ward for all the halls." They met three guards, but all three watched without speaking, faces grim when they passed. One managed a slight nod.

It was only a couple minutes short of fifteen before they reached the corner to the short passage leading to the study. Cael slowed and stopped. Again he made a series of movements with his fingers, slowly, as if he was feeling his way through something invisible.

Daryl heard a muffled snap. Cael held up two fingers and tapped the hilt of his sword. Krager moved up next to him, pointed to himself and Cael, and stepped around the corner.

Daryl needed to tell Cedar to stay behind, but her face told him that wouldn't work. He grabbed her hand, and they headed for the door. Both Krager's swords were out and working. He held the two guards off while Cael worked at the wards on the door lock. Two minutes, two long minutes, and he was up, sword out, helping Krager keep the guards away.

Daryl threw up a shield and stepped into the study, Cedar half-hidden behind him. There was his father's desk with its wide, polished surface, but there was no vase overflowing with flowers. And it was Readen who sat there, not his father. Daryl wanted this to be over. He wanted to sit behind his father's desk and see a tall slender vase with a single rose—one of his father's roses.

But it was Readen he saw. He looked up and smiled. "I heard the swords. I was wondering when you'd appear, brother." His voice was scratchy.

Daryl hesitated. The face was Readen's, the body was Readen's, the voice, even with the slight scratch, was Readen's.

"Not Readen," said Cedar. Daryl barely registered her voice.

Readen smiled, "Welcome back, brother." He didn't even glance at Cedar, almost as if he couldn't see her.

A probe slid off Daryl's shield, and he flinched. Readen shouldn't be able to do that.

Readen went to the sideboard, ran his fingers along the short row of bottles, selected one, and poured amber liquid into two crystal glasses like delicate bubbles.

"That isn't Readen," Cedar said again, her voice soft, insistent. He ignored her. Who else could it be?

Readen placed a glass on Daryl's side of the desk and lifted his own. "En garde." And Daryl was back at the Fort Tree, a small boy playing swords with his older brother and Krager.

"Not Readen. It's not Readen in that body." The urgency in Cedar's voice finally reached Daryl.

This thing that looked like his brother, sounded like his brother, was not his brother. He jerked his head in a sharp nod.

"You have two choices, Readen." He didn't touch the glass. "You can use that beautiful dagger in your belt on yourself, or I can kill you." His voice sounded thick in his head. The words seemed to form in front of him and float across the desk.

"No. There is a third choice." Readen said. "I made a mistake. I know that now. I know with me behind you, you can be a great leader. You can't do this alone. You need me. With my help, you can be the leader this quadrant needs." His mouth twisted into a smile. "I can give you the time for the quiet, studious life you love, time away from the heavy responsibility of the guardianship." He sounded so reasonable, so rueful, so...

Daryl wanted to offer a third choice. He wanted to say, "Just leave Restal and never come back." But that was no longer a choice he could give. Readen was no longer just his brother. He was also the monster who would call more of his kind to spread their devastation across the continent, who would destroy Adalta. A monster who looked so much, sounded too much like his brother.

The moment stretched longer and longer until Cedar whispered, "Not Readen, Daryl. However he looks, it's not Readen," and Daryl's hand moved, without his volition, to his sword hilt. In the half-second that took, he heard Altan's words from so many tendays ago. "We need to attack him now, Daryl. Now is our chance," and he saw the face of Minra Shreeve, dead because he hadn't taken that chance.

Readen touched a finger to the silver medallion on his chest.

Daryl recognized it. He had worn it since he was a child. A pearlescent shield shimmered into place around Readen, a shield that belonged to the alien, not to his brother.

"You have two choices, Daryl," Readen said, his tone friendly. "You can leave now and live, or you can die here in this room. Restal is mine. I will not give it up."

Daryl's shield surrounded Cedar and shoved her into a corner behind him. She made herself as small as possible and took an experimental breath in through her nose. Readen stepped from behind the desk and drew his sword. A big man, a powerful man who seemed to grow bigger as he moved.

Neither shield blocked the harsh metallic odor of the Itza Larrak. Behind what she would call arrogance, if it were human, was a sharp smell of a struggle for survival that didn't smell like Readen. It carried an odor alien to the planet, a mechanical smell too close to familiar. Like the spaceship's. To Cedar, it was the stink of arrogant certainty. A stink that said, "Kill this brother-creature, and this world is mine." The words were so clear they echoed in her head and disoriented her, the smell of them so alien, so pervasive, so invasive. It was difficult to push them away, but she fought and struggled against them. It was Readen she needed to find inside that head. She couldn't fight these odors, so, ethics be damned, she let them surround her and began searching the spaces between, reaching deeper into Readen's scents. Doing what she'd been told never to do.

Readen struck first with a flurry of strikes that was an unbelievable blur to Cedar, it happened so fast. It seemed all Daryl could do to defend against it. Cedar knew it was hard for him to fight back, to attack, and she was terrified for him. She could smell the hope that still lived in him. A hope for his brother that had to die—or he would die, and she'd be next.

Readen kept after him, with precise, rapid strikes. Daryl kicked a chair out of his way, defending, not attacking, staying away from Cedar's corner.

She could smell his fear for her. Wrapping her arms around herself, Cedar breathed deeper, fighting her own fight with fear, and went searching past the mechanical odors. There was no smell of desperation, no sense of fear. Only an implacable need for survival larger than one entity, so large she barely held on to her sense of self. She fought past disorientation, searching deeper and deeper. Fighting past the strange mechanical odors for the complex human smell of Readen, Cedar searched for what seemed forever. She found it and lost it, found it and almost lost it again trying too hard.

Then she caught the faint odor of human fear from the struggle inside Readen, his fight to break the Itza Larrak's hold on him. The smell of his fear and desperation clashed with the machinelike stink of the Larrak's unrelenting struggle for survival. That small piece of Readen was fighting the alien intruder inside him, fighting the fear of losing himself, fought the Itza Larrak inside him, and Cedar fought to grab hold of that piece. But it was the Larrak moving his body, the Larrak trying to kill Daryl. She hoped she was reaching for the right piece. The rapid clash of metal on metal was terrifying. So far outside of her experience, she hoped she wasn't panicking and doing the wrong thing. The thought of Daryl's death was—it was like bars springing up between her and what she had to catch. It wouldn't be pushed away. She had to work through them.

The clang of Readen's sword against Daryl's rang over and over. Daryl could, would only defend. An overpowering smell of "This is my brother, this is my brother," radiated from him in waves of futile hope, pushing at Cedar's fear for him, assaulting her concentration. She tore loose from it.

On the back of her tongue in the scents that were from Readen, she began to taste despair—to taste the fear and desperation in the words she could almost hear inside his head—"If the Itza Larrak kills my brother, I am lost. I will be gone. I will no longer exist."

Through his smell of desperation, she found the path. The fight became Cedar's, the bars of her fear broke, and she struck. Ghost-like, she moved deeper and deeper into Readen, penetrating through smell after smell, searching for the key to his humanity. Hatred, resentment, anger, jealousy—she sifted through them all, strengthening, augmenting, directing them toward the Itza Larrak, while the ring of steel against steel rang too close above her head.

Krager entered, slipped around the fighters and stood in front of her, both swords drawn. His odor of fear for Daryl pushed against her. He wanted to join the fight, and the sharp smell of frustration that he had to let Daryl fight this fight was so strong she almost missed the faint, faint perfume of Readen's remorse.

She let go of everything else and grabbed it and fed power into it. She held the end of it with every shred of strength and determination she could find. It wiggled and squirmed, fought her, tossed her around like she held the end of a flailing rope.

Hand over metaphorical hand, she pulled herself farther into the desperate, ugly depths of Readen's anger and resentment, sliding through the filth looking for the key she knew was there, she hoped was there, searching for what anchored it at the other end. Then she found it.

Betrayal. An enormous cloud of betrayal by the Itza Larrak, a miasma of stink that pulsed out of Readen's mother's womb with the sudden gush of his birth. And, like a thread of copper woven through the betrayal, sometimes bright and gleaming, more often green and corroded, was Readen's scent of Daryl. The smell of brother love.

There was a flash of a small toddler, big eyes and laughing mouth wide with trust and laughter, arms reaching high. She knew it was Daryl's face, the memory Readen had hidden deep inside, encased in a shell like a pearl in an oyster, love its grain of sand.

Now she had to do what she could never tell anyone she could do. With the hard, sharp edge of her talent she could never tell anyone about, she cracked the shell. She grabbed the shining pearl, pulled it free, and attached the faint scent of remorse and the baby's redolence of trust. She braided them into the bitter scent of betrayal, working, working them until she felt the ache in her mental fingers. Then she twisted it around and into the forefront of Readen's mind, between him and the Itza Larrak and held it there.

Her body slid down the corner where she leaned, and she crumpled to the floor, holding, holding, holding the slippery rope wrapped tight inside Readen, fighting to stay conscious, feeling no guilt for her invasion of another's mind.

Daryl reached into Adalta for strength. Not for physical strength. As machine-fast as the Larrak was, Daryl was the faster, stronger fighter. His body wasn't borrowed. He had honed it for years, and it was enhanced with talent.

"This is not Readen. This is not my brother. This is the monster who corrupted him." The thought pounded through him, fought the love still inside him. He knew his brother was not the one fighting him. Readen was locked into a small space inside himself. Daryl knew he had to kill the Larrak, but his sword wouldn't cooperate, wouldn't make the killing strike. He could. He'd been able to defeat Readen since he was eight years old. He'd felt sorry for Readen then, and his grief now, his almost debilitating grief, wouldn't let him get past that sorrow. Had this being he fought ever been just Readen? Had the brother he'd loved ever been just Readen?

Readen's sword glinted. Pain seared across Daryl's upper sword arm. Blood soaked through his sleeve—too fast. Too much. He snapped his attention to the outer fight. He wasn't so much better than Readen/Larrak that he could let his grief take control. He blocked another strike, and another, pushing away the pain and growing weakness in his arm. Then the Larrak in Readen's body faltered and stepped back. Its face swam in Daryl's vision, and Daryl saw what Readen had become. He saw the grotesque, the mechanical, insect-like features that distorted his brother's face. The mouth that moved and contorted, trying to speak.

Then, in the eyes that were for an instant Readen's eyes, Daryl saw true remorse, saw true regret, saw the true and terrible recognition of what Readen had lost, surface.

"Readen, it's Readen," Cedar's voice was so faint Daryl barely caught her words.

It couldn't be. It was the Larrak. It was the Larrak.

Then the face changed again, to a younger Readen, to the face of the brother racing side by side with him, laughing. "I'm going to win. I'll get there first."

Readen's sword thrust toward him again, and Daryl's was slow to block it, his sword hand slick with the blood dripping down his arm. Both swords sliced across the perfect, smooth, polished-to-a-mirror-finish surface of their father's desk. Daryl stepped back and stared at the two crossed scars like crossed swords carved where the vase of flowers should have been. The blood running down his sword had run into one bright cut. Too much too fast. Dazed, he couldn't look away for too long a second.

Readen didn't stop and didn't look. Daryl had trouble blocking his strikes.

Until that face changed again to the dark, barely human face of what Readen was becoming. His sword dropped slowly, as if it fought him, fought to keep fighting. He pressed down on it, gripping it with his other gloved hand. Daryl's focus narrowed to the claws tearing through the leather of the glove.

Then he looked up again. The eyes that he recognized as Readen's eyes spoke the thought that the grotesque rictus of his mouth finally spoke aloud. A hoarse, tortured, whispered scream from Readen's lost soul. "Kill me. Kill me now. If you ever loved me, please, kill me. If you love Adalta, kill me before I destroy it."

Cedar's soft voice said, "There's Readen, Daryl. There's your brother."

Daryl couldn't look at her, didn't dare take his eyes from the monster face that shouldn't be his brother's. How could he do this? To his brother? If he were a true brother he should, could save him.

Then the face changed back into that of the older brother who chased Daryl and Krager through the forest with the wooden practice blades they'd filched from the armory—and smiled.

Daryl did the one thing that could save his brother. With his wounded arm he swung his sword and sliced off his brother's head.

An ear-piercing scream cut into him. The air-rending mechanical squeal went on and on. Grew faint, faded, and died, and his head filled with blank, empty silence. The Itza Larrak, the last Larrak was gone. Finally. Gone. And his brother was dead.

Cedar grabbed a handful of her dress and pressed it to her nose. Daryl stumbled to her, reached out and fell. They wrapped around each other, Krager standing over them, still guarding, while Daryl sobbed and Cedar held him.

Blood spread across the floor and along the seams of the stones. Bright crimson blood marbled with gold.

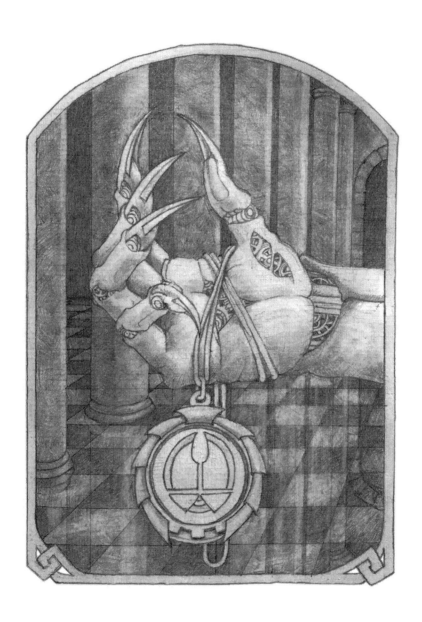

CHAPTER THIRTY-SIX

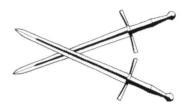

Daryl grabbed the wicked slash in his arm, found the strength to close his eyes and close the blood vessels before he passed out and collapsed. He doubted he ever would heal it completely. He'd wear the scar outside as well as inside.

"Let's go to the library. I need to be alone." But he never let go of Cedar's hand. The library, his favorite room. Away from the blood, from the bright scar on his father's desk.

They sat in silence for a very long time, his hand tight on hers as if she were the only solid thing in the slowly spinning room. Then she told him what she'd found inside Readen, that which destroyed him and that which saved him. She told him about the small pearl she'd found. She gave him back the brother he'd never had.

Two hours later, Krager rapped on the door to report.

Daryl started to lift his injured arm to push his hair back, but he simply shook his head instead. "You can report in the morning. We have a quadrant to patch up."

"Yes." Krager looked away, as if he were looking at the future, and it didn't make him happy. "There's nothing so urgent it can't wait till morning."

"And we have a state funeral to plan," said Cedar.

Both men looked at her, unable to speak.

"You want to give that monster a state funeral?" Krager was incredulous.

Daryl was silent. His hand tightened on hers. How did she know him so well?

"Readen was the son of the former guardian of Restal Quadrant, the brother of the current guardian," she said.

Daryl thought about the polished top of his father's desk, now marred by two crossing sword scars.

Yes. Yes. "Readen had many people who believed in him. He might not have had friends, but he had people who thought they were friends. There are few who would believe a story about Readen being taken over by the Itza Larrak. every one thought it was already dead."

They wouldn't be burying the alien with honors. They'd be burying his brother. The image of the three boys swinging wooden swords at the tree fort flashed in his head. His brother, the last of his family but him. The thought didn't land on his shoulders like the usual mountain-sized boulders of responsibility. In fact the boulders piled there for so long were rolling off. Now—now he could start rebuilding, restoring what his family had come close to destroying. They'd be placing the noxious evil into the earth of Adalta for cleansing, for renewal.

Three days later he stood at the apex of an arc of all the major holders, the members of Restal Council, Anuma's Guardian Ballard Me'Kahrl, and Toldar's Guardian Heir Altan Me'Gerron, Marta and Tessa in the small meadow where the Fort Tree stood. On the other side of the giant tree an arc of Karda, including Abala and one enormous, magnificent gold Karda standing next to Ket.

Daryl watched as Galen knelt, pulled the earth out from under Readen's shrouded body, and it sank into the ground. Cedar squeezed his hand as the earth began to close. Daryl let every memory he had of Readen play through his mind, good, bad, but mostly good. He refused to let in anger and resentment, his foolish gullibility, his denials, his avoidance of what Readen had become, his regret that he hadn't been able to save his brother sooner. He let the clean forest humus smell mix with the memories and cleanse them.

He watched as the small sprout of a darisa tree poked up from the center of the mound, grow taller, spread lacy branches, blossom white. It let its petals fall, covering the grave with a blanket of white petals as it covered itself with bright new-green leaves.

"Renewal," he said and heard it echo around him in voice after voice, some filled with honest promise, some filled with anger, some filled with shame, but all filled with relief and hope. When the last petal fell, Daryl turned and started the long walk back to the gates of Restal Prime.

He and Cedar made their way back to the library in the hall, Krager, ever watchful, right behind them. He stopped at the door. "Right now, the two of you need to take some time to...do whatever it is you have to do. Do I need to back all the way out, Guardian Daryl, or can I just leave without bowing?"

Daryl wanted to throw a book at him, but it would just harm one of his precious books. The door closed behind Krager, and he heard him tell their guard, "They are not to be disturbed until they ask for something."

The two of them sat together for a long time, shoulders touching, gaining strength from each other. Daryl disengaged his hand and went to a tall, narrow cabinet tucked between two bookcases. He opened and closed several drawers before he found what he wanted. A palm-sized soft leather pouch, so old the color was bleached pale tan, but still supple.

"These are very old. They come from so far back in my family —" he stopped for a minute. "My family, that I can't even remember how many great, greats. They don't have the blaze and light and color of new ones. But they radiate warmth when the bond is strong —all the time, not just occasionally."

"I don't know what you're talking about, and I've shut my filter so tight I don't even have a smell-guess."

He untied the pouch strings. They were a little stiff, and the knot was tight. He tumbled a tangle of gold chains into the palm of his broad hand. A pair of stones, each encircled by two plain gold rings, glowed soft white. He untangled them with fumbling fingers, clasped one tight in a fist and held the other out to her, dangling from his hand. "They're not fancy like Marta and Altan's. I can have them reset into something…"

It took her a moment to speak. She touched the dangling pendant almost fearfully. Her voice was so soft he leaned closer to hear her. "How old are these settings?"

"They are the first bonding stones found. Centuries."

She breathed a long sigh. Her eyes were wider than he'd ever seen them.

"One for me. One for you, the you essential to my being. They've been in my family for centuries. They don't glow and flash like some. They will be warm, always. They will be warm for as long as we live. If you agree."

She took it and started to clasp it around her neck, her head down. He couldn't see her face, but for the first time in longer than he could remember, he was home. She was his home.

The laughter inside him wouldn't be stopped. "Cedar, wait. You're always in such a hurry. I'm supposed to put one around your neck then you put the other around mine." He reached around her and closed the clasp. This was joy. This was the essence of joy.

"All right, then. Hurry up and give me the other one." She untangled it from his shaking fingers. "Turn around." She fastened it around his neck, put her arms around his waist, and pressed her face against his back, her hair brushing his neck. Soft words tickled his ear, "It warms my whole body. You warm my whole body."

He pulled her around into his lap. They held each other for a long, long time, just resting, just being warm together.

"Daryl."

"Yes?"

"I want your baby."

"I'll go lock the door."

EPILOGUE

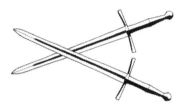

Daryl stood gazing out across the Circle of Disorder, ignoring the soft rain that fell where no rain had fallen for centuries, Cedar's arm brushing his. Bleak, bare ground surrounded them for kilometers, but here and there small tufts and spears of green dotted the space where there had been no green for centuries, where there had been destruction and death for centuries.

With them in a wide arc stood Abala, Marta and Sidhari, Altan and Kibrath, Tessa, golden Ket beside her. Galen, empty seed sack hanging from his shoulder, walked toward them from where the Itza Larrak's long rift had blazed with ugly orange fire until its death, its final death.

Two years. They'd fought the desperate battle for a long time. It seemed longer. He glanced at each of them. At each face, at eyes glistening with grief for friends lost in the battles they'd fought, with relief that the horrific threat of alien invasion was gone.

It would be a long time before he saw Altan and Marta again. They were on their way back to Toldar, all but one wing of Altan's troops already gone. He wondered what kind of life Marta would have there. And he grinned to himself—he suspected it might soon be complicated by a third.

Galen and Tessa. They'd found the first victims of the urbat at the village of Ardencroft. Ket would be carrying them all over Adalta for a long time helping restore the circles and making certain the last of the urbat were gone. He wondered if there would be another Karda for Tessa, but he knew it would be a long while before she would be willing to think about that. Though they were only together for a too short two years, he knew her bond with Kishar had been as close as his and Abala's.

He'd miss this small group of friends. They'd said their good-byes, reminisced with laughter and tears and pain about their battles, about their fellow fighters, the ones still living and the ones lost.

He watched Galen brush the last of the tiny seeds from his hands, kneel on the ground, his hands flat, his head down for several long moments and the ugly space began to green with new life. Then Galen moved to stand close behind Tessa, put his arms around her, his chin on her head, his eyes blinking fast, like Daryl's own, like all the other's.

After a long, silent moment, Tessa spoke. "For Kishar, for all the Karda lost, all the people lost. Renewal," and the soft word was repeated nine more times. every one heard every word, even the one's whispered in their heads.

"Renewal."

A profusion of glistening green sprouts stretched in a wide, wandering line in front of them. The shoots strengthened, length-ened—a wild profusion of grass, of reaching vines, of supple infant trees slowly stretching toward the sun until they grew tall enough to play with the breeze.

So the breeze sang,
And new green life danced
Renewal.

ACKNOWLEDGMENTS

Thank you to my son Kurt Nilson for his amazing illustrations. To my sister Alice V. Brock, ruthless critique partner, chief encourager, and sounding board. (She is the author of two mid-grade novels—*A River of Cattle* and *Mystery on the Pecos*.) And brother Phillip Vincent, author of the thriller, *Varuna*.

To beta reader and proofreader Stephanie Kuersten for her invaluable suggestions and impeccable ability to catch my many mistakes—and not just the spelling and typo ones.

To editor Eliza Dee who also found my mistakes. Also to Dawn Husted. To Jason Sitzes for helping me deepen the characters in the story.

And to the too many to name members of my family for their support and encouragement, especially Jeri Fleming and Abbie Peraza, and, of course, Kurt Nilson for the great cover and insightful illustrations. Also to three of my grandchildren Ethan, Mia, and Mirjana for the use of their names.

Now I have to write more books for the rest of them. Can't leave anybody out.

ABOUT THE AUTHOR

Award winning author Sherrill Nilson has been an environmental activist, horse breeder, cattlewoman, tarot card reader, as well as mother and grandmother. She has a Ph.D. in East West Psychology. She's settled back in Tulsa, Oklahoma now, after moving around from Santa Fe and Ruidoso, NM, San Francisco, and Austin hauling too many books with her.

Visit her website at www.sherrillnilson.com. You can sign up for her mailing list there. She sometimes posts working-version scenes and chapters from her next book, new illustrations, new book covers, even the occasional poem, and she will appreciate your comments. Join her on her Facebook page: Facebook.com/SLNilson, at Twitter @sherrillnilson and @sherrill.nilson_author on Instagram. You can email her at SherrillNilson@gmail.com.

ALSO BY SHERRILL NILSON

Karda: Adalta Vol. I

Hunter: Adalta Vol. II

Falling: Adalta Vol. III

Printed in Great Britain
by Amazon

59437124R00272